UNHALLOWED

James D Thorn

Unhallowed
Copyright © 2021 by James D Thorn

All rights reserved. No part of this publication may be reproduced, distributed, or transmitted in any form or by any means, including photocopying, recording, or other electronic or mechanical methods, without the prior written permission of the author, except in the case of brief quotations embodied in critical reviews and certain other non-commercial uses permitted by copyright law.

Tellwell Talent
www.tellwell.ca

ISBN
978-0-2288-6141-6 (Paperback)
978-0-2288-6142-3 (eBook)

ACKNOWLEDGEMENTS

I would like to express my deepest thanks to my friends and family that helped me along the way as I explored the writing process, and discovered my voice as an author. Your contributions and feedback helped mold this story along the way.

Additionally, I would like to thank those who made such generous contributions to my GoFundMe, making this dream become a reality. Hopefully, you all can take as much pride in seeing your names in print as much I do. Thank you to Dan Owens, Heather and Pete Watt, Margaret Keenan, Doug and Sue Dresser, Chris Colangelo, Carol and Gord Ball, Lisa Aucoin, Robert and Catherine Campbell. And to Linda and John Powell, Danny, Michael, Gaylene, and Sion, thank you for your extremely generous donation. None of this would have been possible without all of you.

1

"What the fuck!" he said as he leaned on the nearby brick wall to steady himself, retching at what he had just seen.

"You good, kid?" said his partner in his thick South Boston accent.

"Yeah, just need a minute," he said.

"It never gets easier, kid, this job is fucked," said his partner.

Ozwald David Shields, or Oz as he was called by almost everyone since he was just a small boy, stood 6'3" tall and had a warrior's build, with fair but tanned skin, and certainly had an attractive look to him. He had piercing blue eyes and short, thick, chestnut hair that was usually kept very neat and styled but was a mess from the current conditions.

Oz had recently passed his detective's exams, was top of his class, and had been assigned to the Homicide Division at the Boston Police Headquarters. He was now 29 years old and in his fifth year as an officer with the Boston Police Department. After all his time as a beat cop, or 'Troopah', as they would say in Boston, he thought he was ready for this, but nothing could prepare him for what he was looking at? Collecting himself, he stood up and walked back towards the body.

It was pouring rain, as it did so often in the early spring in Eastern Massachusetts. It was about 10:30 pm on a Thursday in late March. The rain was so cold as it poured down on them, the kind that immediately soaked and chilled right to the bone. As the rain fell, it flickered in the light of the halogen bulb mounted on the wall above them.

"It looks like they used a fucking wood chipper, man," said Oz.

"Would be hard to get a wood chipper in here, kid. Just enough room for us and the garbage," said his partner.

"What if it wasn't done here?" said Oz, as he fought back a few more heaves.

Oz's partner was a Boston Police veteran named Terry White. Terry was well in his forties at this point and had been in Homicide for 12 years now. Hardened from all that he had seen, not only during his time as a cop but just growing up in "Southie", he showed no emotion to the horrific scene before them. Terry was shorter than Oz, he only stood at 5'10". He was in pretty good shape for a man his age, fit, with only the slightest bit of a belly, most likely from the "few lahgahs" that he would have on the weekends. His salt and pepper hair kept very short and tight to his head. He thought the gray wouldn't be as noticeable this way. Terry had hazel, fatherly-like eyes, the kind that would reveal so much more about what he was thinking than his expressions would.

"Are you alright? Can we do our job now?" asked Terry.

"Yeah, just give me a second. I wasn't ready for this," Oz said.

"You never are, kid. You never are," said Terry. "So, what can you tell me about what you see here?"

"Well, from what is left, I would say we have a Caucasian female, in her mid-twenties to her early thirties. Not married or engaged, as there is no sign of a ring on her finger. I would guess that she was dumped here, as I don't see any blood splatter on the walls or anything, though with this rain, who knows? There doesn't appear to be any signs of sexual assault at first glance, as her clothes… uh… for the most part, are intact."

"What about how she was killed?" Terry asked.

"Uh, the fact that her head and upper torso are beyond recognition would tell me that the cause had something to do with that. But I'm no doctor. I just hope for her sake she was dead, before whoever did this to her," Oz said, trying to make light of what he was seeing. Although he still wanted to vomit every time, he looked at the gruesome scene before him.

"Doesn't look like we're gonna get any help from surveillance cameras, since there are none here in the alley," Oz continued. "The officer first on the scene reported that there were no witnesses. Just the kid who saw the body when he was putting out the trash, that called it in. Do you think he'll be able to tell us more about what he saw?"

"Nah, plus we'll have to get permission from his Ma to talk to him since he's a minor," said Terry. "And I know his Ma, she's a real wicked Cu…"

"I get it, Terry!" Oz said, cutting him off.

Oz reached into the pocket of his coat and pulled out a pair of nitrile gloves and put them on. They were hard to get on because his hands were so wet from the rain. Crouched, he looked up at the crime-scene photographer and asked, "You good?"

"Yeah, go ahead, I've got all the generals already," said the photographer, another South Boston local.

Oz patted the pockets of the jeans on the young woman's body, feeling for anything that will help identify her. Sliding his hands around under the body, feeling the rear pockets, still trying not to disturb the body too much. *Nothing here.* "No ID on her person," he said. He choked back another wretch as he looked around for a purse or something, though that was doubtful, since his theory was that she was dumped here. He grabbed a nearby trash bag, probably the one dropped by the kid when he saw the body before he ran off. When he moved the bag, stunned by what he saw, there was a small purse. "Got a purse," he yelled.

The photographer rushed over and snapped a couple of shots. The flash illuminated the area with each shot. The photographer gave Oz a nod to let him know he could now grab the purse and inspect it.

The purse was a small brown leather bag with a long, thin shoulder strap. A single tarnished metallic closure on the flap. Oz opened the purse and searched its contents. *How do women fit so much in these things?* He wondered. He found a small wallet with a student ID in one of the card slots. The ID was from Suffolk University. "Chloe Elizabeth Wilson," Oz yelled out. She was an attractive young woman. "Brunette. Twenty-one years old. Local girl, from Bunker Hill." *So young, so much life left to live*, he thought.

"Guess we got some bad news to deliver," said Terry.

"Jesus, Terry! Do you have a heart, man?" said Oz.

"Nah, lost that years ago, kid. You'll lose yours too," said Terry.

Oz reached into his jacket and pulled out an evidence bag and put the purse and ID in it. He walked over and handed it to the officer on the other side of the police tape.

"We done here, Terry?" he asked.

"Yeah, kid. The geeks can take over from here. Let's go get a coffee and warm up," Terry replied.

The forensics team had yet to arrive on-site, or 'the geeks' if you asked Terry. That was his pet name for the Forensic Science Division. 'Weird Science' was what Terry called forensics. He never could wrap his head around how they could get so much information from a single swab. Some of his thoughts and opinions made Terry seem like a much older man than he was, reminiscent of someone born back in the early 1900s, rather than that of a man in his 40s.

Oz lifted the yellow plastic tape. Terry crouched under it, followed by Oz. They walked over to their car, a 2015 Chevy Impala, black, opened the doors, and got in. Now in the driver's seat, Oz started the car and reached over to crank the heat. "Don't think I'll ever get used to these cold rains, man," Oz said.

"No? Doesn't it rain like this back in Michigan?" Terry asked.

"It rains, but this seems different, colder, or something," Oz replied.

"Maybe your balls just need to drop," jabbed Terry.

"Really, Ter? You're all over me tonight," said Oz.

"Aww, kid. Did I hurt your feeling?" joked Terry. "Dunkees? Or do you wanna find one of them fucking Starbucks?"

Oz chuckled as he replied, "Nah, 'Dunkees' will be fine."

The banter continued between the two detectives as they drove away. Neither one brought up what they just saw. That could wait for coffee.

***

Inside a Dunkin' Donuts around the corner from the crime scene (because in Boston, you can't spit without hitting a Dunkin'), the two detectives sat sipping their coffees and reviewing the notes of what they just witnessed.

"You ever seen anything like this before, Ter?" asked Oz.

"No, not like that, kid," replied Terry. "I've never seen anyone thrashed like that before. I mean, I've seen some wicked awful shit before, especially after the Marathon bombing, but this is twisted, kid."

"Thank God! I hoped I hadn't made a horrible career choice. I never thought I'd see anything so horrific and brutal," said Oz.

"God has nothing to do with this, kid, this is something far beyond God," Terry said.

"So, I was clearly wrong about the body being dumped there," said Oz. "There is no way that the killer would drop the body there and then the purse. Whatever happened there, happened right there, and the rain must have washed any splatter away. Pretty much gonna make forensics' life hell."

"You got that right. I'm still trying to figure out what the frigging guy used to kill that girl," said Terry. "And how strong is he? There was hardly anything left of that poor girl's upper body. What did he use to do that?"

"First thing we should do is notify the next of kin," said Oz.

"Fuck that, kid. Let a trooper do that job," Terry said. "We are gonna have to talk to the parents at some point, but I ain't gonna be the one to tell them their baby's dead."

"Aww, Terry, there is still a heart in there," joked Oz.

"Don't tell anybody you cawksuckah, I got an image to keep," said Terry, resuming his hard exterior.

"Your secret is safe with me, man," laughed Oz. "Alright, finish your coffee. I wanna get back to the station and start the paperwork on this one, so I can get home tonight."

They downed the last bit of their coffee and headed out. Neither really saying a word to the other. It stayed this way all the way back to the station. Oz parked as close to the doors as he could, since the rain still poured down.

"I'm gonna bounce if you got this, kid?" said Terry, getting out of the car.

"Yeah man, go ahead. Like I said, I just want to get the paperwork started before I head home. Have a good night, Ter. I'll see you in the morning," said Oz as he closed the door of the Impala.

Terry walked off to his car in the far corner of the lot as Oz went up the stairs into the back of the station. Oz opened the door and headed inside, shaking off the rain, running his hands through his hair to squeeze out the excess water. He dropped the keys off with the motor pool before going upstairs to the detective pool to his desk. Taking a deep, cleansing breath, he looked around. There were only a couple of other detectives there working at their desks, but otherwise, the office was quiet. Oz turned on his computer, logged in, opened a case file, and started to write his report.

Oz looked up at the clock on the wall to see what time it was. *Twelve thirty! Fuck me! I gotta get home and get some sleep. Where did the night go?* He looked back at the glowing computer screen and the blinking cursor, waiting for his next input. He recorded what he and his partner had seen, trying to be as descriptive as possible without making himself sick again. As he typed, he hoped that something would pop out at him, something that maybe he missed.

Outlook dinged, notifying Oz that a new email had just arrived. He opened up his Outlook app and saw that the photographer had sent the crime scene photos to him. Opening the email, he braced himself to relive what he saw tonight. One by one he went through the images. Looking at each one closely. *Jesus! Who could have done this?* He wondered. One image showed that the young woman's head was completely non-existent, at least in any recognizable form, anyway. Her neck and shoulders appeared to be shredded. Something severely tore the flesh. *What the fuck! Even the bones are thrashed! What the fuck did that?* The pictures reminded him of the aftermath of a grizzly bear attack. *That can't be possible. The closest thing to bears in Boston are the Bruins!*

Oz sat back in his chair and rubbed his eyes. His eyes felt hot and stung a bit as he rubbed them. *Fuck it, I'm far too tired to figure this out tonight. I better head home and get some sleep, if that is even possible after seeing this.* He saved his file and shut down his computer, got up, grabbed his coat and threw it on, and headed out of the station to his car.

The night was eerily silent for such a metropolis. No sirens or horns, just the sound of the rain slapping against the pavement, joining the already large puddles that amassed in the parking lot. Oz walked to his car and got inside. Closing the door, he started the car.

Oz only lived a few miles from the station. Most days he would walk or ride his bike, but he was glad he had his car on days as miserable as this. It was the first car that he ever bought, a 2013 Ford Mustang GT, Deep Impact Blue Metallic, with dual white racing stripes from the hood to the trunk. He remembered when he bought it a few years ago before he came to Boston. He walked into the Ford dealership in Lansing. The salesman who approached him was your typical sleazy car salesman, he remembered thinking to himself. Oz remembered telling the salesman that he wanted the Mustang GT that was up on the ramp at the front of the dealership. Immediately, he began telling Oz that he was going to get so many chicks in that car. It was, as he put it; 'super flash' and 'the ladies will love it', that 'it's a total panty dropper'. What a douchebag. He laughed to himself, reliving that day in his mind.

Oz pulled into the underground lot at his apartment building and reversed into his parking spot. He got out of the car, hit the lock button on his remote. The honk from the car when it locked echoed in the garage. He walked through the garage, his footsteps echoing off the concrete walls throughout the garage, to the steel man door leading into the apartment stairwell.

He climbed the four flights of stairs to the top floor where his little two-bedroom apartment was, unlocked his door, and walked inside. *Ahh, it's good to be home*, he thought, flicking on the light over the foyer. He kicked off his shoes and hung up his coat on one of the empty hooks on the wall by the door.

His apartment wasn't big by any means, but it didn't have to be, after all, it was only him. The apartment had been modestly decorated and very clean. He was a bit of a neat freak. Not that he would admit that to anyone, especially the guys on the force. Oz had been so focused on work since he arrived in Boston that he didn't have much of a social life. He'd met a few women since moving to Boston, but none of them could handle how dedicated he was to his job, so they didn't stick around for long. He couldn't blame them. Being a cop was everything to him. It was all he ever wanted to be since he was a kid, growing up just outside of Lansing, Michigan. He always picked the cops' side when playing cops and robbers with his friends in the neighborhood.

Oz worked very hard at being a police officer, and even harder to become a detective. It was always what he wanted to be. He wanted to be just like the guys on TV and in the movies. Of course, in reality, it was nothing like that in real life. There was no roughing up the bad guy to get information, at least not without getting heavily reprimanded for it. No high-speed police chases through the streets of the city. No shootouts, guns blazing outside the bank as the robbers exited. But he was a detective now. *This is where the actual police work happened,* he told himself. *This is where the crimes really get solved. Not now, though.* Now it was time to get some sleep.

2

Ring... Ring... Ring...

"Detective Shields, Homicide," said Oz, half-awake answering his cell phone.

"You're still in bed? Get your ass up!" the voice on the phone said.

"Terry? Is that you? What time is it?" Oz replied.

"7:30, kid. Come downstairs, I'm driving today," Terry said.

"Yeah, alright, Ter, I'll be down in five," Oz said as he sat up in bed and rubbed his eyes. He yawned and stretched, got up and ambled down the hall and into the bathroom. Catching a look at himself in the mirror, it looked like he'd had a rough night. His hair was all disheveled, and clearly, he needed a shave, but there was no time for that this morning. *A whore's bath is gonna have to do this morning, Ozzy*, he thought to himself.

Downstairs Terry waited patiently in the Impala, sipping his coffee, and looking around at the activity on the street. Reminiscent of his days as a patrolman sitting in the car waiting for the next call to come over the radio. Observing all the people in the neighborhood, always on alert for suspicious activity. Though it had to be pretty suspicious for Terry to take notice, after all, he grew up in South Boston. You had to ignore the strange behavior of the everyday drunks and junkies. If you wasted your time arresting them all day, you'd never be done filling out the paperwork.

Oz opened the passenger door and got in.

"You good, kid?" Terry asked him.

"Yeah, Ter, I'm good. What's up?" Oz replied.

"We gotta get down to the coroner's office. He said he had something to tell us," said Terry. "Oh, there's a Dunkees for you in the cup holder, kid. You look like you really need it."

Oz chuckled, "Thanks, Ter, it's not true what they say about you."

"Heh, not all of it, kid, but most," joked Terry.

"So what did the coroner say?" asked Oz.

"Not much, kid. Just that he needed to see us ASAP," said Terry.

Oz grabbed the coffee from the cup holder and took a drink as Terry pulled out from the curb. *Ugh, I feel like shit this morning,* he thought to himself. *Hopefully, this coffee does the trick.*

***

Arriving at the Medical Examiner's office, Oz wondered what they were going to be told. He'd not slept very well after seeing the state of that poor woman the night before. They walked into the building to the reception area and up to the receptionist sitting there. She was a fair-skinned woman in her thirties, green eyes, brown hair pulled back into a tight bun. Trying her best to look attractive, but she was the kind of woman that you really wouldn't give a second look, even at closing time at the bar after a few too many.

"Welcome to the office of the Medical Examiner. How may I assist you, gentlemen, today?" she said, in her thick Boston accent.

"Hi ma'am, we are from the Homicide Division, and we were called to come down to see the Coron… uh… the Medical Examiner. I'm Detective Shields, and this is my partner, Detective White," Oz said, trying his best to sound professional and not like a rookie detective.

Oz and Terry pulled out their badges and showed the receptionist.

"Yeah, thank you. Mister Walker is expecting you. Through those doors there, and I'll arrange for him to meet you on the other side," she said.

"Thank you, ma'am," said Oz, and he and Terry walked over to a set of double doors to the right of the reception desk and waited for her to buzz them through. As they walked through the doors, there was the medical examiner, as the receptionist said he would be, waiting for them in the doorway of an office.

"Detectives," shouted the man as he waved and approached them. "Thank you for coming so quickly. This really couldn't wait for the report to be filed."

"You almost sound excited?" said Oz, shaking the man's hand. "I'm Detective Shields, and this is my partner…"

"Detective White, yes, we spoke this morning. Thank you again for coming so quickly. I'm Brad Walker, the Medical Examiner, obviously," he said nervously, laughing.

Brad Walker was an awkward man. More so than you would expect for a man who spends the majority of his time with the dead. He looked a bit like George Costanza from the TV show Seinfeld. Same build, balding, and glasses, but he walked more short stepped, like those wind-up robot toys from years ago. He was in his late 40s or early 50s and single, most likely not by choice.

"This way, gentlemen, I need to show you this," Brad said.

The detectives followed him down the hall to one of the autopsy rooms. Inside on the cold stainless-steel table was the body of Chloe Elizabeth Wilson. There was a sweet, sickly smell in the air, not quite definable. It just lingered there. A white sheet covered Chloe's body, just waiting for the medical examiner to pull it back, revealing the horror that they had left not even twelve hours ago.

"Do you guys have any clue what did this?" asked Brad.

"We were kinda hoping you could tell us that," said Oz.

"The cause of death was obviously the mass trauma to the head and upper torso," replied Brad.

"You need a special degree to tell us that?" chirped Terry.

"Well, no," said Brad awkwardly. "It's what caused this massive trauma that I can't figure out. I even went through a bunch of files and pictures online to see if I could find anything that looked remotely close to what caused such damage. I looked at animal attacks, workplace accidents, mutilations from serial killers, you name it, and I came across nothing on record like this!"

"So what was so urgent that we had to come right down here?" Oz asked.

"This…" Brad said, as he pulled out a report from the file folder on a nearby table.

"What's that?" asked Oz.

"This is the toxicology report that I got back early this morning. When I was going over it, I saw something that perplexed me," Brad said.

"Doesn't seem like that would take much," muttered Terry under his breath.

"And what was that exactly?" Oz asked.

"Well, the report showed traces of an unidentifiable barbiturate in a saliva-like substance that I collected from the tattered flesh," Brad stated, acting as if he didn't hear what Terry had said about him.

"So she was eaten?" Oz asked.

"Not exactly… er… or at least by anything that I have ever seen before," Brad said. "The saliva didn't have any typical DNA properties that we would normally see. As I'm sure you are aware, we can extract DNA from saliva and analyze that DNA for matches to people and animals. DNA has three types of chemical components: phosphate, a sugar called deoxyribose, and four nitrogenous bases—adenine, guanine, cytosine, and thymine. Two of the bases, adenine, and guanine, have a double-ring structure characteristic of a type of chemical known as a purine. The other two bases, cytosine, and thymine, have a single-ring structure of a type called a pyrimidine. The chemical components of DNA are arranged into groups called nucleotides, each composed of a phosphate group, a deoxyribose sugar molecule, and any one of the four bases. It is convenient to refer to each nucleotide by the first letter of the name of its base: A, G, C, and T…"

"English, Mister Walker," chirped Terry.

"Right, sorry. We use the DNA to identify species, using a short section of the DNA from known species and comparing the two. Since this saliva didn't contain any DNA, which is bizarre enough in itself, we couldn't make that comparison," stated Brad, nervous about how the detectives would respond.

"So this wasn't saliva then?" asked Oz, perplexed but not trying to show it.

"That's the weird part, other than the missing DNA properties. Chemically it contained everything to classify it as saliva, other than the barbiturate, that is," said Brad.

"You mentioned the barbiturate before, what's with that?" asked Oz.

"Yeah, barbiturates depress the central nervous system. They reduce the activity of the nerves, causing muscle relaxation. They can reduce the heart rate, slow breathing, and drop blood pressure. Oddly, this barbiturate doesn't match chemically to any known chemical barbiturate in the scientific world. It is entirely new, and only from the actual chemical makeup could we really determine that it was a barbiturate. Probably the purest form ever, like naturally occurring, if that makes any sense. The levels in this saliva were also the perfect amount, essentially rendering the victim in a medically induced coma. So, there is the chance that she felt nothing," Brad stated.

"Looking for a silver lining here?" joked Terry.

"No, but when you talk to her parents, you could mention that for their comfort," Brad said oddly sympathetically.

"So, let me get this straight. Your report is going to declare the cause of death if the massive trauma caused by an unknown species, with traces of an unknown chemical barbiturate? So, basically, we know nothing and keep digging?" Oz asked, feeling frustrated and exhausted.

"I mean, yeah, I guess that is pretty much all that I can determine at this time. Sorry, it isn't of more help for your investigation, but I thought you should know," Brad said, hanging his head. Clearly, the detectives were not as intrigued by the findings as he was.

"What about the gouges in the bone and the torn flesh?" asked Terry.

"Also a mystery, unfortunately," said Brad. "There were no traces of any substances left behind in the gouges. If it was done by metal, claws, or anything really, there should at least be something left behind, but there was nothing. So, unfortunately, I can't even fathom a guess at this point, but what I can say is that whatever made these marks, was extremely sharp and strong, sharper than anything surgical that I have."

"Right. Well, thank you, Mr. Walker. This has been… informative," Oz said, too tired to be any more pleasant.

"Again, sorry, I couldn't shed more light on things for you. But thank you for coming down here so quickly," replied Brad.

Terry had already turned around and headed for the door. Clearly frustrated by this visit. He didn't even care enough to say goodbye or let Oz know he was heading to the car. Oz saw Terry leaving and knew that this meeting was pretty much over.

"Sorry about that, it's been a long night. Thank you, Mr. Walker, we'll be in touch if we have any more questions," Oz said, trying to mend the situation. He reached out and shook Brad's hand, and exited the room after Terry.

Oz left the room and rushed after Terry. Terry was at the double doors by the time that Oz caught up to him. Terry opened the door and walked through. Oz was right behind him as they entered the reception area.

"Do you fucking believe that guy? Hurry and come down here, so I can tell you fuck all," Terry said angrily and mockingly.

"It wasn't that bad, Ter. I mean, I did learn something," said Oz.

"You could have learned that from the Discovery Channel!" chirped Terry.

"So, where to now, Ter?" Oz asked, quickly trying to change the subject.

"Let's go see the kid that called this in," said Terry.

"But I thought you said that was a waste of time?" asked Oz.

"After chatting with Dr. Fuckhead, nothing could be more of a waste of time," said Terry.

"You're the boss, Terry. You want me to drive?" asked Oz.

"Nah, I got this, kid!" said Terry.

They got in the car and headed back to the scene of the crime. Once again, not much was said the entire way there. Oz thought it was best to leave Terry to his stewing. They hadn't been partners very long, but this was something that Oz had learned rather quickly. Once while trying to fill an awkward silence, Oz asked Terry what he was thinking about, and Terry had responded: "What are you, my fucking wife? Can't a man just enjoy the fucking silence now and then?" Oz laughed it off and made a mental note: Terry talks when Terry wants to talk. These silent periods didn't bother Oz anymore, in fact, he would often use these times to process his thoughts. This particular moment would give him time to process all that they had just heard at the medical examiner's office. Try to make some sense of what they were just told because it seemed like something out of a sci-fi movie or something.

***

They pulled up to the building beside the alley where Chloe Elizabeth Wilson's body was found. The police tape was still up across the entrance to the alley. The Forensic Science team was still in the alley doing their thing.

"Don't say I didn't warn you about the kid's Ma," said Terry, breaking the silence.

"Yeah, Ter, I remember. How is it that you know her?" asked Oz.

"Doesn't matter, kid. All you need to know is: I know her," said Terry.

"This should be fun then," replied Oz.

They exited the car and went to the front door of the building. Terry approached the buzzer and pressed the button for the boy's apartment. Waiting impatiently, Terry pressed it again, not even ten seconds after the first buzz. The speaker crackled and a woman's voice came on.

"Yeah, quit hitting the buzzer. I'm here. What do you want?" the woman's voice said.

"Charming," said Oz.

"Told you so, kid," said Terry, before pressing the talk button to reply to the woman. "Yeah, Miss Hill. This is Detective White and my partner, Detective Shields. We are here to talk to you and your son about last night."

"Ugh, yeah, come on up," replied the woman, obviously frustrated. "Like I fucking need this shit today," she said, before letting go of the button on her end.

The door buzzed and clicked as the lock released. Terry grabbed the handle and opened it for Oz to go through first. As Oz walked past him, he said, "This ought to be fun!" They walked up the stairs to the second floor of the building. All the doors on this floor had a number and the letter B, this builder's way of letting you know that you were on the second floor. They walked almost to the end of the hallway to a door on the left marked 5B. Terry knocked on the door with three quick raps. A voice on the other side of the door shouted, "Yeah, I'm coming!"

"Tell me she is far more pleasant in person," said Oz.

"Nah, kid. This is as good as it gets," replied Terry.

The woman unlocked the door and removed the chain before opening the door for the detectives. When the door opened, they saw a woman about five feet tall, with her dirty blonde hair pulled back in a ponytail. She had no makeup on and an expression of irritation on her face. She had the potential to be a pretty woman if she cared enough to clean herself up. But this morning she was dressed in an old, sloppy, loose-fitting gray t-shirt with whatever was printed on the front of it almost entirely washed away at this point, and a pair of baggy, black track pants. On her feet was a tattered and well-worn pair of slippers. There was a faint smell of marijuana in the air that was slightly overpowered by a fresh spritz of a cheap spring meadow scented air freshener.

"Miss Hill?" asked Terry, knowing full well this was her.

"You know who I am, Terry. Don't be fucking ignorant," she said.

"Sadie, this is my partner, Detective Shields," said Terry.

"Ma'am," said Oz, greeting her, trying to make a good first impression, hopefully making her a little easier to deal with.

"Hi, look at you!" she said, eyeing Oz up and down. "I wish Terry had told me he was bringing his hot new partner by, I would have done more to make myself presentable."

"You look fine, Miss Hill," Oz replied kindly.

"You're a horrible liar, but you're sweet. C'mon in," she said. "You guys wanna coffee or water or something?" she asked, as the detectives entered the apartment.

"Nah, Sadie. Thanks, though. We shouldn't be here long. We just need to ask Jessie some questions about what he saw last night," said Terry.

"Kay," she said. "Jessie!" she yelled. "Get your butt out here. The detectives need to talk to you."

Jessie Hill came out of a bedroom down the hall in the apartment. Jessie was a boy about thirteen years old, a good-looking kid, tall for his age, and a natural athlete's build. He had dark hair and brown eyes. Jessie was a solid kid, and tough, definitely wasn't the kind of kid that took any flack from anyone close to his age. Despite this, he was a good kid. He did well in school and stayed out of trouble whenever possible. He played baseball any chance he could, and hockey through the winter months, either on the street with his friends or in league ice hockey down at the local rink.

"Hey, Jess," said Terry, seeing the boy emerge from the hall into the living room area. "How was hockey this year, kid?"

"Yeah, good, Ter. Started playing goalie this season," Jessie said, almost happy to see Terry.

"That's great, kid! Goalies are super important," said Terry. "Kid, this is my partner Oz, we just wanna ask you about what you saw last night."

Oz gave the kid an acknowledging nod with a comforting smile. He was still trying to figure out how Terry fit into this whole dynamic. Although he was grateful that he had a connection, it seemed to take the edge off this situation. Questioning children was never easy. You always had to be aware that the parents were right there and could shut it down at any time, being protective of their child. Just hovering around like a helicopter waiting to swoop and take the kid out of there, like the choppers swooping in to pull the Marines out of a field in Vietnam.

"Oz is from Michigan, so talk slow, he's still learning how to speak proper," joked Terry.

Jessie laughed and asked Oz, "Are you a Red Wings fan?"

"Yeah, shouldn't everyone be?" joked Oz.

"Na-ah, the B's are way better! Clearly, you know nothing about hockey," Jessie snapped back.

"He's got you there, kid," Terry said to Oz. "So, Jess, I gotta ask you, about last night. What were you doing down in the alley?"

"Ma asked me to take out the garbage, 'cause it stunk from the onions and garlic from supper last night."

"Ma still hasn't figured out cooking yet?" joked Terry.

Jessie laughed and said, "Nah, it ain't like that, Ter. It was spaghetti, that stuff's always a bit stinky!"

"Tell me what happened when you got downstairs?"

"Well, it was raining wicked hard, so I knew I was gonna run. I opened the door and ran out to the alley to toss the garbage in the bin. When I got around the corner, I saw this woman laying there," Jessie continued. "I shouted out at her, figuring that she was sleeping or something. As I got closer, I saw the body on the ground," Jessie started to shake talking about what he saw next, bouncing his right leg nervously as he sat on the chair.

"It's ok, kid. We saw it, so you don't have to tell us everything," said Terry, trying to comfort Jessie.

Jessie resumed telling the detectives what he saw. "Well, as I started to creep closer, I saw that her head was missing. It was fucking gross."

"Jessie Hill! Watch Your Fucking Mouth!" shouted his mother.

"Sorry, Ma, but it was!" Jessie said.

"Yeah, Ma, go easy on the kid. It was really fucking gross!" Terry chimed in, winking at Jessie, letting him know that he had his back with his mother.

Jessie smiled at Terry and continued his story. "I dropped the garbage and legged it back into the apartment. I was freaking out when I got back here, and Ma asked me what was wrong. So, I told her to call the cops, there's a dead woman in the alley. Ma freaked. She was like, "what?

What are you talking about?" I told her again, and that's when she called the cops."

"Did you see anything weird or hear any weird noises before you saw the body?" asked Terry.

"Nah, nothing like that. All I could hear was the rain falling," said Jessie.

"Was there anyone else on the street when you went outside?" asked Oz, finally feeling comfortable enough to contribute.

"Nah, not that I noticed, anyway. I was just trying to book it 'cause it was raining so hard," answered Jessie.

"Right. Thanks, kid. You did the right thing, booking it like that and getting your Ma to call us," said Terry. "How are you doing? You okay after seeing that?"

"I think so, Ter, it was just a little worse than a scary movie. More real though, you know?" said Jessie.

"Yeah, kid, I hear you. You did better than Oz there, he was gagging when he saw it," joked Terry "If you're ever bothered by what you saw, you call me, okay? I can line up someone for you to talk with."

"We can't afford for him to go to some fucking headshrinker, Terry," said Sadie.

"Sadie, for Christ's sake. Did I say that it was gonna cost you anything? No, I said that I would line it up. There are things set up for kids like Jess here, to talk to someone after seeing something traumatic like this," said Terry, angered by Sadie. "Alright, kid? You just call me, okay?"

"Yeah, thanks, Ter," replied Jessie.

"Good, kid," Terry said, standing up from sitting on the couch. "Say 'hi' to your Pa for me, when you see him, alright?"

"Yeah Ter, will do," said Jessie.

Terry mussed up Jessie's hair as he turned to walk past him to leave the apartment. Oz got up, gave Jessie another nod, and followed Terry.

"Thanks, Sadie. If you guys need anything, just gimme a call, alright?" said Terry.

"I'd rather call your partner here, but yeah, alright, Ter. Thanks," said Sadie, giving Oz the eye again. Oz smiled awkwardly back at her. Almost like he had never been flirted with before.

"Keep your hooks out of him, Sadie, I like this kid," said Terry. "Take care, Sadie, thanks for letting us chat with the kid."

They left the apartment and headed downstairs to the car.

"So, are you gonna tell me about how you fit in with these people, Ter? Or are you gonna make me dig into your shady past on my own to uncover your dark secrets?"

"She was married to my good friend for years before it went to shit," replied Terry. "She is a bit of a fucking whack job, kid. Keep your distance."

"Oh, I wasn't asking for that reason," said Oz.

"Sure, kid. Sadie can clean up alright, but she's still a fucking mess underneath it all," Terry said, laughing as they got back into the Impala.

"Where to now, Ter?" asked Oz.

"To the office, kid. I hate going to that fucking open concept Google hippie shithole! Gimme some cubicle walls or something. Nothing worse than a bunch of cops all trying to make calls with nothing to block the noise, you know?" groaned Terry.

"Want a 'Dunkees' before we head to the station?" Oz asked, smirking, knowing the answer before Terry would respond.

"Is the fucking Pope Catholic?" said Terry excitedly. "It's your round too, kid."

"Sure thing, Ter," Oz said, chuckling.

***

Back at the station, Oz and Terry sat at their desks. 'Desk' is a loose term for the setup. These desks were little more than tables with three and a half-inch high frosted dividers that spanned the length of the sides and the back of the desk, and a few drawers for you to store pens and other items. Or, in Terry's case, a bag of Kerr's Scotch Mints that he would offer to anyone close by when he brought them out. Their desks were across from each other at the end of a double row of four desks, side by side. Terry demanded that he be at the end of a row when they brought in the "open concept office" to the station, as part of a modernization initiative by the city for the Boston PD because, as he put it: "There is no fucking way that I'm gonna be in the middle of a cop sandwich in this stupid set-up." Rather than argue with him, which was usually more frustrating once you found out how much Terry loved to argue just for his entertainment, the lieutenant just agreed and moved on.

The office was definitely more alive with activity today than it was the night before. There was chatter buzzing all around the room. Some detectives were on the phone making or taking calls. While some were off over in the kitchenette, chatting while having a cup of coffee. They were close enough to Oz that he could hear them talking, but still far enough away that he couldn't quite make out what they were talking about. In the distance, you could hear one of the desk phones ringing.

"What do you think, Ter?" asked Oz.

"I don't know, kid. We have no motive, no leads. A sketchy report from the coroner that really doesn't tell us shit, and no witnesses," replied Terry.

"How long do you think forensics is gonna be before we hear anything from them?" asked Oz.

"Who knows, kid. Could be days, and even then, with the rain last night, I highly doubt they are gonna find anything that will help us," replied Terry.

"White! Shields! You fellas got a minute?" the lieutenant yelled from his office.

Lieutenant Jim Roberts was in one of the two offices in the detective pool. The office had frosted glass walls from floor to ceiling and a frosted glass door that was just as tall, with a brushed stainless handle on both sides of the door. In his early sixties, the lieutenant was close to retirement, though he had no intention of retiring any time soon if you asked him. He was an average height man, handsome and with white hair. He looked like he was right out of the TV show Mad Men, in his three-piece suit, was a real suave-looking gentleman with a great temperament. Always so even-keeled and political. In his position nowadays, you had to be. He was a brilliant talker, and a born leader. His wife had passed away three years earlier after a long eight-year battle with Non-Hodgkin's Lymphoma.

The funeral was a wonderful celebration of life for this strong, beautiful, caring woman who had battled so long and hard against such a terrible and painful disease. As though it wasn't tough enough just being a cop's wife, she had to fight her disease as well. Laura Roberts was a remarkable woman, as well-loved and respected by the boys on the force as her husband was. They had been together since high school, and could often be seen poking fun at each other as much as you could see them being affectionate.

All the detectives under Jim were at the funeral, as well as several of the officers who'd had the privilege to meet her. Jim returned to work the week after the funeral, and gathered all the detectives under him, and told them all that he was fine, and thanked everyone for their support. Now that his Laura was at peace, he could now focus on supporting this family, his brothers and sisters in arms. The consummate professional.

"You wanted to see us, sir?" said Oz as he and Terry walked into the office and sat down in the chairs in front of the lieutenant's desk.

"How are you getting on with this case?" Jim asked.

"This is a toughie, Jim. At this point, we have nothing to move on," replied Terry.

"How bad was it?" asked the lieutenant.

"Fucking horror show. Never seen anything so brutal in all my life!" said Terry.

This stunned Oz. Since so far, Terry hadn't shown even the slightest bit of emotion or reaction from the moment that they arrived on-scene.

"Yeah, I saw the pictures this morning when I got in. Pretty brutal," said the lieutenant. "Wished I'd waited until after my coffee to see that shit. Anyway, how are you, Shields? How's Terry treating you?"

"Yeah, good sir," Oz said before Terry chimed in.

"Wasn't so good last night, heaving on loafers at the crime scene," Terry said, giving Oz a playful elbow, laughing.

"Stop picking on the kid, Terry, and let him speak, would you?" said the lieutenant.

"All good, sir, I can take it," Oz said. "Other than almost tossing my cookies, things are going well. Terry is a great mentor. I'm really learning a lot from him. And again, thank you for this opportunity, sir."

"Yeah, yeah alright, Shields. Get your lips off my ass before I crush your head," the lieutenant said jokingly. "You can be straight with me son, I may be your superior officer, but I'm just a guy, alright? What did the Medical Examiner have to say?"

"Yes, sir. Well, he wasn't able to tell us much. At least not anything that would shed some light on the sicko that we are looking for," said Oz. "Obviously, the victim was killed by the trauma to her head and upper torso. He said that he scoured the internet looking for a similar wound that would shed some light on what actually killed her and found nothing."

"Then he started to go on about DNA and some other sciency shit, that still didn't tell us anything," said Terry.

The Lieutenant just looked at Oz, waiting for him to shed some light on this, since he knew that Terry was not a fan of this stuff.

"The Medical Examiner said that he found traces of a chemical barbiturate in this saliva-like substance at the tattered edges of the wound," Oz reported. "Oddly, the saliva and the barbiturate were like nothing ever seen before. The saliva contained no DNA properties that they could trace, and the chemical makeup of the barbiturate didn't match the chemical makeup of any barbiturate known to the scientific world. But he did say that it was possible that because of it, the victim may not have felt a thing."

"Make sure you tell the parents that part when you break the news to them," said the Lieutenant. Oz looked at Terry, waiting for him to say something, but it didn't look like he was going to.

"Yes, sir. Will do," said Oz.

"Alright! Dismissed, gents. Good luck with this one. Keep me posted. I have faith that you'll figure this one out," said the Lieutenant. The two detectives stood up and exited his office.

"Ter, I thought you said that a patrolman was gonna break the news to the parents?" Oz whispered to Terry when they were out of the Lieutenant's office.

"Yeah, guess we can't get away with that now that the Lieutenant has told us to do it," Terry said jokingly. "Best get on that computer and find out where her parents are."

Oz sat down at his desk, turned on his computer, and logged in. Terry continued to the kitchenette, most likely to get another coffee. *All that coffee is gonna be the end of him one day*, he thought as he waited for the computer to finish loading up. Oz opened up the NCIC database to search for the next of kin for the victim. He typed in "Chloe Elizabeth Wilson" and hit the tab key and entered her date of birth, then selected Massachusetts from a drop list to refine the search. The database showed her name on a list. He clicked on the first Chloe Elizabeth Wilson on the list, and up came her file. The picture from her Massachusetts State driver's license was a lot like the one that he had seen on her student ID. Parents: David and Mary Wilson, Medford, MA. *Looks like we're going for a drive to Medford, this should make Terry happy*, he joked to himself. Oz jotted down the address for the victim's parent's house, in Medford, in his notebook. Clicked his pen, and tucked both the notebook and pen in the inside pocket of his sport coat.

"Terry! I found them! We're heading to Medford," Oz shouted to Terry in the kitchenette.

"Ahh, fucking Medford? Really? You're driving, and we're gonna need a Dunkees for the road," said Terry.

3

The drive from the station to Medford was only a twenty-minute drive, but with a "Dunkees" stop it added a few more minutes. *Worth it to make Terry happy before getting to the victim's parent's house*, Oz thought to himself.

"You ever done this before, kid?" asked Terry between sips of his coffee.

"Not myself, no. I was with somebody once that had to deliver the news. But I stayed outside when he went in and broke the news to them," replied Oz.

"Chicken shit!" Terry said, laughing. "I guess I'll take the lead on this then. You can be there for moral support. Maybe hand them the tissues."

"Jesus, Terry! That's cold, man," Oz said, shocked at the words coming from his partner. He knew that Terry was emotionally reserved, but he didn't think he was like this.

"I'm just fucking with you, kid," Said Terry, recovering from his untimely joke. "This is the part of the job that I hate. That's why I was hoping to send a Trooper to break the news."

"Blame the Lieutenant for that, Ter," Oz said, chuckling.

"Yeah, Jim's a great guy, really likes us to put ourselves right in the job. He says doing this stuff keeps us from detaching emotionally from the world, you know?" said Terry.

"Speaking of which," Oz started, "how do you shut it off when you leave work?"

"It's different for everyone, kid. Some guys hit the bottle, some guys box, some guys just don't say anything to the old lady when they get home," Terry continued. "Some play those frigging video games. The trick is figuring out what works for you, whatever that is, and do that."

"What do you do, Ter?" asked Oz.

"Me? I'm a fucking machine, kid. Nothing breaks me," Terry said, having a laugh.

"I think the machine could use a few hours at the gym or lay off the Dunkees and the donuts for a while," Oz said, taking a jab at his partner.

"Ah! You little cawksuckah!" Terry said, laughing. "That was sharp, kid. Good one!"

The two of them had a good laugh. Probably wasn't the best idea, considering what they were about to do. But as Terry was telling Oz, you have to figure out what works for you, or this job would really eat away at you.

They pulled up to a small raised bungalow-style house, pretty typical for this area. The house was beige, black shingled roof, and a single bay window in the front just off to the left of the stairs leading up to the front door. There was a long, recently paved, single-car-wide driveway on the left side of the house that ran from the road to the back of the property. The American Flag flapped in the breeze on the flagpole in the front garden. Oz pulled into the driveway and parked the car. The two detectives got out of the car and walked around to the front door. Oz took a deep breath, exhaling as he reached to ring the doorbell.

The doorbell chimed inside the house, faintly heard by them on the porch. The door opened and a woman in her late 40s answered. She was maybe 5' tall, petite, and had a very uneasy expression on her face as she looked at the two men there before her. Her hair was short, curly, and dark brown, which was neatly styled.

Oz instantly saw the resemblance between her and the picture of Chloe. *Fuck me, this is not gonna be easy*, he thought to himself. "Mrs. Mary Wilson?" asked Oz, hoping that she would say 'No, sorry, you have the wrong address.'

"Yes," the woman replied uneasily.

"Ma'am, I'm Detective Shields, and this is my partner, Detective White. We are with the Boston PD. Is your husband home? We'd like to speak with you both if possible," said Oz, for some odd reason taking the reins on this, when Terry said that he would. But there was Terry, silent as ever, more than happy to let Oz take the lead on this.

"Yes, David is here. May I ask what this is about?" she said nervously.

"Ma'am, I feel that this is better discussed inside and not here on the porch. May we please come in and speak with you both?" stated Oz, remarkably calm considering how uneasy he was feeling.

"Oh, alright. C'mon in, please," she said as she opened the door fully and stepped aside, letting the detectives inside.

"Who are you guys? Why are you here? Mary? Why are these guys in our house?" said David from the living room off to the left of the entrance, as he stood up from the chair he was sitting in.

David was of average height and build. Looked like he could be a tradesman of some kind, but most likely wasn't considering that he was home on a Friday afternoon. His hair was short, salt, and peppered in color. His face had a couple of days' growth around his thick Tom Selleck-like mustache. He was wearing jeans and a t-shirt.

"They are detectives, Hun. They are here to talk to us," she replied.

Oz and Terry both pulled their badges from their belts and showed them to the couple. "Sir? Ma'am? Please have a seat," said Oz as he clipped his badge back on his belt.

Mary closed the door behind them, and joined her husband in the living room, sitting on the arm of the chair David sat in. With her right arm draped over his shoulders and holding his right hand with her left, they sat there, waiting nervously for what the detectives were about to tell them. Terry and Oz sat on the couch, facing them.

"Sir? Ma'am? There is no easy way to tell you this," Oz began. David and Mary's faces were now pale and almost nauseous looking as they anticipated the words that he was about to say. "I'm terribly sorry, but your daughter, Chloe, was murdered last night."

Mary wailed and buried her head in David's chest, sobbing. *The pain this woman is feeling, God, this is brutal,*

Oz thought. David tried to remain tough and strong for Mary as he wrapped his arms around her.

"How did this happen?" asked David, his voice shaking with grief.

"Well sir, we aren't exactly sure yet," *Don't fuck this up now, Ozzy*, he thought as he continued. "We are fairly certain that she felt nothing when it happened, if that should be of any comfort to you." *Smooth asshole.*

"Can we see her? Don't we have to come into the city to identify her?" asked David.

"Nah, that is not needed. Her pocketbook was beside her with her ID in it… and… uh… we would strongly advise that when you arrange for the funeral that it's a closed casket," said Terry.

"Closed casket? What the fuck happened to her?" cried David.

"Sir, again we are truly sorry, and we are doing everything we can to get to the bottom of this. We will find who did this to your daughter, sir. They will be brought to justice," Oz said, trying to recover from Terry's interjection.

"God, why did this happen to my baby?" David cried, no longer able to hold back the tears.

"We are so genuinely sorry, and you both have our deepest sympathies. I'm going to leave you my card," Oz said, pulling a business card from his inside breast pocket, and placed it on the coffee table. "Please do not hesitate to reach out if there is anything you need. We'll leave you two to process this. Again, our deepest sympathies. We'll let ourselves out."

Terry and Oz stood up and headed for the door. David and Mary stayed seated in a huddled mess, sobbing, searching for something to make sense of what they were just told. Oz opened the door and followed Terry out, closing the door gently behind them. They walked back to the car and got in.

"Bwoah! That was fucking rough, kid," said Terry, as they got back in the car, and Oz started to back out of the driveway. "I need a Dunkees after that, kid."

"Are you fucking serious, man? What the fuck was that? That was hard enough. Why did you have to say that shit about a closed casket?" Oz said, annoyed.

"What? It's true?" replied Terry.

"I thought you said that you had done this before?" chirped Oz.

"I have, but most of them were either shot or stabbed. Nothing this brutal before. Sorry, kid. You were the hot ticket in there, though. Good job!" said Terry. This was as close to an apology as Oz was going to get out of him.

"Thanks, Ter," said Oz.

"So… are we gonna hit Dunkees?" Terry said boyishly.

"Yeah, Ter. We'll get you your 'Dunkees', you junkie," Oz said, chuckling at his partner.

"Hey! Easy there, cawksuckah, I'm still your superior, you know," Terry laughed.

***

Oz pulled the Impala into the parking lot at the station and parked in one of the designated spots for the officer's vehicles. "Are we cutting out early today, Ter?" asked Oz.

"Yeah. Why not, kid? Not like we are gonna do much more today anyway," replied Terry.

"You have anything planned for the weekend?" asked Oz.

"Who the fuck knows, kid. Mo will most likely tell me at some point what she has planned," replied Terry.

Maureen was Terry's wife. She was an absolutely lovely woman. At least that was the impression that Oz got when he met her that time that Terry forgot his wallet at home, and they had to swing by to get it. Though to hear Terry talk about her now and then, you'd swear that she was a nasty nag. He was pretty sure that was just Terry being one of the guys. And how you're supposed to complain about your old lady. Deep down Oz was pretty sure that he loved her, and he was happy, well happy for Terry, that is.

Maureen was a couple of years younger than Terry, but they had been together since his senior year of high school. Other than the gray that she hid by getting it colored as close to her natural red as she could at the salon, she still looked as young and beautiful as she did when they met. She was about 5' 7", tall and curvy. A real hourglass figure, the kind that da Vinci himself would have used as a model. She had captivating, compassionate, green eyes, like something out of a comic book, just unreal.

Terry and Maureen never had any children. Oz had asked once when he was first partnered with Terry. Terry explained that they tried for the first couple of years after they were married, but nothing ever took. They had seen a fertility specialist and find out why they were having such a hard time conceiving, learning that the problem was with Terry's "swimmers", as he put it. He was crushed that he could not give Maureen what she had always wanted. However, as much as Maureen wanted children, and wanted to be a mother, she only ever wanted them with Terry, and if he wasn't able to give her one, then clearly the good Lord had other plans for them, and they weren't meant to have them.

"What about you, kid? You're not gonna hang around here all weekend, are you?" asked Terry.

"Hadn't really thought about it, man, I might. I don't really have anything else to do," said Oz.

"Go out to the bar, meet a lady, get hammered. Something other than coming into this place, kid," preached Terry.

"Yeah, we'll see, man, no promises," laughed Oz.

"Hang on a second, kid," said Terry, reaching into his coat pocket and pulling out his phone. He tapped the screen a few times and put it to his ear.

"What are you doing, man?" asked Oz.

"Shh, gimme a sec," said Terry. "Hey, Hun. How are you?"

Oz couldn't hear what Maureen was saying on the other end of the phone, but clearly it was her. Terry wouldn't call anyone else, Hun, would he?

"What are we having for supper? Uh-huh... Is there enough for one more? Yeah... Oz... yeah! That's what I said to him, too. Uh-huh... Yeah, we are pretty much done for the day. Yeah... alright Hun, yeah, love you too... alright... bye," said Terry as he hung up the phone. "You're coming to the house for supper tonight, kid. So, there's your Friday night, figured out, now you'll have to listen to Maureen push you to not work all the time, and get out and do something."

"Terry, I wasn't fishing for an invitation…" Oz said, getting cut off.

"Did I say you were? I just made plans for you, you're welcome," said Terry. "Now let's get going, so we can have a few lagers before supper."

"Ter, seriously man, I don't wanna impose," said Oz.

"You're not, kid. I invited you, besides Maureen was bugging me to have you over anyway, so this kills two birds with one stone. She'll get off my ass about it, and you'll have something to do," joked Terry. "So can we go now? It's been a fucking day and a half, kid?"

"Sure, Ter. And thank you, man, this means a lot!" said Oz.

"Whatever, kid. It's nothing. Let's call it a day. You remember how to get to the house? Or are you just gonna follow me?" asked Terry.

"I remember the way. I'll be right behind you. Just gonna make a quick stop first," said Oz.

"Alright, kid. See you in a few then," said Terry as he got out of the car and headed across the lot to his car.

Oz took a breath. *Well, this was unexpected, but should be a good time. Maureen is a sweetheart, and Terry… well, Terry can be fun… right?* He thought. *Shit, I didn't ask what we were having… oh well, I'll just get something that will work for whatever we could be having.* Oz got out of the Impala, locked it, and went inside to drop the keys with the motor pool. He hung the keys up on the hook with their car ID above it, "DET 35", and left the building. He crossed the lot to his car, and thought, *just go and have a good time, at least it won't be soup or takeout for dinner.*

4

Oz pulled up to Terry and Maureen's house about a quarter after five. The sun was setting. The sky changed colors from the gray that had been pretty much all day to the now almost lavender-colored sky. He reached across to the passenger seat, where he grabbed the bottle of Fat Bastard Chardonnay and Fat Bastard Cabernet that he had picked up at the liquor store on his way. He also grabbed the arrangement of flowers that he had picked up for Maureen. Oz's mom would kill him if he showed up empty-handed to someone's house. *That's not how you were raised, Ozwald.* He could hear his mom saying. Oz got out of the car and walked up the front steps to the front door.

Terry and Maureen's house was in Cambridge. It was a nice house. Two and a half stories, siding painted a lovely blue, a little darker of a shade than a robin's egg blue. The garden in the house's front was full of flowers and bushes and was very well kept when they were in bloom. That wouldn't be long from now when it started to get warmer. Now, though, there was still a bit of snow leftover and hanging on after the massive rains that they had just had.

There was a small double-wide driveway to the left of the house, where Terry's Chevy Malibu and Maureen's Mini were parked.

Oz rang the doorbell to the right of the large, dark-stained, and heavy wood door. The bells chimed in the house. A few seconds later, the door opened. There was Maureen, to greet him. A massive smile on her face.

"Oz, Hun," she said, sweetly greeting him. "How are you? Come in, come in."

"Hi, Maureen," said Oz, as he'd been warned when he met her to call her Maureen, not Mrs. White, not ma'am, just Maureen, or Mo. Whichever he felt comfortable with. Anything else made her feel old, and she wanted none of that. "I'm great, thank you. You look lovely as ever, and, is that dinner? It smells lovely."

"Oh, aren't you a charmer," she said.

"Oh, these are for you!" Oz said as he handed her the flowers. "And I brought wine, white and red. I forgot to ask Terry what you were making."

"They are lovely Oz, thank you," she said, raised herself up on her tip-toes, leaned in, and gave him a little kiss on the cheek. "Look Hun, Oz got me flowers! When was the last time you got me flowers?" said Maureen, taking a playful jab at Terry.

"When I told you to find a woman, I didn't mean go after mine. I don't wanna have to shoot you, kid. I was just starting to like you," replied Terry, jokingly.

Terry approached the door from the living room, off to the left of the door. He took the bottles of wine from Oz and walked towards the kitchen at the rear of the house.

Maureen closed the door behind Oz and followed Terry to the kitchen. "Hun, can you get me that vase from the cupboard up there?" she said to Terry. "I wanna put these beautiful flowers in that, so I can keep them alive and have a reminder that I'm still a desirable woman," she said, taking another dig at Terry as she winked and smiled at Oz.

Oz laughed as he followed them to the kitchen.

"Good choice on the wine, kid," Terry said, laughing. "Fat Bastard!"

"Terry, he's our guest. Don't talk to him like that," Maureen said.

"Hun, it's the name of the wine, look," said Terry, showing her the bottle of the Cabernet.

"Oh," she said, laughing, slightly embarrassed. "Where did you find that? That is hilarious."

Oz laughed with them. "I had a pretty good laugh when I saw it in the store. Hopefully, it's good."

"Lager, kid?" asked Terry.

"Sure, Ter. That'd be great," replied Oz.

Terry opened the fridge and pulled out two bottles of Samuel Adams Boston Lager and opened them. He handed one to Oz; they clinked bottles and took a drink.

"You boys go talk shop and let me finish getting supper ready," ordered Maureen. She hated people in her kitchen when she worked.

"Come on, kid. Let's leave Maureen be," Terry said, escorting Oz out of the kitchen into the living room.

"I really appreciate this, Ter," said Oz.

"Stop, it should have happened sooner, kid. After all, you're my partner. If we don't look out for each other, who will?" said Terry reassuringly.

Oz was definitely seeing a different side of Terry tonight. He was pretty sure that it wasn't just a show that Terry was putting on for Maureen. This seemed like the real Terry. The one that he let few people see. Oz sat on the couch while Terry sat in the armchair that faced the television. The TV wasn't on, but you could hear the static crackling on the screen as though someone had recently shut it off.

"I don't wanna talk about this case in front of Maureen, okay?" Terry whispered.

"Yeah. Sure thing, Ter. I think we've both had our fill of it for now, anyway. Not much else to go on at this point," said Oz.

"So do you think the Sox are gonna take it this year?" said Terry.

"I dunno, haven't really followed baseball much since I left Michigan. I used to go to the odd Tigers game there," replied Oz.

"Have you seen a game at Fenway yet?" asked Terry.

"No, not yet," replied Oz.

"What? How long have you been in Boston now? Four? Five years?" Terry said, shocked that anyone hadn't been to Fenway to watch a game.

"Almost six years, yeah, I know, I need to go," said Oz, a little embarrassed. He really had done little of anything since he got to Boston. He worked every hour he could get as a patrolman and spent a lot of time studying and preparing for his detective's exams. Then he made detective, and he didn't even go out to celebrate.

"For fuck's sake, kid! It's happening then. We are gonna do at least one game this season. If we play our cards right, maybe we can get paid to be at the game," Terry said, laughing.

"Yeah, that would be cool, Ter," laughed Oz.

"Don't mention it, kid. It'll be fun. I remember my dad taking me to games there as a kid. Sometimes sitting up on the Monster. Nothing like a game at Fenway, kid. It's pretty much a religious experience," Terry said, laughing.

"Hope you boys are hungry," said Maureen, walking into the room. "Shouldn't be long now."

Maureen sat on the arm of the chair that Terry was sitting in. She looked lovely as ever, even if she was only wearing jeans and a button-down plaid shirt, with the sleeves rolled a quarter of the way up her arms. Somehow, she could even make this look sexy. She put her arm around Terry and leaned towards him. "So, Oz… have you met a nice Boston girl yet since you've been here?" she asked.

"Jesus, Maureen, straight at it, huh?" joked Terry.

"What? I can't ask a question?" she said.

"No, not really, Maureen. Haven't really had much time," Oz replied.

"How long have you been here now?" she asked.

"Almost six years," Oz replied, just waiting for Maureen to say something.

"Six years and you haven't had time? What the hell have you been doing?" she asked with a slight look of disappointment on her face.

"Hasn't even been to Fenway, Hun," chirped Terry.

"That's sinful," she joked.

"Mostly just focused on work, to be honest," Oz replied, chuckling awkwardly at being grilled. "All I ever wanted was to be a cop, so I just threw myself into it completely."

"Well, you are one now, so let's see if we can't get you fixed up with a nice girl," she said. "Oh shit, supper!"

Maureen hopped up from the arm of the chair and ran to the kitchen.

"She's serious, you know… you're now her little pet project. You're fucked now, kid," Terry said, laughing.

"Supper fellas, c'mon over to the table," Maureen shouted from the kitchen.

Oz took a swig from his beer and followed Terry to the table. The round dining table, set for three, with the fourth chair, tucked into the table with no place setting. Oz sat in the chair off to the left of Terry, who sat in the chair with his back to the living room that they just came from.

Maureen entered the room with two plates for the boys. Each loaded with steaming-hot food. Maureen had made oven-roasted, seasoned, bone-in chicken breasts, long-grain rice that was flavored with chicken broth, and her special blend of seasonings that she wasn't willing to reveal, steamed broccoli, cauliflower, and carrots. It had been longer than Oz cared to mention since he last had a home-cooked meal, and this meal smelled incredible. Maureen brought in her plate last, along with a bowl of freshly mixed salad. *This is quite the spread. I really hope she didn't go through all of this trouble just for him*, he thought.

"There's French and Italian dressing for the salad, here. I think there's ranch dressing in the fridge if you'd prefer that?" said Maureen.

"No, thank you. This is perfect. I really hope that you didn't go through any extra trouble just for me?" Oz said, smelling the food in front of him.

"No trouble at all, Hun. Just means Terry, won't have any to snack on later," she said, laughing.

The food was delicious. Everything exploded with flavor in Oz's mouth. It was the most incredible meal that he'd had in a long time. The chicken was juicy, and the veggies had been cooked to perfection.

"Maureen, this is absolutely incredible," remarked Oz.

"Glad you like it, Hun. So, you guys were working late last night. Big case?" she asked.

"Not really, Hun. Just another case, nothing special," said Terry, taking another mouthful of his supper.

"So, Maureen, what do you do?" asked Oz, quickly trying to change the subject.

"Me, I do a few hours down at the florist a few days a week and interior design from time to time. But mostly I just look after my Terry. He wouldn't make it without me. Isn't that right, Hun?"

"Yeah, babe, that's right. I'd be completely lost without you," said Terry, looking adoringly at Maureen as he reached for her hand to give it a loving squeeze.

"How did you two meet?" asked Oz.

"We met in High School. Terry was a senior, and I was a sophomore. For weeks, I would see him walking the halls. I didn't think he ever saw me. At least it seemed that way. He would walk by my locker and not even a glance my way," said Maureen.

"Gotta play it cool, kid," said Terry.

"Yeah, okay, tough guy. Anyway, for months this went on. He'd walk by, and I'd just stare at him. My friends would poke fun at me. They'd see him coming and tease me, 'Mo, here comes your boyfriend', they'd say, and loud, too, so there was no way that Terry didn't hear them. But he'd just walk by like always." Maureen giggled and blushed as she relived the story. "Before senior prom, he scared the shit outta me. He came up behind me at my locker and said 'hey'. I spun around to see him looking at me. I blushed and said 'hi' back. He said, 'I'm Terry. I know you don't know me but, for months I've been working up the courage to come and talk to you, and… well, I was wondering if you would like to go to prom with me?' I was frozen. I couldn't believe this was happening. I couldn't speak, I just kept staring into his eyes, then one of my girlfriends said, 'if she doesn't say yes, I'll go with you.' Immediately, I came to my senses and told her to shut up, and I said 'yes, absolutely I will!'. Then he asked what my name was." This made Oz laugh.

"She was all flustered and said, 'Me? I'm uh… uh'," said Terry. "She forgot her name, kid. It was hilarious. I'd never had that effect on a girl before. That was pretty much when I knew I wasn't gonna do any better than her." Terry lifted Maureen's hand and kissed it.

"Yeah, been together every day since," said Maureen.

"Aww, that's so sweet, Ter. I had no idea you were such a softy," said Oz, taking a jab at Terry.

"Don't tell anybody, or I'll fucking kill you," Terry said, laughing.

The conversation continued throughout dinner. Maureen got up and cleared the plates and brought both men a fresh beer from the fridge. When she returned, she sat back down and joined the boys in joking and laughing.

Time seemed to fly by as they all got to know each other. Eventually, they opened the Cabernet and had a couple of glasses of that. Hanging out with Terry and Maureen was like hanging out with old friends. It was comfortable, and the conversation flowed freely. There were no awkward silences, just good laughs, and great stories.

Around 11:30 pm, Terry's cell phone rang in the kitchen on the counter. Terry got up from the table to answer it.

"Detective White, Homicide," he said as he answered. "Yeah… Uh-huh… at the Harbor?… Right… well, I can't come down now. I'm a bit fucked up at the moment. Wasn't expecting to leave the house tonight… Oz? I'll see if he can make it… Yeah, I'll get a hold of him… Yeah, alright, Jim… Yeah… Yeah… Okay, you too… G'night."

"Who was that, Ter?" asked Maureen, beating Oz to it.

"That was the Lieutenant. Apparently, they found a body down at the Harbor," replied Terry. "Are you ok to drive, kid?"

"Yeah, Ter, I was taking it easy, since I was driving home, anyway. Are you coming? I can handle it solo if…" said Oz, before being cut off.

"Nah, Jim wants both of us down there," said Terry.

"Let me make you guys some coffee before you go," said Maureen, already on her way to the kitchen to put a pot on.

"That's alright, Hun. We'll just grab a Dunkees on the way. Right, kid?" said Terry.

"Yeah, for sure, Ter. Maureen, thank you again so much for tonight. Everything was delicious!" said Oz, getting up from the table.

"You're welcome, Hun. Glad you liked it. Please come back anytime. You boys be careful, alright?" said Maureen, as she gave Terry a kiss on the cheek.

"Let me hit the pisser before we go, kid," said Terry as he walked off to the washroom.

"Oz, you look after my Terry, please! Make sure that you bring him home safe to me, alright?" said Maureen.

"Yeah, Maureen, of course. I'll get him home safe," said Oz, putting his hand reassuringly on her shoulder.

"Oz, I don't just mean tonight," she said.

"I won't let you down, Maureen. I'll always look out for him, I promise," replied Oz.

"Thank you," she said, and gave him a kiss on the cheek. "Now, go get the bad guys!"

"Thank you again for everything, Maureen. It really was incredible. Spending time with you both was the most fun I've had in a long while. I feel bad leaving you with the cleanup, though," said Oz.

"Don't be silly. You're doing all the dishes next time," she joked. "Go on, you guys have a job to do."

Oz laughed and replied, "Deal. Thanks again."

Terry came out of the washroom and came back to the kitchen. He grabbed his phone, badge, wallet, and his keys. He gave Maureen a kiss on the lips, and said, "Alright Hun, we're off, hopefully, we aren't out all night. I love you."

Terry grabbed his sport coat and his shoulder rig with his police issue SIG Sauer GSR buckled into the holster from the closet by the door. He swung it on around his shoulders, shrugging it into position before putting his coat on.

"I love you too," she replied.

Oz walked out the door with Terry right behind him. Maureen watched them go down the stairs and get into Oz's car. She waved goodbye to them as they pulled away.

***

Terry's cell phone buzzed in his coat pocket. He reached into his coat, retrieved it, unlocked it, and read the text message from the Lieutenant. All that the text said was 'Pier 6'.

"Pier 6, kid," said Terry. "Best to take First to Eighth, take a right, and go all the way to the rotary."

Oz continued driving, following Terry's directions. They arrived at the 8th street roundabout, near the pier. When they pulled up to Pier 6 three squad cars blocked it behind yellow police tape, lights flashing, illuminating the surroundings in flashes of blue and red lights from atop the cruisers. Oz parked his car just outside the police tape. As they were got out of the Mustang, an officer approached them.

"Hey, you guys, gotta get outta here. Get back in your car and bang-a-U-ey," said the officer.

"Detectives White and Shields," Terry shouted at the officer. "We were told there's a body here."

"A body?" said the officer. "Not quite."

"What?" said Oz as they approached the officer.

"Well, it's not so much a body as it is a part of one," said the officer. "Go about halfway down the pier on your right, past the blue roofs. There's another detective there with some troopers."

"Thanks," said Oz as he and Terry crossed the police tape and walked down the pier.

They walked down to where the officer told them, and they saw two other officers there and a man who had to be the detective. The detective was short and skinny with pale skin and had an aimless feeling about him. He had deep brown eyes and short, frizzy, light-brown hair was unkempt, as if he needed a haircut and just couldn't be bothered to go and get one. He was definitely dressed like most detectives nowadays, a gray blazer over a white button-down shirt and jeans, and was smoking a cigarette and talking to the officers.

"Detective?" Oz called out.

The man turned and looked their way, threw his cigarette down on the ground, and stepped on it to put it out. He exhaled a plume of smoke as he approached them.

"Detectives Shields and White, Homicide," Oz announced as he reached forward to shake the man's hand.

"Boys," the man said as he shook both of their hands. "Detective Mickey McCarthy, Narcotics."

"Narcotics? What the fuck are you doing at a homicide?" asked Terry.

"I came down here to meet a CI of mine," started Mickey. "When I got here, my C.I. booked it past me, yelling something about this body down here and that they were outta here. I thought they were outta their fucking mind, tripping, or something. I walked down here and that is when I found it. Just like you see it. I called it in. The troopers showed up a few minutes before you guys did and taped off the area, and we've just been here waiting for you to show."

"You didn't stop them and get a statement?" asked Oz.

"No, like I said, he was legging it," replied Mickey.

"Can we get this C.I.'s name? We are going to need a statement from him," said Oz.

"I'll try to call him, and see if I can get something from him. But I can't give you his name," said Mickey.

"Thanks, Mickey. Let us know what you find out," said Oz.

"No worries, kid. The body is just over there," he said, pointing just off to the West side of the pier. Mickey turned away from them and pulled out his phone to make the call.

"Hopefully, the photographer shows up soon," said Terry as they walked toward the location of the body.

As Terry and Oz approached the location of the body, Oz pulled out his Maglite and turned it on, lighting their path as they turned the corner of the structure. Nothing could've prepared them for what they saw when the light hit the body. Now, what the officer had said made more sense to them. Laying on the ground was only part of what used to be a person. There was an arm, part of a leg from the thigh down, and what looked like the middle part of the torso and pelvis with the entrails spilling out of it in a large pool of blood.

"Fuck's sake!" cried Oz at the scene before them.

"Your not gonna puke again, are you?" joked Terry.

"No, man. Fuck you! That happened once," said Oz, taking every bit of his willpower to not toss the wonderful meal that Maureen had just made them.

"You only gotta suck one cock to be a queer," joked Terry.

"Fuck you! I'm not gonna puke," laughed Oz.

"Aww, don't be so sensitive Oz, I'm just having a little fun at your expense. You know, giving the new guy a hard time," said Terry.

"Fucked up, ain't it?" said Mickey, scaring both Terry and Oz, not knowing that he had followed them there.

"Jesus. You can't sneak up on people like that," said Oz, his heart racing.

"Sorry. The photographer is here," said Mickey. "And I got a hold of my CI."

"And?" said Oz, trying to get Mickey to spill it.

"Right," said Mickey. "He said he got here a few minutes early and walked down the pier, and on his way back up from the end, he saw the body parts. He said that he thought it was just some bum laying there, until he got closer and saw that the body was all faked up like… well, that. Then his words were, 'I shit myself and fucking booked it outta there'."

"He didn't see anyone else down here? Or hear anything?" asked Oz.

"Nah. He said it was creepy quiet, and he was making sure that he was alone like we always do."

"Thanks, Mickey. We'll be in touch if it turns out that your CI is lying to us," replied Oz. "You can take off now. We've got this from here."

"Are you kidding me? I'm not going anywhere? I gotta see this," said Mickey, sounding excited by all of this.

"Okay," Oz said, confused by this odd little man. He turned to Terry and said, "I don't think we are going to be lucky enough to find an ID this time."

The photographer came around the corner and said, "Whoa. I wasn't expecting that." He snapped several pictures from various angles. The flash lit the pier with each snap. The photographer gave the detectives a nod to let them know that he had finished and that they could proceed with a closer inspection.

"Have at it, kid," said Terry. "Tell me what you think."

Oz crouched close to the body parts, shining his light on them to have a better look.

"It looks like we have a light-skinned African-American woman. No clue about the age of the victim. She seems to have been in fairly good shape, judging from the muscle tone in her leg and abdomen." He shined his light at the edge of the upper thigh. "Looks like the same tattered flesh as our last victim. Could these be related?" Oz moved his light to the wall of the structure, looking for blood splatter or spray. "Nothing on the wall of the structure, but it appears as though someone killed right here her, from all the blood."

Where are her clothes? If she was killed here, her clothes should still be here, or at least parts of them, he thought to himself. "She may have been out here for a run. She has a running shoe on her foot, no sign of the other shoe, though. Or her clothes." Oz stood up and walked over to the edge of the pier and looked over the edge for anything floating in the water, being careful not to step into the pool of blood. "I don't see anything in the water, but that doesn't mean that something didn't either fall in or get thrown in," he shouted back to Terry. "Wouldn't hurt to get some divers in to do a search."

"Yeah, kid. We'll tell the geeks when they get here," said Terry.

Going back to the body parts, Oz kneeled again. This time inspecting the arm that lay there. Blood ran down the arm from where it had been torn from the shoulder. *Torn from the shoulder, that's crazy. Who could rip off a person's arm like this?* He thought. "The victim is wearing one of those Fitbit things. Maybe we can get some information about her identity from that?"

"Got me, kid. Don't those things just count your steps?" asked Terry.

"They track everything. Steps, heart rate, blood pressure, sleep, and who knows what else at this point. Some of them even have GPS to track routes and whatnot," said Oz.

"Well, that sure would help. If it does all that, then we could find out where she lives, right?" said Terry.

"Definitely a possibility," said Oz.

"Anything else?" asked Terry.

"I'm no doctor, but shouldn't there be more blood than this?" asked Oz. "I mean, there is a lot here, but it just seems like there should be more. It's not raining, and it's still quite cool out, but it didn't run off the pier and into the water." Oz shined his flashlight around the edges of the pool of blood. The blood had begun to congeal because of the cool air and slight breeze. "I dunno Ter, this seems really bizarre, man. Like last night, there is something that just doesn't make sense."

"Well, I don't think we're gonna figure anything else out tonight. Let's call it and get outta here," said Terry, clearly eager to get home.

"Yeah, sure, man," Oz said, still very puzzled by the two crime scenes.

Oz stood up and he walked over to where Terry was. Mickey McCarthy was still here, right beside Terry. Hanging on to every word being said. Totally captivated by all of this, like he was watching a movie play out before him.

"That's it?" Mickey said. "You guys are leaving?"

"Yup, not much that we are going to find out tonight. Forensics will do their thing, and we'll wait to hear what they say," said Oz.

"Shit, I was kinda hoping for more than this," said Mickey, totally disappointed.

"You can hang out with the geeks if you want. Otherwise, keep your eyes on the papers, Mick, see how it plays out," said Terry.

Terry and Oz walked back up the pier towards Oz's car. Oz lifted the police tape and Terry went under it, followed by Oz. The Forensic Science team was just arriving on scene. Their big white truck looked like an RV with its pickup truck front end, but behind the cab was this massive camper. On the sides of the camper were navy-blue decals that read 'Forensic Science Division'. The truck stretched about twenty-six feet in length, was climate controlled, and had a full electronics suite with a generator. This unit gave them the ability to control and work on-site to process the collected evidence. It also contained photography equipment, tools to collect and preserve physical evidence, evidence collection supplies, packaging, and identification kits, and a ton of personal protective equipment. There was even a small shower inside in case one of the forensic personnel got contaminated, or worse.

"The geeks are here," said Terry.

"Yeah, let's see what they can put together for us," said Oz. "You guys may want to call in the divers," shouted Oz at one of them.

"Thanks, asshole, it's not our first rodeo!" one forensic officer yelled back.

"Fucking geeks. Think they are better than everyone else, should've never given them a TV show," Terry said.

Oz just laughed and brushed off the guy's comment. They got into Oz's car and drove away from the crime scene. It was now well after 1 am when Oz pulled up to Terry's place. There was a light shining through the window on the upper floor of the house.

"Looks like Maureen is still up," said Terry.

"Yeah, thanks again to the both of you for tonight, Ter. I really appreciated it," said Oz.

"Don't mention it, kid. Thanks for coming. Don't be so weird about it next time. You're always welcome over here, kid," said Terry. "Have a good night. I better get in before Maureen thinks you're putting the moves on me out here," Terry laughed.

"Fuck you, Ter!" Oz laughed. "I'll see you later, man. Thanks again."

Terry got out of the car and headed up the stairs to the front door. He unlocked the door, opened it, and entered the house. He turned and waved to Oz and closed the door. Oz waved back and drove off, headed for his apartment. *That was definitely an interesting Friday night*, he thought to himself.

5

The next morning, Oz awoke to the sun shining into his room through the blinds. He sat up in his bed, yawned, and stretched as he turned his head to look at his alarm clock to see what time it was. His alarm clock read 10:45 am, which meant that it was really only 10:30 am, as he set the clock fifteen minutes ahead so that when his alarm goes off, it tricks his brain into thinking it's later than it actually was. It was a thing that he had done since high school. By now it should no longer work, but for Oz, it did. He never hit the snooze button because of it.

Oz reached for his phone on the nightstand, where it was plugged in charging, to see if there were any messages or missed calls. There was none, but this wasn't unusual. If there was any, it would most likely have been from his mom, complaining that he hasn't called or texted her in a while. *I should probably call her and see how they are*, he thought. *They aren't getting any younger.* He put his phone back on the nightstand and got out of bed.

He walked into the bathroom and turned on the shower. Making sure it was just the right temperature before kicking off his boxers and getting in. *Oh yeah, this is undoubtedly what you needed, Ozzy.* As he washed and scrubbed his hair and body, he felt all tension leaving his body. At this moment, there was nothingness, just complete relaxation. He rubbed some soap on the little mirror stuck to the wall of the shower, lathered his face, getting ready for a shave. Splashed a little water on the mirror, and grabbed his razor from the little holder on the mirror, and shaved.

After the shower, he got out, dried himself off, quickly applied some antiperspirant and a splash of Old Spice aftershave, and went back to his bedroom. He threw on a fresh pair of boxer briefs, some socks, a fresh pair of jeans, and a navy-blue crew neck t-shirt. Oz made his bed, making sure to have a four-inch fold over the sheet and cover at the top of the bed, with almost military-like precision. He swept his hands across the top of the bed, making sure that all the wrinkles and ripples had vanished.

In the kitchen, he grabbed a bowl from one of the upper cupboards. Poured himself a bowl of Honey Nut Cheerios, closed up the bag, folding it over, and pressing it tight before closing the box and putting it back in the cupboard. He grabbed the jug of milk from the fridge and poured it over the cereal, swirling it counterclockwise over it, as he always did. He grabbed a spoon out of the drawer, put it in the bowl, took it over to the small breakfast bar behind him, and took a seat on one of the stools on the other side.

I should head to the station after this and open the case file for the second murder, and see if there is anything from the Medical Examiner or the Forensic Science Division. Terry will kill me if he finds out that I was at work. I won't stay, though.

Just a quick in and out. As if this would make a difference when Terry found out.

Oz finished his breakfast, rinsed his bowl, and put it in the dishwasher. He grabbed his phone off his nightstand and his keys off the counter. Made sure that he had his wallet and ID, and left the apartment. It was nice outside; the sun was shining, and it was roughly 60° F. *Perfect day for a walk*. Oz pulled out his phone and called his Mom.

"Hello?" the voice on the other end of the line said.

"Mom, hi, it's Ozzy," he said.

"Oh Ozzy, so great to hear from you. How are you? How are things in Boston?" his mom said.

"Good, yeah. Things are going well. I have a couple of cases on the go. No leads yet, but things are good. How are you? How's Dad?" said Oz.

"We are good. Dad was at the doctor's the other day. Nothing serious, just a check-up. He still has to watch his blood pressure, and the Doctor keeps telling him to cut back on the greasy foods, but you know your father," his mom said. "That is pretty much it with us. Your sister and Will were here with the boys last weekend, they're getting so big. Will just got promoted at his work as Regional Manager. So, they are all good."

"Tracey was there? Nice. Glad you had a great time with them. When you are talking to her next, send her my love," said Oz.

"They were all asking about you. You should call her sometime. I'm sure they'd love to hear from you," said his Mom, as she laid on the guilt.

"Alright, Mom, I'll try to find time to call her," said Oz.

Oz and his sister used to be much closer. Tracey was only a couple of years younger than him. She got married the year before he moved to Boston. Will was a good guy, hard-working, and always treated his sister well. She and Will had their first boy, Thomas, not long after, most likely a honeymoon baby. Oz remembered being there the day Thomas was born. He was there in the waiting room with his Mom and dad. When they were allowed in to see Tracey and the baby, Oz was the first to hold him. He had to get to Thomas first, otherwise; he would never get him from his Mom. He remembered how great he felt becoming an uncle. Their next son Michael was born three years later. Oz was already in Boston by this point and only saw pictures of Michael until he got home for Christmas that year. He missed them all so much, but work always came first.

"Have you done anything exciting lately?" she asked

"No, not really, Mom. Pretty much just working. I had dinner with my partner, Terry, and his wife, Maureen, last night. That's about the most exciting thing I've done," said Oz.

"Oh well, that was nice, Hun. You two are bonding?" his mom said.

"Yeah, I think so, Terry is a tough read, but he's what I imagine having an older brother would be like."

"That's so nice to hear, Ozzy. We always worry about you there all by yourself. I'm glad that you are starting to finally bond with someone, though. I wish you were back home though and not so far away," said his Mom.

"Yeah, anyway, Mom, I just wanted to call and see how you guys were. I'm just on my way to work for a few. Give my love to Dad and everyone, and I'll talk to you soon, okay? I love you," Oz said.

"Oh, okay, Ozzy. We love you too, don't work too hard, okay? Bye," she said.

"Bye, Mom," said Oz, and he hung up.

That should be good for a while, he thought. Not that he didn't enjoy calling home, but the calls always went the same way. His Mom would eventually make him feel guilty for moving to Boston and for not calling enough. She did it out of love and not malice, but it was still irritating.

Oz got to the station and went inside and up to his desk. He nodded at a couple of the other detectives there on his way to his desk. He sat down and turned on his computer, logged in, and filled in the details of the crime scene last night after he opened a new case file. Then he opened up his Outlook to see if there was anything from the Medical Examiner or from the Forensic Science Division. Not seeing anything, he thought, *Shit! There is no way that forensics has found nothing yet, especially with the scene for the first victim. There has to be something there that we didn't see.*

Oz sat back in his chair and looked up at the ceiling. *Think Ozzy... think! There has to be something you're not seeing. Something you're missing. Think back to your training. Are there questions that you didn't ask yourself at the scene?*

"Shields? What are you doing in? You're not on shift today, are you?"

"Lieutenant... uh no sir, not on shift. I uh... just wanted to start the case file on the victim from the pier last night," said Oz, startled by the Lieutenant.

"Right, how was that?" said Jim as he walked over to sit at Terry's desk.

"Brutal sir. There wasn't much left of the victim there. There were some similarities to the victim from the night before, but there is really nothing to link the two, other than how savagely they were killed and that they were both females. Still no witnesses other than those that found the bodies. No motives. No signs of a recognizable murder weapon. Nothing. Not even anything from FSD yet," Oz said, frustrated.

"Listen, kid, I know that you really wanna solve these cases, but it takes time. There's nothing you're missing, so get that outta your head. You're a good detective, and one day you're gonna be a great one," Jim continued. "Just be patient, kid. These things can't be rushed. Some will fall right in your lap. Some will never get solved. It's just that way it is. But you can't let it consume you like this. If you do, the only thing that will happen is you'll drive yourself mad. Then you're no fucking good to me," he chuckled and smiled at Oz. "You'll find that most cases get solved when you're not thinking about them at all. You know what I'm saying?"

"Yes, sir, thank you. I appreciate this," said Oz.

"Great!" Jim said as he slapped his hands on the desk. "Now, get the fuck outta here and go do something. Hit the gym, the bar, go get laid, anything for fuck's sake, just get outta here and don't think about this place until Monday, alright? That's an order!"

"Yes, sir, thank you, sir," Oz chuckled and smiled.

Jim got up and winked at Oz before heading back to his office. "Quit calling me sir! I'm not your father, and I'm not that fucking old," Jim yelled out jokingly as he entered his office.

Well, that was different. That's the first time that I've ever had a boss tell me to stop working before, especially when it was basically unpaid. Oz laughed to himself, shut down his computer, pushed his chair in, and left the station. He reached into the pocket of his jeans and pulled out a pair of Bluetooth earbuds and put them in. He hit play on his phone and the music started playing. *Clear your head, Ozzy. That's what the Lieutenant said.* Oz started walking back to his apartment, enjoying the beautiful spring day in Boston, letting his mind clear as he just listened to song after song the entire way home.

***

Ring… Ring… Ring…

Oz's phone rang, waking him up from a dead sleep. He had drifted off watching TV. He grabbed his phone from the small wooden table beside the couch. Looking at the screen, he saw it was Terry.

"Hello?" Oz answered, sounding like he had just woken up.

"Oz, it's Terry," he said

"Yeah, Ter, what's up? What time is it?" asked Oz.

"We got another body," said Terry. "It's 9:30. I'll be there in twenty minutes to get you. Be downstairs."

"Yeah, sure man, no problem," said Oz.

Terry hung up. Oz stretched and got up off the couch. He slid his phone into the back pocket of his jeans. *9:30, fuck me, really wasted the day, Ozzy. Well, at least I'm well-rested. I'd better get my ass moving, so Terry isn't waiting for me.*

Oz walked over to the kitchen and grabbed a chocolate chip protein bar from the cupboard, felt his jeans to make sure that he still had his wallet and keys on him, snatched his badge off the counter, and clipped it to his belt. He went into his bedroom closet and opened the small gun safe, upon the shelf, that he kept his service pistol in, a Smith & Wesson Glock Model 27. He made sure the safety was active, released the clip, checked the magazine, slid it back in, and pulled back the slide, and checked the chamber. With his pistol checked, he walked to the front door and grabbed his black nylon shoulder rig that hung on the hook, slid his pistol into the holster and snapped it in and put it on. He threw on his BPD windbreaker jacket, which was hanging on the hook, before he left his apartment, locking the door behind him.

Oz waited outside the building for about five minutes before Terry pulled up in his Malibu, which gave him time to eat the protein bar. Terry pulled up to the curb, and Oz got in the passenger side.

"Hey, Ter, what do we know?" he asked.

"Hey, kid, I know this is fucking up my weekend," said Terry, pulling away from the curb. "The B's are on. It's the final fucking games before the playoffs!"

"Inconsiderate fucks," joked Oz.

Oz could hear the game on the radio. WBZ-FM 98.5 The Bruins Radio Network. Judd Sirott called the play-by-play and Bob Beers did the usual color commentary. From the sounds of it, the game was a close one. The Bruins had secured their playoff spot at this point, but as a fan you always want them to finish the season strong, heading into the playoffs. They would most likely face the Maple Leafs again in the first round.

"You got that right, kid," replied Terry.

"So where are we heading this time, Ter?" asked Oz.

"Charlestown," said Terry, keeping his answers brief, trying to listen to the last moments of the game.

Oz didn't say anymore, letting Terry enjoy the rest of the game as they drove to the crime scene. They arrived at the Charlestown Community Center, where Terry pulled into the parking lot on the North-Eastern side of the building. The parking lot was vacant except for the three police cruisers, lights flashing, that were parked near the openings in the chain-link fence to the track and field. Right near the building the officers had run the yellow police tape from the fence to the electrical conduit that ran up the wall of the building, blocking access to the field there. Just East of that, the officers had taped off the opening of the fence where the path from the parking lot led to the field.

"Where's the fire boys?" asked Terry as he and Oz approached with their badges presented. "Detective White and Shields, Homicide."

"Detectives," one officer said, greeting them. "South of the track in the trees there."

"Thanks, give us a holler when the photographer gets here," said Terry.

"He's already down there, sir, with a trooper," the officer said.

"Fuck, he's keen," said Terry. "Alright, thanks, boys."

Terry and Oz went under the tape as the officer lifted it for them. They put their badges away and started walking on the red synthetic track surface. "Feeling up to a few laps, kid?" joked Terry.

"If I didn't think you would drop from a heart attack after half a lap, I'd say bring it on," chirped Oz.

"Ahh, you cocky fucker. I never pegged you for a shit talker, Oz. But you're not half bad at it. I'm gonna have to up my game," Terry said, laughing.

Oz laughed, "Just learning from the master, Ter."

They walked off the track towards the trees in the South corner of the Community Center. There they saw the officer chatting with the photographer. As they approached, the officer gave them a nod, and the photographer turned around to see who the officer was acknowledging. Almost as if he was in the middle of an offensive story or joke and needed to see who was approaching, as they might have been offended by what he was going to say. "The scene's all yours, detectives," said the photographer.

"Thanks!" Oz replied as he and Terry approached the body.

"Alright, kid, let's do this," said Terry.

Oz pulled out his Maglite and turned it on, lighting their way. "Looks as though this victim was dragged here from the track," Oz said. "You can see the marks on the grass leading this way. Looks like there was a bit of a struggle, the way that the grass is ripped up here."

When they got to the body, there was a pool of blood around what was left. "This one is a male, Caucasian," said Oz. "Looks like he was out here using the track, judging from the running shoes he's wearing. If I had to guess, I would say that he is of average height, maybe a little on the heavier side." Oz continued to describe what he saw. "The head has been crushed. Christ! His face… has… uh… it's been removed? I think those are the words I'm looking for." Kneeling closer to the body, to get a closer look, Oz continued to call out exactly what he saw. Terry was taking notes in his little notebook that he, and every other officer, kept on them.

"No signs of what was used to crush his head," said Oz, shining the light in the area around the body. "The right arm is missing, and there are long, claw-like lacerations across the chest of the victim. They appear to be pretty deep, the t-shirt is ripped and heavily soaked in blood."

"Whatcha thinking, kid?" asked Terry.

"I have no clue, Ter. This is the third victim that we have been called to that has been… well, just absolutely brutalized, but by who or what?" Oz said, as he stood up and turned back to Terry, shining his light on the ground, tracing the drag marks back to the track. "Looks like he was grabbed from the track and dragged here. Then they caved his head in, ripped off his face and arm, not necessarily in that order. Why take the face and the arm?"

"Doesn't make any sense, kid," said Terry. "I think you're spot on with your theory about how he was killed, though."

"My gut tells me these three murders, are connected. And whoever is doing this is incredibly strong. But two of the victims were female, this one is male. So, there is no connection there. Two appear to have been out for a run, similar but insignificant," Oz continued to theorize out loud. "Everything is more coincidental than connected. All three were killed violently, and mercilessly."

Oz turned off his flashlight and put it back in his coat pocket. He reached up and started scratching his head while he was deep in thought. "Officer," he yelled to the officer nearby.

"Uh-huh," the officer replied.

"Who found the body?" asked Oz.

"It was a woman and her dog. They were walking on the walkway there on the other side of the fence," said the officer. "She said the dog started going crazy. They are from the houses there, on Old Ironside Way."

"Did we get her name?"

"I didn't, but Jenkins did, he's up in the lot there," said the officer.

"Thanks," said Oz. He turned back to Terry. "We should talk to her at least and find out what she saw before she phoned it in."

"Uh-huh," said Terry.

Oz pulled out a pair of blue nitrile gloves from his jacket pocket and put them on. He knelt back down beside the body and patted down the pockets of the jogging pants the victim was wearing. "I'm not feeling a wallet, or even a phone, for that matter. Who leaves home without either of those things these days?" Oz reached up to the left arm, slid the sleeve up, looking for a watch or something. "This guy doesn't appear to be wearing one of those fitness devices, so we aren't so lucky tonight. No wedding ring, so I'll assume not married. Must be from around here, probably comes down to the track quite often for a run.

But again, no witnesses, just someone who found the body. Fuck!" Oz yelled in frustration.

"Easy, kid. I get that you're frustrated, but you can't let it better you," said Terry, almost repeating what the Lieutenant said earlier.

"Yeah, sorry, Ter," Oz said, hanging his head. "How many more people are gonna get murdered like this before we get a clue… or… or… a motive or something… fucking anything?"

Oz stood back up, peeled off the gloves, and balled them up in his hand.

"Come on, kid, let's go talk to this trooper, Jenkins, and then go get a Dunkees before going to see the woman who called it in," said Terry, trying to calm Oz down. "The geeks are here now. Let them do their thing."

"Yeah. Alright, Ter. Sorry, man," said Oz, as he walked towards Terry.

"Quit apologizing. This happens to all of us, kid. Trust me, you're gonna feel a hundred times better once you get a Dunkees in you," said Terry.

This made Oz laugh. "You mean you'll feel better once you get your 'Dunkees', you junky."

"Same, same, kid. Same, same," Terry said, laughing.

The two detectives walked back the way that they came to the parking lot, where the officers still kept guard of the entrance. The forensics team was suiting up in their white Tyvek suits, to collect physical evidence, if any, before they move the body and take it to the Medical Examiner's office.

"Jenkins," Terry yelled out as they approached the officers.

"Yes, sir," said one officer, turning around to face them.

Oz tossed his gloves into the trash bin by the fence. They hit the shield and slid down and through the six-inch hole and into the garbage.

"We were told that you took the statement from the woman walking her dog that called this in?" inquired Terry.

"Yes sir," Jenkins said.

"What can you tell us?" asked Terry.

"She was walking her dog on the walkway on the other side of the fence. Her dog started acting all crazy, barking and pulling on the leash, trying to get to the fence. When she got to the fence, she saw the body lying there. When they didn't move or react to the dog barking, she pulled out her phone and turned on the flashlight. That's when she saw how fucked up the guy was, screamed, and then called 9-1-1," said Jenkins.

"Did she see anyone else or anything near the body?" asked Oz.

"I asked her that, and no sir, she saw nothing, just the body," said Jenkins.

"What's her name?" asked Terry.

"Uh… her name was uh…" said Jenkins, thumbing through the notebook pulled from his uniform shirt pocket. "Ah, here it is… her name is Lulu Johnson. How the fuck could I forget that?" Jenkins said, elbowing the other officer there.

"Thanks, Jenkins. And the other trooper said that she lived in the houses just behind us, there?" asked Terry.

"Yes sir. I have her cell number if you want it?" asked Jenkins.

"Did you ask her out on a date, Jenkins?" said Terry, making a joke.

"What? No, it was for the report to match up with the 9-1-1 call records," Jenkins replied quickly.

"I'm fucking with you, Jenkins. Good job. Let's have that number," said Terry.

Jenkins chuckled and said, "Sure, it's 617-555-0167."

"Thanks, kid. Again, great job," Terry said to Jenkins. "Let's go, Oz."

Oz followed Terry to the Malibu and got in. "Wanna talk to this Lulu tonight?" asked Terry.

"I think we should," said Oz.

"The trooper took a pretty good statement," said Terry, as he tried to talk Oz out of it.

"Yeah, I know, but I think I'll sleep better knowing that we didn't miss something," said Oz.

"Alright kid, it's your show. You gonna call her, and let her know we are coming?" asked Terry, holding out his notebook for Oz.

"Yeah, I think we should," said Oz, as he punched the number into his phone from Terry's notes. The phone rang.

"Yeah," said the woman's voice aggressively on the other end of the call.

"Is this Lulu Johnson?" asked Oz.

"Yeah, dis her. Who dis?" she said.

"Ma'am, this is Detective Shields with the Homicide division of the Boston Police Department. You gave a statement earlier to Officer Jenkins. My partner and I would like to come by and follow up with you?" said Oz.

"Why? I already gave my statement to that other cop. Why I gotta talk to you now?" she asked.

"Ma'am, this is just a follow-up. It's just protocol that we make sure that there was nothing missed by the other officer. It shouldn't take long. We should be in and out in no time at all," Oz said, trying to ease the tension in the call.

"Ugh. I guess, but you ain't coming up in my house, I'll meet you outside on the street," she said.

"Thank you, ma'am," said Oz. "We will be right there, we are just leaving the Community Center now."

"Yeah, whatever," she said, and then hung up the phone.

"But what about Dunkees, kid?" said Terry, whining like a kid.

"Yeah Ter, after man. This woman didn't sound super pumped about having to talk to us. She is even gonna meet us outside, and said she didn't want us coming in the house," said Oz.

"Alright," said Terry, clearly disappointed. "She doesn't want us in her house, probably because she is a crackhead or something."

"Terry, come on man, you don't know that?" said Oz.

"C'mon, kid, it's not like we are going to the Rozzie or something, we're in Charlestown and going to the project houses."

"You may be right, but still," said Oz.

"Alright, kid. Let's go talk to Lulu," said Terry, as he pulled out of the parking lot and headed to go and see the witness. It literally was around the corner. They turned off Medford Street, left, on to Old Ironside Way.

As she had said on the phone, Lulu Johnson was standing right there on the sidewalk with her dog, a pit bull with the largest head Oz had ever seen on a dog. Standing there, she was about 5' 4" tall, and heavily built, with dark skin. She had a harsh feeling about her, though after talking with her on the phone, Oz already had that impression of her. She had dark brown eyes and her short, straight, black hair braided with a few fly-aways, and was dressed in unwashed, casual clothes that were ill-fitting for a woman of her build.

Terry parked the car in one of the empty spots along the curb on the south side of the street. Oz got out of the car and approached Lulu cautiously as her dog growled at the sight of him. Terry wasn't far behind him, but he sure wasn't going to take the lead on this one. This was Oz's show. Oz pulled out his badge and displayed it for Lulu to see.

"Ma'am, I'm Detective Shields. We spoke on the phone," he said, approaching gingerly.

"Yeah, that's why I'm out here. What do you want?" Said Lulu, just as pleasant as she was on the phone.

"Yeah, ma'am, can you restrain your dog, please?" asked Oz.

"Lucius, knock it off!" She yelled. Lucius whimpered and retreated behind her legs, and sat down.

"Thank you, ma'am," said Oz. "Good boy! That's such a well-trained dog."

"Uh-huh, are you gonna get to the point, so I can go the fuck home?" She said.

"Yes, of course, my apologies," said Oz. "So, the officer told us you were walking your dog on the walkway just over there, is that right?"

"Yeah, that's right," she said.

"And what time was that?" asked Oz.

"I dunno, like 8:30, 8:45, something like that," she said.

"And the officer said that your dog sensed the body first?" asked Oz.

'Yeah, Lucius started pulling me like crazy. I thought he was gonna tear my muthafuckin arm off. He was growling and barking and shit. When we got close, that's when I saw the body," she said.

'And the officer mentioned you turned the light on your phone to get a better look?" asked Oz.

"Yeah, that's right. It was fucking gross! Wish I hadn't seen it," she said.

"Did you see or hear anything near or around the body, or before you approached the fence?" asked Oz.

"Nah, it was like quiet as fuck here. That was kinda weird. Like all the world was put on mute or something. Then all I heard was Lucius going nuts," she said.

"Right. Well, thank you, ma'am. I really appreciate you taking the time to speak with me. I know it's late. I'm going to leave you my card, and if you remember anything else, anything at all, you can call me directly, alright?" said Oz as he pulled a card from his inside coat pocket and handed it to her.

"Is there a reward or some shit, for like useful information or whatever?" she asked.

"No, ma'am, not at this time, but I'll be sure to let you know if that happens. Again, thank you for your time. You have yourself a good night, ma'am," said Oz.

"Uh-huh, I bet you will," she said.

Oz turned around to find Terry already heading back to the car. They got in the car and Terry pulled out of the spot, following the street around, where it exited back onto Medford Street. Terry swung out onto Medford Street, headed for the nearest Dunkin' Donuts.

"Good job back there, kid. She clearly didn't want to talk to us. But you handled that like a pro," said Terry.

"Thanks, Ter. I appreciate that," said Oz.

"Whatcha thinking?" asked Terry.

"Something she said… about it feeling like the world had been muted. It was unusually quiet and calm at the pier last night too, wasn't it? And the night before in the alley… it was super quiet too. All you could hear was the rain pouring, right?"

"Can't say I was really paying attention. What about it?" asked Terry.

"When was the last time you remember Boston being so quiet at night? Especially Charlestown?" asked Oz.

"I dunno, kid. Can't say I ever really gave it much thought. Growing up here, it is just normal noise, you know?" said Terry.

"Yeah, maybe it's nothing," said Oz.

Terry pulled up to the Dunkin' Donuts and went inside to get the coffees. Oz stayed in the car, still thinking about the odd silences. *Can that be a weird coincidence too? Didn't Jessie say something about that, too? C'mon Ozzy, don't overthink this. It has to just be an odd coincidence. Nothing can cause the world to go silent.*

Terry returned to the car with the coffees. "Here, kid," said Terry, handing Oz the coffee.

"Thanks, Ter," he said as he popped the top and took a sip.

"Let's call it a night, kid. I'll drop you off, and we'll talk more tomorrow or Monday," said Terry.

"Yeah, alright," said Oz, deep in thought as he stared out the window.

6

Oz awoke to the sound of screaming.

"YAHR SUCH A FAHKIN' CAWKSUCKAH!" yelled the voice, the sound muffled as it came from the hall outside Oz's apartment.

"AHH GO FAHK YAHSELF!" another voice yelled back.

Oh good, the neighbors are up and in a great mood. They haven't fought like this in a while. The yelling and screaming continued, and the slurs and the name-calling escalated. He woke up on the couch, a notepad, and a pen on the coffee table in front of him. Oz looked at the clock on the wall, it was 10:15 am. He never made it to bed after Terry had dropped him off. He rubbed his eyes and stretched out his arms, curving his upper body backward. *Fuck!* Oz leaned forward to see what he had scribbled on his notepad, trying to remember what he was doing before he passed out on the couch.

Written on the notepad were random thoughts:
- *Mauling?*
- *Limb removal?*

- *Claws?*
- *Eerie silences*
- *How much blood is in the human body?*
- *Barbiturates*
- *Venom?*
- *Boston urban legends and myths — this is a stretch!*

These murders have been extremely violent. But each one is quite different. They don't increase in violence or perversion. What is the connection? Is there a connection? There has to be. What else could be so violent each time? Only in the movies does someone have the strength to rip limbs off. And what about the marks on the victim's chest last night? What rips through a man's chest like that? Are we hunting Freddy Krueger? There has to be something I'm missing. Something I'm not seeing. What the fuck is taking forensics so long to tell us something? Anything… Even nothing, for fuck's sake! Ozzy, you gotta stop this man. Quit obsessing, remember what the Lieutenant said. You're gonna drive yourself mad.

"Fuck!" Oz said out loud.

Get out and do something today. You're in Boston, for fuck's sake. There's lots to do, lots to see, especially since you don't have the entire time that you've been here. Just get out there… explore… wander. Get out of this apartment and just do something.

Oz got up off the couch, went and took a shower, changed his clothes, made sure he had his phone, wallet, keys, and his leather jacket, and walked out of the apartment. The sun was shining brightly again, and there was a gentle breeze that cooled him off slightly from the heat of the sun. It was a perfect spring day. He was glad that he decided to walk rather than take the car, as he strolled down Tremont Street, turned right at Roxbury Crossing station for "The T", the Boston subway system. He watched the people coming and going, as he just casually kept walking, making random turns down streets, exploring his neighborhood, for the first time.

Oz found himself at Kevin W. Fitzgerald Park. In full bloom, the trees in the park were lush and green. The winding path was a great place to just wander for a bit of peace and tranquility in the city. It wasn't The Boston Common, but it was really close to his apartment. *I really need to take advantage of this place more often*, he thought. People were playing with their dogs off-leash, throwing balls and sticks. Some just let their dogs have a good run around. He eventually ended up walking through a parking lot for a plaza with a Stop & Shop and a Walgreens. Oz cut through the lot to Calumet Street, and turned right on the sidewalk, and headed back towards Tremont Street. *I can't believe all of this was right near me the whole time, and I never paid attention, not once. Not a good sign for a detective. You should be more observant, Ozzy*, he thought, and laughed to himself.

As he strolled back down Tremont Street, he noticed a pub across the street. There was a small chalkboard sign out front with the daily specials handwritten on it. *That looks like a pretty nice pub*, he thought. He pulled his phone from his pocket and tapped the power button on the side so that the screen turned on, 3:45 pm, *why not?* Oz looked in both directions for an opening in the traffic and ran across the street.

He grabbed the brushed stainless handle on the door and opened it, walked inside, and took a brief look around. There were booths along the one wall with the windows to the street, the bar was opposite to the booths, and off to the left were a few tables; some sat four, and others two. This was obviously to accommodate larger parties of people when they came in. Behind the bar was a young woman, in her early to mid-twenties. She wore a tight-fitting black tank top tucked into her skinny jeans, with a thin brown belt with a silver buckle. Her long brown hair pulled into a ponytail. She had smooth, fair skin and an inviting smile, certainly perfect for her line of work.

There were only a few other patrons in the bar at this time on a Sunday. Oz took off his coat and draped it over one of the stools at the bar and had a seat. The bartender tossed a coaster in front of him; it spun as it landed and came to a stop in the perfect spot for his drink to be placed. This was clearly a trick that she had mastered.

"What can I get you, Hun?" she asked.

"I'll have a double scotch, neat, please. And a menu when you have a second," said Oz.

"Out-of-towner, huh?" she said coyly, noting his non-Boston accent. "Do you have a preference for the scotch?"

"Uh… yeah," Oz laughed. "Glenfiddich or Glenlivet would be great, but any will work, thank you."

"Coming right up, Hun," she said as she reached for the bottle of Glenlivet 12-year, single malt on the tempered glass shelf behind her, while simultaneously pulling out a small glass from under the bar. She brought the bottle and the glass together and started to pour. As the scotch poured from the bottle spout in a stream, she pulled the bottle away from the glass, then back to it. She did this motion twice, as it seemed to be how she measured the amount to pour into the glass. Once she completed the pour, she put the bottle back on the shelf and placed the glass on the coaster. Her next motion presented Oz with an open menu.

"You're good," said Oz.

"Don't forget it, Hun. I'll give you a minute with the menu. If ya have any questions, I'm Tiff," she said, then walked over to the cash register and tapped in his drink, and opened his tab in the point of sale system for the pub.

Oz looked over the menu. It contained the usual pub fare, wings, nachos, soup, and sandwiches. *Can't be in Boston and not have a bowl of clam chowder*, he thought. *That will work nicely.* The bartender walked back over to Oz, seeing that he had put the menu back on the bar, and appeared he knew what he wanted.

"What'll it be, Hun?" she asked.

"Is the clam chowder any good?" he asked.

"You're in Boston, Hun. That's like asking if the B's play hockey. Of course, it's good. One of the best in town, I promise," she said. Oz couldn't tell if she was flirting with him, or just making fun of him.

Laughing, he said, "Alright then, if you promise, I'll take a bowl of chowder, please."

"One chowder coming right up, Hun," she said, and walked over to the register and entered the order, adding it to his tab.

Oz looked around the bar again, taking in the atmosphere. As he looked down the bar, he saw an extremely attractive woman a few seats away sitting by herself. She had long auburn hair that seemed to shimmer as if it were made of the purest strands of silk flowing down to the middle of her back. She had flawless, milky white skin, and was very petite, but slightly bustier than most women of her size. She wore a tight-fitting, dark pine green dress that clung to her body in all the right places, and red stiletto heels. Not something that you would expect a woman to be wearing in a pub in the middle of the afternoon on a Sunday. It looked more like an evening dress, or something actresses might wear to a movie premiere. Oz didn't really care, though. He was too bewildered by how stunning she was. She looked up from her drink, sensing that someone was watching her. When her eyes met Oz's, he saw she had the most enrapturing green eyes. His normal reaction would have been to turn away. Instead, as if he were no longer in control, he found himself acknowledging her.

"Afternoon," he said, and gave her a smile. *Ozzy, what the fuck are you doing, man? This woman is so out of your league!*

"Hi," she said in her alluring voice with a slight rasp.

"How are you today?" he asked her. *Seriously, dude, what are you doing?*

She laughed. "Yeah, pretty good, thanks. How about you?" she asked.

"Very well now," Oz replied. *Okay, seriously, man, have you completely lost it? Can you not stop yourself? You're going to embarrass yourself. She feels sorry for you, that is the only reason that she is answering you.* "What brings you in here on a Sunday afternoon?"

"Just didn't feel like being at home, thought I'd do some window shopping. Saw this place, and thought I'd check it out," she replied.

"You went out window shopping dressed like that?" asked Oz. *And here we go, ladies and gentlemen. Watch this fool go down in flames!*

"What? You don't like it? Don't I look good?" she asked, turning towards him, arching her back ever so slightly, pushing her exquisite bust out, giving him a better look at her.

"No, not that at all. You look great. Stunning, in fact," said Oz.

She laughed, noticing how flustered Oz had become. The woman picked up her drink, her little purse, and switched seats to be closer to him. *She even walks sexy,* thought Oz.

"I'm Donna," she said, smiling and extending her hand to him.

"Oz. It's a pleasure to meet you," said Oz, gently shaking her hand. *Holy fuck, this is really happening!* "Can I get you a refill?" he asked her.

"Sure, if you're offering," she said.

Tiff returned with his bowl of chowder and set it down in front of him. She placed a spoon and a white cloth napkin folded neatly in a rectangle beside the bowl. "Can I get you anything else?" she asked.

Oz took the last sip of his scotch. "Yes please, the lady here will have another glass of the red that she was enjoying, and I'll have another scotch," said Oz.

"Would you like a bowl of chowder as well?" asked Tiff.

"Maybe just another spoon?" she said to the bartender.

"And would you mind adding her tab to mine as well? Thank you," said Oz.

"That's not necessary," said Donna.

"It's my pleasure. Honestly," said Oz.

Tiff brought another spoon and napkin for Donna and another glass of red wine. She grabbed the bottle of Glenlivet from the shelf and refilled Oz's glass. Donna finished her first glass of wine, then gently pressed her red lips together and cleared any wine left behind with her tongue.

Oz moved the bowl of chowder in between them on the bar. He picked up one spoon and Donna grabbed the other. They both dipped in for a spoonful of the thick, creamy chowder. Oz blew on his spoonful, as did Donna on hers, to cool it ever so slightly. They both ate their spoonful.

"Wow! That is really good," said Oz.

"Mm, it really is," said Donna.

They continued to share the soup until Donna threw in the towel, with about a quarter of the bowl left. They laughed and chatted while Oz finished the bowl of chowder and ordered them another round of drinks when Tiff came by to collect the dishes.

"So I'm guessing that you aren't from Boston either since you don't seem to have "tha hahd" accent?" Oz said, doing an awful Boston accent.

Donna laughed and said, "No, I'm originally from Ohio. I just moved here this past week. What about you? Where are you from? Judging from your terrible Boston accent, it isn't here?"

"Was it that bad?" Oz joked. "I'm from Michigan originally, just outside of Lansing. I moved here nearly six years ago."

"Oh wow. So, is this your usual hang out?" asked Donna.

"It may surprise you to hear this, but this is actually the first time that I've ever set foot in here," said Oz, chuckling.

"Really?" said Donna.

"Yeah," said Oz. "I've been so focused on work since I moved here, that I really haven't done anything else."

"Oh? What do you do for work?" Donna asked.

"I'm a Homicide Detective," replied Oz.

"Really? I wouldn't have pegged you for a cop," Donna said.

"No? What did you have me pegged for?" asked Oz.

"I dunno, a teacher maybe?" Donna said, giggling.

"No, definitely not a teacher," Oz said, laughing. "What do you do?"

"Well, I was an admin for an accountant back in Ohio," said Donna. "But since I moved here, nothing. I'll start looking tomorrow."

"Well, I don't think you'll be out of work long," said Oz.

They continued chatting, laughing, and flirting with each other. The hours passed like seconds. Oz could hardly believe his luck. He would've never imagined connecting with someone in this random pub just down the street from his apartment. Not to mention someone as drop-dead gorgeous as Donna was. Things were going so well, too. There was definitely a powerful attraction between them.

Donna was laughing, and she put her hand on his upper thigh. Oz momentarily tensed up. This caught him totally off guard. She was definitely a very confident woman, making a move like this. She looked at Oz. Their eyes locked on each other. Her green eyes were incredible. So hypnotic. There was a predator-like hunger in her eyes, yet gazing into them, he felt so calm and safe.

"How far away is your place?" Donna asked, almost sounding ravenous.

"Just down the street," replied Oz.

"Why don't we get out of here then?" she said.

"Tiff," Oz said. "Check please."

Donna leaned in and whispered into Oz's ear, "I want you to take me now!" She flicked his earlobe with her tongue and sucked on it as she squeezed his thigh with her hand and moaned. She sat back on the stool and grabbed her purse.

Tiff brought the bill, and Oz took a quick glance. The bill was just over $45. He pulled out his wallet and grabbed a hundred-dollar bill out of it and put it on the counter. He turned to her and said, "Thank you, Tiff. Have yourself a great night!"

"Uh-huh, I'd tell you to do the same, but it seems unnecessary. Come back again soon," said Tiff.

Oz got up off the stool, grabbed his jacket, and put it around Donna's shoulders and his arm around her tiny waist after she hopped from her stool, and they left the bar.

***

Oz pushed the button, calling the elevator. He'd never used the elevator before, but there wasn't a chance in hell that he was going to make her take the stairs. The elevator chimed, and the doors slid open. Oz put out his arm, insisting that Donna head inside first. She obliged, and he followed her in. He hit the button for the 4th floor, and the doors slid closed. As the doors closed, he leaned in and gently kissed her soft, full lips, her back pressed against the wall of the elevator car. She reciprocated the kiss and reached her arms up and around the back of his neck. Oz put both of his hands on her tiny waist as they kissed again. She tasted so sweet. There wasn't a trace of the Cabernet that she'd been drinking. Her perfume was intoxicating, like nothing he had ever smelled before. It was as though this magical scent filled him with even more desire for her. The passion and intensity increased with each kiss. Her tongue now flicked inside his mouth as they continued.

The elevator stopped and chimed, letting them know they had arrived at the 4th floor, and the doors slid open once again. Parting like fighters at the end of a round, Oz picked up his jacket, as it had fallen from her shoulders when she put her arms around his neck. He put his hand on the small of Donna's back and guided her out of the elevator and down the hall to his apartment. He kissed her again as he pulled his keys from the jacket pocket and unlocked the door. Oz opened the door and continued kissing her as he backed her into the apartment, one hand on her waist again. Once inside the apartment, Oz kicked the door closed behind him with his outstretched foot.

Donna dropped her purse and kicked off her shoes. Oz's jacket fell to the floor, freeing up his hands as he grabbed her tight, perky ass. Her hands slid up Oz's chest to his head as she curled her hands behind it. He kicked off his shoes towards the wall where the coat hooks hung. Oz then moved his hands to her soft, silky thighs, slid her dress up to just past her hips. She gasped in ecstasy, between passionate kisses. Oz continued to guide her to his room. Donna ran her hands up underneath Oz's t-shirt and lifted it up over his head and off. The world could have been ending around them, and neither would have noticed. They were just so focused on each other at this moment. The t-shirt fell to the floor in the hall as they continued into his room.

Donna's hands worked to undo his belt and the button of his jeans. Her hands slid around the waistband to the sides and down into the pants, forcing the zipper open and the pants to fall. Oz stepped out of them as he lifted her almost effortlessly. Donna wrapped her legs around his waist, and her arms around his neck, as he carried her the rest of the way to the bed, and laid her on it. He moved in to kiss her cheek, then her neck, then down to her chest. Her legs released him from their grasp and fell to the bed on either side of him. Donna gasped as he kissed down her body. He kissed his way down, just below the navel, grabbed the thin strings of her lace thong, and pulled them down. As Oz pulled them down past her butt, she raised her legs into the air, and Oz pulled her panties up her legs and off, dropping them on the floor.

He grabbed her legs and spread them as he kissed his way down the left leg to her thigh. Her legs lowered to the bed as he kissed further and further. He kissed her thigh, then her inner thigh, her hip teasing her. Her hands-on his head, with her fingers, weaved through his hair. He kissed around to her other thigh, and then her inner thigh, teasing her. Finally, he tasted her. She was so soft and warm, and perfect. Donna moaned as Oz continued to devour her. Her hips quivered. She gripped his hair in her fists. Her moans got louder, her breathing became more erratic. She cried out, "Oh fuck!" as she released. Her legs squeezed his head, and she convulsed from his efforts.

Oz kissed his way back up her body. She sat up as he reached her taut stomach. He ran his hands up her dress and lifted it up over her head as he kissed her heaving chest. Donna unclasped her bra. The straps fell off her shoulders, and then into her lap, and she tossed it aside. Oz kissed his way to the nipple of her left breast. Her skin was so soft and smooth, completely flawless. Then he crossed over to her other breast to share the attention.

"Kiss me!" Donna demanded between panting breaths.

Never wanting to disappoint a lady, Oz fulfilled her request. He kissed her trembling lips passionately. Donna sucked in his bottom lip and bit it. Oz growled as he moved her up the bed. Donna bent her legs and grabbed his boxers with her toes, and pulled them down. She reached down with her hand and stroked his throbbing member.

Donna pushed on Oz's right shoulder and transitioned so that he was now laying on his back. She kissed him. Then slid her way slowly down his body, kissing him as she moved. She kissed his firm, muscular chest, then his sculpted abs. She now stared up at him from behind his rock-hard shaft. Her eyes glowed like two perfect jade stones in the moonlight that seeped through the blinds on the window. Her small, soft hand gently grasped him and slowly stroked. She moved towards it and licked from the base to the tip. Oz moaned. She then took him in her mouth. Oz jolted each time she took him in deeper and deeper. Her soft hand stroked and twisted.

She released him from her mouth, and crawled her way back up to his face, and kissed him long and hard. She straddled him; her sculpted legs on either side of him as she sat on his stomach.

"I want you inside me now!" she whispered between kisses.

Donna grabbed him and guided him inside her. She gasped as he entered, feeling every inch of him as he slid deeper and deeper inside her. She was so wet and ready for him. He had his hands on her hips as she moved. He slid them up to her magnificent perky breasts, grabbed them, and squeezed them, massaging them in his strong masculine grip. Donna sat up, moaning loudly, him deep inside her. She worked her hips back and forth, grinding into him.

Oz sat up, wrapped his arms around her. He kissed her lips as he lifted her up and laid her on her back. He was now on top of her. It was his turn to control things again. He pulled his hips back, then plunged himself deep inside her. *God, she feels so incredible. This is insane*, he thought.

"Fuck me, Oz!" she said. Her fingernails raked his back down to his ass, where she pulled him in deeper. She moaned and repeated, "Fuck me!"

Oz kissed her neck as he began thrusting. She moaned and yelped with each thrust. She wrapped her legs around him and guided him to her perfect rhythm. "Yes... Yes... Yes..." she cried out. "Right there... right there... yes... fuck me!"

They panted and moaned. Their bodies clashed. The sounds of flesh slapping against flesh filled the room. The air in the room was hot from them. Oz could feel that he was so close to exploding. "I'm gonna…" he said. Her legs gripped tighter around him.

"I want it…" she said, then gasped. "Inside me," she said with her next breath.

"Yeah?" said Oz, slightly hesitant.

"Yes!" she moaned. "Now. I'm gonna cum too!"

Oz kissed her again on the lips as he thrust closer and closer to exploding with ecstasy. Donna moaned and squeezed him with her legs. He pressed right against her, deep inside, as he erupted within her. He felt her clench around him as he throbbed inside her. Oz groaned in pleasure with Donna as they shared this euphoric moment. He kissed her again. Brushed her cheek with his hand as he collapsed, falling beside her in bed. His leg and arm draped across her as they laid there, panting.

"That was fucking incredible," Donna said.

"Amazing," said Oz. He moved his leg. She rolled so that her back was to him. He pulled her tight into him. She grabbed his arm and embraced it in between her breasts, her hands holding his. Oz kissed her shoulder.

Donna moaned and wiggled her bottom into him as they embraced.

7

Oz awoke shortly after midnight to find that Donna was out of bed and gathering her clothes. "You're leaving?" he asked.

"I have to," she said.

"Let me get dressed. I'll take you home," he said, sitting up in bed.

"Don't be silly," she said. "I'm a big girl, I can find my own way home."

"I don't doubt that at all, but I wouldn't be able to live with myself if something were to happen. So, I'm taking you home," Oz demanded. He hopped out of bed and collected his boxers and his jeans.

"Really, Oz, I'm good," she said.

"Do you not want me to know where you live? I'm a cop, remember? I can find out anything I want about you," he joked. "Don't be silly. I'll take you home. Please, I insist."

Oz, now half-clothed, walked up behind her and wrapped his arms around her, and kissed her on the shoulder. Whatever tension she had seemed to melt with his kiss.

"Well, if you insist. Who am I to say no," she said.

"Good," he said. "Now, where is my shirt?"

"I think we left it in the hall," Donna joked.

Oz exited the room and found his shirt on the floor. He collected it from the floor, pulled it on over his head, and saw Donna exit the room, slinking her little green dress down over her legs.

"Now that is a shame," he said.

"What is?" she asked.

"You, getting dressed," he said.

Donna smirked at him with a half-smile, her head tilted to the left. "Haha, aren't you funny," she said sarcastically.

She collected her purse and slid her feet into her stilettos. Oz picked up his jacket, removed the keys from the pocket, hung it up, and put on his shoes. They left the apartment and took the elevator down to the main floor. He kissed her again in the elevator.

"Be careful, or you'll get me going again," she said.

"And what's the downside?" he asked.

Donna pinched his arm playfully as the elevator stopped on the main floor and the doors opened. They exited the elevator and walked to the stairwell to access the garage. Donna's heels clicked and echoed as they walked to his car. Oz unlocked the doors with the remote, opened the passenger door and Donna got in. He closed the door once she was comfortably inside, walked around to the driver's side, and got in. He started the car and pulled out of his spot. The exhaust roared and echoed in the garage as he exited to Tremont Street.

"Where to, ma'am?" he said jokingly.

"Don't call me ma'am!" she said, laughing. "Darling Apartments over by the Park. Do you know where that is?" she said.

"I think so. That's really close," he said.

"I told you I could've made it on my own," she said.

"Don't be silly, I just didn't think that we were so close to each other," he said as he pulled out onto Tremont Street, heading North-West.

"Don't you go stalking me, now that you got some," she joked.

"I just might," he laughed. "I may just quit my job to do it."

She laughed and swatted him with the back of her hand playfully. Then she grabbed his right hand from the shifter and weaved her fingers between his.

"Turn left on Calumet," she said. "You can just drop me off on the sidewalk in front of the second building on the right," she said.

Oz pulled up to the curb in front of the building and parked the car.

"So, will I get to see you again?" asked Oz.

"Maybe," she said

"I don't even know your last name," said Oz.

"Did we skip that part?" Donna giggled. "It's Richardson,"

"So, Donna Richardson, can I call you sometime?" Oz smiled and said.

"Let me have your phone," she said.

Oz reached down and grabbed his phone from the little console pocket by the shifter, unlocked it, and handed it to her. Donna entered her number into his contacts and sent herself a text message.

"There you go, Tiger. Now you can get me anytime you want," she said.

"Perfect," said Oz.

He leaned in to kiss her. She put her hand on the side of his face while they kissed goodbye.

"Thank you for the great welcome to Boston, Detective! I look forward to you serving and protecting me," she said, staring deep into his eyes and gave him a wink, and one last kiss.

Donna opened the passenger door and spun in the seat, putting her legs out, and elegantly exited the vehicle. She turned around and before closing the door, she said, "Goodnight Oz, sweet dreams!"

"Goodnight, Donna. I'll see you soon," said Oz.

"Mm, you better," she said, and closed the door.

Oz watched her walk to the door of the apartment, unlock it, and head inside. She turned around and blew him a kiss before she disappeared inside the building.

***

The next morning, as Terry walked into the Detective's pool at the station, coffee in hand, he saw Oz there sitting at his desk. This wasn't totally unusual. Depending on how busy Dunkin' was in the morning, Oz would occasionally beat him to work. Terry walked around to his desk, pulled out his chair, and sat down.

"Morning, kid! How was the rest of your weekend?" asked Terry.

"Morning, Ter! Yeah, it was good. Had a nice quiet Sunday," said Oz.

"Really? You didn't come in here, did you?" asked Terry.

"No, shockingly, I managed to stay away," said Oz. "The Medical Examiner's report came through for the other two victims this morning." Oz switched topics to prevent Terry from inquiring any further.

"Yeah? What did they have to tell us?" asked Terry.

"Same as the first victim, really. Unknown, barbiturate, and saliva residue on the second victim from the pier, but not on the one from the Community Center. I'm pretty confident that they are all done by the same person. But still are clueless when it comes to exactly who that is," said Oz.

"Did he say what crushed that third victim's head?" asked Terry.

"Sadly, no clue there. And since there were no rocks or large branches near the body, and no mineral residue in the wound, he assumed hand or paw did it. In the report, it said that it found marks behind the ears that were similar to the entry pattern on the scratch marks on the chest," said Oz.

"A hand or paw? What the fuck does that mean, kid?" asked Terry.

"Well, when I called him this morning to follow up, he said that the pattern of the scratches aligned with a hand. But a hand with fingers that would be roughly, and he was guessing when he said this, about eight to ten inches long. That would include the claws or nails, as there was definitely a sharp razor-like entry to them," said Oz.

"When you called him? What fucking time did you get here this morning?" asked Terry.

"Early, that's all you need to know," laughed Oz.

"Alright, so what now?" Terry asked, after a slight chuckle.

"Well, I called FSD, and they said they are baffled," said Oz. "They've spent nearly twice the amount of time at these scenes looking for any physical evidence, and have found nothing, apart from blood and tissue from the victims. The divers recovered nothing from the water down by the pier. So, what we saw there was all that there was of our Jane Doe. They also confirmed exactly what the Medical Examiner told us about the barbiturate and the saliva."

"What about the Fitbit thingy, on the arm of the second victim?" asked Terry.

"FSD released it for the tech guys to look into this morning. We may hear something today or tomorrow on that," said Oz.

"Jesus, kid. You're all over this," said Terry.

Oz laughed and said, "Anyway, last night was the first time that we were free from a victim since these killings began.," said Oz.

"So what, the killer doesn't work on Sundays?" said Terry. "Are they religious or something?"

"Don't throw that idea away, Ter. That could be a thing if we don't catch them first," said Oz.

"Too bad it's not football season. I'd love a killer that doesn't fuck with me watching the Pats," joked Terry.

"I was thinking about going to the Library," said Oz.

"What, you suddenly need to check out a book?" Terry asked.

"Funny. No, I wanted to look into some things that might help us. Could just be a waste of time. I just don't really want to hang around here this morning. I need to get out and do something," laughed Oz.

"Alright, don't be mad if I let you go do that yourself," said Terry.

"Don't like the Library, Ter?" joked Oz.

"Nah, too fucking early for that shit," Terry said.

"Yeah, alright Ter. That is where I'll be if you need me. Just gimme a call if something comes up," said Oz.

"Alright, kid, have fun!" Terry said sarcastically.

Oz got up from his desk, pushed his chair in, grabbed his notebook and his ballpoint pen, and put them in the inside breast pocket of his charcoal gray sport coat. He gave Terry a nod, and walked out of the office, and left the Station. He walked to the Parker Hill Branch of the Boston Public Library. This was actually the first place Oz visited when he moved into his apartment on Tremont Street. The only reason that it was the first was because it was basically across the street.

Oz walked up the stone steps and through the thick black doors of this historic-looking stone building. There was a row of desks with computers on them. Each desk was old, dark stained hardwood with large dividers for privacy. He walked up to one of the desks, sat down, pulled the notepad and pen from his pocket, and set them on the desk. The screen illuminated when he moved the mouse, opened the web browser, and typed in the search bar: Boston Urban Legends.

He saw a link that led him to 'Nine Urban Legends in Massachusetts'. There were, of course, the witches of Salem and the Gloucester Harbor Sea Serpent, but there were a couple that he never heard of. There was the 'Black Flash of Provincetown' in the late 1930s. It was first reported by two men who recalled seeing an eight-foot-tall, unusually thin figure, clothed in black. A figure that they said could leap over high fences. But sightings of this creature stopped in 1945. Then there was the 'Hoosac Tunnel' that was nicknamed 'The Bloody Pit'. This was a railway tunnel that ran between North Adams and Florida, and as legend told, over 200 people died during its construction in the mid-1800s. Tales of spooky sounds and sightings in and around this tunnel had been reported for over 150 years. Neither of these really seemed to fit.

He clicked another link, where he read posts from Bostonians sharing stories of ghost trains and haunted houses. There was even a post that said that they once heard that the B Line ran quickly and on time. *Oh, you gotta love Boston sarcasm*; he thought. He saw a post that mentioned something called the 'Dover Demon'. Oz moved the mouse over the search bar and typed in 'Dover Demon' and hit enter, and opened the Wikipedia page. This was a creature reportedly spotted in Dover, MA back in 1977. This creature had not been associated with any killings. They described it as a large-eyed creature with tendril-like fingers and eyes that glowed. It was never reported again by anyone after 1977. *This doesn't really help much. I knew this was a stretch*, he thought.

Oz then examined some of the other things that he had written on his notepad. He typed in the search bar

'How much force to crush a skull' and hit enter. The top of the search results showed a study published in the Journal of Neurosurgery, that a skull would require 520 pounds of force to crush it. The article also stated that this is likely twice as much force as human hands can typically muster. *Just like I thought, this would have to be some freak to be able to do this*, he thought. He wrote this down on his notepad.

Then he searched 'Force to rip off an arm'. The results populated, and one link stated it takes roughly 1500 to 2000 pounds of force to remove a human arm. *That is over three times the amount to crush a skull. What in the world could be this strong?* Oz wrote this down as well.

He spent the next hour or so researching the remaining items he had written and made notes beside each one. When he hit the end of the list, he looked at his notepad as if he were studying for a test.

- *Mauling? — but nothing like what's happened to the victims*
- *Limb removal? 1500–2000 lbs of force — Jesus!*
- *Claws? The most dangerous claw belongs to a cassowary, and it only has 3 toes.*
- *Eerie silences — nothing outside post-apocalyptic fiction*
- *How much blood is in the human body? 1.2 to 1.5 gallons*
- *Barbiturates — just like the ME said — acts as a sedative*
- *Venom? Most known venom are slow-acting that work like powerful sedatives*

- *Boston urban legends and myths — this is a stretch!*
- *520 lbs force to crush a skull*

Oz's phone vibrated in his pocket. He reached into the inside pocket and pulled out his phone. It was a text from Terry. *'Coming to get you. You at Parker Hill?'* the message read. Oz called Terry. The phone rang twice before Terry answered.

"Hey kid, where are you?" Terry asked.

"Hey, Ter. Yeah, I walked over to Parker Hill," said Oz.

"Alright, kid. I'll be there in five. We'll go get a grinder and go check out the common location from the second victim's fitness thingy," said Terry.

"Alright, Ter. I'll meet you out front," said Oz, and he hung up.

Oz cleared the search history of the web browser, stood up, and pushed in the chair. He put away his notepad and pen, and walked out of the library, and waited by the curb for Terry to pull up. He opened the messaging app on his phone and typed in a message to Donna that read; *'Morning Gorgeous! Just wanted to thank you again for a wonderful day yesterday. Hope you have a great day!'* and hit send. He put the phone back in the inside breast pocket of his sport coat. The phone rang. He pulled it out and swiped the screen to answer it.

"Detective Shields, Homicide," he said.

"Mm, good morning, Detective," said the voice seductively on the phone. It was Donna.

"Hey there! How are you?" he asked.

"I'm fantastic," she said. "I'm still in bed. Why don't you come over and keep me company," she said.

"As much as I would love to, unfortunately, my partner is coming to get me, and we have to go and see someone for a case we are on," he said.

"Can't he drop you off and wait downstairs for you to finish?" she said.

"Fuck me!" he said, shocked by her response.

"That's what I am trying to do," said Donna, giggling.

"As tempting as that is, I still have to decline. Maybe I can see you later, though?" he asked.

"We'll see, Tiger. For now, I guess I'll just have to take care of myself," she said.

"You really know how to make a guy feel guilty," Oz said.

"I didn't think you were the kind of guy to neglect a woman in need," she said.

"Aww, that is so not fair," said Oz.

Donna giggled. She seemed to enjoy torturing him, getting him flustered like this. Oz struggled between his desire for her and his sworn duty to the job.

"Have a good day, officer!" she said.

"Fuck! You're driving me wild over here. My mind is racing. You're insatiable!" he said.

"Don't forget it, Tiger. Bye, Ozzy," she said, and she hung up the phone.

"Bye Donna," said Oz into a vacant call.

Holy fuck, Ozzy. Did you hit the lottery with this one or what? He thought. Oz stood there stunned at what just occurred and stared at his phone. Terry pulled up in front of Oz, standing at the curb. He tucked his phone in the inside pocket of his jacket, opened the door, and got in. Terry looked at him and began laughing.

"Did someone just get a naughty phone call?" he said.

"Huh? What?" said Oz, his face all flushed.

"Did Oz get laid this weekend? There some horny broad saying nasty shit to you after you gave her the executive treatment this weekend?" joked Terry.

"What? No, man. Let's go get that sandwich," said Oz.

"Whatever you say, Romeo. But I know that wasn't your mother on the phone." Terry laughed harder as they drove away.

8

"So, where are we heading, Ter?" asked Oz.

"Over to 9th Street in Charlestown," said Terry, finishing the mouthful of sandwich before continuing. "The tech geeks hacked that fitness thingy and said the common location was on 9th Street. It's close to where we found the body on the pier. They've had no luck getting the ID of the victim yet, but they said that would take a little longer."

"Those guys work quick," said Oz.

"Yeah, about time we had a bit of luck on this shit," said Terry.

"So we know roughly where, but not who. What are we hoping to find there?" asked Oz, thinking about where else he could be right now.

"There are apartments there. Hopefully, someone has noticed not seeing our victim around for a couple of days, and maybe we get a name," said Terry, as he took another bite of his sandwich.

"Crap shoot," said Oz.

"That's true, kid. But what the fuck else are we doing?" said Terry.

If you only knew, Terry. If you only knew. They finished their grinders and left the shop, headed for the Impala. "Ter, do you know of any urban legends or myths in Boston?" asked Oz.

"What, like Tom Brady or Bobby Orr?" joked Terry.

"No, seriously, do you?" said Oz.

"Nothing comes to mind, kid. Why?" asked Terry as they got into the car.

"I read that the amount of force required to crush a man's skull like that is over five hundred pounds, and to remove a limb takes over three times that. This is way more than any man can do. So, I have this weird feeling that we are looking for something else," said Oz.

"What, like a monster?" said Terry. "The only monster in Boston, kid, is the big green one at Fenway."

"I know it sounds fucked up, man, but I'm serious. I don't think what's killing these people is human," said Oz.

"So, maybe it's an animal? Maybe we should bring in the Parks and Wildlife guys? See what they think?" said Terry, half-serious as he pulled out into traffic headed for Charlestown.

"You joke, man, but what could it hurt to consult them?" said Oz.

"I think you're gonna end up in the fucking loony bin, talking like that. And I'll be needing a new partner," said Terry. "Do you hear what you're saying, kid?"

"Yeah. You're right. Maybe I'm just frustrated, reaching for anything that might remotely make sense," said Oz.

"Besides, kid, this ain't Hollywood, it's Boston. The fucking real world," said Terry. "That kinda shit just doesn't exist."

"How do you explain the claw marks, though?" asked Oz.

"For all I know, kid, there is some whack job trying to be Freddy Krueger or Edward Scissorhands, but I'm sure as shit not saying that out loud to anyone," said Terry. "Oz, we'll catch who's doing this. It's just gonna take some time. You gotta relax."

"Alright, Ter," Oz said, feeling a little ashamed.

"So, tell me about this Stylene?" said Terry.

"Stylene?" said Oz.

"Yeah, a Stylene. You know, a whore, a slut, a skank. The broad that has you all fucked up this morning?" said Terry.

"She's not a 'Stylene', man!" said Oz.

"Ahh, but there is a chicky, I knew it," said Terry.

"What?" said Oz, surprised.

"You said 'she's no Stylene', that means there was a 'she'," said Terry. "Can't get by me, kid, I'm a fucking outstanding detective. Stick with me and one day you will be too."

"Fuck!" said Oz, accepting defeat. "Alright, I met someone"

"Spill it!" said Terry, laughing.

"There is 9th Street, on the left there," said Oz as he quickly diverted from having to say anymore.

"You're gonna tell me, we got the whole ride back to the station. I want all the details," said Terry as he pulled up to the curb on the right and parked the car.

Across the street from them was an apartment building. Three stories in total, but long. It ran almost the entire length of the street to the roundabout at the South end of the street.

"Still feeling lucky, kid?" asked Terry. "Think we can find a super or someone that may be able to tell us something?"

"Here's hoping, man," replied Oz.

They got out of the car, crossed the street to the apartment, walked up the walkway to the main entrance, and entered the lobby. There was an apartment phone on the wall just to the right of the entrance, with a list of all the apartment numbers and last names. Studying the board, they saw a number marked 'Office'."

"Let's try that one," said Oz.

Terry picked up the receiver and dialed '0#'. The phone began to ring. It rang four times before someone finally picked up. Oz couldn't hear what the voice on the phone said, he could only hear what Terry was saying.

"Yeah, hello. This is Detective White from the Boston Homicide Unit. My partner and I would like to talk with you about possibly a tenant of yours?" said Terry. "Uh-huh… yes sir… no sir, nobody here is suspected of anything. We just wanna talk with you to see if you can help us… Thank you."

Terry hung up the phone, and the door in the lobby buzzed and clicked. Oz grabbed the handle, and they went inside. From around the corner came a short, portly man with an awkward limp. He was rough looking, with at least three or four days growth on his face. His gray hair unkept where it peaked out from under his green plaid scally cap. His eyes were gray and bloodshot.

"Detectives," he said in a very hoarse voice and thick Boston accent. Very raspy from years of smoking and hard living. "I'm the building super, Mister O'Reilly," he said, extending his stubby thick hand, fingers stained brownish-yellow from the nicotine.

"Detective White, and this is my partner, Detective Shields," said Terry as he and Oz shook his hand. "Thanks, for taking the time to talk with us."

"Sure," said Mr. O'Reilly.

"Sir, you may have read about it in the papers, but there was a body found down on pier 6 on Saturday evening," said Oz.

"Yeah, fucking shame," said Mr. O'Reilly.

"Well, sir, we have reason to believe that the victim may have been a resident here at your building," said Oz. "We know she was a lighter-skinned African-American female, and was often out running."

"Well, we don't track the movements of our tenants. Just if they complain, or don't pay their rent," said Mr. O'Reilly.

"So you haven't noticed any of your tenants missing, then that may fit that description?" asked Oz.

"No sir, but rent is due this week, so I might know more soon if someone is missing," said Mr. O'Reilly.

"Right, we appreciate you taking the time to talk to us, and if you have any info that may help us, we would really appreciate it," said Terry as he handed him his business card. "Here's my card. Please call if you have anything. Thanks for your time."

"Sure, will do," said Mr. O'Reilly.

They shook his hand once more and exited the building, heading back to the car.

"That went about as well as we could have hoped," said Oz, once they were outside, disappointed.

"Can't all be touchdowns, kid," said Terry.

They crossed the street and got into the Impala. Oz grabbed his phone from his coat pocket. There was a message from Donna. *Really, hit the jackpot with this one, Ozzy.* He swiped to unlock the phone and tapped on the messaging app. Donna has sent him a photo. She was laying in bed, her white covers draped over her. She had one leg out of the covers bent with her foot flat on the mattress, one hand was holding the phone, and her other hand was down in the covers, touching herself. There was a very erotic and lustful look on her face, with her biting her bottom lip. The message after the picture read; *'Wish you were here!'*. Oz felt his temperature rise. *Fucking hell, Ozzy! This woman is so hot! Why aren't you there right now? Why is work more important?*

"What you got there, kid?" asked Terry as he reached across and snatched Oz's phone with his left hand. Terry used his right hand to keep Oz away as he looked at the screen. "Fucking hell, kid! Is this your lady friend?"

"Ter, come on man, give it back!" said Oz as he tried to get his phone back from Terry, like a little brother trying to get his toy back from his older brother.

"How long have you been hiding this one kid?" Terry said, his eyes fixed on the picture.

"I just met her, man. C'mon seriously, give it back!" said Oz. He struggled more than he imagined he would in this position. "How can someone, so old, be so strong?"

"Oh, you cawksuckah! I'm older, but I'm not fucking old. Maybe I'll just send this pic to my phone," said Terry.

"Go ahead, man. I'm sure Maureen would love that!" said Oz.

"Muthahfuckah!" Terry laughed, and handed Oz back his phone. "Why do you gotta bring my old lady into this?"

"You gave me no choice, man. I had to do it," joked Oz, grateful to have his phone back. "Seriously, though, are you on roids or something? How the fuck are you so strong?"

"Remember that, kid. I can take you any fucking time," laughed Terry. "So, now that I've seen the goods, are you gonna spill it?"

"Fuck!" said Oz. "Her name is Donna. I met her on Sunday. That's all you're getting."

"Just 'met' her on Sunday, huh? Alright, champ, I'll let you have this for now, but I will make you tell me more later," said Terry.

Terry pulled out of the parking spot and onto the street, heading for the roundabout. The pair of them laughing and smiling, like a couple of high school friends messing with each other. Oz texted Donna back before putting the phone away in his pocket. They headed back to the station, stopping for a coffee on the way back, since it had been at least 10 minutes since Terry had his fix.

***

Back at the station, Oz sat at his desk, slumped in his seat. Terry sat at his desk drinking his coffee, looking at the hockey scores and news from the night before. Oz reached into his coat pocket and pulled out his phone. It was close to quitting time, and nothing had happened for the last couple of hours. Oz was just thinking about the things that he learned at the library this morning. He put his phone back in his pocket.

"I think I'm gonna bail, Ter," said Oz.

"Hot date?" said Terry. He didn't even look up from the computer.

"No!" Oz said defensively.

"Uh-huh, whatever you say, kid," laughed Terry.

"You don't stop, do you?" said Oz.

"You miss 100% of the shots you don't take, kid," said Terry.

"Whatever, man, I'm gonna take off. I'll see you tomorrow. Have a good night man, say hi to Maureen for me," said Oz.

"I will. Take it easy, kid. Enjoy your lady friend," teased Terry.

Oz got up, pushed in his chair, gave Terry a salute, and left the office. He started walking home, thinking about the day before and how incredible the entire day was. He couldn't believe how lucky he was, couldn't stop thinking about her, how extraordinary she was.

In no time, he was back at his apartment. He unlocked the door and went inside, kicked off his shoes, took off his sport coat, and tossed it over the arm of the couch as he went into the kitchen. He opened the fridge and pulled out a bottle of water, opened it, and took a swig. Re-capped it and put the bottle on the counter. He grabbed his sport coat off the couch, walked down the hall and into his bedroom.

"Hey there, Tiger!" said Donna. She was laying in his bed, the covers pulled up, and tucked under her arms. Her hair, draped over her shoulder, shimmered in the setting sunlight that came through the blinds. Her stunning green eyes stared up at Oz.

"What… How… Hi! How did you get in here?" said Oz, shocked.

"Are you not happy to see me, Ozzy?" she said, changing her expression to that of a sad puppy. Her bottom lip pouted out.

"No, shit, of course, I am. Thrilled. I've been thinking about you all day," said Oz. "But how did you get in?"

"Are you mad, Ozzy?" asked Donna.

"Am I mad? No, not at all, just surprised," said Oz. But how did you get in here? Do I need to run a background check on you?"

"No, your building super let me in," said Donna. "You're mad. I'm sorry. This was a bad idea. Please don't hate me." Donna pulled the covers tight to her chest and moved to get out of the bed. Tears pooled in her eyes.

"Hate you? God, no," said Oz. "Until you called this morning, I honestly thought yesterday was a dream. Something I completely conjured up in fantasy."

Donna moved back into the bed. She looked up at him with those entrancing green eyes of hers, blinking away the tears. She blushed as Oz spoke to her.

"I still am just so blown away that you are real, let alone in my apartment," said Oz.

"Aww, Ozzy!" she said. "Yesterday totally happened, and you totally rocked my world last night. I couldn't stop thinking about you all day. Every time that I did, I just wanted you to touch me again, kiss me again, hold me again."

"I thought about you all day, too," said Oz.

"So, are you more interested in talking? Or are you going to join me over here and find out just how real I am?" asked Donna.

She flipped off the covers, exposing her naked body, laying on her side, her right leg slightly bent at the knee and her foot tucked behind the calf of her left leg.

"You don't have to ask me twice," said Oz as he dropped his coat, shrugged off his shoulder rig, removed his shirt, and undid his pants. He kicked off his boxers as he climbed into bed, kissed her, and wrapped his arms around her. Donna swung the covers back over them.

9

Oz and Donna lay there in the afterglow of another heated and passionate session of lust. Donna had her head on his chest, and with her left hand rubbed his bare chest. Oz ran his fingers up and down her spine with his left hand.

"Shall we go out for dinner?" asked Oz. "I'm pretty sure that I have nothing here to make us."

"Mm, where should we go?" she asked.

"McDonald's?" joked Oz.

Donna gently bit his chest.

"Ow! I'm kidding, totally kidding," laughed Oz. "What are you craving?"

"Besides more of you?" she said.

"Plenty of time for that after dinner," said Oz.

"How about we just order in? I really don't want to get out of this bed," she said.

"Yeah? We can totally do that. Pizza? Chinese?" asked Oz.

"Hmm, I could go for Chinese," she said.

"I'll get my phone," said Oz as he sat up.

Donna pushed him back down. "Not yet," she said, and moved to straddle him.

***

There was a knock on the door of the apartment. Oz went to the door. He had on a pair of track pants and a t-shirt. He opened the door; it was the delivery kid with the Chinese food.

"That'll be $32.65, sir," said the delivery kid, as he handed Oz the bag of food.

"Here you go," said Oz, giving him $40. "Have a good night," said Oz, closing the door.

"Thanks, you too," said the kid.

Oz brought the food into the kitchen. Donna sat at the breakfast bar wearing nothing but Oz's white button-down shirt he had discarded on the floor. Oz grabbed a couple of plates out of the cupboard and cutlery from the drawer. He dished out the chicken fried rice, chow mein, chicken balls, and beef and broccoli on both of their plates. He put Donna's plate down on the breakfast bar in front of her.

"What can I get you to drink? Water or water?" he asked.

"Water would be lovely. I think I need to rehydrate anyway," she said, giggling.

Oz pulled out a bottle of water from the fridge, cracked open the lid on her bottle, and put it in front of her. He grabbed his plate and his water that he had left on the counter, and walked around the counter to join her at the breakfast bar.

"Hell of a date," joked Oz.

"Yeah, we really should go on one of those," Donna laughed.

The conversation continued through dinner, and while Oz cleaned up and did the dishes, as he insisted. She was so incredibly easy to talk with. They could talk about anything and nothing, and none of it was strained. Not only was she incredibly beautiful, but she was intelligent, funny, very witty, and so incredibly warm-hearted.

"So, I guess you didn't get to look for work today?" joked Oz.

"No, I really didn't. I was a little too preoccupied today," laughed Donna. "Tell me about this case you are working on."

"Not much that I can tell you, really," said Oz.

"Well then, why don't you tell me why you got into Homicide?" she asked.

"That I can do," Oz laughed and said. "I think that unlike drugs, burglary, or missing persons, homicide is the most heinous and dramatic thing that one human can do to another. And chasing down and bringing those people to justice, though it will never replace the loved ones that people have lost, always seemed the most rewarding work to me. If that makes any sense?"

"It does. I think that is honorable of you," said Donna.

"I don't know if it is honorable, but it motivates me, it drives me?" said Oz.

"But I'm still curious about your case. Please tell me?" Donna said.

"Why can't I say no to you?" said Oz.

"Because you adore me," she said and giggled.

"You might be right there," joked Oz.

"Might?" said Donna. She pouted out her bottom lip.

Oz leaned in and kissed her. "What do you think?" he said.

"So, are you gonna tell me about it?" she asked.

"I really can't say much because it's an ongoing investigation, but I can tell you that we're following up on three very grizzly murders that occurred recently," said Oz.

"Oh my God! What happened to them?" asked Donna.

"It wasn't pretty. They were probably the most gruesome scenes that I have ever seen," said Oz.

"Do you have any leads?" she asked.

"Leads?" he laughed. "Watch a lot of cop shows, do you?"

"Shut up! Is that not the right word?" she said.

"It works, but no, we don't have any leads. So far, we haven't been able to find any evidence that would point at who is doing this. It's pretty frustrating, I just need to find one thing, just one thing that will give us something to go on," he said.

"What about your partner? Does he have any ideas?" she asked.

"Terry? No, he is just as puzzled as I am. But he's had a lot more years to figure out how to handle his frustration," he said.

"What about that CSI stuff? In those shows, those guys were always so good at finding stuff," she said.

"They are more stumped than we are. They haven't been able to find anything that would point to a suspect," said Oz.

"Aww, Ozzy," she said, getting up and walking around the counter to cuddle him. "Maybe I can help you get some of those frustrations out?"

"You still haven't had enough?" joked Oz.

"Is that a bad thing?" she said as she looked up into his eyes.

"With you, never," he said.

Oz scooped her up in his arms. She squealed and laughed. She wrapped her arms around his neck as he carried her down the hall into the bedroom, kissed her soft, sweet lips, and laid her on the bed.

***

Ring… Ring… Ring…

"Detective Shields, Homicide," said Oz. He was groggy, woken by the call.

"Oz, it's Terry. They struck again," said Terry.

"Seriously? What time is it?" asked Oz.

"It's 12:20, kid. I'm leaving shortly to come to get you. Lieutenant said this one is bad," said Terry.

"How bad?" asked Oz.

Donna, now awake, snuggled into Oz, looked up at him. She whispered, "Do you need to go?"

Oz nodded yes.

"Real bad, kid. You better bring a barf bag," said Terry.

"You're hilarious. Alright, so what, you'll be here in twenty? Thirty?" asked Oz.

"Why? Do you need more time?" laughed Terry as he asked.

"No, man. I'm good. I'll meet you out front," said Oz.

"Alright, kid, see you in twenty," Terry said, and hung up the phone.

"Fuck," groaned Oz. He sat up, moved to the edge of the bed, rubbed his eyes, and tried to get focused.

"What is it, Ozzy?" asked Donna

"The killer struck again. We have to go to the scene," said Oz.

Oz stood up and collected his clothes. He picked up his shoulder rig and placed it on his dresser. "Are you going to stay here? Or do you want me to take you home?" asked Oz.

"Do you mind if I stay?" she said.

"Not at all. It'd be a nice change to come home to something so incredibly beautiful, after what I'm about to go and see," he said as he leaned in and kissed her on the forehead. "You gonna be ok here by yourself?"

"Don't worry about me, Tiger. There is nowhere safer for me to be," she said.

Oz smiled at her before he exited the room, headed for the washroom. He splashed his face with water, and quickly brushed his hair and teeth, before he went back into the bedroom, put on his shoulder rig, and grabbed his sport coat off the floor. He shook it and gave it a quick pat-down before putting it on.

"Mm, I can't wait for you to come back," she said.

"You sure you are going to be ok?" Oz asked as he walked over and sat beside her on the bed.

"Positive, Ozzy. You just be safe, and come back to me," she said and stared into his eyes.

"I will," he said, and kissed her goodbye. "Call me if you need anything, okay?"

"I will," she said, slowly releasing his hand as he got up and walked out of the room.

Terry pulled up to the curb just as Oz walked out of the building and got into Terry's car.

"Hey, kid," said Terry. "Were you having a good night?"

"Where are we headed?" asked Oz, brushing off Terry's joke.

"We're heading to a ballpark off Medford Street in Charlestown," said Terry.

"You said this one is bad?" asked Oz.

"Yeah, the Lieutenant said this one was pretty rough. So be prepared for anything," said Terry.

"What do we know?" asked Oz.

"Just that a trooper on patrol called it in," said Terry.

"So still no witnesses?" asked Oz.

"Nah, doesn't look like it, kid," replied Terry.

"How is this possible? I mean, if we were in the sticks, I'd understand, but in the middle of the city? Really?" said Oz.

"I know, kid. It's fucking bizarre, but not impossible," said Terry.

They drove down Medford Street to the Tobin Memorial Bridge. There were four squad cars, lights flashing, parked, one blocked the entrance to Brien Court from the southbound lane of Medford Street. Another partially blocked Medford Street from the north. They had a wooden police barricade beside the car blocking the Southbound lane so that they could quickly move it to let authorized vehicles through. The other two squad cars blocked traffic at the south end of Medford Street at Decatur St. The FSD truck was on-site already as they pulled up. Terry made a U-turn and parked on the East side of the Northbound lane just up from the squad car at the North end of Medford Street. They got out of the car with their badges, ready to show the officer at the blockade.

"Detectives Shields and White, Homicide," Oz said, as they presented their badges.

"Head to the ballpark, detectives. They're waiting for you guys down there. The trooper there was the first on-scene," said the officer.

"Thanks," said Oz.

He and Terry proceeded to the ball diamond. The forensic officers were suiting up, getting their gear ready to go to work as Terry and Oz walked past them. Getting close to third base, they saw the body; the lieutenant was right. This was so much worse than the others. This victim had been tied to the cage behind home plate, about six or seven feet off the ground, looking like it had been crucified. As they approached, the scene only got more horrific as details came into view. The head and legs were missing. The intestines and bowels hung out of the torso like deli sausages hung in a butcher shop window. The flesh on the chest had been flayed and peeled back, revealing the musculature and sinew. The flesh that had been peeled back was hooked to the fence cage under the arms. This was truly sadistic.

"Holy shit!" said Oz.

"There ain't nothing holy about this, kid," said Terry.

Oz turned and saw the Trooper standing back near the pitcher's mound. "Officer?" he shouted out.

"Yes, sir," the officer replied.

"Were you the first on the scene?"

"Yes sir. I called it in," said the officer. "I was on patrol and I saw this thing hanging there on the fence. I couldn't make out what it was, so I shined the spotlight from the squad car over here, and saw that it was a body. I immediately radioed dispatch and called in a 10-23, Officer on Scene at Barry Field, and a possible 10-31-Charlie, Homicide. When I got closer, I saw it was awful, and radioed in a 10-78, Request Assistance…"

"Sorry, what's your name?" asked Oz.

"Martin, Martin Farrell, sir," he said.

"You're a rookie?" asked Terry.

"Yes sir, three months outta the academy," said officer Farrell.

"I figured. Martin, when you're talking to other cops, you don't need to tell us what the codes mean," said Terry.

"Oh, uh… yes, sir," said officer Farrell.

"Did you see anyone in the area?" asked Oz.

"No sir. It was super quiet, not a soul for miles," said officer Farrell.

"What time did you call this in?" asked Oz.

"It was… uh… after midnight, about 12:15," said officer Farrell.

"Thanks, Martin. Good job. Stay close, alright?" said Oz.

"Yes sir, will do," said officer Farrell.

Oz and Terry walked towards the body. The smell was sickly sweet and lingered. The ground below the body was muddy from blood. Drops of blood would occasionally drip from the torso above. Oz pulled out his Maglite and turned it on, shining the light on the ground, lighting their path to the muddy pool of blood.

"There doesn't appear to be a blood trail or tracks leading up to the fence or away. How the fuck is that possible?" asked Oz.

"That's odd, kid. Where are the head and legs?" asked Terry.

"No clue, none of this makes any sense," said Oz. "If the killer brought the body here, there should be blood or tracks leading to the fence. Similarly, if the killer took the head and the legs away from here, then there should be blood or tracks leading away from here, right? But there is absolutely nothing. How hard would it be to mount a body up there by yourself?"

"I'm thinking, pretty fucking impossible," said Terry.

"That's what I'm thinking too," said Oz. "How does someone do all this with no one seeing? I mean, this kind of work would take time, right?"

"Yeah, I'd say so," said Terry.

Oz shined the light at the right wrist, sweeping across to the left. "Looks like the wrists have been in place by steel wire. The wire seems to go through the wrists, then wrap around them, strapping it to the fence. How high off the ground would you say that is… seven feet?" asked Oz.

"How tall are you?" asked Terry.

"I'm 6'3"," said Oz.

"Yeah, I'd say at least seven feet then," said Terry

"The victim appears to be male. Caucasian, maybe Latino or Italian. No clue of age. The chest flesh looks like it is held to the fence with the same steel wire, but done with small loops, like chain mail links through the skin and around the fencing," said Oz. "The blood on the fence looks consistent to the wounds and runs down to the pool on the ground. So, I would assume he was alive, or not dead long before getting hung up here. But still, how do you get the head and legs away from here without leaving a trail?"

One of the forensic officers approached them. He was completely covered up in his Tyvek suit, safety goggles, and mask on. He was the lead forensics officer on-scene, and roughly the same height as Oz, hard to tell his build in the puffy white suit, but underneath, was the body of a man who worked hard at staying fit. His name was Jared Hughes. Jared was a black male, in his 30s, and he'd been with the FSD since coming out of college. He worked very hard honing his craft, and now led teams on site, for the last two years.

"You guys about done?" he asked.

"Pretty much," said Oz. "Let me ask you something. Can you guys pull a print from something as small as that wire?"

"It's not impossible. We may only get a partial. It depends on how much the killer handled it," said Jared.

"Right, that makes sense," said Oz. "What's your take on this?"

"I mean, this is some sick shit, like something out of one of those Hellraiser movies or something," said Jared.

"Yeah, that's what this looks like," said Oz. "We'll get out of your way. I look forward to seeing what you guys find."

"Yeah, thanks," said Jared.

Jared turned and waved at the other forensics officers, who came in carrying their toolboxes and halogen lights to help them see everything. Oz and Terry walked away from the scene. Oz stopped near the pitcher's mound and turned around for one last look. He stared at the scene from a distance. *Why the ball diamond? Why a crucifix pose? Why remove the head and legs? Why flay the chest?* He thought.

"Oz? You alright?" asked Terry, grabbing onto Oz's arm.

"Yeah, Ter. Just thinking, man," said Oz.

Oz turned to officer Farrell, who waited there near the pitcher's mound. "Thanks, Martin. We'll get a hold of you if we have any more questions. Good work!"

"Thanks! And… yeah… whatever you guys need," responded officer Farrell, still a ball of nerves.

Oz and Terry walked back towards Terry's car.

"Those buildings there, Ter," said Oz, pointing at the buildings opposite the ballpark. "We should see if there were any witnesses."

"We can come back tomorrow and talk to some of them. I think only those on the first floor there and there," said Terry, pointing at the windows on the East end of the two buildings. "They would've had a view of the ballpark. Those trees thick and grown, and would've blocked the view of those on the upper floors."

"Yeah, you're probably right there," agreed Oz. "That will at least cut down how many we need to talk to, for sure."

They arrived back at Terry's car, got in, and headed back up Medford Street for home.

"I've been a detective for 12 years, kid, and I ain't ever seen anything like this before," said Terry, breaking the silence. "This wacko is something else. A real twisted fuck."

"You can say that again, Ter," said Oz. "Hey, remember this morning when you said that the killer might be religious?"

"Yeah, I don't think this guy is a Catholic, kid," said Terry.

"Me either, but what if this is some satanic shit? Like these are ritual sacrifices or something?" said Oz.

"I mean, it could be possible," said Terry. "People do fucked up shit for their religions."

"Yeah, they sure do," said Oz. "Do you know of anyone that might be able to tell us about Satan worship here in Boston?"

"Not off the top of my head at two in the fucking morning. But I'll think about it," said Terry.

"Yeah, I don't think that either of us is capable of much at this point," said Oz.

Terry pulled up in front of Oz's apartment.

"Get some rest, kid. I'll see you at the office in a few hours, and we'll head back to those apartments and see what we can find out," said Terry.

"Yeah, you too. Careful on that drive home, man," said Oz, as he exited the car.

"For sure, kid. Thanks," said Terry.

Oz closed the door, gave Terry a wave, and turned and walked into his building. He couldn't wait to get back into bed. He was exhausted.

10

Oz's alarm clock blared.

Oz reached over Donna and turned off the alarm. Donna moaned as Oz rolled back over onto his back. Oz blinked his eyes slowly, trying to wake up, and stretched out as much as he could with Donna on his left arm.

"What time is it?" asked Donna as she yawned and stretched.

"Seven… well, really it's 6:45… don't ask," said Oz. "You wanna take a shower here before I take you home, and go to work?"

"Mm, are you going to join me in there?" she asked.

"I'll be late for work if I do that," he said, kissing her on the forehead.

"Party pooper," she said. "They don't cut you a break, for working in the middle of the night?"

"Sadly no. Crime doesn't stop," he said. "We have to go back to the scene this morning and see if we can find a witness."

"Ugh, that really sucks!" she said. "I'll just have a quick wash before you take me home. I'll get all pretty there and start my job hunt."

"You're already perfect," said Oz. "Alright, I'm gonna take a quick shower and get ready, then I'll make us some breakfast."

"Mm. Now who's the perfect one?" she said, leaning over and kissing him.

"You really don't make it easy to get out of bed," he said, smiling at her.

"Good," she said, smiling back.

Oz hopped out of bed, walked to the dresser, pulled out a fresh pair of boxer briefs and a pair of black dress socks, and put them on top of the dresser. Donna watched him as he went over to the closet, grabbed a light blue collared shirt, a brown sport coat, and a fresh pair of jeans, and laid them on the small upholstered chair in the corner by the window. He grabbed the socks and underwear from atop the dresser as he left the room.

Donna fell back asleep while Oz was in the shower. She awoke to him fully dressed, shoulder rig on, and threading his brown belt through the loops of his jeans and buckled it. She stared at him in the early morning sunlight coming through the blinds behind him, giving him a sort of angelic aura.

"Mm, don't you look handsome," she said.

"Can I make you an omelet or something for breakfast?" he asked.

"Aren't you adorable? Some toast with butter and a glass of OJ will be beyond perfect," she said.

"Are you sure?" he asked.

"Absolutely!" she said.

"Alright, toast and OJ, it is," he said. He kissed her and left the room for the kitchen, sport coat in hand.

Donna slid out of bed, grabbed her clothes, and went into the bathroom. Oz grabbed two glasses out of the cupboard and began preparing breakfast for them. There was a fluidity to his movements, especially this morning. He was happy and at ease. He grabbed a butter knife from the utensil drawer, dropped the bread in the toaster, and plunging the lever down, starting the toaster.

The toast popped up just as Donna exited the bathroom and rounded the corner. Oz turned to see her coming towards the breakfast bar. Even dressed as casually as she was in a green v-neck t-shirt and tight-fitting jeans that hugged her shapely curves, she still looked absolutely incredible. Her hair pulled back into a ponytail. Oz buttered the toast, cut it diagonally, and put the plate down in front of her at the breakfast bar. He grabbed one of the glasses that he took down, opened the fridge, removing a jug from the shelf. He put the glass down in front of her and filled it with orange juice.

"Thank you!" she said. "You're in an incredible mood this morning, Ozzy."

"Why wouldn't I be?" he said, buttering his toast now. "Woke up to a beautiful woman beside me in bed. The sun is shining. Feels like today is going to be a great day."

"Aww, aren't you a charmer," she said.

Oz poured himself a glass of orange juice, put the jug back in the fridge, and brought his plate and glass around the counter, and sat on the stool beside her. They ate their simple yet delicious breakfast, with the sun now a little higher in the sky, shining through the living room blinds behind them.

"When did you get back last night? I didn't look. I was just happy to have you to cuddle up to," she asked.

"Close to 2:30, I think," said Oz as he took another bite of toast.

"Ugh! How are you even functioning?" she asked. Donna took a sip of her juice.

"Like I said, it just feels like it's going to be a great day," said Oz.

They finished their breakfast. Oz cleared it all away, doing the dishes quickly and putting everything back in its place. Donna asked to help, but Oz insisted she leave it to him. He went quickly into his room and grabbed his service pistol from the safe, did his usual checks, and holstered it in the shoulder rig as he came back out of the kitchen.

He grabbed his sport coat from the arm of the couch, put it on, and grabbed his badge, and clipped it on his belt. Donna slipped into her black, flat shoes she had with her, and they left the apartments. Oz locked the apartment behind them.

"Not that this keeps anyone out," he joked.

Donna pinched his arm as they laughed and headed downstairs to the garage to get in his car. Oz opened the passenger door for her and closed it behind her once she was safely inside. He jogged around to the driver's side and got in. He started the car, and they drove out of the garage, headed for her place. Oz pulled up to the curb at the very place that he had dropped her off before.

"Thank you for everything, Ozzy," she said. "Will I hear from you later?"

"Absolutely," he said. "I'll message you around lunch to see how things are going. Good luck with your job hunt today."

"Thanks. Hopefully, I don't get distracted again today," she laughed.

Oz leaned over and kissed her on the lips, long and passionately. He sat back in his seat and Donna lingered a moment in bliss. She exhaled deeply and grabbed the handle, opening the door, and slipped out of the car.

"I'll talk to you soon," he said.

"Thank you, Tiger. Be safe, okay?" she said.

"Always!" said Oz.

Donna closed the door and walked up the walkway to her building, blowing him a kiss as she went inside. Oz put the car into gear and drove off.

***

Oz pulled into the lot of the police headquarters and backed his car into a spot. Terry pulled into the lot just as Oz turned off his car and parked a couple of spots over from Oz. Oz got out of his car and waited for Terry to get out of his.

"Morning, kid," said Terry, groaning as he got out of his car. "How are you?"

"Better than I thought I'd be. How about you?" asked Oz.

"Could've stayed in bed a few more hours this morning," said Terry as they headed into the building.

Oz stopped by the motor pool and signed out the keys for their car before joining Terry up at their desks. He sat at his desk, turned on his computer, and logged in, opening a case file for the victim last night. He was filling out the details of the report when Terry looked up and broke the silence.

"When do you wanna head over to those apartments this morning?" asked Terry.

"9:30 or 10?" said Oz.

"Sounds good, kid," said Terry, taking another big swig of his coffee.

"You wanna drive or do you want me to?" asked Oz.

"I'm so tired. I shouldn't have driven my ass here this morning. Do you mind?" said Terry.

"Not at all, man. How's Maureen?" asked Oz.

"Crazy broad, stayed up until I got home, and still was up this morning making me breakfast," said Terry.

"That's a damn good woman you got there, Ter. Better hang on to her," said Oz.

"She ain't going nowhere, kid. She's too crazy about me," said Terry.

"I have no clue why," joked Oz

"Aww, you cawksuckah!" laughed Terry. "Take your shots while I'm tired, kid, I'll make you pay later."

Oz laughed and continued to write up the report for last night. When he finished, he opened up his email and hoped to find something there from either the Medical Examiner or the FSD, but there was still nothing. *Guess they're still struggling to find something.*

"Ready to go, Ter?" asked Oz.

"I'm hit the pisser. Meet you at the car," said Terry.

"Alright man, see you in a couple then," said Oz.

Oz grabbed his phone and sent Donna a quick message before heading down to get the Impala. As he opened the driver's door, she responded. Oz got in and pulled out his phone to see that she had sent him a kissing face emoji. He smiled, returned his phone to his pocket, and started the car. Terry came down and got in, and they drove to the apartments near the crime scene from last night.

They pulled up in front of the apartment building off Decatur, got out and walked up to the West entrance of the building, and went inside. They walked to the apartment at the end of the hall and knocked on the door. A skinny blonde woman answered the door. She had on a pair of gray track pants that sat right above her pelvis, a gray hoodie that looked like it was for a toddler, it was so short on her, and a pink shirt under the goodie. Her midriff was exposed, displaying her navel pierced and a tribal tattoo of an orchid.

"Yeah," she said.

"Ma'am we are with the Boston PD. I'm Detective White, and this is my partner, Detective Shields. We'd like to ask you some questions about what happened across the way last night," said Terry. He and Oz had their badges out on display for her to examine.

"Fine. You can tell those assholes to turn their lights off at night. All fucking night, that shit flashed in here," she said in a thick Boston accent, as she opened the door completely to let the detectives inside.

"Yeah, sorry about that, ma'am. I'll mention that to the Lieutenant," Terry said, clearly lying.

"Uh-huh," she said, sitting down on the couch in the living room of the apartment, lighting a cigarette.

"Can we get your name, ma'am?" asked Oz.

"Oh, this one speaks," she said, eying Oz up and down. "Shailene."

"Can you please spell that for me?" asked Oz

"Pretty, but not smart, huh," she said, looking at Terry and thumbing at Oz. "S-H-A-I-L-E-N-E."

"Thank you, ma'am," said Oz, ignoring her comment.

"Do you know what happened across the street last night, Shailene?" asked Terry.

"Someone found a body or something," she said.

"That's right. Did you hear or see anything strange or out of place last night?" asked Terry.

"Nah, it was really quiet around here last night. I was out for a smoke out back there last night about ten or eleven, and there wasn't even a dog barking," she said.

"Do you remember anything else?" asked Oz.

"Not really, not until the cops showed up with their lights on, keeping me awake all fucking night," she said.

"Have you seen any weird or suspicious people around lately?" asked Terry.

"In this neighborhood, are you fucking kidding? They're all fucking wackos here," she said, laughing.

"Right, well, thank you for your time, ma'am. Here is my card. If you can recall anything else that might be helpful to us, please call me," said Oz as he handed her his card.

"Sure, cutie, will do," she said.

Oz and Terry left the apartment, headed down the hall to the door where they came in.

"That was about what I expected," said Oz.

"Yeah, typical Stylene, kid," said Terry.

"Do you want to talk to anyone else in this building before we go over to the other one?" asked Oz.

"Nah, I'm thinking this is a waste of fucking time," said Terry.

Oz and Terry left the building and walked around North to Brien Court, just off Medford Street. Forensics was still in the ballpark, but it appeared as though they were wrapping up their search for evidence. Terry and Oz entered that building and headed for the apartment that had an unobstructed view of the ballpark on the East side of the building. Oz knocked on the door and reached for his badge to present it. Terry had his badge out already.

The door opened slightly, as far as the chain latch would allow. They could see the face of an elderly black woman, her hair gray and wrapped in a handkerchief headband.

"Can I help you?" she asked.

"Ma'am, I'm Detective Shields, and this is my partner, Detective White. We'd like to ask you some questions if we could about what happened across the street last night?" said Oz.

"Oh, sure, please come in," she said.

She closed the door to release the chain and opened it again to let the detectives inside. The woman was frail and slightly hunched. She was well into her 70s and was dressed in maroon-colored slacks and a silky floral shirt. She walked over to an armchair in the living room and sat down, leaving the couch for Oz and Terry to share.

"Thank you, ma'am. Can I start by getting your name?" asked Oz.

"Mary Ward," she said.

"Thank you, Miss Ward. Do you live here by yourself?" asked Oz.

"Yes, sir, for the last eight years since my Husband, Davis, passed away," she said.

"Sorry to hear that, ma'am. Were you home last night between 10:30 and 1?" asked Oz.

"Well, I wasn't out at the dance hall, if that is what you're hinting at," she laughed and said.

"You're sure about that?" asked Oz, chuckling.

Mary smiled at him. He was attempting to make her feel more comfortable by going along with her joke.

"You may or may not have heard, but there was a body found last night, across the street. Did you happen to see or hear anything suspicious last night?"

"Oh my! I hadn't heard, but I guessed it was pretty serious. I was sitting by the window in my bedroom about 11 or so having my usual cup of tea, listening to some jazz on my radio, like I normally do. And I saw this weird shadow on the ballpark there," she said.

"Weird shadow?" repeated Oz. "Can you describe it?"

"It's going to sound crazy, but do you remember the old horror pictures with the werewolves and such?" she said.

"Kinda," said Oz.

"He was like that, but really oddly shaped. He didn't walk so much as it seemed to float, and he was awkwardly hunched. Like he was hurt or something."

"Which way was this person heading?" asked Oz.

"That way there," she said, pointing North. "He was so very strange and looked very tall."

"Did you happen to see if this person was white, or black or Hispanic?" Oz asked.

"No, I never saw him like that. He seemed to always stay in the dark, never touching the light," she said.

"But you're sure it was a man?" asked Oz.

"Well, I've never seen a woman built like that in all my years, but I suppose it's possible," she said.

"Was this the first time that you had seen this person?" Oz asked.

"Oh, my yes. You would forget seeing something like this," she said. "He was very creepy. I remember shaking, hoping that he wouldn't see me watching him. It took me forever to fall asleep after that. Worse than any scary movie."

"Ma'am, is there anything else you can tell us about him?' asked Terry.

"His legs seemed to bend again after the knee, but in the other direction, like an animal's legs, you know?" she said, making gestures trying to show how it looked. "I guess that is why I think he was like a werewolf or something. But it was so dark, it was really hard to get a great look at him."

"Did he look like he was carrying something?" asked Terry.

"No sir, nothing like that at all, at least not that I can remember," she said.

"Would you be able to call us if you ever see it again?" asked Oz.

"Oh, I hope that I never see him again. That was terrifying enough for one lifetime," she said.

"You said this was around 11:00?" asked Oz

"Mm-hmm, it wasn't long after that the police were there with their lights flashing. Then more police showed up, and then you couldn't get away from the flashing lights. That didn't help me get to sleep either."

"We apologize for that, ma'am. Can you tell us anything else about what you saw last night?" asked Oz.

"That was pretty much it. And to be honest, I wish I hadn't even seen that much," she said.

"I understand, ma'am. Thank you so much for your time. If you remember anything else, please call me directly," said Oz as he handed her a business card.

"I will. Good luck with your investigation, detectives," she said.

"Thank you, Miss Ward," said Oz.

Oz and Terry left Miss Ward's apartment and strolled out of the building, headed back down Medford Street. On their way back to the car, the forensics officers were stripping out of their Tyvek suits. Oz gave Terry a nod and a nudge to get him to head over towards the FSD truck.

"Detectives," greeted Jared Hughes. Jared looked exhausted from the long night they had just put in.

"How'd it go?" asked Oz.

"I have no idea who is doing this shit, but they seem to know almost as much as we do about collecting evidence," said Jared.

"What makes you say that?" asked Oz.

"The scene is clean. I mean fucking clean," said Jared. "Not a print, not a hair, a fiber, nothing that didn't belong to the victim that was hanging there. It's impossible, and ridiculous, of me to say, but it's like the victim put themselves up there, or were put there by magic or some shit. You know what I mean?"

"Seriously?" said Oz.

"Yeah, it doesn't make any sense," said Jared. "How about you guys. Any luck?"

"We think we finally have a witness," said Oz.

"Yeah?" said Jared.

"A woman saw a shadowy figure leaving the ballpark last night about 11," said Oz.

"Good luck sketching that shit out," joked Jared.

"Yeah, thanks. Go get some rest, man," said Oz.

"Thanks, good luck on your lead," laughed Jared.

Oz and Terry walked back to the Impala, got in, and headed back to the station.

11

Back at the station, Oz and Terry sat at their desks. Oz's desk phone rang. The number on the display was from an internal extension.

"Shields," Oz said, answering the phone.

"Detective, it's Steve from Tech. We got a name finally off the Fitbit," he said.

"You're kidding? What is it?" said Oz.

"No sir, the information that we pulled from the device said her name was Kanesha Parker, D.O.B.: 18 April 1997," said Steve.

"That is amazing, thank you!" said Oz, and he hung up the phone.

"What's up, kid?" asked Terry.

"Got a name for our Jane Doe. Her name is Kanesha Parker," said Oz. "I'm gonna call that building super over there and see if she lived there."

"Good thinking, kid," said Terry.

Oz quickly googled the number for the building complex and then dialed it from his desk phone.

"Hello, Mr. O'Reilly? This is Detective Shields, we met yesterday… yes sir… that is why I am calling. Do you happen to have a tenant by the name of Kanesha Parker? You do? Would it be possible to let us into her apartment? Yes, I understand you are supposed to give written notice for that sort of thing… but considering that we believe she is our victim, sir. I doubt she will complain… right… thank you, Mr. O'Reilly… We'll see you shortly." Oz hung up the phone. "Let's go for a ride, Ter."

***

Oz and Terry pulled up to the apartment on 9th Street, got out of the car and headed into the lobby, and dialed the office extension. Mr. O'Reilly answered the phone, and remotely unlocked the door for them, and they met him inside.

"Her apartment is on the second floor," said Mr. O'Reilly.

"Lead the way," said Oz.

Mr. O'Reilly took them up in the elevator, and they followed him down the hall heading North of the elevators to an apartment about halfway down the hall on the right side. The number on the door was 216. Mr. O'Reilly knocked on the door, and announced his presence. Hearing no response, he used his master key to unlock the door and let the detectives inside.

It was a small studio apartment, spotless, and well-organized. The furniture was mostly from Ikea; the tenant used their furniture to make the most of the small space. There were two closets, side by side, with bi-folding doors on the right when you walked into the apartment. Opposite the closet was the bathroom. A little further in was the kitchen on the left, with a breakfast bar that separated the kitchen from the rest of the apartment.

"It definitely looks like no one has been home for a few days," said Oz. He pulled out a pair of blue nitrile gloves from his jacket pocket and pulled them on. Terry grabbed his notebook and pen.

"Yeah," said Terry as he followed Oz into the apartment.

Oz walked to the breakfast bar and picked up a small pile of mail sitting there on it and thumbed through it.

"She definitely lived alone. All the mail here is addressed to her," said Oz.

He walked into the living room/bedroom area, looked at pictures she had on her bookshelf. There was a picture of what appeared to be her with her parents on graduation day, and a couple of school pictures of nieces and nephews.

"Was a pretty person?" asked Oz.

"Super, quiet. She was a real sweetheart," said Mr. O'Reilly. "She brought me a tin of cookies she made last year for Christmas."

"Did you know her well, Mr. O'Reilly?" asked Oz, as he turned to face Mr. O'Reilly, still by the door.

"Not super well. I fixed a couple of burnt bulbs a few times for her. She was always smiling, said hello every time she saw me. Just a super sweet, kid, you know?" he said. "Who would kill a sweet kid like her? She never bothered anybody?"

"That's what we are going to find out, Mr. O'Reilly," said Oz.

Oz walked back to the closets and looked through them. He moved clothes back and forth that hung in the closet. Looked through the hanging closet organizers in there. "She really didn't seem like she needed very much," said Oz. "You wouldn't happen to know her parents, would you, Mr. O'Reilly?"

"I think her Mother is the Emergency Contact on her tenant agreement," said Mr. O'Reilly. "We can check when we get back downstairs to my office."

"That would be great. Thank you. I'm not seeing anything here like an address book or anything," said Oz.

"You kidding, kid?" said Terry. "Do you still keep an address book? Most people have that shit on their phones now."

"Yeah, you have a point there, Ter," said Oz. "Alright, I think I'm done here. I don't see anything here that would lead us to her killer. Let's see if we can get her mom's name."

"Sounds good, kid. I'm not seeing anything jump out at me neither," said Terry.

They left the apartment with Mr. O'Reilly and followed him back downstairs to his office, where he sat in his little office chair and wheeled himself over to the filing cabinet. He pulled out a drawer near the middle of the four-drawer cabinet, put his reading glasses near the tip of his nose, and flipped through the folders for Kanesha's file. When he found it, he pulled it out and used his forearm to keep the place as he opened her file.

"Uh… Emergency Contact… uh, here it is… Tariana Parker, phone number 417-555-4106," said Mr. O'Reilly.

Terry wrote it down in his notebook.

"Thank you again for all your help, Mr. O'Reilly. We really appreciate it," said Oz.

"Yeah, no problem. You guys just catch the cawksuckah that killed that sweet girl," said Mr. O'Reilly.

"That's the fucking plan," said Terry.

"Have a good day, sir. And really, thanks again," said Oz. He and Terry left the building and got into the Impala.

"I'll notify the Springfield PD," said Oz. "We'll have them deliver the news."

"How do you know she's in Springfield," asked Terry.

"I have a weird thing about remembering area codes, don't ask," said Oz.

"That's a fucked up talent to have, kid. Glad it's coming in handy for you, though," said Terry.

Oz drove away from the apartments. They stopped for a quick bite to eat on the way back to the station, and another coffee for Terry. While Terry was inside getting his coffee, Oz gave Donna a quick call to see how her job hunt was going. The call went through to voicemail, so he left a brief message. Terry came back to the car, smiling like a kid leaving the candy store. Oz just laughed at him and shook his head.

Back at the office, Oz emailed Brad Walker, the Medical Examiner, to let him know they discovered the name of the Jane Doe brought in on Friday night, and to now identify her as Kanesha Parker. He also copied Jared Hughes on the email so that they could update their file as well. Oz opened his case file from Friday night and updated it.

Oz's phone vibrated in his pocket. He pulled it out to see that Donna had sent him a text. He opened the message, and it read; *'Guess who got herself a job! Can't wait to talk to you later! xx'*. Oz replied, congratulating her, and that he would call her when he finished work.

The Lieutenant came out of the office and sat in the chair next to Terry. "How's it going, boys?" he asked.

"Hey, Jim, got a couple of hits today. We found out who our Jane Doe was from Friday night. We have a witness that reported to us she saw a shadowy figure leaving the ballpark around 11," said Terry. "It's not much, but it's something."

"Just the one guy leaving the scene at the park? How did one guy do that to that body?" asked Jim.

"We spoke with Jared from FSD, and he said that they have no clue about that either. No prints, no fibers, nothing. He said that this killer knows almost as much as they do about forensics," said Oz.

"C'mon, those CSI shows weren't that good. How is this fucking possible?" asked Jim.

"No clue, sir… uh… Lieutenant," said Oz.

"What am I supposed to tell the public. They are starting to ask questions. Four murders and no connection, no motive, no evidence. Fuck all," said Jim.

"Well, Lieutenant, why not tell them just that?" said Oz.

"Are you outta your mind, kid? They'll eat me alive," said Jim. "Tell you what, Oz, come up with something, and I'll put you in front of the cameras in two hours. How about that? Perfect… I'll be there as your back-up," said Jim. He got up and went into his office.

"Put your foot in it this time, kid," said Terry.

"Fuck, I don't wanna be on TV," said Oz.

"Doesn't look like the Lieutenant gave you a choice," laughed Terry.

***

Standing at the podium in the Police Headquarters Press Room was Lieutenant Roberts. He thanked the press for coming and then introduced Oz to tell them about the murders. Nervously, Oz stepped up to the podium. The Lieutenant shook his hand and whispered, "Good luck, fucker." Then he took a position in the background behind Oz.

"Ladies and Gentlemen of the Press, I am Detective Ozwald Shields from the Homicide Division. Over the last several nights, we have been witness to four of the most horrific murders that Boston has seen in a long time, quite possibly ever. We are currently procuring leads and following up on them as they surface, but this is a very slow process. Unfortunately, as the killer appears to be very skilled at leaving little to no evidence at the scene," said Oz, more confident than he thought he would be. "We will release more details to the press as we get them, but for now, we ask that the press give us the space to do our investigation. We kindly ask that the citizens of the great City of Boston be super vigilant at this time, do not leave your houses alone if you can avoid it, especially at night. Be good to each other and look out for one another. Together, we will catch this killer. Thank you."

The press room erupted with noise. All the reporters were desperate to have their questions addressed. Oz stepped away from the podium and took a deep, cleansing breath. The Lieutenant went back to the podium, thanked everyone for coming, and mentioned that a press release would be coming shortly. Jim and Oz exited the room and went back up to the detective pool.

"Great job, kid. That was excellent!" said Jim, he punched Oz in the arm.

"Thanks, that was hell," said Oz.

"You keep performing like that, and I may have you do all of these press events for me." Jim laughed. "Terry, we got a superstar here. The kid is a natural."

"Don't say that in front of him, Jim. We don't want him to think we like him and want to keep him around," laughed Terry.

"Yeah, yeah, laugh it up guys," said Oz.

"Go on, you guys get outta here for the day. You've put in more than enough hours," said Jim.

"Don't gotta tell me twice," said Terry, hopping up from his desk. "Let's get the fuck outta here, kid."

Oz grabbed his keys from his desk drawer and followed Terry out of the office. Walking through the parking lot to their cars, Oz said, "Have a good night, Ter. See you in the morning."

"Yeah kid, you too. Good job today!" said Terry.

"Thanks, Ter, take it easy," said Oz.

12

"Hey, Donna!" said Oz. "How'd it go today?"

"Hey, Tiger!" she said. "I had a great day. I woke up with you, I got a new job, and now, here you are calling me. Could it be any better?"

"How about we go out to dinner to celebrate, then?" said Oz. "Do you like steak?"

"Mm, that sounds wonderful. What time?" she said.

"Pick you up around 7? I'll call and get us a reservation," said Oz.

"Sounds great," she said.

"Great. I'll see you shortly then," said Oz.

"Same here, Tiger," she said, then hung up the phone.

Oz called a restaurant right on the water that he had heard about but had never been to. It was a converted, old historic building, now one of the top restaurants in Boston. Oz booked them a table for 7:30. If they got there early, he figured they could grab a drink at the bar while they waited for their table.

He pulled out of the lot and headed home to get ready. On his way, he thought about the statement that Miss

Ward gave them. The shadowy figure that she described. He thought about what he read at the library the day before. The urban legend about 'The Black Flash of Provincetown' came to his mind. The tall black shadowy figure could leap tall fences, but it still didn't seem to fit. They were nowhere near Provincetown, and what was described was still more like a man than what she described. She described something like a werewolf. *A fucking werewolf?*

Oz pulled into the garage and backed into his spot, like always. He kept thinking about the little information that he had about these cases. Just trying to connect the dots. Walking up to his apartment, he grabbed his phone from his pocket and dialed the Medical Examiner's office. The phone rang.

"Office of the Medical Examiner," said the receptionist. "How may I help you?"

"Hi, this is Detective Shields, is Mr. Walker in?" asked Oz as he unlocked the door and entered his apartment.

"He is. I'll pass you over to him," she said. There were about ten seconds of instrumental elevator music before Brad picked up the call.

"Brad Walker," he said.

"Brad, its Detective Shields," said Oz.

"Yes, Detective, how can I help you?" said Brad.

"Brad, what I'm going to ask you is probably going to sound… well… for intents and purposes, absolutely insane. Like some X-Files type of shit," said Oz.

"Go ahead, Detective, I don't judge," said Brad.

"Well… uh… we interviewed an elderly woman today who was a witness for the victim with the flayed chest that came in last night," said Oz.

"Uh-huh," said Brad.

"Well, she described something that looked like a werewolf. Like I said, I know this sounds crazy, but have you ever heard of anything like this ever?" asked Oz.

"Well, to be totally honest, no, but... but... but... that doesn't mean that it's entirely impossible," Brad continued. "Now who sounds crazy?"

"Not at all. You mentioned scouring the internet for pictures and what not to match our first victim. What about for all the victims?" asked Oz.

"Well, Detective, I haven't done this for all the victims, but I hear what you are saying. I'll tell you what, I'll do a deep dive into this, and I'll get back to you. Because, like you, I have to know who or what is doing this," said Brad.

"You will?" said Oz.

"A... a... absolutely!" he said.

"Thank you, Brad. I really appreciate this. I'm just at a total loss of where or what to look for," said Oz.

"Don't mention it, Detective. I'll send you over everything that I can find that may help."

"Thanks again, Brad. I'll be in touch," said Oz, hanging up the call.

Relieved by how well that call actually went, Oz put his phone, badge, and wallet on the breakfast bar, before heading to his bedroom to set out a change of clothes for tonight, and to put away his gun. He hopped in the shower and got ready for his evening with Donna. It was time to stop stressing over the cases that he had no path forward on and just enjoy his life outside of work.

***

Oz pulled up to the front of Donna's building and parked the car. He got out and called her, waiting by the passenger door.

"Hey, Tiger! I'm ready, I'll be right there," said Donna.

"Sounds great!" said Oz.

Oz was wearing a black blazer with a white V-neck t-shirt, a nice pair of dark blue washed jeans with natural crease lines by the fly and pockets, a brown belt with a brushed nickel buckle, and a pair of brown leather boots. He looked like he was right out of GQ magazine.

Donna appeared at the door of her building. She looked absolutely radiant. She was wearing a dark red, velvety, tight-fitting evening gown that hung off her upper arms. Her lips painted a seductive color of red, her silky auburn hair was down and slightly curled, as some of it draped over the front of her left shoulder. The gown was long, and you couldn't see her shoes, but they were definitely high heels. She walked elegantly towards him.

"Wow!" he said, putting his hands around her waist. "You look incredible!"

"Thanks, Tiger. You look pretty damn great yourself," she said. "Are you sure that you are a cop?" she giggled.

Oz gave her a kiss, and opened the door to his car, and helped her down and inside, holding her hand, and making sure that she got all of her dress in before closing the door for her. He walked around the front of the car, let a vehicle pass before opening his door, and got inside.

"You're in a wonderful mood today, Ozzy," she said.

"I'm about to have dinner with the most attractive woman in Boston. How could I not be?" he said as he pulled away from the curb.

"You're too sweet," she said. "How was your day?"

"We confirmed the identity of our second victim, and interviewed a few people about the case from last night," said Oz, as he tried not to give her too many details. "Made more progress today than we've been able to in quite some time."

"So you are close to catching this guy?" she asked.

"Not exactly," said Oz. "But I'm getting some help from someone that will hopefully find something that will help us."

"So cryptic. You can open up to me, you know?" she said.

"Yeah, I know. But really, I can't talk about an ongoing investigation." he said.

"Is that the law?" asked Donna.

"Kinda, yeah. Tell me about your new job?" said Oz, changing the subject.

"Well, I walked into this law firm this morning to give them my resume. I like to do that, so they see me, rather than blindly emailing it to them. I think it seems more ambitious and driven," she said. "And well, there was a lawyer at reception when I dropped it off. He must have been a partner or something because he said that they weren't currently looking for anyone, but he had recently heard that the DA was looking for someone."

"So you are a DA now?" he said playfully.

"No, silly," she laughed. "He called the DA's office, and I talked to the DA directly, I guess, and then he said that I should head down there for an interview at 11:30."

"Wow, that is outstanding!" said Oz.

"Yeah, I know. So sweet of him. I was being interviewed when you called. And I got the job right there and then," she said.

"That's incredible. Congrats!" said Oz. "So, when do you start?"

"He said to come in Thursday morning to get a feel for things, fill out the employment paperwork, blah blah blah. Then I'll do a few hours on Friday, but by Monday, I will be in full swing," she said.

"Nice," said Oz. "I'm so proud of you. I told you you wouldn't be out of work long."

"Yeah, yeah," she said. "It feels good."

"Good," said Oz. "And who knows, I may even see you from time to time at work."

"Easy, Tiger, I work for lawyers now. It will be super easy to get a restraining order," she joked.

"Says the woman who broke into my apartment," joked Oz.

"Aww, hey, I was let in there," she said.

They laughed as Oz pulled into the parking lot behind the restaurant. The parking lot was rough and bumpy, shaking them as they drove slowly through the potholes. Oz found a spot in the lot where the pavement was more flat and even. He got out of the car and jogged around to the passenger side and opened the door for Donna, and helped her out. He closed the door behind her, locked arms with her, and they carefully navigated the parking lot to the door of the restaurant.

"Reservation for Shields, 7:30," Oz said to the hostess.

"Yes, sir," said the young woman. "It will just be a few minutes. Would you two like to grab a drink from the bar, and I will come and get you when your table is ready?"

"Sure, that would be fine. Thank you," said Oz.

He and Donna walked over to the bar. Oz ordered a scotch neat and Donna a glass of Pinot Noir. Not long after their drinks arrived, the hostess came over to them, menus in hand, to escort them to their table. The hostess, in her tight-fitting black dress, led them through the restaurant to a nicely set table lit by candlelight. The restaurant had elegant lights with antique-looking bulbs that hung from the ceiling, combined with the candle-lit tables. The setting was very romantic. Oz pulled out Donna's chair for her. She sat down, and he pushed her chair closer to the table. He sat in the chair across from her, and the hostess handed them the menus.

"Are we celebrating anything tonight? A special occasion? An anniversary? A birthday perhaps?" asked the hostess.

"A blossoming relationship and a new job," said Oz.

"Oh, wonderful!" she said. "Your server will be over shortly. Enjoy your evening." The hostess left them and went back to the front of the restaurant.

"Blossoming relationship, huh?" said Donna. She took a sip of her wine.

"Isn't it?" said Oz. He smiled at Donna.

"If you're lucky," she giggled.

The server came to the table and introduced himself. "Good evening, folks. My name is Jason, and I'll be taking care of you this evening. Thank you for joining us tonight. Would you care to know the specials before diving into the menu?"

"Sure," said Oz.

"Absolutely. Tonight we have our signature prime rib, a 10-ounce portion, roasted to a delicious medium rare, served with your choice of side, and salad or soup to start, for $35. If you are feeling a little hungrier, we also have a succulent, locally caught, 8-ounce, Atlantic lobster tail, with a 7-ounce filet mignon grilled to your satisfaction served with your choice of side, and soup or salad to start, for $45. And our soup of the day is New England Clam Chowder," said the waiter flawlessly.

"Sounds lovely," said Donna.

"I'll give you a few moments to decide, and while you do, I'll be right back with water and our complimentary sourdough loaf and whipped butter," said Jason, as he left them to decide.

"I hope you are hungry," laughed Oz.

"You have no idea!" she said

Jason returned with a warm, fresh from the oven, loaf of bread that he placed on the table between them, and a jug of ice water to fill the two short, almost spherical glasses already on the table. "Have you two decided?" he asked.

Donna and Oz looked across the table at each other, confirming that indeed they were both ready.

"We have," said Donna.

"Splendid. For the lady?" asked Jason, ready to memorize her order.

"I'll have the 7-ounce filet mignon, medium rare, with steamed asparagus, please," said Donna.

"Wonderful. And for the gentleman?" asked Jason.

"I'll have the 14-ounce Peppercorn NY Strip, medium rare, with a baked potato, please," said Oz

"Excellent choice. You will both thoroughly enjoy them," said Jason as he left to put in their orders with the kitchen.

They waited for the food, having a lovely conversation about the rest of Donna's day, after her interview and landing the job. She had gone and purchased herself a couple of outfits to wear to work, as a reward for landing such a great position. She told Oz how she couldn't wait for him to call after work so she could share the news with him.

Jason arrived with their meals, their steaks still sizzling from the grill, as he placed them in front of them. The smell of the perfectly seared and grilled steaks, exquisitely seasoned, that radiated from the plates was mouthwatering.

"May I get you both another beverage from the bar?" asked Jason.

"That will be perfect," replied Oz.

Jason left to fetch their drinks.

"This looks great," said Donna.

"It really does," said Oz.

They excitedly cut into their steaks and tasted their first bites. Both of them had euphoric expressions on their faces. The first bites were so savory and tasty. Jason returned with their drinks and asked if everything ha been cooked to their liking, which of course it was.

They enjoyed another lovely evening together. They laughed and shared stories of their families and growing up in Michigan and Ohio. The time seemed to fly by, as it usually did with them. The rest of the world faded away into the background, and it seemed as though they were the only two people left on the planet.

At the end of their meal, Oz paid the check and left a generous tip. He reached across the table, held Donna's hand, and stared into her eyes. His phone rang inside the breast pocket of his blazer. Oz let go of Donna's hand and retrieved his phone from the pocket, answering it.

"So sorry about this," said Oz. "Detective Shields, Homicide."

"Kid, it's Terry. Hope I'm not interrupting anything?" said Terry.

"What is it, Terry? Is everything ok?" asked Oz.

"'Afraid not, kid. We got another body," said Terry.

"You're kidding? What time is it?" asked Oz.

"Quarter to ten," said Terry.

"Shit. Alright, where are we going this time?" asked Oz.

"To a church at Saint James and Clarendon," said Terry

"Okay, Ter. I'll meet you there, just have to drop Donna off first," said Oz.

"Sorry about that, kid," said Terry. "Duty calls, right?"

"Yeah, Ter, no worries," said Oz as they hung up.

"You gotta go to work again?" asked Donna.

"Yeah, Hun, I'm so sorry," he said.

"Don't be. I've had a lovely evening with you," she said as she grabbed his hand. "Why don't I just come with you? I'll stay in the car."

"What? No. That's crazy. I have no idea how long I'll be," said Oz.

"I don't mind Ozzy, besides it will turn me on to see you work," she said.

"You are something else," he said. "Are you sure?"

"Definitely, and we can just go back to your place together after," she said. "I'm not ready for our evening to end yet."

"If you are sure," said Oz.

"Absolutely," she said.

"Alright, shall we get going?" said Oz.

He got up from the table and pulled out Donna's chair, helping her up. They exited the restaurant the way that they had entered, arm in arm, all the way to Oz's car.

13

Oz pulled up to the church. Police barricades and patrol cars blocked off the street and access to the church. People gathered at the barricades, trying to catch a glimpse of the victim. Officers manned the barricades, trying to keep order and the citizens far enough away from the crime scene, so they didn't bear witness to the horror that awaited the eyes of Oz and Terry.

"Are you sure you don't want me to just take you home?" asked Oz.

"Babe, I'm positive. I'll be fine, really. Just go, do your thing," said Donna.

"Alright. I'll leave you the keys, listen to the radio, turn the car on for heat, whatever you need. I'll be back as soon as I can," said Oz.

Oz popped the trunk of the car from the button on the remote before handing the keys to Donna. He leaned in and gave her a kiss on her succulent red lips.

"I'll be right back. Please keep the doors locked until I return," he said.

"Ozzy, I'll be perfectly fine. Stop worrying. Now go," said Donna.

Oz lifted the trunk lid and opened a small black nylon bag that he had in the trunk. He pulled out a couple of pairs of blue nitrile gloves that he put in his blazer pocket, a spare Maglite from the bag, and a small notepad and ballpoint pen. He slid the Maglite into the right front pocket of his jeans, and the notepad and pen inside the breast pocket of his blazer. The trunk lid closed, and he headed over to the barricade that blocked Clarendon Street near the southeast corner of the Church.

"Officer," Oz said, presenting his badge. "Detective Shields, Homicide. Do you know if Detective White is on scene yet?"

"I'm not sure, sir. There are troopers near the walkway at the back of the church there," said the officer, pointing at the east side of the church.

"Thanks, officer. Can you keep an eye on my car there, the blue Mustang? There is someone very precious to me waiting in it," said Oz.

"Sure thing, Detective," said the officer.

"Much appreciated," said Oz.

Oz headed towards the officers guarding the covered walkway at the East side of the Church, keeping people from getting near the crime scene. Just to the left, behind the officers, was the scene of the crime. There was an entrance to the back of the church with exquisite concrete work that made a beautiful archway just to the right of the doors. The stonework of this centuries-old church was extraordinary and stood up to the test of time.

Oz still didn't see Terry. There was no point in waiting for him. FSD would be here soon, and they would want to take control of the scene. Oz approached the officers.

"Officers, what do we have?" he asked.

"We have the body of a male. Just there by the doors," said one officer.

"Any witnesses?" asked Oz.

"Just the homeless guy who harassed a passer-by to call the cops," said the officer.

"Where is this gentleman now?" asked Oz.

"He's in the back of my car, just over there," said the officer, pointing at the Boston PD Crown Victoria parked just on the other side of the street.

"Thank you. I'll want to talk to him shortly," said Oz.

Oz pulled the Maglite out of his pocket and turned it on. He was just about to approach the location when from behind him, he heard, "Hey Oz, you're starting without me?" It was Terry. He had just arrived.

"Hey, Ter, I was just about to take a look at the victim. You wanna join me?" asked Oz.

"I saw your car there, with your new lady friend inside. She's even lovelier in the flesh," said Terry. "And friendly, too. I waved hello"

"Easy, Ter, be respectful," said Oz.

"I said nothing," said Terry, laughing.

They walked together, entering the covered walkway. Oz shined his flashlight towards the door to their left, initially only seeing a pool of blood on the tiles leading to the set of double doors. He moved the light up from the pool of blood illuminating the decorative archway to the right of the doors and there, crucified upside down, was the skinless body of what used to be a man. The hands and feet had long metal spikes driven through them into the intricate concrete work that made up the decorative archway.

"I don't believe what I am seeing," said Oz.

Terry said nothing, just stared at the horrific scene before them. As usual, Oz tried to call out what he was seeing for Terry to take notes.

"Uh… looks like we have a male, unknown race, and age, all the skin has been peeled off the body," said Oz. "There is metal through the palms into the concrete, and through the top of the feet together."

"That crucifix of St. Peter," said Terry.

"What?" said Oz.

"When Peter, one of Jesus' Apostles, was crucified, he asked to be crucified upside down, 'cause he felt unworthy of being crucified the same way as Jesus," said Terry.

"How the fuck do you know that?" asked Oz, surprised.

"Forty-plus years as a Catholic, kid. Bound to retain something," laughed Terry.

"So what significance does that have here?" asked Oz.

"Maybe that killer is telling us that he deems this victim as unworthy," said Terry.

"Unworthy of what, though?" asked Oz.

"Gotta figure out who this is first, to find that out," said Terry. Terry turned and yelled at one officer nearby. "Trooper?"

"Yeah," one officer yelled back.

"Was there anyone in the church when this happened?" asked Terry.

"Three sisters live in that monastery right there," said the officer, pointing at the building to the north.

"Did anyone talk to them yet?" asked Terry.

"Uh… No sir, I don't think so. Why?" said the officer.

"For real? A fucking body gets nailed to a fucking building and you two idiots don't have the brains to talk to anyone that may have been inside, or may have heard something? For fuck's sake," said Terry. "Do you need more time here, kid?"

"Nah, Ter, I've seen more than my eyes care to handle. Let's go talk to the nuns," said Oz.

Terry and Oz walked to the monastery at the other end of the covered walkway, where the entrance was on the East side of the building. They knocked on the big wooden door. The door opened, and a nun dressed in full habit greeted them.

"May I help you, gentlemen?" she said in her soft and very calming tone of voice.

"Ma'am, I'm Detective Shields and this is my partner, Detective White. We need to ask you and anyone else that is here about what has occurred here tonight," said Oz.

"Oh, of course. Please give me a moment, and I will collect the other sisters. Please come inside," she said.

Oz and Terry entered the building, and she closed the door behind them. She turned and went down a hallway on the right. She returned a couple of minutes later with two other women. Both women dressed in their habits. One of them, Mother Margaret Mary, was in her 50s. She was the Mother Superior for this monastery. On the right and slightly behind her was the nun who answered the door, Sister Teresa Marie, who was twenty-four, and beside her on the left was Sister Mary Anna Joseph, who was forty-two.

"Detectives, have you found Father Fitzpatrick?" Mother Margaret asked.

"Father Fitzpatrick?" responded Oz.

"Yes, I assumed that's why you're here. I called almost two hours ago, to report Father Fitzpatrick, missing. He went out for his usual walk after supper and never returned," said Mother Margaret.

"Is this not normal behavior for him?" asked Oz.

"Oh no. Father Fitzpatrick is a man of routine. You can set a clock to him. He is always back by 6:30. When he still wasn't here by 8:30, I was worried and called the police," said Mother Margaret.

"I'm truly sorry. But that's not why we are here. There was a body discovered at the back of the church," said Oz.

"Oh, my!" said Mother Margaret.

"Did you ladies hear anything in the last few hours?" asked Oz.

"Not that I can recall. The sisters and I were doing our evening prayers after I made the call to the police. Then we went to our chambers. I left my door open so that if Father Fitzpatrick came back, I would hear him. But I heard nothing until you gentlemen came by," said Mother Margaret.

"Nothing? No banging? Or screaming?" asked Oz.

"No. I'm sorry. Nothing like that," said Mother Margaret.

"And you ladies have been here all night?" asked Oz.

"Yes, sir, all night," said Mother Margaret.

"Thank you so much for your time," said Oz. "We'll be in touch if we hear anything about Father Fitzpatrick. You ladies enjoy the rest of your night."

"God bless you, gentlemen. Be safe," said Mother Margaret.

Oz and Terry left the building. The FSD truck was passing through the barricade as they exited the church. Oz turned to Terry and asked, "Think our victim could be the missing Father?"

"Yeah, kid. I do," said Terry.

"I'm just gonna check on Donna, and then we should go talk to the homeless guy. Would you mind telling FSD to see if they can get some DNA for the Father from the Sisters?" asked Oz.

"Sure, kid. I'll say it more proper like so the geeks don't go swabbing the sisters," said Terry.

"Dude, that's fucking gross!" said Oz.

"What? You said it, kid. I just cleaned it up," laughed Terry.

Oz walked over to the passenger side door of his car and tapped on the window, and Donna rolled it down.

"Hey, Tiger!" she said.

"Are you still okay?" asked Oz. "Shouldn't be much longer. We have one more witness to talk with."

"Absolutely Hun. Go do your thing. I'm fine," said Donna.

"You're one in a million, for sure," said Oz. "I'll be quick, and we can head home."

Oz leaned in the open window and gave her a kiss. He walked back through the barricade and caught up with

Terry at the FSD truck, talking with Jared. Jared was suiting up in the Tyvek jumpsuit.

"Oz, that was quick. Can't say I would've lasted any longer," joked Terry.

"Really, Ter? I was just making sure she was alright, man," said Oz.

Jared was laughing at Terry, giving Oz a hard time.

"She's more than alright, kid," said Terry.

"Alright... Alright. Jared, did Terry here tell you we think the victim may be the priest?" asked Oz, as he changed the topic.

"Yeah, he just said that before you came over. We'll ask the nuns for his hairbrush or something. That will be the easiest way to confirm," said Jared.

"Perfect. Let us know if you guys find anything. Good luck!" said Oz.

"Yeah, thanks," said Jared, already doubtful that they would find anything.

Oz and Terry walked over to the police cruiser, where the homeless man was sitting in the back seat. The man looked very uneasy sitting there. Not because he was in the back of a police car, but more like he thought something was out to get him. Oz opened the door of the squad car. The man slid over to the passenger side door, pinning his back against it.

"Whoa! Easy there, we're Detectives, we just wanna ask you some questions. Can we do that?" said Terry, very calmly.

The man nodded.

His stench billowed out of the car when they opened the door. He hadn't washed in years. His beard was dark gray and matted. His hair was the same, full of tangles and matted masses. There were even trash remnants in his hair and beard. His clothes, layered and tattered. A collection, years in the making by rummaging through the trash and from the occasional trip to the Salivation Army.

"What's your name, pal?" asked Terry.

"J… J… Jerry," said the homeless man.

"Jerry, I'm Terry, and this is my partner, Oz. Why don't you tell us what you saw tonight?" said Terry.

"I… I… It was that Devil, man! Fucking Satan, himself!" said Jerry.

"C'mon, pal, we can't help you if you're gonna make shit up," said Terry.

"I'm not lying, man. It was him!" said Jerry.

"You're telling me that the Devil did this? The guy with that fucking horns and that tail, and all of that?" said Terry.

"The fucker I saw didn't have horns or a tail, but it was him! You gotta believe me, man!" said Jerry. "I was sitting in the corner of that cut in there across from the church. I was eating a sandwich that one sister gave me before, like they do now and then, you know. And I looked up and there he was, man. Eight feet tall at least, on these weird legs, like goat's legs or something. He was huge, man. I… I… I hid behind my carriage and saw him. He grabbed this guy right off the street, like a fucking rag doll or something. Dragged the guy screaming down the walkway, there. The screaming stopped just like that, like the Devil, sucked the sound right outta him, you know."

"Sucked the sound out of him?" said Terry.

"Yeah, man. Like a vacuum, he just sucked the scream and the life outta him," said Jerry. "He was still alive 'cause you could see him still trying to get away and shit, but when the fucking Devil has you man, there's no getting away. Then with his right hand, the Devil used his nail to carve down his face, opening him up peeling off his fucking skin, man."

"And then what?" asked Oz.

"I hid, man," said Jerry. "I couldn't watch anymore. I was terrified. I rolled into a ball behind my carriage and prayed like I never prayed before. When I thought it was safe to come out, I peeked around my carriage, and he was gone. Then I walked across the street and down that walkway there and that's when I saw that body on… well, you saw it. So, I legged it and razzed some guy walking by to call the cops. He must have called them on me because the cop that showed up didn't even know about that body. I had to tell him everything. Then he brought all of you guys."

"Right. Thank you, Jerry. This was very helpful," said Oz. Terry looked at Oz as though he was crazy. "The officer will take you to the hospital, get you checked out, okay? We'll be in touch. Thank you again!"

Oz closed the door of the squad car and waved over the officer. The officer jogged over to them.

"Yes, sir. What can I do for you?" the officer said.

"I want this man taken to the hospital, tell them to do a physical and mental wellness check on him," said Oz. Oz pulled out a business card and handed it to the officer. "Get them to contact me with all the results. Thank you."

Oz and Terry began walking back towards their cars.

"You don't buy this nut's story, do you, kid? The fucking Devil?" asked Terry.

"I believe he believes that is what he saw. That's why I want the doctors to look him over. If he's crazy, then the statement is useless, and we wasted our time talking to a nut. But if he's not, then I think we have to kinda run with it. Not like we have anything else to go on at this point," said Oz, trying to rationalize what they just heard.

"I guess so, kid. But c'mon… the Devil?" said Terry. "We're gonna be a laughingstock. A big fucking joke."

"Then we better get this right then, man, so that doesn't happen," said Oz.

They arrived at Oz's Mustang, and Oz knocked on the window of the passenger's side door. Donna rolled down the window again.

"Donna Richardson, I'd like to introduce you to my partner, Terry White. Terry, this is Donna," Oz said.

"Nice to finally meet you, Donna. I've heard so little about you," said Terry as he leaned in to shake her hand.

"Nice to meet you too, Terry. Are you the one teaching Ozzy everything he knows?" she said, giggling.

"As much as anyone can," laughed Terry. "You kids enjoy that rest of your night. I gotta get home to Maureen. She'll be so jealous that I got to meet you first," joked Terry. "Pleasure to meet you, Donna. Make sure you go easy on him tonight, Oz still needs to get up for work tomorrow," he laughed, stood up, and looked at Oz. "See you at that office, kid. Have a great night!" Terry winked at Oz and slapped him on the shoulder, and walked over to his car. He gave one last wave to Oz and Donna before getting in his Malibu.

Oz got in the Mustang and started it. "That went as well as I'd hoped it would."

"He's funny," said Donna. "Is he always like that?"

"All day, every day," said Oz. "Like an older brother. Let's get outta here."

"Mm, let's... Your bed is calling!"

***

Oz and Donna laid in bed, cuddled up, her head on his chest, his left arm wrapped around her, his hand caressing her soft skin. She traced his muscles with the fingers of her left hand. Both laying there satisfied, and completely calm.

"How bad was it tonight?" she asked.

"Worst yet, I'm afraid," he said.

"You're joking," she said.

"Afraid not. We have a missing priest, and a body at the back of the church," he said, trying not to reveal too much.

"What happened to the body?" she asked.

"You really don't want to know. It was horrible enough just seeing it," he said.

"Ozzy, I asked. I want to know," she said.

Oz took a deep breath and sighed. "The victim had been skinned alive before being crucified," said Oz reluctantly.

"Oh, my god! How do you not just vomit seeing that?" she asked.

"It's not easy. I have to fight puking every time," said Oz.

"What kind of sicko does that?" she asked.

"That is what I'm trying to figure out. Each one of these murders is becoming more horrific and bizarre with each one that we get called to. And the homeless guy who witnessed this whole thing, thinks that the Devil did it," said Oz.

"The Devil?" she said, confused.

"Yeah. Satan, himself. He was mortified when we went to talk to him. He described it to us, said that he was so terrified, that he curled up in a ball behind his buggy and hid until it was all quiet. I've sent him to the hospital for an evaluation," said Oz.

"He actually saw it?" she asked.

"Poor guy," Donna said. "Do you believe the guy?"

"I don't know what to believe. I know what my eyes saw, and this is so far beyond anything that my brain can comprehend as physically possible for any man to do," he said.

"Then keep your mind open to any possibility then," she said, trying to ease his frustrations.

"Even that it could be the Devil? Seriously? How can I believe that?" he said.

"Ozzy, things happen in this world sometimes that go far beyond normal explanation. Maybe there is something to this. Maybe the Devil and angels and all that are real. We don't know. But you said, yourself, that no man could do this stuff. Maybe it's time to start thinking that maybe it isn't a man that you are looking for," she said, and kissed his chest.

"Do you believe in Heaven and Hell, and all that stuff?" asked Oz, being soothed by her touch and kisses.

"I do. But I was raised Catholic, Sundays in church, and all that. Don't you?" she replied.

"I mean, I'd like to think that there is more to this world, and this life than just existence," he said.

"I think I believe more now than ever before. I mean, there had to be some divine intervention to bring us together. You just happened to be in a bar that you've never been to before. Me, in a new city, just happened to pick that same bar. It's unexplainable, but I feel like we were meant to be there together. And if that is possible, then anything can be possible," she said.

"Maybe you're right," said Oz. He hugged her tight and kissed her head.

Donna hugged him back. Then she moved, kissing his chest and down his abs, before disappearing under the covers. Oz moaned.

14

Oz dropped Donna off at her apartment in the morning before heading to the station. It was another sunny spring day. The rising sun illuminated the streets of Boston as he drove to the station. Traffic was light. It was a peaceful drive to work. He backed his car into a parking spot at the station, parked the car, and got out of the car, locking it behind him. The horn honked as he crossed the lot to head into the station.

Oz got up to the detective pool, and went straight into the kitchenette, pulled out a mug from a cupboard above the coffee machine. A fresh pot had just finished brewing. He poured the rich aromatic brew into his mug, added a bit of cream, two spoonfuls of sugar, and stirred it. He dropped the spoon into the utensil tray in the dishwasher, grabbed his coffee, went to his desk, and turned on the computer, waited for it to boot up, and sipped his coffee. *Ahh, that's what I needed.* He logged in and opened a new case file for the body found last night, wrote in the details from the scene, and the interviews with the nuns and the homeless man. He sipped on his coffee between entries.

The detective pool slowly filled up, but he was so focused on what he was doing that he paid no attention to all that was happening around him. Terry walked up behind him and gave him a pat on the back before walking around to his desk.

"Morning, kid. How are you doing?" asked Terry, before taking a sip of his coffee.

"Morning Ter. I'm good, yeah," said Oz.

"I bet you are, kid," Terry said, laughing.

"Always the comedian, Ter," said Oz.

"What do you have in mind for today?" asked Terry.

"Well, hopefully, we hear back from the hospital today about Jerry," said Oz.

"Jerry?" asked Terry.

"The homeless man," said Oz.

"Right, the bum," said Terry. "I don't think we can really put any stock in what he said, kid. Probably crazier than a shit house rat."

"What about what Miss Ward told us? The shadowy figure that she saw? Is she bat-shit crazy too?" asked Oz.

"Well, no. I'm not saying that. But maybe she was tired. It was late. Maybe she didn't see what she thinks she saw," said Terry.

"Then what, man?" said Oz. "This is the second witness that said that they saw a man-like creature at the scene. I don't think that can be ignored. They don't know each other, two completely separate crime scenes."

"I dunno, kid. But I gotta believe that it wasn't monsters. There has to be a better explanation," said Terry.

"I'm all ears, man," said Oz.

"Try to go through this logically," said Terry. "We have five victims. Not a single connection between them, other than that they have all been killed horribly. Not a shred of evidence. Each kill is different from the others. We finally get a couple of witnesses, and they think they're seeing monsters. The whole thing stinks."

"Still waiting for an alternative theory from you," said Oz.

"We're looking for a guy, a sick fuck, maybe a couple. The more they kill, the more insensitive they become to it all. That is why they keep getting more horrific," said Terry.

"How do you explain how good this guy or these guys, as you put it, are with not leaving a shred of evidence at the scene? Or on the victims?" asked Oz.

"I dunno, kid. I can't explain any of it," said Terry. He took a drink of his coffee. "I still don't think that we have anything to go on. I do know we're Detectives, not Ghostbusters."

"Do you believe in Heaven and Hell?" asked Oz.

"What?" said Terry.

"I'm just asking. You said you were raised Catholic," said Oz.

"You're asking if I believe in God?" asked Terry.

"I guess, yeah," said Oz.

"I mean, all my life I've been told that there is a God. I've never seen him or spoken to him, but I think he keeps me safe, grants me the good things in my life," said Terry.

"So do you believe in the Devil with the same blind faith?" asked Oz.

"If you're asking me if I think the Devil is real, and he is doing this shit, then no, I don't. People do bad things, there's no source of evil making 'em do it," said Terry.

"Alright, man. I'm not grilling you. I just think we should stay open-minded," said Oz.

Terry just drank his coffee. He didn't say a word. Oz sat back in his chair, deep in thought. He grabbed the mouse and opened up his Outlook. He saw an email from Brad Walker, with the subject: Victim #5 — John Doe. Oz clicked open the email and began to read what he had been sent.

Brad placed the time of death after 10:00 pm. *After ten? How is that possible? I was there around that time. He was alive when the officers showed up. How did they not notice that he was still alive?* Oz kept reading the email. *Cause of death: Traumatic Cardiac Arrest (TCA). Can this be right, he was skinned alive and crucified. He had to be dead before we got there.* Oz continued. *Extreme blood loss leading to hypovolemia and diminished delivery of O_2.*

"Whatcha got, kid?" asked Terry.

"The ME's report for the victim last night," said Oz.

"What's it say?"

"What time did we get there last night?" asked Oz.

"You were there before me, and I think I pulled up just after 10. Why?" asked Terry.

"He puts the time of death after 10," said Oz.

"So, he was alive when we were there?" replied Terry.

"According to this… yeah. He has the cause of death as Traumatic Cardiac Arrest," said Oz.

"A heart attack?" said Terry, shocked.

"From massive blood loss," said Oz.

"Well, there was no skin to keep the blood in. So, that part makes sense," said Terry.

"Do you know anyone in Missing Persons?" asked Oz.

"Yeah, why?" asked Terry.

"Vic three, community center John Doe, his identity is still unknown. You would imagine by now that someone would be looking for him, right?" asked Oz.

"Yeah, I'll make a call," said Terry.

"Thanks, Ter," said Oz.

Oz pulled a full-size notepad from his desk and started to jot down everything that they knew. He wanted to make sure that they were not forgetting anything as the caseload piled up. Oz pulled out his ballpoint pen from his jacket pocket and started writing everything down.

Thursday, March 29 - 10:30 Pm — C03/29/1224 — Victim #1

- *Chloe Wilson — Alley, Bunker Hill St.*
- *Caucasian*
- *Female*
- *20s*
- *Head, neck, and shoulders thrashed*
- *No witnesses — Jessie Hill called it in*
- *No forensic evidence was collected*
- *Unknown barbiturate in saliva-like liquid*

Friday, March 30 - 11:30 Pm — C03/30/1255 — Victim#2

- *Kanesha Parker — Pier 6*
- *Black*
- *Female*

- *20s*
- *Dismembered — Arm, leg, and partial torso*
- *No witnesses — Ci First Saw It — Det. Mickey McCarthy called it in.*
- *No forensic evidence was collected*
- *Unknown barbiturate in saliva-like liquid*

Saturday, March 31 - 9:30 Pm — C04/03/1289 — Victim#3
- *Name unknown — Charlestown Community Center*
- *Caucasian*
- *Male*
- *Age unknown*
- *Skull crushed, face removed, claw slashes on chest*
- *No witnesses — Lulu Johnson found vic — Called it in*
- *No forensic evidence was collected*

Monday, April 2 - 12:20 Am — C04/02/1301 — Victim#4
- *Name unknown — Barry Field*
- *Caucasian W/Tan?, Italian?, Hispanic?*
- *Male*
- *Age unknown*
- *Head and legs removed, skin on chest flayed, crucifix pose*
- *Mary Ward — Tall shadowy figure — Werewolf?*
- *No forensic evidence was collected*

Tuesday, April 3 - 9:45 Pm — C04/03/1336 — Victim#5
- *Father Fitzpatrick? — Church — St. James & Clarendon*

- *Race unknown*
- *Male*
- *Age Unknown*
- *Skin removed, crucified upside down*
- *Jerry (Homeless Man)*
- *Waiting for forensics*

"Whatcha doing, kid?" asked Terry.

"Jotting down everything that we know about the victims," said Oz.

"So, a short list, then?" joked Terry.

Oz went back to his computer, opened Outlook, and scanned his emails. He scanned all the emails from FSD over the last few days. Each one of them showing the same thing, no fingerprints found, no foreign material, only victim blood and tissue located on the scene. Oz picked up the phone and dialed Jared Hughes' extension. The phone rang three times before Jared picked up the phone.

"FSD, Jared Hughes," said Jared.

"Jared, it's Shields, I have a question for you?" said Oz.

"Sure, man, what can I help you with?" said Jared.

"How long does it typically take to get DNA results?" asked Oz.

"You mean like matching the skinless body and the hair samples that we got from the sisters for the priest?" asked Jared.

"Yeah, exactly that," said Oz.

"Could be as little as 24 hours or as much as 72. As soon as I know something, you'll know something," said Jared.

"Thanks, man. I appreciate it," said Oz. He hung up the phone.

Terry was getting off the phone at the same time. He looked up at Oz and said, "Nothing reported with Missing Persons. However, dispatch has a wellness check for a man who hasn't shown up for work yet this week. He lives close to the Community Center. I told them we would take it rather than sending a trooper there," said Terry.

"So we are heading back to Charlestown this morning?" said Oz.

"If you're feeling up to it," said Terry.

Oz said nothing, just gave Terry a look, showing his disapproval of the comment. Terry opened the drawer of his desk and grabbed a mint from the bag inside, got up, pushed in his chair, and headed out of the Detective Pool. Oz logged out of the computer, put his notepad back in the drawer, grabbed a sharpie, and put it in his pocket with his pen. He re-tucked his shirt, rotated his shoulders, and adjusted his sport coat, then walked out of the office and down to the parking lot. Terry came out shortly after him.

"The usual car, kid. Get in," said Terry.

***

Terry pulled onto Trenton Street and parallel parked into the first spot he could find on the Southside of the street. The north and south sides of the street were walled with townhouses running the length of the street. The townhouses all stretched up to three stories high.

Terry and Oz walked to a house with a heavy black wooden door about halfway down the street on the Northside. Oz knocked on the door with three hard raps.

They wanted a few seconds before Oz knocked on the door again. There was no response or sound of movement.

"What's his name, Ter?" asked Oz.

"Jon Collins," said Terry.

"Mr. Collins! This is Detective Shields with the BPD! We have been called to do a wellness check. If you are in there, please respond!" yelled Oz, as he knocked on the door again.

There was still no response. Terry reached into his back pocket and pulled out his wallet. He opened the brown leather bifold wallet and pulled out a lock pick set. Terry nudged Oz out of the way and started to pick the lock.

"What are you doing, man?" asked Oz.

"He's not responding, could be passed out in there, or not able to answer the door," said Terry.

"Where did you learn to do this?" asked Oz.

"I wasn't always a cop, kid," said Terry. "Now shut up and let me work."

Terry continued to work on the lock until he could turn the barrel of the lock. The deadbolt released and tried the handle. The door opened.

"We're in, kid," said Terry as he opened the door further and walked in, announcing their presence. "Mister Collins! Can you hear us? Please respond!"

They continued into the house. Oz pulled out a pair of blue nitrile gloves and put them on. Right inside the house were 4 stairs up to the main floor.

They walked up to the main floor and looked around. It appeared as though no one had been home for quite some time. Oz walked past the living room and straight into the kitchen.

On the counter were a wallet and cellphone. Oz grabbed the phone first. When he pushed the power button on the side, the phone didn't respond to the button. It desperately needed a charge. Putting the phone back on the counter, Oz grabbed the wallet and opened it, looking for an ID.

He found a driver's license in one of the slots. Oz slid it out of the wallet and examined it. Jon Collins, born April 8, 1990, and an organ donor. *I bet that is something that they wish they knew before the autopsy.* Oz looked at the picture on the driver's license. Jon had short dark hair in the picture, either brown or black. It was hard to tell. He had a round face, not chubby, just more round in shape, and his eyes were hazel. In the picture, he sported a tightly kept goatee. Oz put the license back in the slot and returned the wallet to the counter.

"You see anything, Ter?" asked Oz.

"I'm gonna just take a guess and say that our guy here is single. There aren't any of those knick knack-y things that women usually buy. You know?" said Terry from the living room. "What about you?"

"Found his wallet, and his cell phone is here, but it's dead," said Oz. "I was just about to head upstairs to see if there is anything up there."

"Alright, I'll keep looking here and catch up with you," said Terry.

Oz walked up the staircase to the second floor. This floor had a bedroom and a bathroom. The bedroom had been converted to an office. There was a wooden desk with an all-in-one computer on the top. It was very clean, except for the thin layer of dust that had accumulated on it. Opposite the desk was a couch that could be pulled out into a bed when a guest would stay over. The bathroom on this floor was clean and neatly kept, but was definitely not the primary washroom.

Oz continued to the top floor, to the master bedroom with an en-suite bathroom. Oz looked around the master bedroom. He saw a queen-sized bed, neatly made, a long six-drawer dresser on the wall that faced the foot of the bed. On the dresser were a couple of pictures in frames of what looked like nieces and nephews, and a family picture from Christmastime. Oz walked around to the en-suite doorway and saw another clean and organized bathroom. This was definitely the primary washroom, as his powered toothbrush was there on the charger plugged into the wall socket. There was a safety razor on a stand, with a badger hair shaving brush on the other side of the stand. Beside the stand was a container of shaving soap.

"Oz! Where are you?" shouted Terry.

"Here Ter, in the master bedroom," replied Oz. Oz turned around to see Terry entering the master bedroom.

"You find anything?" asked Terry.

"No. It definitely looks like no one has been here for a bit," said Oz.

"Do you think this is our guy from the Community Center?" asked Terry.

"Could be. Let me call Jared and see what he will need," said Oz.

"Smart, kid," said Terry.

Oz pulled out his cellphone and called the number for headquarters. He was greeted by the automated system, where he dialed the FSD extension. It rang three times before someone picked it up.

"FSD, Sharon speaking," said the voice.

"Sharon, this is Detective Shields with Homicide. Is Jared free?" asked Oz.

"Not at the moment, Detective. Can I help you?" she asked.

"Sure, we are at the home of our suspected third victim, the gentleman who had his head crushed," said Oz.

"Yeah, I remember that one. What do you need?" she asked.

"What can I grab from here that you can use to confirm his identity with DNA?" asked Oz.

"Well, can you find a hairbrush? Or hair in a waste bin or something?" she asked.

"Let me take a look. I'm right near the bathroom here," said Oz.

He went into the en-suite and opened one of the drawers. He found a hairbrush, picked it up, and examined it to see if there was hair in the bristles.

"I have a brush, with some hair. Will that work?" said Oz.

"If it's his hair, it should. Is there anything else there that you see?" she asked.

"There is his powered toothbrush and a safety razor," said Oz.

"Can you bag both of those as well?" she asked.

"Uh, yeah, I think I have enough bags on me," said Oz.

"Great. If we can get any DNA from those, then we can match it to the samples taken from the victim," she said.

"Great. Thanks for your help, Sharon. Hopefully, this is our guy, otherwise, we're robbing some poor guy of his toothbrush," joked Oz.

"Only one way to find out," she said, laughing.

"Thanks again," said Oz, then he hung up the phone.

Oz pulled three ziplock evidence bags from his sport coat pocket. He put the brush into one, the razor into another, and the toothbrush into the third. He closed all the bags and pulled out a sharpie from his inside breast pocket, and wrote 'Jon Collins' on all three of the bags, with the date. He capped the sharpie and put it back in his pocket, and grabbed the bags carefully from the counter.

"You good, kid?" asked Terry.

"Yeah Ter. Let's get out of here, and get this stuff back to the station and see if this is our John Doe," said Oz.

Oz followed Terry down the stairs and out of the apartment. They walked back to the Impala and got in. Oz put the bags on his lap carefully so that the razor didn't cut open the bag or him. Terry pulled out of the spot carefully and headed back to the station.

***

Back at the station, Oz descended to the basement, to the FSD lab, while Terry went upstairs to his desk. Oz entered the reception area of the FSD. No one was there to greet him, but one of the techs looked up to see Oz standing there. They stopped what they were doing and headed over to the door, removed their gloves, pulled off their safety glasses and their mask, and opened the door to greet him.

"Can I help you?" she asked, opening the door.

"Yes, I'm Detective Shields," said Oz.

"Hey! Sharon," she said. "Is that the stuff you collected for us to run?"

"Yeah, it is," said Oz. "I put the guy's name on the bag, so if it turns out to be our victim, we have it."

"Great. Might be a day or two before we know anything, but it's not like he's going anywhere," she said.

"Yeah, definitely not. Thanks again for your help," laughed Oz.

"No problem, have a good one," she said.

"Yeah, you too," said Oz. He turned and left, heading back up to the office.

Oz got back to his desk, sat down, logged into his computer, and pulled out the notepad that he was jotting his notes on before they left the office. He saw that there was an email from Dr. Mohammad Baddour, with the subject line reading 'Jerry Moore'. Oz opened the email and began to read it. *Detective Shields, I have examined Mr. Moore as you had requested. Apart from a minor infection partly caused by living on the streets that I have provided treatment for, Mr. Moore is in great physical condition. There are no signs of severe intoxication or prolonged drug use. We performed a preliminary psychiatric evaluation as you requested, and he appears to be of sound mind, other than the trauma that he witnessed tonight. There are of course some signs of PTSD that make perfect sense, for what he claims to have witnessed. We have released Mr. Moore as of the time of this email, as there was no medical reason to keep him here. I do hope that this email helps you in your investigation and wish you luck. If you have any further questions, please do not hesitate to contact me. Sincerely, Mohammad Baddour B.Sc. M.D.*

"So, our homeless guy is sane, not intoxicated or on drugs," said Oz.

"You're kidding me?" said Terry.

"Nope, got it here in writing from a doctor. Just a little PTSD after what he saw, but otherwise, totally sane," said Oz.

"I don't know what to say to that, kid. I'm shocked," said Terry. "I still doubt though that we're chasing the Devil."

"I didn't say that we are. I was just letting you know that you were wrong about Jerry," said Oz, smiling at Terry.

Oz looked over the notes that he had jotted down earlier. He picked up his desk phone and made a call.

"Brad, its Detective Shields, BPD," said Oz.

"Detective Shields, how are you? How can I help you?" said Brad.

"Brad, I have a question for you about our victims," said Oz.

"Sure, what do you wanna know," said Brad.

"Are you still finding the saliva-like substance on them?" asked Oz.

"Not since the second victim from the pier," said Brad. "The remaining victims didn't even have a trace of the barbiturate in their systems."

"Do you think they were all killed by the same person or thing?" asked Oz.

"Oh, there isn't a doubt in my mind," said Brad. "Whatever they used to cut the skin... the instrument, claw, or whatever, remember? I said it was extremely sharp. The flaying of the last two was unquestionably the same. The precision with which the skin had been cut and removed was incredible. There weren't any hesitation cuts," said Brad.

"Hesitation cuts?" asked Oz.

"Yeah, typically people will hesitate when they cut another human, not always, but mostly. When they hesitate, it makes rough or several slight cuts, but this was surgical, very precise. With the last body, the one that came in skinless, none of the muscle or sinew had a single cut. That is almost impossible. Even I knick something now and then, but this guy, it was like he knew exactly how deep to cut… everywhere," said Brad.

"Thanks, Brad. I appreciate the info," said Oz.

"No problem, oh, and Oz? I haven't forgotten the other thing you asked me for. I'm still working on it," said Brad.

"Thanks again, Brad. I'll talk to you soon," said Oz, and he hung up the phone.

"What was that about?" asked Terry.

"I was just going over the notes, and I thought that I'd missed something for the last three victims, but I didn't," said Oz.

"Like what?" said Terry.

"That saliva and drug thing that the coroner mentioned. It was not found on the last three victims," said Oz.

"Does that mean we have another killer?" asked Terry.

"No, that's just it. Brad said that he is almost positive it is the same killer," said Oz.

"So what, he's just stopped drooling on them or whatever?" asked Terry.

"Yeah, something like that," said Oz, pausing for a moment to think. "Almost like he no longer needs to. He may have needed the barbiturate to incapacitate the victims, but now the killer is… stronger? More calculated?" said Oz.

"So, now our guy can just overpower anyone? Do whatever he wants? He doesn't need to knock 'em out first?" said Terry.

"That's the way the evidence, or at least, the little that we have anyway, is saying," said Oz.

"That's a scary fucking thought," said Terry. "The first two victims never felt a thing, but the last three felt everything until the lights went out?"

"Yeah, I guess that is totally possible," said Oz.

"Fuck, kid!" said Terry.

They sat there for the next hour and a bit, not saying a word. Oz wasn't sure what Terry was thinking about, but he was thinking about what Terry said. *Did our guy get stronger? Is that why he doesn't need to incapacitate them anymore with the barbiturate? Are the victims now being tortured before they are being killed? How sadistic is this killer?*

Oz's cell phone vibrated in his pocket. He pulled it out and unlocked it. There was a message from Donna. *'Whatcha doing, Ozzy? Almost done for the day?'* Oz looked at the time, it was nearly 5:00 pm. He was almost done for the day. He messaged Donna back.

'Just getting ready to get out of here. Call you when I get home?' replied Oz.

'Sure thing! Talk soon xx' responded Donna.

Oz put the notepad and the sharpie back in his desk drawer and grabbed his keys from the tray in the drawer. He logged off his computer, got up, and pushed in his chair. He gave Terry a salute, letting him know he was taking off for the day. Terry looked up at him, gave him a nod.

"Have a good night, kid," said Terry.

"You too, Ter," said Oz.

15

Keys jingled as Oz pulled them from the front pocket of his jeans and unlocked the door to his apartment. He pulled his phone from the inside jacket pocket, and his badge from his belt, and put them on the breakfast bar. He took off his sport coat and untucked his shirt as he walked down the hallway into his bedroom.

Oz slid open the door of his closet, and reached up, and entered the code to unlock his gun safe. He removed his pistol from the holster, discharged the clip, and placed it in the safe. He hung his shoulder rig on an empty hanger and his sport coat on the right side of his closet, where the sport coats from the previous days hung. *I'll need to bring them to the dry cleaners tomorrow so that I can get them back for next week*, he thought to himself.

He unbuttoned and removed his shirt, tossed it in the laundry hamper beside the dresser. He opened the middle drawer of his dresser, pulled out a plum-colored v-neck t-shirt and put it on, and walked back out to the breakfast bar, grabbed his cell phone, and called Donna.

"Hey, Tiger! Are you home?" asked Donna.

"Yeah, just got in," said Oz.

"Have you eaten yet?" she asked.

"No, not yet. I guess I should soon, though. Do you have plans?" he asked.

"I was thinking that I would make us dinner tonight," she said.

"Really?" said Oz, surprised.

"Yeah, I can cook. Don't sound so surprised," she said.

"I'm not surprised, just wasn't expecting that," said Oz. "Do you want me to come to pick you up?"

"No, I'll drive over. I can do that too, Ozzy," she said.

"Alright, what can I do?" he asked.

"Turn your oven on to 350 °F and let me in when I get there," she said.

"That's it?" he said.

"Hope you're hungry, Tiger! See you shortly," she said and hung up the phone.

Oz got up from the couch and went into the kitchen. He tapped the bake button on the control panel of the stove, turning the oven on. Then he punched in 3-5-0 on the keypad and hit start. He grabbed cutlery and plates and placed them on the counter, tore two pieces of paper towel from the roll, and folded them into two rectangular napkins. He took the napkins and the utensils over to his small square dining table and set them on the two gray cloth placemats that were always on the table.

I wish I had some candles; he thought. He walked back into the kitchen and grabbed the salt and pepper grinders and took them over to the table. *I don't even know what she is making. What else can I set out? Do I have any wine? Red or white? Relax Ozzy, just get a couple of wine glasses down, worse case scenario, you'll fill them with ice water.*

He walked back into the kitchen and pulled out two wineglasses from an upper shelf from the cupboard that held all of his glassware. He examined the glasses in the remaining daylight coming through the open blinds. The glasses had water spots on them, so he washed and dried them before putting them on the table.

Knock… Knock… Knock…

Oz walked over and opened the door. There was Donna standing there, hair up in a ponytail, wearing a pair of tight blue jeans and a faded yellow t-shirt. In her hands was a foil pan with a sheet of aluminum foil covering the top of it.

"Hey there," he said. "Come in, let me take that from you."

He grabbed the tray from Donna, leaned in, and gave her a kiss as she came into the apartment.

"Hey Ozzy, so good to see you!" she said. "Take the tinfoil off and get it in the oven."

Oz removed the tinfoil, revealing a delicious-looking homemade lasagna. He opened the oven and slid it inside. He reached up to the hood above the stove and turned the exhaust fan on low.

"That looks so good!" he said.

"I thought after a long hard day you could use a nice night in with a good home-cooked meal," she said.

"You are incredible. Do you know that?" he said.

"Aww, Ozzy. You know just what to say to make a girl's day," she said and gave him a kiss.

"Can I get you something to drink?" he asked. "I don't think I have much, a bottle of water, a beer. Maybe there is beer?"

"Ozzy, you're adorable. You've already got me, just relax. A bottle of water is perfect," she said, holding his face in her soft, gentle hands.

He smiled at her, grabbed her hands, and kissed them. "Water it is," he said as he walked over to the fridge, pulled out two bottles of water, and opened them. Donna sat on the couch, her legs tucked up under her. Oz handed her the water.

"Good day?" he asked.

"Yeah, pretty productive. I got everything together for tomorrow, went to the market, and grabbed what I needed to make the lasagna. Came home and put it all together, then pretty much just waited for you to finish work. How was your day? How's your investigation coming?" she asked.

"Well, we're still waiting for forensics to link a couple of things for us. Could be a day or two before we hear about that," he said. "Terry and I broke into a man's house today."

"A suspect?" asked Donna.

"No, we picked up a wellness check for a man who hadn't shown up for work yet this week. He lives near where we found our third victim, so there's a slim chance that this guy is our victim," said Oz.

"And you guys broke into his house. What kind of cops are you?" she joked.

"It was a wellness check," laughed Oz. "When he didn't answer the door, we broke in to see if he was maybe incapacitated or worse."

"How do you find out if he is your victim?" she asked.

"Well, Terry and I took a hairbrush, his toothbrush, and his razor and gave it to forensics to test and compare the DNA."

"You stole his stuff?" she asked, laughing.

"Collected," said Oz. "The house didn't look like anyone had been there for days. His wallet and cell phone were on the counter. The phone was completely dead," said Oz.

"You're pretty sure this guy is the third victim?"

"Almost positive. My gut tells me it's him," he said. "Speaking of my gut, that smells delicious."

"Should be ready shortly," she said. "So, other than breaking into that guy's apartment, what else happened today?"

"Well, I talked to the ME…" laughed Oz.

"ME?" she asked.

"Medical Examiner, these are things you are gonna need to learn working for the DA, that is the District Attorney," laughed Oz.

"Haha, aren't you funny," she said, as she reached over to pinch Oz. "So what did the *Medical Examiner* say?"

"He was about this substance found on our first two victims that would have incapacitated them, but the last three, this substance wasn't there at all," said Oz.

"What does that mean for your case? It's not the same killer?" she asked.

"He said it's definitely the same killer. There are other similarities. So, it's almost as if our killer has gotten stronger or more sadistic," said Oz.

"How does that fit with what the homeless guy told you?" asked Donna, getting up from the couch to go and check on the lasagna.

"The Devil thing? I mean, other than finding out that he isn't crazy, the Devil thing still seems like a massive reach," said Oz.

"Nearly every night you guys get a new victim, and they just keep getting worse, How does one man do this so quickly?" she said.

"That's the most frustrating part. I can't figure out how this guy is doing the things that he is doing," he said.

"You will, Ozzy. You'll catch him," she said. She pulled a knife out of the knife block that was sitting on the countertop. She cut the lasagna into portions. "Where's your flipper?"

"Flipper?" he said.

"Yeah, you know, a flipper… a spatula," she said.

"Oh! The drawer on the left there," he said, pointing at the drawer on the left of the stove.

Donna opened the drawer and pulled out a black-handled, stainless-steel spatula from the drawer. "Plates?" she asked.

Oz got up from the couch and walked into the kitchen to lend a hand. He reached around her and opened the cupboard just on the left of the range hood, and pulled down two plain white dinner plates for her, and set them on the counter. He leaned down and kissed her on the neck, brushing her hair to the side.

"Mm. There is time for dessert later, Ozzy," she said.

Donna put a piece of lasagna on each plate. Oz picked up the plates and brought them over to the table and placed them on the placemats. He pulled out her chair, and she sat down. Oz sat in the other chair, facing her.

"Sorry, I didn't have any candles," he said.

"Oh, shush. This is perfect. I hope you like it," she said.

"It smells amazing!" he said, cutting into the lasagna, taking the first bite, and blowing on it before putting it in his mouth. "Oh, my god! This is incredible."

"You're just saying that," she said.

"No, I'm serious. This is delicious. So much flavor," he said, finishing his first bite.

They ate the wonderful meal that Donna had made for them. Oz enjoyed it until the very last bite. It was such a hearty piece of lasagna that by the end of it he was so full. Donna could only manage to eat a little over half of what she portioned out. Through dinner, the conversation was light. Mostly just sweet banter between the young couple. They sat at the table for a few minutes after finishing their meals, just chatting away. Oz was the first to get up from the table. He grabbed both of their plates and cleared them from the table.

He emptied the leftover bit on Donna's plate into the waste bin under the sink. He rinsed and washed both plates and the silverware, placing them on the drying rack beside the sink, before grabbing them, drying them, and putting them all away.

"Looks like there are lots of leftovers," he said, looking at the pan on his stove.

"Just put it in your fridge. Have it for lunch," she said, giggling. "I still haven't learned how to cook just a little food."

"Aren't you going to take any with you?" he asked.

"You making me leave already?" she said.

"No, hell, no. Stay all night if you like," he said, backpedaling.

"Oh Ozzy, you're so easy," she said, laughing.

They went back over to the couch and sat down together. Donna cuddled into him, her head on his chest and her hand resting on his stomach. Oz wrapped his arms around her and hugged her tight.

"You're such a little shit disturber," said Oz.

"Me? No way, I'm an angel," she said. Oz just laughed and kissed her on the head. "Let's say for argument's sake that it is the Devil, or a demon, or something that is doing this. How do you go about catching them or stopping them? Are you trained for this kind of thing?"

"If we were trained, I must have missed that day. I don't think that demon-slaying was ever part of the job description," joked Oz.

"I'm serious. If this is something otherworldly, how do you stop it?" she asked.

"I have no clue. We can't even get close to the killer at this point," said Oz. "There isn't even a trend to the killings so that we can predict where and when they will strike next. The only thing that I can say is that if things go as they have been, I bet I'll be getting a call tonight."

"Guess I had better tuck you into bed then, so you can get some sleep," joked Donna.

"Yeah, somehow I don't see that happening if you were tucking me in," laughed Oz.

"Well, maybe that would help you sleep, too," she joked.

"You're insatiable," said Oz. "What is your plan tonight? Are you spending the night?"

"Do you want me to?" she asked.

"Of course, I want you to stay," said Oz. "But you have a big day tomorrow, so I would understand if you don't."

"Why don't we just enjoy our time and see where it goes?" she said.

"Always the wise one," said Oz. "Are you excited about tomorrow?"

"I am. Not just to be working, but I think working for the DA is going to be a challenge, but something that I'm so ready for."

"You'll do great," said Oz. He put his hand under her chin and lifted her head to look at him. Their eyes met. He kissed her soft, supple lips.

"Mm. Are you trying to seduce me, Mr. Shields?" she asked, smiling.

"Not at all, just letting you know how much I appreciate you," he said. "Do you want to watch a movie or something?"

"Sure, let's see if we can agree on something to watch on Netflix," she said. "First couple challenge," Donna laughed.

Oz turned on the TV and opened the Netflix app on his smart TV. They browsed through a few titles before settling on a Comedy Special for a comedian that neither of them had heard of before, but Netflix gave them a special. How bad could it be? They snuggled up on the couch, watching the special, laughing together, for a little over an hour. It had been forever since Oz even watched anything on Netflix.

He loved to be around her. She was so incredibly easy to talk with, and joke with. There was this childlike playfulness between them, as well as amazing passion. It almost didn't matter that they had only met just days before. He felt as though he had always known her, that she had been a part of his life for years.

Ring... Ring... Ring...

"Here we go again," he said.

Oz grabbed his phone from the end table beside him. It was Terry calling. He looked quickly before answering, seeing that it was 10:35 pm. He swiped the screen and answered the call.

"Hey, Ter. What do we have?" he said.

"Hey, kid. We have another body," said Terry.

"Where is this time?" asked Oz.

"To the Common. The Parkman Bandstand," said Terry.

"Alright. Meet you there?" said Oz.

"Yeah, I'm gonna stop at Dunkees on the way. You want something?" asked Terry.

"Sure, I'll take a Regular," said Oz. "Thanks, Ter. See you there."

"Yeah, kid. Oh, and Oz... leave your stomach at home. The Lieutenant said this is bad," said Terry.

"Thanks for the heads-up. See you there," said Oz, and he hung up the phone.

"Is our time up?" asked Donna.

"It seems like it, I'm sorry," said Oz.

"No need to apologize, Tiger. It's your job. Where are you heading to this time?" she asked.

"To the Boston Common," he said.

"Don't let this wreck that place for you. I'll want you to take me there one day," she said.

"Nowhere can be ruined if I'm there with you," said Oz.

"Aww, so cheesy." she giggled and moved in to kiss him. "Keep that coming, Tiger."

"I'll grab my stuff and walk you out?" said Oz.

"Yeah, I should probably go home, be all bright-eyed and bushy-tailed for tomorrow," she said.

Oz got up from the couch and went into his room, collected his gun from the safe and did his usual weapon check, slid the pistol into his shoulder rig, and put it on. He came back out to the kitchen, grabbed his badge, notepad, and pen from the breakfast bar, and put them in the inside pocket of his police windbreaker leather jacket. Donna joined him over at the front door.

"Aren't you going to that incredible lasagna to take with you? I have some containers that I can put some in for you," said Oz.

"No. You keep it. Maybe we'll have another piece for dinner tomorrow night, while I tell you all about my first day," she said, as she slipped on her shoes.

"Sounds like a plan," said Oz. "Shall we?"

He slipped on his shoes, grabbed his jacket, and held out his arm for Donna to hold on to as they left the apartment. Oz walked Donna all the way out to her car, opened her door for her, and she got in. He leaned in and kissed her goodbye.

"Drive safe, Hun," said Oz. He kissed her again.

"Mm, be safe, Ozzy," she said and kissed him one last time.

Oz stood up and closed her door, walked around to the sidewalk, and waved goodbye to her as she checked her blind spot and pulled out into the street. She waved back as she drove off, headed home. He went back into the building, through the stairwell, and into the garage, unlocked the doors of his car. Oz threw his jacket on the passenger seat and got in. The rumble of the exhaust echoed in the once silent garage, as he pulled out, headed for the scene.

***

Oz pulled up beside a couple of BPD cruisers and SUVs parked along Tremont Street, just North of Boylston Street. The police had barricades up at the entrances to the park paths, restricting access to the Parkman Bandstand. Oz grabbed his jacket from the passenger seat and got out of the car. He put on his jacket and started walking towards one of the barricades.

"Detective Shields, homicide," he said, presenting his badge to one officer at the barricade.

"Detective, the body is at the bandstand, just on the other side of those trees," said one officer.

"Thanks. Any witnesses?" he asked.

"Not as far as I know, but the Trooper at the bandstand was the first on-scene. Maybe he knows something," said the officer.

"Is FSD is here yet?" asked Oz.

"Not yet, they're about ten minutes out," said the officer.

"Great. Thanks," said Oz, before he headed through the trees to the bandstand.

Oz arrived at the bandstand and was greeted by the officer that was first on scene, Gabe Adams. Gabe had a razor-shaved head, dark skin, and stood a little over 5'10" tall, dressed in full uniform. He was a handsome guy and had only been with the Boston PD for the last 3 years.

"Detective?" Gabe asked.

"Yes, sir. Detective Shields, Homicide," replied Oz.

"The scene is as it was found. I radioed for half the force to come and help secure the perimeter," said Gabe.

"Great work! Any witnesses?" asked Oz.

"Uh, yes, sir. Sort of," said Gabe.

"Sort of? What does that mean?" asked Oz, trying not to sound upset.

"There was a homeless guy who flagged down my cruiser. He's in the back of it, still out there on Tremont. He was ranting something about a demon or the Devil or some shit. I don't think he'll be much help to you. He sounded pretty crazy," said Gabe.

"You don't believe him?" asked Oz.

"No. Shit no. The Devil? C'mon man… I mean, this shit is something out of Predator or something, but I don't think it's the Devil," said Gabe.

"Where's the body?" asked Oz.

"Up there on the bandstand," said Gabe. "Hey! Who goes there?" he shouted out towards the trees behind Oz.

"Detective White, Homicide," shouted Terry.

"Sorry, Detective," said Gabe.

"Oz, are you gonna come get your coffee, or what?" said Terry.

"Yeah, sorry man, I totally forgot," said Oz, jogging to grab the coffee from Terry. "Thanks, Ter."

"Trooper, I'd have brought you one, if I knew you were gonna be here," joked Terry.

"Yeah, thanks, Detective," said Gabe, laughing at Terry's bad joke.

"What do we have, kid?" asked Terry.

"So far… Another homeless witness, and a body up there on the bandstand. Haven't made it there yet. FSD is about 10 minutes out."

"Alright, shall we?" said Terry, making a gesture for Oz to lead the way.

They left Gabe on the walkway. Seeing what they were about to see was more than enough for him. As they approached the bandstand, they could see the horrific scene more clearly. They walked up the stone steps to access the bandstand stage. In the middle of the stage, on the floor, laid the naked body, arms and legs spread, like da Vinci's Vitruvian Man. The body laid out chest down, flayed open down the back, arms to the hands, and legs to the feet. The bones from the arms and legs, arranged like the structure of a teepee, where the lower back would be, perfectly pointing up to the swaying skull and spine that was suspended from the ceiling of the bandstand. Around the body was a perfect circle drawn in blood, making the scene almost look like a pentagram if you were looking at it from above.

"Just when I thought it could get any worse than it was last night, but clearly I was wrong," said Oz.

"This is fucked, kid!" said Terry.

"I don't even know how to call this one out," said Oz.

"Use your imagination, kid," said Terry.

"The victim appears to be male, Caucasian, judging by the hands and feet that remain intact. No ring on the left-hand ring finger. I would place the height of the victim around 5'10" maybe 5'11". Age unknown, but I would guess in his thirties. The skull and spine have been removed and hung from the bandstand ceiling by what looks like an electrical wire pulled from the light in the center. The bones from the arms and legs have been arranged in a conical shape directly below the hanging skull and spine," said Oz. "This has the look and feel of a ritualistic killing. Like some satanic sacrifice or something."

Oz snapped on a pair of blue nitrile gloves, and crouched to the body, as close as he could get without disturbing the scene, since the photographer or FSD were not on scene yet. He stabilized himself with the fingertips of his left hand and examined the body. A sickly, sweet, and slightly sulfurous smell permeated the air and lingered, as there was only a slight breeze.

"The cuts through the skin and muscle are clean and precise. This is meticulous work, not rushed in any way. Why leave the hands and feet intact? Why just remove the major bones from the arms and legs?" said Oz, thinking out loud. "Why here? It's well lit, very open, very exposed. Witnesses would have been highly probable. There's no splatter or droplets of blood outside the circle. No footprints to or from the body."

Oz stood up and stepped back near Terry, where he set his coffee down. He picked up his cup and sipped it as he circled the scene. He looked at the wrought-iron railings with decorative rams heads at the ends of each top rail that appeared to attack the stone columns that circled the bandstand. The Eastern railing opposite of the stairs that led to the stage, appearing slightly bent. Oz approached the rail for a better look, eying it from different angles as he approached.

"Ter, look at this railing," he said. "Does it look bent to you?"

Terry approached, looking at the railing. He crouched to look at it straight on, his knees cracked as he crouched. Sports had taken their toll on him over the years.

"Looks like it bows down, yeah," said Terry. "The top rail is what… an inch thick? That would take some weight to bend that, or some force to bow it like that."

"That's what I'm thinking too," said Oz. "Maybe we'll get lucky and FSD will get something like a print or something from it. This is either the way that the killer came in or exited the scene. Let's talk with the witness."

"The odds are slim that we get two sober, or sane homeless guys, kid. Don't get your hopes up," said Terry.

"Come on, Terry, where is your optimism? Anything is possible," joked Oz, knowing Terry had very little faith in people.

"Yeah, ok, kid," laughed Terry.

"How busy is it here at night, usually?" asked Oz.

"Depends on the night, and what's going on around town. At night, there are usually bums and drunks wandering through. What's today? Wednesday?

"Yeah," said Oz.

"Can't imagine it being too busy here tonight. When this happened, it's not impossible that no one was around to see," said Terry.

The Tyvek troops marched through the trees and out of the shadows with their toolboxes in hand. Jared was slightly ahead of the rest of the crew and had a camera around his neck. The officer didn't even try to stop them from coming. There was no question who they were.

"Taking up photography, Jared?" shouted Oz.

"It's kinda my hobby," he joked back. "The usual photographer couldn't make it tonight. League night or something."

"Didn't take him for a bowler," said Terry.

"Not quite… Dungeons and Dragons," laughed Jared.

Oz and Terry left the stage and met Jared over by the officer. Oz peeled off his gloves, balled them up in his hand, and tossed them in the waste bin at the edge of the walkway and down the path that led back to Tremont Street.

"The scene's all yours," said Oz. "The railing on the West side of the bandstand looked bent to us. Let me know if you get anything from that."

"Sure thing. Thanks for letting me know," said Jared. "How bad is this one?"

"Looks like a ritual killing, a sacrifice, or something," said Oz.

"Wonderful," said Jared, waving to the team to start setting up. "You guys have a good night!"

"Thanks, you too. Good luck!" said Oz. "Let's go see our witness, Ter."

"Yeah, alright, kid," said Terry.

Terry gave Jared a pat on the shoulder as they parted. Probably the most the FSD guys were ever going to get from Terry, as far as a sign of respect. They exited the park onto Tremont Street. There, by a cruiser, was an officer standing guard over the witness.

"Trooper," shouted Terry.

"Yes, sir," said the officer.

"Is that the witness?" asked Terry.

"Yes, sir," said the officer.

Oz and Terry walked over to the cruiser, and the officer opened the rear door for them. Terry leaned into the car. "Hey pal, how are you tonight?" he asked. "I'm Detective White. What's your name?"

"Uh… yeah… uh… muh… muh… my name is Sam… Sam Finn," he said.

"Sam, nice to meet you. This is my partner, Detective Shields," said Terry. Oz gave Sam a smile and a wave. "Can you tell us what you saw tonight?"

"W… w… well, I saw this… this… this thing… it was like eight or nine feet tall. An… an… and it wore this ripped up robe," Sam said, shaking.

"Where were you when you saw this thing?" asked Terry.

"I… I… I was over b… b… by the tennis courts," Sam said.

"You got a good look at this thing from all the way over there?" asked Terry.

"Yeah man… this th… th… thing was fucking huge, man," said Sam.

"What did you see it doing?" asked Terry.

"It w... w... was hunched over, kinda bobbin' up and down... you know... like it was working on something... an... an... and then all of a sudden, it stood up and had something in its hands," Sam continued. "I couldn't quite see what it was. Then there was the sound of breaking glass as it reached up, and pulled something down from the ceiling, and hung what it was holding. Then it hunched back down to go back to doing whatever it was doing, you know. Th... th... then when it was done, it hopped on the railing and headed my way, well, kinda my way. It took off between the tennis courts and the sandwich shop. I fell back and hid behind the port-a-potty that is at the courts there. It moved so fast, man!"

"Can you tell me more about it? What it looked like?" asked Terry.

"Well, it wasn't like any man I ever saw before. Way too tall. It had really long arms, and its legs were like animal legs, you know. That's probably why it was able to jump and move like it did," said Sam.

"Anything else?" asked Terry.

"No," said Sam.

"Why were you in the park tonight, Sam?" asked Terry.

"I... I... I used to live here... until tonight... n... n... no fucking way I'm going back there... fuck that!" Sam said.

"I hear you. So, what is gonna happen, Sam, is that the Trooper here is gonna take you to the hospital to get looked at by a doctor. This doctor is gonna make sure that you're alright, okay?" said Terry.

"Sh... sh... sure, as long as I don't have to go back in the park tonight," said Sam.

"Thanks, Sam. Take care, alright," said Terry, before he stood up and closed the door of the cruiser. "Trooper, this witness needs to see a doctor at the hospital for a physical and mental assessment."

"Tell them to call or email me with the results," said Oz, handing the officer his business card.

"Sure thing," said the officer.

Oz and Terry walked away from the cruiser, closer to where they had parked their cars. They didn't say much while they were walking, just drank their coffees.

"Sounds like he saw something similar to the last guy," said Oz.

"I don't care what the doc says, both of them are nuts, kid," said Terry.

"They basically described the same thing, man," said Oz.

"Kid, you're nuts too, if you believe them. There is no way, this is what they are telling us. It can't be. The Devil isn't real. It was made up to scare us into being good. That's it," said Terry.

"What if it is real, though, Ter? Or this isn't the Devil, but some sort of demon or monster or something. Monster stories have been around forever. People seeing unexplainable things, things they've never seen before. Creatures and ghouls and whatnot," said Oz. "They can't all be crazy, man."

"Are you on drugs? Have you completely flipped your lid?" asked Terry. "There are no such things as monsters, kid."

"Then give me another theory then… because, at this moment, all we have are six dead bodies, no clues, no evidence, no leads, and three witnesses all claiming that they saw some kind of monster or creature. I'm open to anything at this point, Ter," said Oz.

Terry hung his head. "I dunno, kid," he said, low and frustrated. "I dunno."

16

Oz awoke to his alarm going off, and sat up in his bed, alone for the first time since meeting Donna. *Had last night all been a dream?* He reached over to his nightstand and grabbed his phone and unlocked it. He opened the call list and there saw the call from Terry at 10:35 pm the night before. *Not a dream.*

Oz got out of bed and made it. He went about his normal morning routine, having his shower, getting ready, and dressed for work. He draped his sport coat over the stool at the breakfast bar, swiped his phone, unlocking it, and made a call.

"Good morning, Ozzy!" said Donna.

"Good morning, Donna, I was just getting ready to head out, and I wanted to wish you a great first day," said Oz.

"Aww, Ozzy. You're so sweet. Thank you! I'm just about to head out myself. I hope that you have a great day too. Can't wait to see you later," she said. "Bye, for now, Detective."

"Talk to you soon," said Oz.

Oz grabbed his sport coat from the stool and put it on. He clipped his badge onto his belt and headed out the door. As Oz headed down the stairs to the lobby, there was a booming crack of thunder from outside. The lights in the stairwell flickered as though the thunderous boom frightened them. Oz reached the lobby and looked out to the street. The rain fell in waves, cars kicked up little tsunamis as they drove through the puddles, splashing and soaking everything on the sidewalks. *Looks like you are taking the car today, Ozzy.*

He went back into the stairwell and through the door to the garage. His footsteps echoed as he crossed the concrete floor of the garage to his car. It was normally quiet in the garage, but this morning things seemed especially quiet, almost eerie. He pushed the unlock button on his car's remote as he approached and made his way to the driver's door. He pulled the handle and opened the door.

"Ozwald!" a voice whispered.

The sound of this halted Oz in his tracks. He looked all around the garage, not seeing a soul. The lights on the wall flickered as he heard the voice again.

"Ozwald!" the voice whispered again.

"Who's there?" shouted Oz. His voice echoed throughout the garage. "Show yourself!" There was nothing but silence. "I'm a police officer, and I'm armed! Come out now! Show yourself!" There was still nothing but silence. *Pull yourself together, Oz. You're all alone in here.* He took one last look around the garage, then got in his car and closed the door. *You're losing it, man.*

THUD!

"What the fuck!" shouted Oz. A massive rat had fallen onto his windshield. His heart was racing. He started the car and flicked on the wipers. The rat scurried across the base of the windshield, chased by the wiper blade, hopped off the car, and ran off into a dark corner of the garage. *That scared the fuck out of me! Gonna have to tell the super about the rat when I get to work.* He pulled out of his spot, exited the garage, headed for the station. His heart rate slowly returned to normal.

The drive to the station was treacherous from the rain. The wipers could barely keep up clearing the sheets of water from his windshield, even on the highest setting. He figured Terry would be a bit later getting in this morning, as his drive would be just as slow. Oz pulled into the parking lot of the station, backed into what he could only assume was a spot, judging from the car on his right. There was no chance of seeing the lines with how hard the rain splashed down in the flowing water of the parking lot.

He quickly exited the car, closed the door, and ran through the lot to the doors. As he got to the doors of the station, just about to head inside, the voice called out to him again.

"Ozwald!"

He went inside and shook off the rain, ran his fingers through his hair, and looked back through the glass door for anything, but saw nothing. *This is definitely all in your head, Ozzy. You're exhausted. Go get a coffee and just take it easy this morning,* he thought to himself.

Oz went upstairs to the detective pool, poured himself a cup of coffee, added his cream and sugar, stirred it, and took it to his desk. He set the cup down and sat down. He sipped his coffee, logged into his computer., and like he had the morning before, opened a new case file for the victim from last night. Oz continued to sip away at his coffee. It soothed him as he sipped it, generating waves of heat inside him that warmed from the cold rain that had soaked him on his way into the building.

Terry patted Oz on the shoulder as he walked past Oz to his desk. Oz nearly jumped out of his skin.

"You alright, kid?" asked Terry. "You look like you've seen a ghost,"

"Yeah, Ter. Just a little off this morning," said Oz.

Oz pulled the notepad from his desk drawer. He clicked the pen and added the latest victim to his notes.

Wednesday, April 4 - 10:35 Pm — C04/04/1348 — Victim#6
- *Name unknown — Parkman Bandstand*
- *Caucasian*
- *Male*
- *Age unknown*
- *Skull and spine removed, along with arm and leg bones — Ritualistic?*
- *Sam Finn (Homeless Man)*
- *Waiting for forensics*

"Did you open a case file for our latest John Doe?" asked Terry.

"Yeah, just finished putting in the details," said Oz.

"Killing it, kid!" said Terry.

"Poor choice of words for a Homicide Detective, Ter," joked Oz.

Terry laughed and pantomimed pulling on his collar uncomfortably. Terry sat back in his chair and sipped away on his coffee. Oz opened his Outlook, and saw the ME's report for last night's victim. Cause of death listed as Mass Trauma — Removal of the skull and spinal column. *Basically, take your pick at the cause of death. Any of the massive trauma to the poor guy could have killed him.*

The next unopened email was from Jared Hughes. The subject tilted: Identity Confirmed. Oz opened the email and read it. *The identity of the skinned/crucified victim, Case File: C4/03/1336, was the missing priest, Father Fitzpatrick. The results of this test confirmed a 100% match to the samples collected by FSD from the victim's belongings. This test is 99.9% accurate.*

"Looks like the victim from the church was the priest that the Sisters reported missing," said Oz.

"Shit, really?" asked Terry.

"Yup. Just read the email from FSD confirming it," said Oz.

"Guess we should notify the Sisters," said Terry.

"Yeah, that isn't a job for an officer," said Oz. "We should head over there shortly."

"Yeah, I'm ready for a refill," said Terry, shaking his coffee cup lightly.

"What was that thing that you said about being crucified upside down?" asked Oz.

"Peter asked to be crucified upside-down because he said he wasn't worthy of being crucified the same way as Jesus," said Terry. "Why?"

"Is the killer telling us that the priest was unworthy to be a man of God?" said Oz. "Is that why the killer did that to the priest?"

"No, I think the killer is just a really sick fuck!" said Terry. "I think the killer was just giving us a clue of the victim's identity, since he took all the guy's fucking skin."

"You could be right," said Oz.

"Think about it, kid. No other victim has been killed in any way that was related to them, what they do, or who they were. Just the priest. The killer isn't smart, he's just sick and twisted," said Terry.

"You have a point there," said Oz. "The locations are totally random too. There's no pattern, no significance to any of them, either."

Oz's desk phone rang. The monochrome LCD displayed the caller ID as; FSD. Oz picked up the receiver.

"Detective Shields, Homicide," he said.

"Shields, it's Jared, with FSD," replied Jared.

"Yeah, Jared. What's up?" asked Oz.

"That railing that you guys mentioned last night," said Jared.

"Yeah?" said Oz.

"It was bent for sure. When we dusted it and pulled a partial print from it," said Jared.

"That's excellent, man! What did you find out?" asked Oz. Terry looked at Oz with a keen interest in the conversation.

"That's the shitty part. It matched nothing," said Jared.

"What do you mean?" asked Oz.

"We analyzed it, and it doesn't come up as a print at all. They don't even look like they came from human feet or hands," said Jared. "I'm at a total loss. The computer crashed twice trying to analyze it. And when we tried it old school under magnification, the ridges were like nothing any of us had ever seen. I sent them to a friend of mine in the lab with the FBI, and even she was stumped. All I can tell you is that something very heavy was on that rail. The deflection in the rail was almost an inch. For that thick steel to bend like that over such a short span, would require a shit ton of pressure."

"Is that an imperial shit ton or a metric shit ton?" joked Oz.

"Yeah, sorry, man," Jared laughed a little. "I wish I had better news, but we aren't quitting on you. We're still trying to figure it out, but I thought you should know where we were at."

"Thanks, Jared. I appreciate it," said Oz, and he hung up the receiver.

"What was that about?" asked Terry.

"FSD pulled a partial print from that bent rail, but it's unidentifiable," said Oz.

"You gotta be kidding me?" said Terry. "Nothing?"

"Nope. Jared said it even stumped his friend at the FBI," said Oz.

"Fuck. Definitely not the time for us to be buying Power Ball tickets," said Terry.

"I'll grab the keys, and we'll head over to the church. What do you think, Ter?"

"Sure, kid. I'll meet you downstairs," said Terry.

Oz put his notepad back in the drawer, got up, and pushed in his chair. He leaned down and logged out of his computer, and headed downstairs to the motor pool, dropping his mug in the dishwasher in the kitchenette along the way. He signed out the keys for "DET 35", their usual car, and walked to the door to the parking lot. It was still raining heavily, with no signs of letting up any time soon.

Oz opened the door and sprinted to the Impala. He quickly opened the driver's door and got inside, started the car, and pulled out of the parking spot. He drove to the door of the station. Terry waited inside the station until Oz pulled up before coming out.

They made the short trip across town to the church. Oz pulled up to the curb beside the church on St. James Ave. They got out of the car and walked up to the two sets of double doors. The doors were dark mahogany stained with two beautifully ornate black steel hinges that spanned nearly the entire width of the doors near the top and bottom of each door. Oz opened one of the doors, allowing Terry to enter the church first. Inside, they shook off the water and wiped their shoes on the floor mat. Terry followed Oz toward the altar, dipped his fingers in the holy water, and made the sign of the cross, before continuing down the main aisle of the church towards the altar. Mother Margaret greeted them as she came down from the altar.

"Good Morning Gentlemen. How may I assist you today?" she said.

"Ma'am, I am Detective Shields, and this is my partner Detective White," said Oz. "We spoke to you the other evening, the night that Father Fitzpatrick went missing."

"Ah yes. I'm terribly sorry, I should have recognized you. How may I help you, Detectives?" said Mother Margaret.

"Ma'am, I'm afraid that we have some terrible news," said Oz.

"Oh dear," she said, taking a seat on the nearby pew.

"Yes, ma'am, the body that was found out back of the church, was confirmed this morning to be Father Fitzpatrick," said Oz. He reached towards Mother Margaret, placing his hand on her shoulder.

Mother Margaret brought her trembling hand to her face, touching her mouth in grief from the unfortunate news. She prayed for the late Father, but low so that Oz couldn't quite make out what she was saying. She kissed the rosary in her left hand and made the signum crucis.

"You are certain that this was our Father?" she asked.

"Most certain ma'am. The officers who collected the hairbrush from you, used his hair to confirm his identity," said Oz.

"I should tell the sisters. We will need to make the necessary arrangements," she said, trying to be strong.

"If you are up to it, ma'am, we would like to ask you a couple of questions about the Father?" said Oz.

"Of course," she said.

"Can you think of anyone that may have wanted to harm the Father? Anyone that he recently had a dispute or disagreement with?" asked Oz.

"Not at all," she said confidently. "Everyone adored Father Fitzpatrick. He was always so sweet and friendly. A true father figure to the community."

"What about the night of his disappearance, were there any suspicious individuals around?" asked Terry.

"Not that I recall. He had a visit from one of the ladies from the American Legion Auxiliary, inviting him to a luncheon this weekend, And a few people came in for confession, but not anyone strange or out of sorts," she said.

"You mentioned the other night that the Father usually went for a walk after supper. Do you know where he would walk to or who he would see on these walks?" asked Oz.

"Usually just around the neighborhood, a couple of blocks down and over. I would go with him occasionally. He would come back by the library and then back to the monastery walking along Boylston," she said. "I don't remember him ever going to see anyone on these walks. They were mostly just for him. His time with God. Occasionally, he would think about the coming Sunday service."

"Do you know a homeless man named Jerry?" asked Terry.

"Yes. He's a lovely man," she said. "The poor man lost everything a few years back. The sisters will sometimes make him something to eat and take it across the street to him. He's always so appreciative, bless him. Why do you ask? He's not involved, is he?"

"No ma'am. Jerry, unfortunately, was witness to it though," said Oz.

"Poor dear. We shall pray for Jerry," she said.

"Would you say that Jerry is normal? Not crazy or anything?" asked Terry.

"Jerry is certainly not crazy. He's just had some hard times," she said. "We have always had great chats."

"Thank you for your time. We will find whoever did this to Father Fitzpatrick," said Oz.

"Bless you, detectives. May the Lord be with you on this search," she said.

***

Oz and Terry walked back into the detective pool, coffees in hand, and sat at their desks. Oz took a sip of his coffee, and logged into his computer, and checked his email to see if anything came in while he and Terry were out. He was hoping to see something from FSD confirming the identity of the victim from the Community Center, but there was nothing yet.

"Boys," said the Lieutenant.

"Hey Jim, how are you?" said Terry.

"I've had easier days," said Jim. "I was just on the phone with the FBI."

"FBI?" said Oz. "What do they want?"

"Funny you ask, kid. They wanna know if we need any help with the string of victims that you boys are looking into," said Jim.

"If they think they can do better with no evidence, hardly any witnesses, and no fucking motives, be our guest," said Terry.

"Easy, Ter, I told them, we have it under control," said Jim. "You do, don't you?"

"We're piecing more together every day, Lieutenant. Just put a name to victim #5," said Oz.

"Alright, I'll stay outta your way, but keep me in the loop, alright?" said Jim.

"Sure thing, Jim," said Terry.

Jim walked over to the kitchenette to get himself a coffee. He stopped off at a couple of the other Detective's desks before heading back into his office. He was just doing his rounds, checking in on his guys as usual. Jim was good at knowing just enough about every case so that if he had to report on it, he could. He knew that his detectives were all more than capable to handle their business, and if they ever really needed help, that they wouldn't hesitate to ask him for help.

"Ozwald!" whispered the voice again.

"Terry, did you hear that?" asked Oz.

"Hear what? What Jim said? Yeah, fuck the FBI, man," said Terry.

"No, not that," said Oz. "A voice. It just whispered my name. Did you hear that?"

"Keep it together, kid," said Terry. "Don't go losing it on me."

"I'm not crazy, Ter. I heard it this morning too when I was in the garage at my apartment," said Oz.

"Kid, it's your mind, fucking with you. All this Devil talk is making you paranoid," said Terry.

"Maybe you're right, man," said Oz.

"Ozwald!" said the voice again, but louder this time.

Oz looked up at Terry. He was just sitting there, looking at his monitor, sipping on his coffee. *He really isn't hearing this*, thought Oz. The voice was gravely and dark. It was the kind of voice that would chill your bones when you heard it. It sounded menacing. Oz looked around the office. *Nothing out of the normal guys working at their desks, people in the kitchen*, he thought.

BANG!

A crow flew right into the plate-glass window to Oz's right. It not only frightened Oz, but a few of the Detectives in the pool also looked up to see what had just happened. Even Terry looked up to see what it was.

BANG! BANG! BANG!

Three more crows hit the window. Jim came out of his office. "What the fuck was that?" he said, looking at the detectives in the office, most of which were now standing watching what was happening.

BANG! BANG! BANG! BANG! BANG!

Crows now flew one right after another, straight into the window. The glass began to crack under the barrage of crows, all dive-bombing the window. No one could believe what they were witnessing.

"It's like something outta that fucking Hitchcock movie," said Terry.

"This is crazy?" said Oz.

Crows continued the attack on the window, then suddenly it just stopped. There was nothing but dead silence. The rain continued to pour down, pelting the windows. Oz cautiously approached the window. When he got to the glass and looked down, he expected to see a mass of dead crows on the ground. What he saw instead was nothing, not a single bird. Not one, but the window remained cracked in several spots from the impact of the birds hitting it.

"You all saw that, right?" asked Oz.

"Saw what? The shitload of crows all committing suicide on our fucking window? Yeah, we fucking saw that," said Jim.

"Right… well… that's just it… there isn't one crow out there," said Oz.

"Get the fuck outta here," said Jim as he walked over to the window to see for himself.

Jim slowly looked up at Oz. There was a horrified and confused look on both of their faces. Terry was still standing back at his desk, just staring in disbelief at the window.

"How is there not one fucking crow out there?" said Jim. "We saw them hit the window!" Jim turned to look at the other detectives in the office. "You all saw it, right?" No one replied. "Right?" shouted Jim.

"Yeah, Jim, we saw it," said Terry.

"Then how the fuck is there not one single dead crow in my fucking parking lot?" said Jim. "What's going on, here?"

"No clue, sir, but it sure falls in line with the other crazy shit we've seen over the last week," said Oz.

"You two, my office, now!" said Jim, walking back to his office. He wiped the perspiration from his brow with the back of his hand. "Close the door behind you."

Oz and Terry followed the Lieutenant into his office. Oz closed the door behind them and sat down next to Terry, across from the Lieutenant.

"Spill it," said Jim. "I don't care how fucking crazy it sounds, tell me everything."

Oz told the Lieutenant everything, the increasing sadistic nature of the killings, the ritualistic poses and dismemberment of the victims, and the strange witness statements that were now coming in. Oz even mentioned the voice that he heard this morning and just now, before the crows attacked the window. Jim just stood and stared out of his office window at the parking lot below. Jim was silent the whole time Oz was talking. What could he say? It all sounded like something out of The Exorcist. He finally turned around and sat in his chair, looking at Terry and Oz.

"I told him, Jim. I told him that this devil stuff was crazy," said Terry.

"Shut up, Terry. Respectfully, let me process this," said Jim. "What has FSD been able to come up with?"

"Nothing, except helping us confirm the identity of a couple of our victims so far," said Oz. "They haven't been able to find a single thing at any of the crime scenes that wasn't traceable to the victims."

"What about the saliva shit from the first victims?" asked Jim.

"Not traceable to anything, and never appeared again on a victim since those first two," said Oz.

"I hate to say it, boys, but I think we gotta bring in the Feds on this now," said Jim. "How many more people gotta die before we figure this out?"

"With all due respect, Jim, the feds won't be able to do any more than we are," said Terry. "The body count ain't gonna just stop because they show up."

"Fine," said Jim. "But I wanna be told everything from now on, no matter how crazy it may be. Am I clear?"

"Yes, sir," responded Terry and Oz in unison.

"Dismissed," said Jim.

Oz and Terry went back to their desks and sat down. The detective pool was dead silent after what they all just witnessed. Terry went back to sipping away on his coffee. Oz sat back in his chair, grabbed his coffee, took a few sips while he sat there in thought. He pulled the notepad from his desk and stared at his notes. *C'mon, Ozzy! You can figure this out! Find the pattern! Where is this thing going to strike next?*

Oz pulled up a map of Boston on his computer. He scrolled over the locations of each of the victims and dropped virtual pins, marking them so that when he zoomed out, he could see if a pattern was developing. There didn't appear to be a pattern jumping out at him. The first 4 victims were all in Charlestown. With his last two killings, the killer was now on the south side of the Charles River. *If he continues in this cluster, the next victim could be on this side of the Charles River. But where?* He suddenly had a gut feeling. He couldn't quite explain it, but something was drawing his eyes to the Hatch Memorial Shell.

"Ter?" said Oz.

"What's up, kid?" replied Terry.

"Do you feel like going on a stakeout tonight?" asked Oz.

"Based on what?" asked Terry.

"A feeling," said Oz.

"You wanna camp somewhere based on a feeling?" asked Terry.

"Yeah. Something is telling me that we need to be at the Hatch Memorial Shell tonight," said Oz.

"Is there a band playing or something?" asked Terry.

"No, it's just a feeling," said Oz.

"No offense, kid, but I'm not camping out based on your hunch," said Terry.

"Alright," said Oz.

Oz couldn't shake the feeling that he had about this spot. *I have to be there tonight!* He thought. *But what about*

Donna? It was her first day at the DA's office. I talked about seeing her tonight. Maybe I can still do both. Maybe I can head there after dinner. Maybe…

"Oz! Yo, Oz!" said Terry, as he waved to get Oz's attention.

"Yeah, sorry. I was off in another world there," said Oz.

"No shit," said Terry. "A staying here all night?"

"What?" said Oz, surprised. "Why?"

"'It's quitting time," said Terry.

"Huh, what? Really?" said Oz.

"Yeah, kid. Let's get outta here," said Terry.

Oz put his notepad in his desk, quickly logged out of his computer, and got up. He pushed in his chair and walked out of the office with Terry.

"You ok, kid?" asked Terry. "I'm not losing you, am I?"

"No, Ter. I'm good. I was just deep in thought, you know?" said Oz.

"Alright, kid, have yourself a good night. I'll see you in the morning," said Terry.

"You too, Ter. Tell Maureen I say hello," said Oz.

"Will do, kid," said Terry.

They got into their cars. Terry pulled away. Oz waved at him as he drove past. Oz took a cleansing breath, started his car, and drove off, headed for home.

17

"Hey, Donna. How'd it go today?" asked Oz.

"Hey Ozzy, it was great! I'm going to be the Administrative Assistant for the DA," said Donna.

"Really? So, things went well then?" asked Oz

"So good! Everyone there was so helpful and friendly. I can tell right away that I am gonna be busy," she said.

"That's great, Hun. So, what are you up to now?" asked Oz.

"Just got home and was hoping that I'd see you tonight?" she said.

"I'd love to see you," said Oz.

"Uh oh… Why do I hear a 'but' coming?" she asked.

"No, no 'but'…" he said.

"Ozzy, I know that we haven't known each other very long, but I know you well enough to know when you have something on your mind. So, spit it out," she said.

"I have a feeling that I know where the killer is going to be tonight," said Oz.

"Really? How'd you figure this out?" she asked.

"I don't know for sure where he is going to be, but it was a very strange day… and… well, let's just call it a hunch," said Oz.

"Ok, let me change into something comfy, and I'll be right over," she said.

"What?" asked Oz.

"We'll chat more over dinner, throw that lasagna back in the oven there, Tiger," she said. "Then after dinner, I'll go with you on your stakeout."

"But it could be dangerous," said Oz.

"Is Terry going to be there with you?" she asked.

"No," said Oz.

"Well, there is no way in Hell, that I'm letting you do this alone. So, I'm coming with you, and that is the end of it," she said.

"But I can't have you there on police business," he said.

"Is it official police business?" asked Donna.

"Not exactly," said Oz. "Just me following a hunch."

"Then it's just you and your girlfriend out on a date," said Donna, before she hung up the phone.

This woman is something else. Why is she willing to risk everything? I don't know for sure that the killer is going to be there, so what can it hurt to have some company. If the killer does show, she can call for backup and stay in the car. She will at least be safe there.

Oz turned on the oven and set it to 350 °F, he pulled the lasagna out of the fridge and set it on the counter. He quickly changed into a black v-neck t-shirt, grabbed his shoulder rig, with his pistol still strapped in the holster, from the bed where he laid it when he was getting changed, and walked back out to the entryway. He hung his shoulder rig on the hook by the entrance and unlocked the door.

The oven chimed, letting him know that it had reached temperature. He went back into the kitchen and put the lasagna in the oven. *There we go, all set,* he thought. *I really need to get more than water, milk, and orange juice for the fridge. It's not just me here anymore.*

Knock... Knock... Knock...

Oz opened the door, and there was Donna. Her hair up in a ponytail pulled through the back of a Cleveland Indians baseball cap, a short denim jacket over top of a navy blue t-shirt, tight jeans, no-show socks, and a pair of navy jersey knit sneakers. A real casual look, yet she still looked so sexy.

"Wow, you look great!" he said.

"Well, are you just gonna stand there, or are you gonna kiss me and let me in?" she giggled.

"Yeah, of course, sorry," said Oz. He leaned in and kissed her soft red lips. "Come, the lasagna just went in a couple of minutes ago. Can I take your coat?"

"So sweet, Ozzy! I got it," she said.

She shrugged off her jacket, and Oz hung it on the hook at the door.

"How about a drink?" he asked.

"Sure, do you have any water?" she said, laughing.

"Don't be cheeky," he said.

"Aww, but you love it," she said.

"So, tell me more about your day," said Oz.

"There's time for that later on the stakeout," she said.

"It was your first day. I want to hear about that," he said.

"Later, now, spill it," she said.

"There is no saying 'no' to you, is there?" said Oz.

"It's good that you're learning that early on," she giggled. "So, tell me how your day went.'

"Alright, my day started pretty much like every day," Oz continued. "I called you to wish you a great day, then headed downstairs. I was gonna walk to work, then saw that it was pouring, so I turned around and headed into the garage to take the car. I went to get in the car, and I heard this ominous voice whisper my name."

"Who was it?" she asked.

"I looked around the garage and didn't see anyone. So, I went to get in my car, I heard it again. I shouted out in the garage, for whoever was there to come out, but there was no one. I got in my car and started it and boom, this rat fell onto the windshield, scared the shit out of me."

"Oh, my god! And that was just the beginning?" she asked.

"Yeah," said Oz.

He headed over to the oven to check on the lasagna. It was ready, so he pulled it out, dished up 2 portions for them, and brought them over to the table. He sat down and continued the story.

"We heard back from FSD," said Oz.

"FSD?" she said, taking a fork full of lasagna.

"Yeah, sorry. That's our CSI group," said Oz.

"Gotcha," she said.

"They confirmed for us that the crucified victim from the church was the priest who went missing just hours before. So, Terry and I made a quick trip out to break the news to the nuns. That all went fine," Oz continued. "Back at the station, we were sitting at our desks when I heard the voice again. I asked Ter if he heard it, and he looked at me like I was crazy. Then I heard it again, only louder this time."

"That's freaky! Terry didn't hear it at all?" she asked.

"No, and it gets weirder," said Oz. "Right after that, a Crow flew into the window."

"A crow?" she said."

"Yeah, then another, and another. Before we knew it, there was crow after crow flying into the window. Each one seemed to hit harder and harder, cracking the window. Then all of a sudden, it stopped. I walked to the window, expecting to just see a pile of dead crows, but there wasn't a single bird," said Oz.

"Not one?" she asked.

"No, It was like it never happened, other than the window being all cracked and that every one of us saw it happen," said Oz.

"That is so scary," said Donna.

"Yeah," said Oz. "If the other detectives and the Lieutenant hadn't seen it happen, I'd be in the nuthouse instead of sitting here with you," said Oz.

"Is this when you got your hunch?" she asked.

"Not long after, yeah. I was looking at a map of Boston and was plotting all the locations of our murders. That's when I was drawn to the Hatch," said Oz.

"The Hatch?" she said.

"Right, sorry, it's a bandshell near the river," said Oz.

"So, that is where we are going?" she asked.

"That was my plan," said Oz. "Donna, this killer is extremely dangerous and sadistic."

"I'll be fine, babe. Don't worry about me," she assured him.

"I would feel terrible if anything were to happen to you," he said. He reached across the table for her hand.

"Aww, Ozzy. That's exactly why I'm coming. If something happened to you because you were all alone doing this, I would be crushed," she said.

"Just promise me one thing," said Oz.

"What's that?" she asked.

"If we do see the killer tonight, you'll stay in the car, lock the doors and call for back-up," said Oz.

"I promise, Ozzy," she said.

Oz got up, walked over to Donna, and kissed her. Then he cleared the dishes, washed, and dried them. Donna came up behind Oz as he was putting the plates in the cupboard and hugged him from behind.

"Promise me that if we see the killer that you will be safe and come back to me," she said. Oz turned around in her arms, wrapped his arms around her, her head nuzzled into his chest.

"I promise!" he said.

***

Oz parked his car in the small parking lot on the east side of the bandshell. The rain had stopped shortly after he had gotten home. The sky was now a reddish-orange as the sunset over the horizon. Donna reached over and grabbed Oz's hand.

"So, now are you ready to tell me about your day?" he asked.

"Well, it was nothing like your day, but I got to meet the DA, Matt Moore," she said. "He is very serious, but nice. He walked me through his typical needs. Asked me if I was willing to put in a ton of hours, and could be called at any time if he needs me. I figured that it isn't much different from the hours that you work, so I said that wouldn't be a problem."

"What if he calls during… well… you know?" asked Oz.

"Can't say it, Ozzy?" she joked. "If he calls when we are fucking?" she laughed. "He'll just have to wait until I get off." Oz Blushed. "Aren't you just so adorable when you blush?"

"Get out of here," he said playfully.

Donna continued to tell Oz about her day down at the DA's office. The sun had set, and the city was blanketed in the dark of night, illuminated only by the glow of streetlights and signs. Oz rolled the windows of the car down slightly so that they could listen for any noises.

Minutes passed like seconds as they sat there, talking and waiting. Oz had brought a small pair of binoculars with them. They took turns looking through them. Donna people watched with them, making up stories about the people that she saw, providing entertainment for them while they sat there.

"*Ozwald!*" the voice said again.

"Did you hear that?" asked Oz.

"Hear what?" she said. "Did you just hear the voice?"

"Yeah, you didn't hear it?" he asked.

"No. What did it say?" she asked.

"Just my name," he said. "Stay here and keep the doors locked."

"Where are you going?" she asked.

"I'm going to have a look around," he said. "Just stay here, please."

Oz got out of the car and pulled out his pistol from the holster. He closed the driver's door gently and quietly. As he walked around the front of the car, he stayed low, looking towards the bandshell. He darted across the parking lot to a tree just to the right of the bandshell near the path, taking cover behind it.

"Ozwald!" said the voice.

Oz glanced around the tree, looking toward the stage. He couldn't see anything but the shadow of the bandshell. Staying crouched, he walked down the path that cut across the front of the bandshell, being careful to not make any noise.

He cautiously approached the stage. He could see something in the middle, but he couldn't quite make it out. There was very little light, just the residual light from the light fixtures that lit the Charles River Esplanade that ran along the bank of the river. Oz pulled his flashlight from his pocket. With it pointed at the ground, he twisted the barrel, turning it on, and focused the beam. Slowly he brought the light and his pistol up together as though they were one item. He shined the light on the shape on the stage. It was a black, tattered robe covering an enormous figure.

"Police! Hands in the air!" shouted Oz, announcing his presence.

The figure rose from its crouched position. It was enormous. It turned to look at Oz, with its glowing eyes like two smoldering embers in the covered darkness of the hood.

"I said hands up!" said Oz.

The figure now faced Oz. The light from his flashlight seemed to disappear, as if the robe somehow could swallow up the light. The figure was hooded, and all that could be seen were these glowing eyes, like two smoldering embers in the covered darkness of the hood.

"Freeze!" shouted Oz.

The figure lurked towards him, as if it did not care who he was or what he ordered it to do.

"*Ozwald!*" the voice said, still in his head, even with the figure right there.

"Stay there, or I will shoot!" shouted Oz.

The figure kept coming. Oz fired a warning shot above the head of the figure. It wasn't phased in the slightest as it kept coming. Oz fired three shots into the cloaked figure. It let out this shrill scream as the bullets seared their way into its flesh. The figure turned, ran, and hopped off the stage, taking off towards the river, disappearing into the darkness. *Holy shit, that thing is fast! I hit it dead square in the chest. How is it not laying there dead right now?* Oz pulled his phone from his pocket and called 9-1-1.

"9-1-1, what is your emergency?" said the operator.

"This is Detective Shields, badge number 2367. Officer-Involved shooting at Hatch Memorial Shell. The suspect fled the location. Possible victim. Ambulance and patrol units requested," said Oz.

"Thank you, Detective. Officers and paramedics are being routed to your location now. Do you require me to stay on the line with you?"

"No, thank you," said Oz, ending the call, and called Donna.

"Ozzy! I heard gunshots! Are you okay?" she said, panicked.

"Yeah, the shots were mine. Are you okay?" he asked.

"I'm fine. I was so scared that something happened to you," she said.

"I'm fine, really. Stay on the call with me, I'm just going to head onto the stage here," he said.

Oz holstered his pistol and walked up to the elevated stage, hoisting himself up on the first concrete level before stepping up to the stage level. Once he was on the stage, he shined his flashlight around, finding a body lying in the center. He rushed over to it and knelt down. It was a young woman, in her twenties, and looked like she was just out for a run on the esplanade. She was still alive. Her shirt had been torn almost completely off, her chest heaving erratically as she tried to breathe. She had her hands over her stomach, and they were covered in blood.

Oz reported what he found to Donna and asked her to pop the trunk and grab the first aid bag and bring it to him. They hung up the phone as Oz focused his attention on the young woman.

She was badly wounded, her stomach had been slashed open, there was blood spilling from the wounds. Oz shrugged off his shoulder rig, pulled his shirt off, balled it up, and put it on the open gash in her abdomen. With his right hand, he applied pressure on the wound, and with his left hand, he grabbed her left hand and squeezed.

"My name is Oz. I'm a police officer. Help is on the way. What's your name?" he said as calmly as he could.

"Sh... Sh... Shannon..." she said, struggling to find the breath and the strength to speak. "Shannon Russo."

"You're going to be alright, Shannon. Don't worry, just stay calm, okay," said Oz.

"Ozzy, I'm here," said Donna, hoisting herself up on the first level of the concrete, that was almost as tall as she was.

"Donna, stay back. You don't need to see this. Just toss me the kit," said Oz.

Donna didn't listen and brought the first-aid kit to him. She handed it to him as she knelt down beside him. She grabbed his flashlight from the stage and shined it so that he could see what he was doing.

"What can I do to help?" she said.

"Donna, this is Shannon. We need to keep her calm and comfortable while I try to field dress her wound, okay?" said Oz as he made eye contact with Shannon.

"Hi, Shannon. You're in good hands," said Donna. "Stay with us, alright, stay calm."

Oz let go of the shirt on her stomach and opened the first aid kit. He tore open some large packages containing padded bandages and swapped them out for the t-shirt. He layered the bandages across the laceration in her stomach and wrapped her abdomen with a tensor bandage he pulled from the kit. Being careful to not move her too much as he passed it under her back.

Sirens could be heard approaching as Oz dressed the wound. Donna kept talking to Shannon, squeezing her hand, while Oz dressed her wound. The bandshell lit up with the flashing lights of the ambulance as it pulled up in front of the stage. Two EMTs hopped out of the ambulance, grabbed bags from the back, and rushed up and onto the stage.

"Shannon, you're doing so great. The paramedics are here. They are going to take over, okay," said Oz.

The paramedics took over assessing the young woman before beginning treatment and prepping her for transportation to Massachusetts General Hospital. Oz picked up his shoulder rig and blood-soaked t-shirt. Quickly, the scene became littered with police cruisers and SUVs, all with lights flashing. Oz walked to the edge of the stage, hopped down, and turned around to help Donna down safely to the ground.

"Are you okay?" asked Oz.

"It hasn't exactly set in yet, what we just did," she said. "There was so much blood," she said. "I've never seen anything like that in person before. That poor woman. How... how did you just know what to do?"

"Training. I've been a first aider since I was a patrolman. We're usually the first on-scene, and you never know what you are gonna see," he said.

"You were just so calm, didn't hesitate at all," she said.

"You were great. You were everything that she needed to see and hear at that moment, and you didn't flinch," said Oz.

"I just did as you told me to. Well, except for staying back. I just wanted to help you. I didn't even think about it," she said. "But now, my God! Ozzy, there was so much blood, she was hurt so badly."

"Hey... Hey... Hey... Shh... It's okay," said Oz as he embraced her.

Pulling her close to him, he rubbed his hands softly up and down her back, trying to calm her down. She wrapped her arms around him.

"Identify yourself," said the voice of an officer as she approached.

"Detective Shields, Homicide," said Oz, breaking their embrace, pulling his badge from his hip, where it was clipped to his belt.

"Sorry Detective. Dispatch said there were shots fired?" asked the officer.

"Yeah, they were mine. Four rounds from my service pistol," said Oz. "Three shots hit the suspect, center mass, but he still fled the scene."

"That's impossible!" said the officer.

"You're telling me," said Oz. "I believe the suspect is the one responsible for a string of murders that I am investigating. And judging from the state of the young woman up there with the EMTs, I'd say I'm right."

"Where is your partner?" asked the officer.

"Home," said Oz. "I was here based on a hunch that appears to have been a good one."

"And you are, ma'am?" asked the officer.

"Sorry, this is Donna Richardson. She is my girlfriend and was here with me, in the blue Mustang just over there in the parking lot," said Oz.

"Ok. Thank you, Detective. I'll get the other officers to secure the scene. You're not going anywhere, are you?" asked the officer.

"No, I'll be around. I may just grab a shirt from my trunk, but we'll both be here. I know the drill," said Oz.

"Absolutely, go right ahead," she said.

The officer turned and walked towards the squad cars and coordinated with the other officers on-scene to barricade off the area. Oz and Donna walked back over to the car, where Oz opened the trunk and pulled a gray t-shirt from a small duffle bag, and put it on. He pulled out a plastic grocery store bag from the duffle bag and put his blood-soaked shirt in it, tied it closed, and left it in the trunk.

"Girlfriend, huh?" said Donna.

"You said it first," asked Oz.

"I did, didn't I," laughed Donna. "I'm fine with it if you are. As long as you're not turned off by my breakdown a minute ago?"

"I don't know many people that would have handled that situation back there as well as you did. The moment hit you afterward, that is totally normal," said Oz.

"You're too sweet. Thank you, Ozzy!" she said.

Donna shivered slightly. Oz wrapped his arm around her shoulder, pulling her close to him. She wrapped her arms around his waist.

"Let's get you the blanket from my trunk and get you warmed up," said Oz.

"I'm okay," she said.

"Now, I'm not taking 'no' for an answer," said Oz.

Oz popped the trunk and pulled a gray fleece blanket out that he kept in there for emergencies. He wrapped the blanket around her shoulders and pulled her close to him.

"I should probably call Terry," said Oz.

A second ambulance pulled up at the scene. The paramedics came straight over to Oz and Donna to check them out, since they were covered in blood. Oz told them they were fine, and that it wasn't their blood. The paramedics then rushed to the stage to see if the other paramedics needed assistance. Oz pulled his phone from his back pocket and called Terry.

"Oz! What's going on?" said Terry.

"I found the fucker, Ter. Had him dead to rights, and he still fled," said Oz.

"Where are you?" asked Terry.

"Hatch Memorial Bandshell," said Oz.

"Are you alright?" asked Terry.

"Yeah, Ter, I'm good. Officers and medics just arrived on-scene," said Oz.

"Alright, I'll be there in ten, kid," said Terry.

"Alright, Ter," said Oz. They hung up the call. Oz looked at Donna. "Are you okay?"

"Yeah, I've calmed down. That was crazy, though," she said. "My heart was pumping like crazy. You were incredible, Ozzy. You're saved that woman's life!"

"Let's see if she makes it, first," said Oz.

Oz put his hand on Donna's back, kissed the top of her head, as they walked back over to the ambulance by the stage. The paramedics had just finished loading Shannon into it.

"How is she?" asked Oz.

"She has a better chance, thanks to you both being here. We're taking her to Mass Gen now. Keep your fingers crossed," said the paramedic in charge.

The paramedics hopped in the ambulance, one in the driver's seat, and the other in the back as Oz helped close the rear doors of the ambulance. They sped off around the bandshell headed for the hospital.

The first officer on-scene approached Oz and Donna. Her name was Olivia Martin. She was twenty-five years old, 5'8" tall with brown eyes, and dark brown hair pulled back neatly into a bun tucked into her service cap.

"Officer?" said Oz.

"Sorry to bother you, Detective, but can I get a statement for my report?" said Officer Martin.

"Absolutely," said Oz.

"You said that you two were here already before the suspect was? Did you see the suspect, and that is why you approached the stage?" she asked.

"We arrived here just around sundown. We watched the sunset as we sat there. I'd say that was around 6:00 pm. We stayed in the car chatting for quite a while. I had a feeling that something was wrong, so I got out of the car, and Donna locked the doors behind me," said Oz.

"A feeling, sir?" she said.

"Yeah, the same feeling I had earlier today at work that told me I needed to be here tonight," said Oz.

"Like a premonition or something?" she asked.

"No, not exactly. Just a hunch that cops get, you know? That feeling that something just isn't right?" said Oz.

"Right. So, you approached the bandshell and what did you see?" asked Officer Martin.

"I saw a large shadowy figure in the middle of the stage. "I drew my pistol and announced my presence and told the suspect to stand up, and put their hands in the air," said Oz.

"Did they comply?" she asked.

"No. The suspect stood up and turned around and began to approach me," said Oz. "I warned the suspect to halt and put their hands up. The suspect didn't comply and continued to approach me. I warned I would shoot, and this still didn't deter them, so I fired a warning shot over their head. FSD should be able to recover it from the bandshell. The suspect continued to approach, so I fired three shots, hitting the suspect center mass with all three. The suspect let out a screech and took off towards the river."

"You didn't pursue?" she asked.

"No. Suspecting that this was the killer that my partner and I have been looking for, I felt it was better to check and see if there was a victim. I called 9-1-1 and reported the shooting before I called Donna, here, as I approached the stage. When I saw the victim, a young woman in her twenties, named Shannon Russo," said Oz. " I asked Donna to bring the first aid kit from my trunk, and began tending to the severely injured woman."

"Thank you, Detective. That should be enough," said Officer Martin.

"No problem. If there is anything else that you need for your report, here is my card," said Oz as he handed her a business card from his wallet.

"Thanks, Detective," she said and turned and headed back to her cruiser, reporting in on the radio along her way.

Oz and Donna walked back over to the Mustang to wait for Terry to show up.

18

"Kid, are you alright?" asked Terry.

"Yeah, Ter. I'm good," said Oz.

"Hiya Donna, Hun, how are you? Are you alright?" asked Terry.

"I'm fine, Terry. Thank you. This isn't my blood," said Donna.

"Good to hear. Now, why the fuck, is she here with you? Why are you putting her life in danger?" said Terry, sounding like a father scolding his child.

"I made him bring me along," she said.

"Hun, that's all well and good, but you could've been hurt or worse," said Terry. "Not to mention, it's against department protocol. You can't have a civilian on a stakeout."

"It wasn't an official stakeout. We were on a date. I wasn't gonna let him come here alone," she said.

"This is one tough cookie you got here, kid," said Terry.

"Don't I know it," said Oz. "She was great, Ter. She locked the doors and stayed in the car when I went to check things out, ready to call 9-1-1 if anything happened."

Terry put his hand on Donna's shoulder and gave her a smile and a wink, then knocked the peak of her ball cap down. "That hat will get you shot in some neighborhoods here, kid," said Terry. "We're gonna have to get you a proper team's hat."

"This is a proper team," she said.

"She's breaking my heart, kid," joked Terry. "So what did you see when you got outta the car?"

"Nothing really until I got closer to the bandshell. Then I saw what the homeless guy last night described. This massive figure in a tattered black robe with a hood."

"For real?" said Terry in disbelief.

"Yeah, Ter. It looked right at me. Its eyes were like flaming coals. It wasn't afraid of me. I fired my gun over its head, and it still kept coming. Didn't even flinch," said Oz. "I shot it three times in the chest. It let out this screech, and then took off towards the river. It moved far too fast for something that big man."

"Fuck's sake, kid," said Terry. "So the bums are not crazy?"

"No, not at all," said Oz. "This thing isn't done, Ter. I interrupted it. It's pissed off."

"It screamed when you shot it, so it can be hurt," said Terry. "How the fuck did you know it was gonna be here tonight?"

"I told you, I had a hunch," said Oz.

"That's some fucking hunch, kid!" said Terry. "Do you know where it's gonna be next?"

"No," said Oz.

"So where is the vic?" asked Terry.

"On her way to Mass Gen, she was still alive when she left here. Donna saved her life," said Oz.

"I really did nothing, it was all Ozzy here," she said. "All I did was bring him the first aid kit."

"She was outstanding, Ter! So brave. So calm," said Oz.

"You did? Good job, kid!" said Terry as he nudged Donna's shoulder. "So if there is no homicide, then what the fuck are we still doing here?"

"I think we should see if this thing bled when I hit it," said Oz.

"Are you cleared to leave the area?" asked Terry.

"Let's check with Officer Martin and go for a stroll," said Oz.

"Trooper Martin?" Terry shouted.

Olivia Martin came running over from her cruiser to Oz and Terry.

"Yes, sir, what can I do for you?" she asked.

"Are you done with my friends, here? Can I take them for other business?" asked Terry.

"Uh… Yes, sir, I got a statement from Detective Shields, so I think we are good."

"Officer Martin, have FSD been called in?" asked Oz.

"No, sir, should they be?" she asked.

"Absolutely. We will need them down here to scrub the scene for evidence," said Oz.

"Yes, sir, I'll call for them now. Thanks!" she said.

"No problem, and hey, good job tonight," said Oz.

Officer Martin nodded at Oz as she headed back to her cruiser. She radioed Dispatch to contact and send FSD to the crime scene. Oz, Terry, and Donna all walked back to the stage. Oz climbed onto the stage first, and pulled

Donna up, then helped pull Terry up onto the first level. They turned on their flashlights and searched for any signs that Oz injured the creature.

"It was hunched over the woman here," Oz said. "I yelled at it to freeze, and it stood up and turned around and started to walk towards me this way."

Oz shined his light on the stage and retraced the steps that he thought the figure walked. Donna stayed close to him, hugging his right arm, and Terry walked alongside him on his left.

"I fired a warning shot over its head first," said Oz.

Oz stopped walking and turned around, shining his light on the bandshell, looking for where the bullet hit. He found a spot on the bandshell that appeared to be damaged.

"There's where it hit," he said, then turned back around. "I fired three more shots, hitting it directly in the chest, or what, I think, was its chest, right about here I think."

Shining his light, it reflected off a small drop of something on the stage. Oz knelt down and looked at it closer. The droplet appeared to be jet black. He shined his light further and saw a few more drops of the same black liquid.

"Does this look like blood to you, Ter?" asked Oz.

"Looks like something," said Terry. "And if that is from the thing, that means it bleeds. If it bleeds, then it can be killed, right?"

"That sounds like pretty sound logic," said Oz.

"Which way did it go after you hit it?" asked Donna.

"It ran off that way," said Oz. "Fast!"

Oz shined the light across the stage towards the river bank. In the beam of light, they could see random drops of the same black liquid trailing off the stage.

"I say we walk that way and see how far we can track it," said Oz.

"Lead the way, kid," said Terry.

Oz stood up and followed the trail of drops across the stage to the edge. He hopped down and helped Donna and Terry down, then picked up the trail again on the pathway at the front of the stage, heading towards the esplanade. The droplets were further apart here as the creature picked up speed, heading for the river. They followed the trail to the river bank, where it disappeared. Oz and Terry shined their flashlights around the bank, trying to pick up the trail again.

"It just disappears here," said Oz.

"Where did it go?" said Terry.

"No clue, Ter. In the Charles maybe?" said Oz.

"I wouldn't jump in the Charles, kid. Not for all the fucking money in the world," said Terry.

"Yeah, but where else could it have gone?" asked Oz.

"Got me, kid," said Terry.

They turned and headed back to the parking lot. FSD was just pulling onto the scene. The officers moved their cruisers so that FSD could park their camper in front of the bandshell. Jared hopped out of the driver's side of the truck and spotted Oz and Terry coming from the esplanade. Oz gave him an acknowledging wave as they walked towards him.

"Jared, how's it going?" asked Oz.

"No offense, but I could go a night without seeing you two," said Jared. "Looks like you've had quite the night?" He said, pointing at the blood on Oz and Donna's clothes.

"Little more entertaining than sitting and watching Netflix," said Oz.

"I would say so, yeah," laughed Jared.

"Vic is off to Mass Gen.," said Oz. "There is a pool of her blood on the stage. I fired 4 shots, one is in the bandshell. That was the warning shot. The suspect took the other three with him."

"What?" said Jared in disbelief.

"Yeah, and there is a black liquid on the stage as well that trails off the way the suspect fled to the river," said Oz, tracing the path in the air as he pointed it out to Jared.

"Black liquid? Oil?" asked Jared.

"Yeah, would be great if you could tell us what it is," said Oz.

"We'll do what we can. You guys taking off now?" asked Jared.

"Yeah. We'll leave you to do your thing," said Oz. "I want to swing by Mass Gen and check on the victim. You wanna come, Ter?"

"Nah, kid. We'll talk with her tomorrow if she makes it," said Terry. "I'm gonna get home to Maureen."

"Alright, Ter. I'll see you tomorrow then," said Oz.

"Sounds good, kid," said Terry. "Donna, don't let him keep you out too late… get him home to bed, alright?"

"You bet!" laughed Donna. She gave Terry a hug.

"G'night, kids," said Terry.

"You too, Ter," said Oz.

"We're going to get going on this, Oz. I'll talk to you later. I don't want to be here all night," said Jared, as he shook Oz's hand, and left to get suited up.

Oz put his arm around Donna, and they headed back towards the car.

"Do you mind going to the Hospital before we go home?" asked Oz.

"Not at all. I'd feel better knowing that she's ok," replied Donna.

"You're incredible. Thank you for being here with me tonight," said Oz.

"Aww, Ozzy, I was happy to come along. Even if I was a total spaz after. Besides, watching you tonight was such a turn-on!" she said.

Oz opened the passenger side door for Donna to get in and closed it once she was safely inside. When he got in, he started the car, leaned over, and gave her a kiss before pulling out of the parking lot.

***

Oz pulled into the parking garage at Massachusetts General Hospital and parked his car in the first spot that he could find. He and Donna got out of the car, walked across the street, and entered the emergency room through a set of automatic sliding doors into the waiting area. They walked up to the check-in desk. Oz pulled his badge from his hip and showed it to the woman behind the desk.

"Ma'am, I'm Detective Shields, with Boston PD. EMTs brought in a young woman with a laceration to her abdomen... Shannon Russo, is her name," said Oz. "Would you be able to give me an update on her?"

"One sec, Detective," she said as she searched the computer in front of her. "Here it is… she is in Trauma 1, for emergency surgery. If you head through the doors there on the left and walk straight to the Nurses' Station, they'll be able to help you more there."

"Thank you," said Oz.

He held Donna's hand, their fingers tangled together, as they walked through the double doors, and down the hall to the Nurses' station.

"How can I help you, Hun?" said one of the nurses behind the desk.

"Detective Shields, Boston PD. I'm here to check on the status of the young woman, Shannon Russo, brought in by the EMTs with lacerations to her midsection?" said Oz. "I was told that she is on Trauma 1."

"Sure, Hun. One sec," she said. She pulled a clipboard from the half wall behind her and examined it. "Just a moment, Hun, let me go see how things are going."

The nurse got up from the chair and walked out of the station and to a sliding glass door marked 'Trauma 1'. She slid open the door and parted the curtain that was drawn to keep anyone from seeing what was going on inside. Oz squeezed Donna's hand, nervously awaiting the news. The nurse reappeared, closing the door behind her, and she walked over to Oz and Donna.

"Are you the officer that administered treatment before the EMTs arrived?" she asked.

"Yes, ma'am. I am," said Oz.

"Well, the doctor said that you being there when you were, saved her life," she said. "She is gonna be fine. The doctor is getting ready to close the wound now. She'll be in recovery for a few days, but she'll be just fine."

"Thank God!" said Oz. He embraced Donna. "Thank you so much! My partner and I will be by tomorrow to see her if she's up to visitors. Thank you again!"

"I'm sure that she will be more than happy to see you. It was a great thing you did for her," she said.

"Thanks again for your help. Please give her our best. Goodnight!" said Oz.

"G'night, Hun. Take care," she said.

Oz and Donna both let out a considerable sigh of relief as they turned and walked out of the Emergency Room. They walked back to his car, his arm around Donna's shoulders and her arm wrapped around his waist.

"Thank you again for tonight, Hun. You reacting as quickly as you did, and not panicking at the sight of all of that blood, probably saved her life," said Oz.

"I just did what you asked me to, Ozzy. You're the real hero tonight. If it weren't for your hunch, that poor woman would have been killed tonight, or worse," she said. "I'm so proud of you."

Oz opened the car door for her, and she got in. She looked up at him with her stunning green eyes and smiled at him. Oz smiled back at her as he closed the car door.

"Ozwald!" said the voice.

Oz stopped dead in his tracks in front of his car, looking around. The night air was eerily quiet and still. He heard the voice call out to him again.

"You will suffer for this!" the voice hissed.

19

Oz woke to the sound of his alarm. He quickly shut it off, trying not to disturb Donna, still asleep beside him. He climbed out of bed and headed into the bathroom to shower. They had stopped by her apartment briefly so Donna could run inside and pack a quick bag before they went to his apartment.

As the water poured down on him from the shower head, pelting away his aches and tension, he couldn't help but remember the end of the night. Returning to his apartment, they stripped out of their blood-soaked clothes and had a long, hot shower together. He washed her smooth, silky skin. Caressing her every curve as he ran the soap across hot skin. Lathering and massaging her as he helped her wash away the blood that had soaked through her clothes.

She reciprocated and washed him clean, her hands moving and tracing his muscles. They kissed passionately and embraced each other as the warm water crashed down on them from above. Their hands continued to explore each other, caressing, massaging, and squeezing. Shutting off the water, Oz toweled her dry before carrying her into the bedroom to make love to her.

Oz quietly returned to the bedroom, where he got dressed in fresh, clean clothes. Like a ninja, he crept to the closet, grabbing his service pistol from the safe and sliding it in the holster. Oz went back to the other side of the room, claimed his sport coat from the chair before he quietly exited the room.

Oz picked up his pen and opened his notepad and wrote a note for Donna. He tore the note from the pad and placed it on the breakfast bar and placed his spare key, which he plucked from one of the small key hooks by the entrance to the apartment, on the note for her.

It was raining again this morning, not quite as hard as it was the day before, but still hard enough to drench the city of Boston for the second consecutive day. Oz exited the stairwell to the garage and walked across the cold, hard concrete to his car. The sound of the rain and low rumble of thunder could be heard inside the garage this morning. He got into his car, started it, pulled out of his parking spot, and exited the garage.

His drive to the station was quiet. Very little traffic for a Friday morning. Not that it ever mattered, as he was always early for work, and it was not very far to drive. He pulled into the station parking lot, backed his car into his spot like always, parked, and went inside and up to the Detective Pool.

He made himself a cup of coffee and sat down at his desk, and logged into his computer and opened his Outlook. There was an email from the Bureau of Professional Standards and Development. I guess I should have been expecting this one; he thought. Anytime an officer discharged their weapon, they would hear from this group. Just part of department protocol. They just wanted to confirm the statement that he had given Officer Martin on the scene last night.

Oz sipped on his coffee as he responded to the email. Recounting the events of the night in as much detail as he gave the officer, and included the details of the 9-1-1 call. Terry strolled in and sat down at his desk.

"Thank fuck it's Friday, kid!" said Terry.

"I hear you, Ter. Been a long, rough, and bizarre week," said Oz.

"You can say that again. So, how's the vic?" asked Terry.

"Doc said that she is going to make it," said Oz.

"Finally, some good fucking news!" said Terry.

"Yeah," said Oz.

"How's Donna?" asked Terry.

"Better. I left her sleeping in the apartment," said Oz. "How's Maureen?"

"She's always good. I still haven't told her anything about this yet," said Terry. "I don't need her freaking out, or dragging me to church or nothing."

"Doesn't she bug you about it?" asked Oz.

"Nah, we've been together since we were kids," said Terry. "She knows if I gotta talk to her about something, I will. Oh! She saw you on TV the other day, and she wanted me to tell you; you looked good." Terry laughed.

"You're damn right, he looked good!" said Jim.

Jim came out of his office and sat at the desk beside Oz and patted Oz on the shoulder.

"Great work last night, kid!"

"Sir?" said Oz, caught off guard by the praise.

"At Hatch last night," said Jim. "Shame our guy got away. Nevertheless, good job. I hear the woman is gonna be just fine thanks to you!"

"Oh! Thanks, Lieutenant," said Oz humbly. "Terry and I were going to head over there shortly to talk with her."

"Yeah, good idea," said Jim. "Let me know how that goes. I'll need to give an update on this story for the news later." He slapped Oz on the shoulder and got up from the desk. "Keep it up, boys, we'll get this cawksuckah!"

Oz and Terry looked at each other. Jim's compliment did not completely throw them off, nor how nice he was being, since that was not out of character for him. They were more than just stunned that he knew as much as he did, since neither one of them had even said a peep to him about it.

"What are you working on?" asked Terry.

"Responding to the email from BPSD about last night," said Oz.

"Fucking brilliant. It's so great answering to those cawksuckahs every time you fire your gun," said Terry.

"Is there any department in the BPD that you do like?" joked Oz.

"Yeah, my department," said Terry.

"Such a crusty old fucker, Ter," said Oz.

"I told you before, I'm not fucking old!" said Terry.

"Just crusty," laughed Oz.

"It's just part of my charm, kid," laughed Terry. "When are we gonna head over to Mass Gen?"

"When do you wanna go? What else do you have in mind?" asked Oz.

"I was just thinking that we could line it up with another round and lunch," said Terry, holding up his coffee.

"Seriously, one day I'm going to hold an intervention for you, with this coffee addiction of yours," said Oz.

"It'll only be a problem if you cut me off, kid," laughed Terry.

Oz's desk phone rang. He looked at the caller ID, which displayed FSD. *That was quick*, he thought, as he picked up the receiver.

"Shields, Homicide," said Oz, answering the call.

"Oz, it's Jared," he said.

"Hey, Jared. What can I do for you?" asked Oz.

"Got a lot for you this morning, brother. Do you have a pen handy?" said Jared.

Oz pulled his pen and notepad from his jacket pocket. He clicked the pen and flipped open the notepad to a blank page. "I'm ready man, fire away," said Oz.

"Alright, first, we have confirmed the John Doe from the Community Center to be the body of Jon Collins. Those samples that you brought us all came back with 100% matches to the DNA of the victim," said Jared. "Second, we retrieved the bullet from the bandshell, and all four casings from the path where you fired the shots. Ballistics is a dead match for your service pistol, so we sent that to BPSD to corroborate your story. Expect a bill from the city for the damage to the bandshell," joked Jared.

"Let them send it, can't get blood from a stone," laughed Oz.

"And that brings us to the third. That black liquid is in fact blood. Depleted almost completely of oxygen, which is why it is black like that. But it was also sludgy, like old blood. Similar to that of a corpse, but oddly still circulating," said Jared. "It also matched that of a known felon in the database."

"So you have an ID for our killer? That's excellent!" said Oz.

"Well, if it is him, the blood matched Nathaniel Price aka Worm. Did a stretch in Walpole for aggravated assault, and weapons-related charges. Paroled three years ago, stayed on BPD radar until last year, when he appears to have just disappeared. No known address, no job, no medical visits, nothing."

"Disappeared?" said Oz.

"Yeah, completely vanished. Like a ghost," said Jared.

"Any known associates?" asked Oz.

"Just one. George "Wheezy" Rose," said Jared.

"Do we have a last known address for Wheezy?" asked Jared.

"It's the halfway house he was sent to after being paroled, 2235 Park Drive," said Jared.

"Thanks, Jared, you're a fucking rock star!" said Oz.

"Anytime, man, good luck!" said Jared.

"Thanks," said Oz, hanging up the phone.

"That sounded promising," said Terry.

"Vic three is Jon Collins, the gentleman whose house you let us into," said Oz.

"At least we don't have to worry about a B&E charge," said Terry.

"Yeah," laughed Oz. "The black shit was indeed blood, but old blood depleted of oxygen, and it matched the DNA of Nathaniel Price, did a stretch in Walpole for aggravated assault and weapons-related charges," said Oz.

"So let's go find Mr. Price," said Terry.

"Therein lies the problem… he disappeared almost a year ago," said Oz. "Best we can do is pay a visit to a friend of his, George "Wheezy" Rose, and see if he's seen him lately," said Oz.

"Looks like we got a full day, then. So much for easing into the weekend," said Terry.

"Yeah," laughed Oz. "Let go to Mass Gen first, pay a visit to Wheezy after that, and then notify the next of kin for Mr. Collins."

"Sounds like a plan, kid," said Terry. "Gotta fit lunch and Dunkees into that plan somewhere."

"Let's go, junkie," said Oz, getting up from his desk.

***

Oz and Terry walked up to the Nurses Station on the first floor of the Surgical Intensive Care Unit, Ellison 4 at Mass Gen. There was one nurse on a computer there when they walked up.

"How can I help you?" she said.

"Ma'am. Detective Shields and Detective White, here to see Shannon Russo," said Oz.

The nurse looked up at the whiteboard on the wall to her right to find the patient's name. "Room 1853, Detectives. Just down the hall here," she said, pointing down the hall on her right.

"Thank you, ma'am," said Oz.

They walked down the hall and on their left they found the room with a placard that said 'Room 1853'. Oz knocked on the partially opened door lightly as they entered the room.

"Hello? Miss Russo?" said Oz.

"Yes," said the voice faintly.

They entered the room and found Shannon laying up in the hospital bed. Blankets pulled up to her chest, hooked up to an IV in her left hand, that was connected to a long clear tube with a large bag of saline and a small morphine drip hanging on the IV pole.

"Ma'am I'm Detective Shields, and this is my partner, Detective White. How are you feeling?" asked Oz.

"Alive," she replied.

Oz presented her with some flowers that he had purchased from the gift shop for her. "These are for you," he said, handing the bouquet to her.

"They're lovely! Thank you! But why is a detective bringing me flowers?" she asked.

"I was the one that found you last night, ma'am," said Oz.

"You?" she said, surprised. "I should be the one giving you flowers. You saved my life." Her eyes welled up with tears.

"Right place, right time, ma'am. That's all it was," said Oz. "Are you feeling up to talking with us about last night?"

"I wouldn't be here if it wasn't for you," she said. "Yes, I'm fine, I'll tell you whatever I can remember."

Oz sat on the edge of the bed by her legs. Terry pulled up a chair that was in the room. She reached for Oz's hand, held it, and squeezed it.

"Let's start with what you can remember, okay? What were you doing down by the bandshell?" asked Oz.

"I was out for a run like I do every night. I love running down by the water, it helps keep me calm."

"Do you normally run alone?" asked Oz.

"Pretty much. I'm training to run in the Marathon again this year, and don't really like to have someone there to slow me down or whatever."

"So you were running on the esplanade, then what happened?" asked Oz.

"I was running, and all of a sudden, this thing swept me off my feet. It stunk, like mold or something. It was so strong, and it carried me to the stage of the bandshell as if I was a feather," she said.

"Did you scream for help?" asked Oz.

"I couldn't. I had the wind knocked out of me by how hard this thing hit me," she said.

"Then what do you remember?" asked Oz.

"It dropped me down on the stage and was hunched over top of me. I was so scared, it was so big. Its eyes looked like I was looking directly into Hell," she said.

She squeezed Oz's hand tightly. Oz could feel the fear in her building as she recalled the events.

"It's ok. Take your time," said Oz.

"It ripped open my shirt and dragged its fingernail across my stomach. It felt so weird, I felt nothing until it pulled its hand away," she said. "Then there was so much pain. I put my hands down there and all I felt was warm and wet. I remember thinking, 'Oh my God, I'm going to die!' I was so scared."

Shannon began to cry. Tears flowed down her cheeks, followed her jaw, and dripped off her chin onto the blankets. She sniffled and wiped away her tears with her left hand.

"It's okay," Oz said, gently squeezing her hand.

"That's when I heard you yell out," she said. "I wanted to cry out for you, but nothing would come out. I panicked, thinking you wouldn't know I was there and that I would die. You fired your gun, and the thing ran off… and then there you were helping me. Then there was a woman there, too…"

"That was Donna," said Oz.

"Yes, that was her name," she said. "Then I remember waking up here, alone, but alive, and so relieved."

"Can you tell us more about this thing that grabbed you?" asked Terry.

"I couldn't see anything, but its eyes, and the black hood it was wearing. I remember seeing its hand. The fingers were long and bony-looking, and the nails were long. It held its hand just like Freddy Krueger used to in the movies, you know?" she said, simulating it with her hand.

"How big would you say it was?" asked Terry.

"It was really tall when it stood up and turned around. Like nine feet or more, maybe? Even standing, it still seemed hunched a bit," she said.

"Thank you, Miss Russo," said Oz.

"Shannon. Call me Shannon," she said.

"We'll let you rest, Shannon. I'm going to leave you my card, and you can call me if there is anything else that comes to you," said Oz.

"Thank you again!" she said. "God, that really doesn't seem like that's enough."

"No thanks needed, Shannon. I'm just happy that you are going to be okay," said Oz. He squeezed her hand one last time before getting up from the edge of the bed. "You just take care!"

"Thank you, Miss Russo," said Terry. "I'll be watching for you in the Marathon."

Terry winked at her and put his hand on her knee and gently shook her leg before he and Oz left the room. They walked down the hall past the Nurses' station, headed for the exit.

"The flowers were a nice touch, kid," said Terry. "Donna gonna be okay with you giving another woman flowers?"

"I put Donna's name on the card," said Oz.

"Smooth," joked Terry.

"She said the thing smelled like mold," said Oz.

"Shocked, that's all it smelled like if it came outta the Charles," joked Terry.

"Jared mentioned this morning that the blood was black because it was depleted of oxygen, and sludgy like that of a corpse," said Oz.

"So what, we got some kinda super zombie or something?" said Terry. "I was having a hard enough time with the Devil thing. Now you want me to think it's a zombie?"

"No, even I don't think that, Ter. But I do think it's interesting," said Oz.

"Interesting? It's fucking weird, kid," said Terry.

"That too," said Oz. "Let's go see what this 'Wheezy' can tell us."

***

The Impala pulled up in front of a four-story red brick building, with a black-trimmed glass door at the entryway. The number of the building etched in gold numbers on the glass pane above the door.

It was still raining, but had definitely eased off from the morning. They walked into the building and off to the right was a reception window where the tenants and visitors would sign in and out of the building. They approached the window and presented their badges to the House Manager.

The House Manager was a former correctional officer by the name of Harrison Randall, but everyone called him Coach. He was a mountain of a man, standing 6'8" and weighed over 300 lbs. He looked like one of those guys who compete in the World's Strongest Man competitions. Certainly, a good pick to run a houseful of former inmates. He had dark brown eyes, dark skin, a long thick black beard, and his black hair was in dreads pulled back into a wide thick ponytail.

"Detective Shields and Detective White, Homicide. Do you have a tenant here by the name of George Rose?" asked Oz.

"I'm Coach. Manager of this house," said Coach. "Wheezy? Yeah, we do. Is he in some kinda trouble?"

"Nah. We just need to talk with him about a friend of his," said Terry.

"Sure, I'll take you to his room," said Coach. "He's here, he doesn't work Fridays."

They followed Coach to a door on the third floor about halfway down the hall on the right. Coach banged on the door with his massive hand.

"Wheezy!" he said in his loud and thunderous voice. "Open up, you have visitors."

From the other side of the door, you could hear him approaching.

"Who the fuck gonna come see me?" he said before opening the door.

The door opened and there stood a scrawny man about 5'11", graying scruff on his dark-skinned face. His short, gray, and curly hair could use a trim.

"The fuck do you want?" said Wheezy.

"Excuse me Wheezy? What did you say to me?" asked Coach, sternly.

"N… N… Not you, Coach! Sorry," Wheezy said, immediately humbled.

"These Detectives are here to ask you some questions," said Coach. "I'll be your witness for the conversation, in case you need legal representation."

"Detectives? I ain't done nothing," said Wheezy. "I stay here, and I stock shelves at the market down the way. That's it."

"We aren't here for you. We wanna about a friend of yours, Nathaniel Price," said Terry.

"Worm? What the fuck you want with Worm?" asked Wheezy.

"When was the last time you saw him?" asked Oz.

"Shit, been a while. Like six months or more. That muthafucka went crazy as shit," said Wheezy.

"Crazy?" asked Oz.

"Yeah, the muthafucka started talking about Satan and shit. Like he was turning into one of those fucking Devil worshipers or some shit," said Wheezy.

"This was six months ago?" asked Oz.

"Something like that. Before Thanksgiving, for sure," said Wheezy. "I told him to get fucking help, and that I didn't want to hear that shit, you know. I was trying to get my shit straight."

"This was new for him?" asked Oz.

"Yeah, man. Worm's always been a little fucked up, you know," he said. "But not like this. This was new. I don't know where it was coming from. But the muthafucka looked like shit. He was all pale and shit, and his eyes were all black like he hadn't slept in forever."

"Was he running with a new crowd or anything?" asked Oz.

"Nah, man. Worm's always been a loner. I mean, we weren't really friends, you know," said Wheezy. "I knew him a little before we ended up in Walpole, but he was just this weird guy from the hood"

"Can you describe what he looks like?" asked Oz.

"Last I saw him, he was really skinny, like a walking skeleton. His skin was all gray and shit. Muthafucka looked like he was already dead and just hadn't laid down yet. You know what I'm saying," said Wheezy.

"How tall is he?" asked Oz.

"Like my height maybe a little shorter," said Wheezy.

"When you saw him six months ago, was he still living here in Boston?" asked Oz.

"Yeah, I think he got kicked outta the place he was living. Muthafucka stunk, so he either wasn't cleaning himself properly or he was living on the streets," said Wheezy.

"Thank you, Wheezy. You've been a big help. I'm going to leave you both my card. If he comes back, or you hear from him, please call me," said Oz, giving Wheezy and Coach his card.

"Sure thing, Detective," said Wheezy.

Coach escorted the detectives back downstairs to the lobby.

"Good luck finding this guy," said Coach.

"Thanks, Coach. Have a good day," said Oz.

He and Terry exited the building and walked to the Impala, and got inside. Oz pulled out onto the street, the tires splashing through puddles as they headed back towards the station.

20

Back at the station, Oz and Terry sat at their desks, polishing off the sandwiches that they grabbed for lunch on the way back to the station. Oz logged into the NCIC database and searched up the information for Jon Collins, the third of their victims that was only identified that morning.

The database pulled up a list, and Oz clicked on the first one. Up came the Massachusetts DMV picture for Jon Collins that Oz saw on his driver's license in the house. Scrolling the page looking for next of kin, the name listed was Judith Collins. Clicking on her name, he was brought to her file. It appeared as though she was Jon's ex-wife. Oz jotted down the number for her.

He finished his sandwich and picked up his desk phone. He dialed the number for Judith Collins. The phone rang twice before a woman answered the phone.

"Hello," she said.

"Is this Judith Collins?" asked Oz.

"Judith Forrest, I've gone back to my maiden name, but yeah, this is her," she said.

"Miss Forrest, I'm Detective Shields with the Boston PD.," said Oz.

"If Jon needs bail, he can fuck off. There's a reason he's my ex," she said.

"Uh, no, ma'am, that isn't why I am calling. I'm calling to inform you that Jon has been murdered," said Oz.

"Oh my God!" she said, suddenly distraught. "When?"

"Saturday evening, ma'am. We only just had his identity confirmed," said Oz. "You are still listed as his next of kin, that is why we are calling you."

"Uh… Yeah, Jon's parents are both dead, and he was an only child," she said. "H… H… How did this happen?"

"Unfortunately, this is part of an ongoing investigation, so we can't release the details," said Oz. "Can you think of anyone that may have wanted to harm your ex-husband?"

"No," she said. "He was just a normal guy, working a shitty job for an Insurance Company."

"I'm very sorry to be the one to tell you this, ma'am. You have my deepest sympathies," said Oz.

"I can't believe this," she said.

"I'm terribly sorry, ma'am. You will need to contact the Office of the Medical Examiner to make arrangements for the body," said Oz.

"Oh God, the body," she said, crying.

"Yes ma'am. Terribly, sorry. We are doing everything we can to find who did this. Please take care, and again I'm truly sorry." said Oz.

He hung up the phone and took a cleansing breath. He reached into his pocket and pulled out his cell phone. There was a text from Donna.

'Hey Tiger! Hope you are having a good day. Thanks for leaving me to sleep. I can't wait for you to come home to me.'

Oz smiled and messaged her back.

'Aww. Shouldn't be long now. Been a very busy day. Looking forward to seeing you, too. Hope you aren't bored there.'

Oz set his phone down on the desk, grabbed and crumpled up the wrapper of his sandwich, and tossed it in the waste bin under his desk. His phone vibrated. There was a new message from Donna.

'Not bored at all, babe, but I do need my hero to help me make this a perfect day. Hurry home! I have a surprise for you!'

'I'll be home as soon as I can, Hun. I can't wait.' he replied.

Oz put his phone back in his pocket. He took a drink from the bottle of water that he had gotten with his sandwich, got up from his desk, and walked out of the Detective's Pool, headed for the Men's washroom. He pushed the door open and walked up to one of the urinals.

"Ozwald!"

Oz tried to ignore the voice. He knew that there was nothing in the washroom with him and that the voice was only in his head.

"You will suffer!"

Oz shook, and put himself back in his pants and zipped them up, went to the sink, and washed his hands. He was rinsing his hands when all four of the faucets on the vanity turned on.

"I will break you!!!

Fuck you! Thought Oz.

Oz pulled his hands out of the water. The faucets sputtered and blood started to ooze from the spouts. The white porcelain sinks now stained red with the flow of blood from the taps. Oz grabbed a couple of sheets of paper towel from the dispenser on the wall and dried his hand. He closed his eyes, knowing that the blood pouring from the tap couldn't be real. *You don't scare me;* he thought. He reopened his eyes to see the single tap that he had turned on was still running. Only water streamed from the spout. He shut off the tap; the sinks were white again, with no signs of ever being bloodied.

Oz grabbed the handle of the door, pulling it open and catching it with the toe of his shoe as he tossed the paper towel into the trash. Oz opened the door fully and walked out into the hall and back to his desk.

***

Ring... Ring... Ring...

"Detective Shields, Homicide," said Oz.

"Oz, it's Brad, Brad Walker," said Brad.

"Yeah, Brad, what have you got for me?" asked Oz.

"Sorry, it took me so long to get back to you. But it took me a while to dig this up. The only stuff that I could find was on the Satanic Temple in Salem, which is basically a group trying to get it recognized for standing up against tyrannical authority, so it was pretty much a dead end. The other stuff I found was from the FBI, and there were a lot of redacted documents about Skinwalkers."

"Skinwalkers?" asked Oz.

"Yeah, again it's not totally relatable, but it's said that some Navajo can transform themselves into animals," said Brad.

"Yeah, that isn't this, either. I actually saw it last night, Brad," said Oz.

"No way! You did?" asked Brad. "Tell me!"

"I interrupted it. It had just pulled a victim onto the stage at the Hatch Bandshell. It was easily nine to ten feet tall. Couldn't see much else since it was wearing a long, black hooded robe. Its eyes were like flaming hot coals," said Oz.

"That's incredible!" said Brad.

"I shot it three times in the chest, and it let out this horrible screech and took off towards the river," said Oz. "FSD said that the bit of blood that it left behind was black and sludgy, like that of a corpse."

"Wow! This is unreal!" said Brad.

"I know, and if I hadn't seen it with my two eyes, I wouldn't believe it," said Oz.

"This is something entirely different," said Brad. "Something more supernatural, demonic even."

"I don't think you need to keep digging, Brad. I doubt we will find anything like this," said Oz. "On top of that, I can hear it in my head."

"The screech?" asked Brad.

"No, this is going to sound even crazier... but this thing speaks to me. Only I can hear it," said Oz.

"Holy shit! What does it say?" asked Brad.

"It calls my name, and now that I have interrupted it, it threatens me," said Oz.

"I'd shit my fucking pants, man," said Brad. "How did you find it last night to interrupt it?"

"I was mapping all the crime scenes, and suddenly, I had this hunch that I had to be at the Hatch Bandshell last night. Just a gut instinct," said Oz.

"Like a premonition," said Brad. "Like there is some otherworldly connection that you have to this thing."

"I just thought it was a gut instinct," said Oz.

"Think about it… without hearing the voice of this thing in your head, I could go with you on it being a gut instinct. But you hear this thing. You had this feeling that something horrible was going to happen at the bandshell. Almost like you felt its thought, or overheard its plan," said Brad.

"That is an interesting theory," said Oz. "So by that rationale, I should be able to see its next move?"

"I wouldn't rule it out of the realm of possibility. You did it once already, why not again?" said Brad.

"Thanks, Brad! Really, thanks for everything," said Oz.

"Don't mention it. Please let me know if I can be of any more help. Keep me posted," said Brad.

"Will do. Thanks again," said Oz. He hung up the phone and sat back in his chair.

"Was that your therapist?" asked Terry.

"No, it was the ME," said Oz.

"That weird coroner guy?" said Terry. "You told him all that?"

"I reached out to him earlier in the week to help me do some research," said Oz. "He was actually pretty helpful."

"If you say so, kid," said Terry. "So, I think I'm gonna get the fuck outta here for the day."

"Yeah, that sounds like a good plan. Odds are probably pretty good that we will be working again later," said Oz.

"Is that your gut telling you that?" asked Terry.

"No, just the recent trend of events," said Oz.

"Well, it would be nice if the fucker could wait till after the B's game tonight," said Terry.

"If I hear from it, Ter, I'll let it know," joked Oz.

"Thanks, kid," said Terry. "Great job today!"

Terry offered Oz a mint. Oz grabbed one from the bag and threw it into his mouth, and Terry grabbed two and tossed them into his. He put his clip back on the bag, returned the bag of mints to the drawer, and closed it.

"Thanks, Ter! Have a good night. Enjoy the game!" said Oz.

"Thanks, take it easy, kid," said Terry.

Oz tidied his desk, put his notepad away in his drawer, got up, and pushed in his chair. He walked out of the office, down the stairs, and out of the building. He messaged Donna, letting her know he was on his way and that he would see her shortly.

21

"Honey, I'm home!" said Oz, opening the door to his apartment. "Wow! Something smells incredible!"

"Ozzy! How was your day?" said Donna.

Oz kicked off his shoes and walked to the breakfast bar, putting his badge, notepad, and pen on it. He walked into the kitchen, wrapped his arms around Donna, lifted her off the ground, and gave her a kiss. She wrapped her arms around his neck and kissed him back.

"Besides you, what smells so good?" said Oz.

He kissed her again and put Donna back down on her feet.

"I hope you like stir-fry," she said.

"If it tastes half as good as it smells, it's going to be great!" said Oz.

"It's Teriyaki Chicken Stir-fry. Fresh chicken breasts, broccoli, zucchini, snap peas, onions, red and green peppers, served over a bed of white rice," said Donna.

"You've really outdone yourself. This is quite the surprise!" said Oz.

"Oh, this isn't your surprise," she said.

"It gets better than this?" asked Oz.

"Just have to wait and see, Ozzy," she laughed. "Dinner will be in a couple of minutes. Go wash up and when you get back, it should be on the table, and you can tell me all about your day."

"Has anyone told you before that you're amazing?" said Oz.

"Get going," she said, as she smacked his butt as he walked out of the kitchen.

Oz put his gun in the safe, took off his sport coat, and hung it up. He shrugged off his shoulder rig and draped it over another empty hanger, then took off his shirt and tossed it into the hamper. Oz grabbed a fresh t-shirt from the dresser and pulled the t-shirt over his head before he walked into the bathroom and washed his hands. Oz came back out to the table and sat down.

Donna had prepared an incredible dinner for them. There was a single white stick candle in the center of the table. The little flame licked the air as it burned. There were two wine glasses filled with a French Pinot Noir, and the dinner she had just plated. A generous bed of steamed white rice blanketed but succulent strips of chicken breast, onions, red and green peppers, shockingly green broccoli florets, and fresh snap peas, all covered in the aromatic teriyaki sauce they were cooked in.

"I'm speechless. This is absolutely incredible!" said Oz. "Why are you going to work for the DA?"

"Oh, shush!" she said. "Did you go see that woman from last night?

"Terry and I went this morning," said Oz. "She's recovering. She was so grateful for you and me being there last night. Oh, and she thanks you for the flowers."

"You brought her flowers?" asked Donna.

"I just delivered them. The card said they were from you," laughed Oz.

"That was sweet of you to do that for her. I'm sure, though, that saving her life meant so much more than the flowers," said Donna.

"Honestly, I just heard my mom in my head saying that I should bring her flowers. It doesn't matter what we did for her, flowers were just to help brighten her spirits," said Oz.

"Such a good man I've snagged," she said.

"Babe, this is absolutely delicious!" said Oz.

"Glad you like it," she said, smiling at him. "Did she remember much?"

"She was able to give us a pretty good account of what happened. And a slightly better description of the thing that attacked her," said Oz, putting another forkful of food in his mouth.

"Poor thing, she must have been mortified reliving it," she said.

"Yeah, she was pretty upset, but like you, very tough. She pushed on through," he said.

"Aww," she said. "You said it was a busy day. What else happened?"

"Well, remember that guy that Terry and I did a wellness check for?" asked Oz.

"You mean the guy whose house you broke into?" she said.

"Yeah, turns out that he was our third victim. So, I had to notify his next of kin. Which turned out to be the guy's ex-wife," said Oz. "Never an easy thing to do."

"I don't think I could ever do that," she said. "It's so hard when anyone loses a loved one, but to be the one who has to break that news to them… to see or hear that devastation… ugh, it breaks my heart just to think about it."

"Yeah. It's rough," said Oz. "That black stuff, we found on the stage, was blood."

"Black blood?" said Donna.

"Apparently when it's depleted of oxygen, it turns black. And it was thick and sludgy like that of a corpse," said Oz.

"The killer is a dead guy?" Donna said, confused.

"No clue, but the blood matched the DNA of a known felon. So, we went to see a friend of his, to see if he had seen him lately and to ask him about the guy," Oz said.

"Wow, what a day," she said.

"And this is by far the best part of it all. Sitting here with you," said Oz as he grabbed Donna's hand.

"Ozzy, if you get any sweeter, my teeth are gonna rot," she giggled.

"What did you get up to?" asked Oz.

"Well, I went out and got a few groceries for dinner tonight. Picked up this lovely Pinot. Stopped by my place and grabbed a few more things for the weekend. Not much really, just had a very nice, quiet day waiting for my man to finish work," said Donna.

Oz devoured the meal that Donna had so elegantly prepared. There wasn't a single grain of rice left when he was finished. Donna, who had plated herself with a much smaller portion, ate all of hers as well. Oz got up and cleared the dishes. He insisted that since she prepared this lovely meal for them she let him clean it all up, and for her to just relax. Oz washed and dried the dishes while they continued to chat.

"Are you ready for your surprise?" asked Donna.

"I still can't imagine how this night can get any better," said Oz.

"Wait right here on the couch," she said.

"Yes, ma'am," said Oz as he sat down on the couch.

Donna headed off to Oz's bedroom, while Oz waited anxiously on the couch.

"Ozzy!" called Donna. "Come and get your surprise."

Oz got up off the couch and walked down the hall towards the bedroom. He could smell her perfume, and it was intoxicating as he approached the bedroom and the door cracked open. He pushed the door open to reveal Donna on the bed. She was wearing a very sexy and flattering, hunter-green, baby doll nightgown with spaghetti straps, and flowing lace from under the bosom to just above her hips. Underneath the baby doll, she wore a hunter-green g-string, so tiny that it barely existed at all. The color of her auburn hair enhanced by the color of the lingerie. She looked incredible as she laid there on her side.

"Wow!" said Oz. His jaw dropped.

"You like it, Ozzy?" she said, cutely, batting her beautiful eyes.

"So much! You look incredible!" said Oz.

She seductively gestured for him to join her with a "come here" motion of her index finger on her right hand. Oz couldn't resist, as if she had him on a rope and was reeling him in. He knelt on the bed and kissed her soft, red lips. She wrapped her arms around him and kissed him back. The temperature in the room shot up with the heat of their desire for each other. His left hand slid up her thigh and under the flowing lace of the top, settling just under her breast, his fingers following the support of the lingerie. Her right leg now wrapped around him as he slid her up the bed, still kissing each other passionately.

***

Vrrrrt… Vrrrrt… Vrrrrt…

Oz's phone vibrated from the back pocket of his jeans heaped on the floor after being discarded. Oz reached down to pull the phone out of his jeans as it vibrated for the second time. He swiped the screen to answer the call.

"Detective Shields, Homicide," said Oz.

"Guess what, kid?" said Terry.

"Not another body?" said Oz.

"So much for you psychic vision," said Terry.

"Fuck! Where is this one?" asked Oz.

"It's Wheezy," said Terry.

"No way!" said Oz.

"Afraid so, kid," said Terry.

"Where was he found?" asked Oz.

"His room," said Terry.

"Shit, I'll meet you at the Halfway House then?" said Oz.

"Yeah, I'm leaving here shortly. You'll probably get there first," said Terry. "Talk to Coach and see what he can tell us."

"Will do, Ter," said Oz. "See you there," said Oz.

"Yeah, kid," said Terry before he hung up the call.

Oz put his phone down on the nightstand and stretched out. He rubbed his eyes with his palms and groaned.

"Another one?" asked Donna.

"Unfortunately, babe," said Oz.

Donna moved herself to Oz's side, draping her arm across him and laying her head on his chest. Oz wrapped his arm around her, hugging her. She kissed his bare chest and caressed his stomach.

"Mmm, I really don't want to go," said Oz.

"I'm not going anywhere. I'll be right here waiting for you," she said.

He hugged her and kissed her on the head. He sat up on the edge of the bed before getting up and heading into the washroom to freshen up. When he returned, Donna laid partially conveyed in bed. Her right leg was on top of the cover. She seemed to know just what to do to ignite the passion in Oz.

"God, you're so incredibly sexy!" said Oz.

Donna giggled playfully as she watched him getting ready to head out the door. Oz pulled up his jeans, zipped and buttoned them, grabbed the v-neck t-shirt from the floor, and pulled it on over his head. He sat on the edge of the bed to pull on his socks. Donna kneeled behind him, wrapped her arms around his shoulders, and kissed his ear and neck.

"You don't make leaving easy," said Oz, his eyes closed, enjoying her touch.

"Should it be easy?" said Donna.

"Mmm, probably not," said Oz.

"Just make sure that you come home to me," she said as she nibbled his earlobe.

"I will be as quick as I can," said Oz. "This place isn't far away."

Oz grabbed the shoulder rig, pistol, and a charcoal gray sport coat from the closet and put it on. He turned around to see Donna, completely naked, still kneeling on the bed, watching him. The light that came through the blinds illuminated her like a divine figure.

He walked over to her and kissed her goodbye, grabbed his cell phone from the nightstand, and slid it into his back pocket before leaving the room to collect his badge. He slid his feet into his shoes and left the apartment, locking the door behind him. Oz took the stairs down to the main floor and entered the garage, unlocked his car with the remote on the way, and got in.

"*Ozwald!*" said the voice as he started his car. "*You got close once… but never again!*"

Oz ignored the voice, pulled out of the parking spot, and approached the garage door. The door slowly opened. He went to pull out of the garage. There was a large flash of lighting, and the figure appeared in front of his car, big as ever, staring back at him with those flaming eyes. There was a second flash of lighting, and the figure vanished.

He's getting in your head, Ozzy! Don't let him get to you! Oz pulled onto the street. The tires splashed in the pools of standing water as it continued to rain; he headed North to the Halfway House.

***

Oz pulled up in front of the halfway house. There were two cruisers on-scene. Oz got out of the car and approached the doors. An officer greeted him at the door.

"Shields, homicide," he said, showing the officer his badge.

"Go on, detective," said the officer. "The house manager is just inside there on the right."

"Thanks," said Oz, entering the building through the door that the officer held open for him.

Oz saw Coach in the office area, speaking with another officer. As he approached the office, Coach saw him and acknowledged Oz by raising his hand.

"Coach," said Oz. "What happened here tonight?"

"Detective, this is fucked up, man!" said Coach. "You guys were just here today talking to him, and now this happens. This whole thing stinks."

"Walk me through what happened," said Oz.

"I was doing my usual curfew check. I got to Wheezy's room, knocked. There was no answer," said Coach. "I checked my clipboard to make sure that he hadn't signed out, and he hadn't. So I knocked again. Still no answer. I hollered out to him. Still nothing, so I unlocked the door, and that's when I saw Wheezy, like… you'll see."

"So he was killed in his room?" asked Oz.

"Killed? This is far more than just killed, Detective," said Coach. "Whoever did this is a sick fuck!"

"Did everyone else check out for curfew?" asked Oz.

"Yeah, all tenants are accounted for," said Coach.

"Did any of them have a problem with Wheezy?" asked Oz.

"Nah, Wheezy pretty much kept to himself. He's probably one of the better tenants, you know. It seems like this time he really was trying to get straight," said Coach.

"You aren't going anywhere, are you?" asked Oz.

"Me? No sir. I live here with them. Helps earn their trust and respect. I'm no better than them," said Coach.

"My partner is on his way. If you could send him up when he gets here, that would be great. Thanks, Coach!" said Oz.

Oz made his way to the third floor and walked down the hallway to where an officer was standing outside Wheezy's room. He had police tape across the door. Oz reached into his pocket and pulled out a pair of blue nitrile gloves and put them on. He showed his badge to the officer, pulling his sport coat to the side. The officer dropped one side of the police tape and gave him a nod. Oz turned the doorknob and opened the door to Wheezy's room.

Inside was a horrific scene that he was not prepared for. Wheezy had been torn in half. His upper body hung from the light fixture in the middle of the room, a noose around his neck. His face had several slash marks, and his eye sockets were bloody holes, as his eyes had been cut out.

His arms hung by his side, sliced from the wrist up to the ditch of the elbow on both arms. Blood oozed from the wounds down to his hands and dripped from his fingertips. His intestines, strewn about the room like party streamers, hanging from whatever they could be draped over and around. On the walls, written in his blood, were the words 'SNITCH' and 'BETRAYAL'.

His lower body laid on the floor below in a pool of blood that had emptied from the lower half. The jeans he was wearing were soaked from the blood.

The sickly sweet odor of death filled the room, worsened by what the killer had done to Wheezy's body. Overwhelmed, Oz stepped back into the hall.

"Pretty fucked up, huh?" said the officer at the door.

"Understatement of the year," said Oz.

"Reminded me of something from that movie... the one about the sins... you know, with Brad Pitt, and that guy that does the voice for everything," said the officer.

"Morgan Freeman," said Oz.

"Yeah, that's him. Love that guy," said the officer.

Oz looked at the door frame, looking for signs of forced entry. But the door frame was clean. No damage to be seen. He glanced across the room to the window. The blinds were closed and drawn all the way down to the bottom of the windowsill. There wasn't a fire escape on that side of the building, so accessing the window would be virtually impossible. *Coach said that he had to unlock the door. Did Wheezy let the killer in? He must have... but who would open the door to that monster? How did no one see it enter the building?*

"Oz, how bad is it?" shouted Terry.

Oz turned to see Terry and Coach walking down the hall. Terry looked so small next to Coach, not just in height, but overall size.

"It's bad, Ter," said Oz. "Coach, did anyone come here tonight that you didn't recognize?"

"No, there were no visitors today apart from you two earlier," said Coach.

"Any chance that someone came in that you didn't see? Maybe through the back door?" asked Oz.

"No chance. I see everyone coming or going. The back door has an alarm that goes off if that door is opened. And there are cameras set up at the front and the back doors and one pointing down the hall on every floor," said Coach.

"Can you show us the footage from this hall?" asked Terry.

"Sure, when you guys get done here, come down to the office, and I'll have it ready for you," said Coach.

"Thanks!" said Terry.

Coach left them to go through the crime scene, headed back downstairs. Terry approached the door to Wheezy's room.

"What the fuck!" said Terry. "I wasn't ready for that."

"No sign of forced entry," said Oz.

"This…" said Terry.

"Yeah, it's pretty bad," said Oz.

"So did Wheezy let the killer in?" asked Terry.

"I asked myself the same thing, but who would let in a ten-foot monster?" said Oz.

"Good point, kid," said Terry. "What about the window?"

"Third floor, no fire escape," said Oz.

"Let's go see what's on camera," said Terry.

"You don't want to go in and look around?" asked Oz.

"Fuck that, kid!" said Terry. "The geeks can play around in that shit!"

"Alright, Ter," said Oz.

They walked down to the office and knocked on the door frame. Coach was on the computer, pulling up the security footage from the cameras. He turned around when he heard Oz knock.

"I have the footage for the front and back doors and the third-floor hall, ready to go," said Coach.

"Perfect," said Oz.

Coach started with the footage from the front door, starting at 19:00, playing the footage at four times speed. They saw tenants come and go, signing in and out. Coach told them that the tenants sign in and out, even when they step outside for a smoke. They watched footage all the way until the officers arrived.

"You didn't see anyone that you didn't recognize?" asked Oz.

"Nope, every one of those guys is a tenant. We don't get many visitors around here until the weekends," said Coach.

Coach pulled up the footage of the back door, and started it at 19:00, and played the footage at four times speed. The minutes ticked away like seconds. Nothing came in or went out of the back door, just like Coach told them because it triggers an alarm, no one even dared to go near it.

He pulled up the footage of the third hallway; he showed them on the screen which door was Wheezy's. The footage rolled from 19:00 again at four times speed. They saw tenants coming out of their room and walking down the hall. They would be gone for ten minutes or so, and they would return to their rooms. Wheezy opened his door at 21:12 and looked out into the hallway, then closed the door.

"What was that?" asked Oz. "Can you roll that back?"

"What?" asked Terry.

Coach skipped the video back to 21:05 and hit play again, at two times speed, until the clock showed 21:10, then he let it play at normal speed.

"Watch again, Wheezy opens his door, looks out into the hall, and then closes the door again. Watch," said Oz. "Can you play it in slow motion?"

"Sure," replied Coach. The video played frame by frame.

"See right there. He opens the door," said Oz. "What made him open the door? What is he looking for?"

"He looks like he heard something," said Terry.

"But what? There's nothing there," said Oz. "One more time, Coach, can you roll that back?"

"Sure," said Coach, clicking the mouse a couple of times. The video played again.

"What's that?" said Oz.

"What's what, kid?" asked Terry.

"What's that weird shadow in the hall there," said Oz, pointing at the screen. "Right there. Wheezy has the door open and the light from his apartment casts his shadow here, but what's that shadow there?"

"Yeah, what the fuck is that?" asked Coach.

"Look, it disappears with Wheezy before he closes the door," said Oz.

"That's gotta be a camera glitch or something," said Terry. "Right?"

"It's unusual, for sure," said Oz. "Can you make sure that the FSD guys get a copy of this and the footage from the front door?"

"Absolutely," said Coach.

"Why the front door, kid?" asked Terry.

"Maybe that shadow was caught on that camera too?" said Oz.

"You think a shadow did this?" asked Terry.

"After what I've seen? I'm not ruling out anything," said Oz.

"What do we have tonight, gents?" asked Jared through his mask.

Oz turned around to see Jared all suited up. "Jared, it ain't pretty," said Oz.

"More like a horror show!" said Terry.

"Great!" said Jared sarcastically.

"Be glad you're not the clean-up crew," said Oz. "Third-floor, officer outside the door, can't miss it. Vic's name is George "Wheezy" Rose."

"The name I gave you this morning?" asked Jared.

"Yeah. We paid him a visit this afternoon. Coach, here, was with us the entire time. He was safe and very cooperative," said Oz. "No signs of forced entry, and Coach has a couple of videos for you to get the tech guys to look over."

"Perfect," said Jared. "I love it when they're easy like this."

"Yeah, good luck," said Oz.

Jared waved to the FSD crew to follow him as they made their way up to Wheezy's room. The crew had their toolboxes and were all completely covered in their Tyvek suits. This was one crime scene that they would be grateful to be wearing all that gear.

"Coach, thanks for everything," said Oz. "If any of the tenants heard or saw anything, please call us, and we'll be more than happy to come down and get a statement from them."

Oz and Terry shook hands with Coach before they walked out of the office and exited the building. They stopped by the FSD truck.

"You really think this thing can turn itself into a ghost?" asked Terry.

"At this point, Terry, I'm winging it. I don't know what this thing can or can't do. We know it is ridiculously big, fast, and strong. We know it can disappear without a trace. Is it really a stretch to think that it can't turn itself into a shadow, or a ghost or whatever?" said Oz.

"I hear you, kid," said Terry. "Guess I'm just clinging to logic."

"Nothing more we are gonna do tonight. Let's get out of here," said Oz. "I'm not sure of much, but I am pretty sure that I will see you tomorrow night at this point."

"Unless you can use your magic and find this fucking thing sooner," laughed Terry.

"Have a good night, Ter," said Oz.

"You too, kid," said Terry.

Terry slapped Oz on the back before walking over to his car. Oz walked to his car and got in. He messaged Donna to let her know he was on his way home.

22

Oz awoke to the smell of something cooking. He stretched and looked for Donna to still be beside him, but she wasn't there. Oz hopped out of bed, grabbed a pair of low-waisted maroon pajama pants from his dresser drawer, pulled them on, and tied the drawstring. He walked out to the kitchen and saw Donna in his t-shirt at the stove, cooking. He walked up behind her, wrapped his arms around her, and kissed her on the cheek.

"Mmm, morning, Ozzy!" she said.

"You look so good in that shirt!" he whispered into her ear.

"Hope you like omelets," she said.

"You haven't made anything so far that I didn't like. What did you do yesterday, stock my fridge?" joked Oz.

"Just got a few things," she laughed.

"What can I do?" asked Oz.

"The omelets are almost done. Why don't you grab cutlery and drinks," she said.

"Coffee or OJ?" asked Oz.

"Mmm, coffee sounds lovely," she said

Oz grabbed a couple of Keurig pods filled with a delicious, and aromatic light roasted coffee. The coffee brewed while he grabbed knives and forks from the utensil drawer and set them on the table. He went into the fridge and pulled out a bottle of hot sauce, and put them on the table.

"How do you take your coffee?" asked Oz.

"Bit of cream and two sugars," said Donna.

"Well, that is easy," said Oz, since that was how he took his.

He added the cream and the sugar to the freshly brewed cup, while he dropped in the pod for the second cup, and placed the second mug under the spout. He stirred her coffee; the spoon clinking the porcelain as it tapped the sides of the mug. He shook off the spoon gently above the cup before placing the spoon on the counter. He grabbed her coffee and brought it over to the table. Oz took salt and pepper shakers over to the table with his coffee. Donna finished plating the omelets and brought them to the table.

"Wow," said Oz.

"Hope you like it," she said.

The omelets contained chopped red and green peppers, diced tomatoes, spinach, small pieces of ham, and cheddar cheese. The smell of this combination made Oz's mouth water. He grabbed the bottle of hot sauce and shook out some sauce all over the omelet. Donna added a little salt and pepper to hers.

"What should we do today?" asked Oz, cutting into the omelet and taking a bite.

"I dunno. Where can we go?" she asked.

"Have you been to Quincy Market?" suggested Oz.

"Sounds interesting," she said. "What is it?"

"It's a historic market with vendors and eateries, and whatnot," said Oz.

"Have you been?" she asked.

"Just as a patrolman," said Oz. "It is also close to the Aquarium, we could go there too if you want."

"This sounds like it's shaping up to be a great date," she said.

"Should be fun. Do you want to take the T there as well? Make a real Boston day of it?" asked Oz.

"Sure, why not," she said.

"This is so good, Hun," said Oz, nearly finished his omelet.

"Thank you!" she said.

"Do you want to take a shower and get ready while I clean up?" asked Oz.

"Only if you promise to join me after you are done," she said.

"Purely for efficiency, right?" joked Oz.

"Oh, absolutely! I was only thinking about water conservation.," laughed Donna.

They finished breakfast and their coffees. Donna got up from the table and headed off to get her things from the bedroom before getting into the shower. Oz watched her walk away, her backside peeking out from the bottom of Oz's t-shirt that she was wearing. He wondered if the desire he had for her would ever fade, or at least ease.

Oz cleared the table, washed and dried the dishes, and put everything away. He walked into the bedroom, made the bed, and set out his clothes for the day. He could hear the water of the shower running, so he undressed and climbed in behind Donna. She turned around and put her arms up around his neck. Oz's hands were on her hips as they kissed under the water that poured down on them. Oz moved his hands to her firm and perky butt. He kissed her deeper and more passionately. She raised her left leg and hooked it around behind him.

"I want you now!" she whispered in his ear.

***

The day was sunny and a comfortable 60 °F; the sky was a brilliant blue with the occasional cloud. There was a lovely, soft breeze that increased as they got closer to the harbor. Oz and Donna walked together hand in hand down to the Roxbury Crossing station, just down the street from Oz's apartment. They hopped on the Orange Line of the T, taking the train through the city, getting off at the State Street Station, just a short walk to Quincy Market at the historic Faneuil Hall.

The marketplace was alive with locals and tourists alike. Oz and Donna window shopped a bit, taking in the sights and smells that the marketplace had to offer. They shopped at a few stores, where Donna picked up an outfit or two for work. She even dragged him into Victoria's Secret to help her pick out a couple of items that, as she put it, if he played his cards right, he would see her in.

They left the Marketplace and strolled along State Street towards Long Wharf, where they cut down Old Atlantic Avenue to Central Wharf. They headed into the Aquarium, taking in the displays of beautiful corals and tropical fish, stopping to laugh and take in the entertainment of the penguins and seals.

Oz couldn't believe that he had been here all these years and not once had he ever had a day like this. In fact, he couldn't remember the last time that he ever had a day like this. He and Donna were just enjoying each other's company so much that they didn't want it to end. She was everything that he could have ever hoped for, and more in a woman.

The sun began to head towards its slumber when they left the Aquarium. The warm day was now cooling off. Donna cuddled into Oz more as they walked.

"Dinner?" asked Oz.

"Thought you'd never ask," she said.

"What are you craving?" he asked.

"I could murder a big juicy burger right now?" she said.

"So not what I thought you would say," laughed Oz. "Such a tiny little thing, like you."

"I'm full of surprises," she said.

"I see that. Definitely keep me on my toes," he said, laughing. "Wanna check out that pub we walked past on the way to the Aquarium?"

"Sure. It looked like a nice place," she said.

They walked into the pub and managed to get a table right away. They ordered a couple of drinks while they looked over the menu. When the waitress returned with their drinks, they were ready to order. Donna ordered the Pub Burger and Oz ordered the Shepherd's Pie. They held hands and chatted about the day until their food came.

The burger was so big that it made her already tiny hands look smaller. Oz's Shepherd's Pie was a large and hearty serving. It barely fit on the plate.

"There is no way that you are eating all of that," said Oz.

"Is that a challenge?" said Donna.

"Nope, but if you do, I will forever be impressed," laughed Oz.

Donna took a bite of her massive burger. The lettuce and onions crunched as she bit through them. The meat was so tender and juicy that juices trickled down her chin. She put the burger down and grabbed her napkin to wipe her chin, trying to smile and chew the mouthful of the delicious burger. Oz just looked at her and smiled, amused by the show.

"How'd it go last night?" she asked, holding her hand in front of her mouth.

"The victim was the man that we talked with yesterday," said Oz, loading his fork with Shepherd's Pie.

"The friend of the guys whose DNA matched the black stuff?" asked Donna.

"Yup. I think our killer had his feelings hurt his friend talked with us," said Oz.

"Was it bad?" she asked.

"Left him recognizable at least, but I think it was a message for us," said Oz.

"How is everything this evening?" asked the waitress.

"Wonduhful! Fank you!" said Donna, with a mouthful of burger.

"Perfect. Can I get you another round of drinks?" she asked.

"Why not?" said Oz. "We aren't driving."

"Another glass of Merlot, and another scotch, coming right up," said the waitress, leaving the table to get their drinks from the bar.

They finished eating their meals. Neither of them came close to finishing the enormous portions. They finished their drinks, and Oz paid the tab. They walked out of the pub arm in arm down State Street to the station and hopped back on the T, taking the Orange Line back to Roxbury Crossing.

Walking back to Oz's place from the station when his phone rang. He pulled the phone from his back pocket, swiped it to answer the call.

"Detective Shields, Homicide," he said.

"Oz! Thank God you answered!" said the woman's voice on the phone, trembling and distraught.

"Maureen?" asked Oz.

"Yeah," she said. "Please tell me that Terry is with you?"

"No, he's not. What's going on?" asked Oz.

"Oh, God!" she said, crying.

"Maureen, take a breath. What's going on?" he asked.

"Ter left about an hour ago after he got a call on his cell. He said he would be right back, that he would be ten minutes tops, he just had to go see someone. I figured he was with you," she said.

"Who called him?" asked Oz.

"I dunno, he never said," she said.

"Okay, Maureen. Don't panic," said Oz.

"He's not answering his phone. I'm so worried, Oz!" she said.

"It's ok Maureen. I'll be right there, okay?" he said.

"Okay," she said. "Please don't let anything happen to my Terry, Oz."

"Maureen, I promise. We will find him," said Oz. "Stay calm, I'm on my way."

"O… O… Okay," she said, hanging up the call.

Oz and Donna walked into his building and up to his apartment. He unlocked and opened the door, and went inside. He quickly glanced at the clock on his wall that said that it was almost 10. Oz quickly grabbed his gun and shoulder rig from the closet, his badge from the counter, and his jacket from the hook.

"I'm coming with you," said Donna. "I'll stay with her as you look for Terry."

"Are you sure? You don't even know her," said Oz.

"It's not even a question, Ozzy. I'm part of this too," she said.

"Alright," he said.

He locked the door, and they rushed downstairs and through the garage to the car. The tires of the mustang screamed as he sped out of the garage and onto Tremont street, heading for Maureen and Terry's house. If his partner was in trouble, there wasn't a second to spare.

23

The mustang roared as it pulled into the driveway behind Maureen's Mini. Oz and Donna quickly exited the vehicle and rushed up the steps to the door. Oz knocked on the door and shouted.

"Maureen, it's Oz," he said.

Maureen opened the door. The poor woman was an absolute mess. Her eyes were red from crying, and her nose from wiping and blowing it.

"Thank God you're here, Oz," she said. "Come in, come in."

Oz and Donna followed Maureen into the house. Oz closed the door behind them. Maureen walked into the living room and sat in Terry's chair. Oz and Donna sat on the couch.

"Maureen, this is Donna. She is going to stay with you while I go look for Terry," he said.

"God, of all days to meet you, it has to be today when I'm a wreck," said Maureen.

"You're beautiful, Maureen. The most important thing is that we find Terry," she said, reaching from the couch to Maureen and grabbing her hand.

"You're a doll," said Maureen. "She's an angel, Oz. A real sweetheart!"

"Maureen, what time did Terry get the call?" asked Oz.

"Um, like quarter to nine, maybe a little later," she said.

"Did it sound like it was work-related?" asked Oz.

"Yeah, which is why I thought he was with you. He took his gun and his badge when he left," she said.

"Okay, Maureen. I will find him. I'm going to leave you with Donna, and I'm going to make a couple of calls," said Oz, getting up from the couch. He walked over to Maureen and kissed her on the cheek, and squeezed her hand. "I'm going to find him, Maureen. I promise."

Oz kissed Donna and mouthed the words "thank you" to her before leaving the room and walking out the front door. He swiped through his contacts on his phone and selected one to call.

"Lieutenant Roberts," said Jim, answering the call.

"Sir, it's Oz. Terry is missing," he said.

"What? For how long?" asked Jim.

"Long enough that Maureen called me in tears, sir," said Oz.

"Fuck! Where is Mo now?" asked Jim.

"At home, sir. My girlfriend is with her," said Oz. "My next call is to get someone to ping his phone for the last known location."

"Call Tech. Let them know I authorized it. If they have a fucking problem, they can call me direct," said Jim.

"Yes sir, will do. I'll be in touch, sir," said Oz.

"Be sure that you are, kid. I'm suiting up now. Let me know the minute you know anything," said Jim.

"Yes, sir," said Oz, hanging up the phone.

"He swiped through his contacts again, finding the direct line to the Tech Division, and called it.

"BPD Tech. This is Davis," said the man.

"This is Detective Shields, badge number 2367. I need you to ping a phone for me," he said.

"Do you have a warrant, detective?" asked Davis.

"This isn't for a suspect. I'm trying to locate my partner. Lieutenant Roberts has cleared this," said Oz.

"Shit, okay. What's the number?" asked Davis.

"The number is 6-1-7-5-5-5-1-1-9-9, please confirm," said Oz.

"I heard 617-555-1199, is that correct?" asked Davis.

"Yes," confirmed Oz.

"Two secs, detective," said Davis.

Oz walked to his car, got in, and started it. His phone connected to the Bluetooth in his car, and he was now in hands-free mode. He began to back out of the driveway when Davis returned to the call.

"Detective Shields?" asked Davis.

"I'm still here," said Oz.

"The phone is on, and is being shown at Cambridge Common, at Harvard."

"Thanks, Davis!" said Oz.

"No problem, detective, good luck!" said Davis.

Oz hung up the call and called Jim back as he drove towards Cambridge Common. It was only a few blocks away. The phone rang once and was picked up right away.

"Shields, tell me good news," said Jim.

"Cambridge Common. Headed there now," said Oz.

"I'm on my way, kid. And I'm bringing backup," said Jim, hanging up the phone.

Oz spotted Terry's Malibu parked on the East side of Massachusetts Avenue, right by a walkway to the Civil War Monument, pulled up and parked behind it, almost forgetting to turn the car off, he was in such a rush to get out and head into the park. He ran along the walkway, calling out for Terry. He approached the monument, heard a gurgling, and he called out for Terry again.

Oz ran around to the southeastern facing side of the monument and saw Terry hanging there in a crucifix-like pose, his arms tied around the columns, and legs dangling. Terry had been badly beaten, his face slashed by two parallel claws from above his right eye across diagonally to the left side of his jaw. Blood dripped from his jaw and chin. His wrists were bleeding from the tension from the ropes that suspended him on the monument. Worst of all was the pentagram carved deep into Terry's chest. Blood still flowed from the wounds.

"Hold on, Ter! I'm coming, man!" shouted Oz.

Oz dialed 9-1-1 as he hopped the short black wrought-iron fence, trampling through the garden and climbing the monument to Terry.

"9-1-1, what's your emergency?" asked the operator.

"Detective Shields, badge number 2367, I have a 999 and require immediate assistance. I repeat 999, officer down, and require immediate medical assistance. We're located at the Civil War Monument in Cambridge Common," said Oz.

"Yes, sir, Detective. EMT and additional units are being routed to your location now. Do you require further assistance?" asked the operator.

"No, thank you! Just tell them to hurry!" said Oz, hanging up the call. "Hang on, Ter, I'm coming, man!."

Oz climbed the monument to the left of Terry to see if he could untie the rope. The nylon rope used to tie Terry up was knotted and burned, preventing it from being untied. He pulled out a small folding knife with a 3" blade from his pocket. He opened the blade, wrapped his right arm around Terry's waist, reached up with his left hand, and sawed at the rope until he cut through it. Oz gently lowered Terry to his feet.

"Oz," said Terry weakly.

"Can you stand, Ter?" asked Oz.

"I think so," said Terry.

Oz went behind Terry, standing in front of the statue, helping brace Terry as he cut the other rope. Terry's arm dropped, and he fell back into Oz. Oz sat Terry down at the feet of the statue and hopped down. He slid Terry off the monument and into his arms and carried him like a bride to the wrought-iron fence, and helped him over it, before hopping over himself.

He sat Terry down and leaned him back against the fence. Sirens could be heard approaching. Oz threw off his jacket and shoulder rig and removed his shirt, and applied it to Terry's chest to help slow the bleeding.

"Stay with me, Ter!" he said. "You're going to be okay, man! EMTs are coming. Just hang in there."

"Oz… I… I'm sorry I didn't believe you…" said Terry.

"Shh… Save your strength, Ter," said Oz.

"M… M… Mo…" Terry began to say.

"Maureen is fine. Donna's with her," said Oz.

Lights flashed and flicker through the trees into the park from Massachusetts Ave. Two paramedics came rushing down the walkway, pushing a yellow frame gurney, their EMS bags on top. Oz yelled at them, letting them know where they were. They came around the southeast side of the monument, finding Oz holding Terry's chest. Oz stepped back, making way for the paramedics to go to work.

"His name is Terry White," said Oz.

"Terry, you're gonna be okay," said the Paramedic in charge. "We're gonna take care of you."

"Oz!" a voice shouted.

Oz looked around to see Jim Roberts running down the walkway towards him. Oz picked up his jacket and shoulder rig and took a few steps towards Jim, not getting too far from Terry.

"Lieutenant?" said Oz.

"How bad is it?" asked Jim.

"He's alive, sir, but he's lost a fair bit of blood. He's pretty weak," said Oz. "He was tied up on the statue when I arrived. I cut him down and applied pressure to the chest wound."

"Was he shot?" asked Jim.

"No sir. The sick fuck carved a pentagram into his chest," said Oz.

"Cawksuckah!" said Jim. "Have you called Maureen yet?"

"No sir, I was tending to him, when the medics arrived, and then you showed," said Oz.

"I'll stay here with Ter, you go get Mo. Bring her to the hospital," said Jim. "Where you are guys gonna take him?"

"Cambridge," shouted the Paramedic in Charge.

"We'll meet you there, kid. No, go get Mo," said Jim.

"Yes, sir," said Oz.

Oz ran back to the car and got in. Two cruisers pulled up, as Oz did a U-turn out of the spot he was in at the curb, and sped off towards Terry and Maureen's house.

***

Maureen saw the lights from Oz's car flash in the front window as he pulled into the driveway. She stood up, shaking with grief and anticipation for what she might see or hear. Donna stood beside her, embracing her, as Oz opened the door.

"Maureen, I found him!" said Oz.

"Oh God, where is he?" she asked in a panic.

"He's on his way to Cambridge Hospital. Lieutenant Roberts is with him. Come on, I'll take us there," said Oz.

"Oz, is my Terry okay?" she asked through tears.

"I'm not going to lie to you, Maureen. He's in rough shape, but I think he'll be okay," said Oz.

"Oh, God! Please save my Terry. I can't live without him," she said, praying.

"He is going to be alright, Maureen. I feel it in my heart," said Donna.

Donna and Oz helped Maureen out of the house and down the stairs. Oz locked the door to their house with Maureen's keys. Donna climbed into the back seat of the Mustang, and Oz helped Maureen down into the passenger seat before and closed the door. He ran around to the driver's side, the car still running from when he pulled up to the house. He backed out of the driveway and sped off towards the hospital, squealing the tires as he pulled away from the house.

"Don't bullshit me, Oz. How bad is it?" asked Maureen.

"He's been beaten and cut up pretty bad, Maureen. He'd lost a fair amount of blood by the time I got there. He was pretty weak, but he was alert and knew who I was," said Oz, reaching over and grabbing Maureen's hand, gently squeezing it.

"Where's your shirt?" she asked, just noticing that Oz only had on his jacket.

"I took it off at the scene and applied it to Terry's cuts until the paramedics showed up," said Oz.

Maureen sobbed, overwhelmed by what she was hearing. Donna reached forward and put her hand on Maureen's shoulder.

"Who would do this to my Terry?" she asked.

"I don't know, Maureen," said Oz, knowing exactly who did this. "But they will pay dearly for this, I promise!"

Oz pulled in front of the doors to Emergency and parked. He helped Maureen out of the car, then Donna from the back seat. Donna took Maureen into the Emergency waiting area, while Oz Parked the car in the first available spot in the underground garage. He ran back to the entrance to the Emergency Room into the waiting area. Jim was there with Maureen and Donna.

"Oz," said Jim, embracing Maureen. "He's back there now. The doctors are taking good care of him. He's a tough bastard, you know that. He is gonna be just fine."

"Did the medics say anything, sir?" asked Oz.

"Just that we should be glad you got there when you did," said Jim.

"Oz, I can't thank you enough," said Maureen.

"You don't have to thank me at all, Maureen. He's my partner," said Oz.

Maureen hugged Oz. Jim, Maureen, and Donna sat down on the chairs in the waiting area. Jim sat with Maureen, holding her hand as he had his arm around her, holding her close.

"Oz, are you gonna introduce me to the lovely lady here with us?" asked Jim.

"Shit, I'm so sorry. Lieutenant Roberts, this is Donna Richardson," said Oz. "I'm such a tool."

"Donna, nice to meet you," said Jim.

"Nice to meet you too, sir. Too bad we didn't meet under more ideal circumstances," she said.

"We're gonna have to teach Oz here, better manners," laughed Jim. "Speaking of which, go get yourself decent, kid."

"Right, yes, sir. I'll be right back," said Oz.

Oz quickly went back out to his car, opened the trunk, took off his jacket and shoulder rig, placing them in the trunk while he pulled another t-shirt from his duffle bag. He pulled the shirt over his head. He shrugged on the shoulder rig, and put his jacket back on, closing the lid of the trunk.

"Ozwald!" said the voice.

Oz looked around the garage, trying to see the figure. He saw nothing but darkness between the projections of lights from the mounted halogen lights on the walls throughout the garage.

"I told you that you would suffer!" said the voice.

"Show yourself," said Oz. "Why are you targeting me?"

"You're weak!" said the voice.

"I'm not the one hiding in the shadows," said Oz.

"You will suffer!" said the voice.

Oz closed his eyes and tried to tune out the tormenting voice in his head. When he opened his eyes, the voice had stopped, and all that could be heard was the hum from the halogen lights mounted on the parking garage walls. Oz walked back to the Emergency Room doors, the doors to the ER slid open as he approached, and he went inside, returning to where Maureen, Donna, and Jim were.

"You alright, Oz," asked Jim. "You look like you've seen a ghost."

"Yeah, just tired. Can I get anyone a coffee or anything?" asked Oz.

"I'd love a coffee, kid. Black, 2 sugars," said Jim.

"Maureen, can I get you anything? Coffee? Tea? Water?" asked Oz.

"Tea please, Hun," she said.

"Absolutely, anything in it?" asked Oz.

"Bit of milk," she said. "Thank you."

"I'll come with you," said Donna.

Oz and Donna followed the signs on the walls to the cafeteria. Oz ordered the tea for Maureen and coffee for Jim. Donna asked for a bottle of water, and he got himself a coffee. Oz paid for the drinks, and put the change in the clear plastic charity collection box at the cash, and picked up the tray of drinks. They walked back the way they came to the waiting area.

"Thanks, Hun," said Oz.

"For what?" she said.

"For everything. For staying with Maureen, who you'd never met. I just left you there," said Oz.

"Ozzy, it was my pleasure. She is the wife of your partner. I guarantee she'd do the same if you went missing," she said.

"Still, thank you!" he said, putting his arm around her shoulder and kissing her head.

They returned to Jim and Maureen. Oz pulled their drinks from the tray and handed them out. He pulled his coffee from the tray and tossed the tray in a nearby waste bin.

"Anything yet?" asked Oz.

"Not yet, kid," said Jim.

Donna sat back down beside Maureen and put her hand on her thigh. Maureen was a wreck while they waited to hear something about Terry's condition. Oz sipped his coffee and paced around.

"Oz, there was nothing more you could've done," said Jim. "Don't beat yourself up over this."

"Should I go back to the crime scene, sir?" asked Oz.

"Oz, Terry needs you here. Not out there. Let the other guys take this one," said Jim.

"Yes, sir," said Oz.

"And quit calling me sir!" said Jim, giving Oz a comforting smirk.

Oz looked at his phone, seeing that it was 12:30. *Surely, we've got to hear something soon.* Oz finished his coffee and tossed the cup in the waste bin. A nurse emerged from beyond the electronically locked door to the emergency room.

"Mrs. White?" called out the nurse.

Maureen and Jim stood and walked toward the nurse. Donna got up and stood back with Oz.

Jim had his arm around Maureen as they stood there bracing to hear the news.

"What's the news?" asked Jim.

"Terry is out of surgery and will be heading to recovery shortly. He lost a lot of blood, so we have him on fluids and have given him several units of blood, while he was sedated," said the nurse. "The lacerations on his face and in his chest were very deep, so we had to repair a lot of muscle and tissue damage. There, unfortunately, will be scarring that a plastic surgeon may be able to repair."

"Oh my God!" cried Maureen.

"But the good news is that he is going to be alright. Thankfully, he was brought in when he was," said the nurse.

"Thank God!" said Maureen, sobbing. "Can I see him?"

"Yes, come back with me. He is still groggy from the anesthetic, but he is alert," said the nurse.

"Oz, come with me," said Maureen.

"Actually, it's best if it is just you, for now, ma'am. He is still too weak to be overwhelmed with visitors," said the nurse.

"If it wasn't for him, my Terry, wouldn't even be here right now," said Maureen.

"Maureen, just go. Have your time with him. We aren't going anywhere. I'll see him later," said Oz.

"Come, ma'am. I'll take you to him," said the nurse.

Maureen stopped fighting, and went with the nurse, through the doors, and into the emergency room. Jim grabbed Oz by the shoulder.

"You did great, kid. I'm really proud of you," said Jim.

"I'm just glad he's going to be okay, sir," said Oz.

"Oz, it's a special kind of person that puts the well-being of others ahead of their own," said Jim as they walked back to sit down. "You're a hero, kid. Just like the other night with that woman. If you didn't act as quickly as you did, they'd both be dead. And that goes for you too, little lady. Not many would have done all that."

"What else was I going to do, he's m partner," said Oz.

"Thank you both from the bottom of my heart," said Jim. "My boys and their families are all the family I have left. And it makes me so proud to see all of you looking out for one another."

Jim patted Oz on the back and stood up. "Anyone want some coin cuisine?"

"No, thanks, sir," laughed Oz.

"I'm good, thank you," said Donna. "That stuff will kill you."

"Hasn't yet, kid," joked Jim as he walked over to the vending machine.

24

Daylight broke through the windows of the Emergency Room waiting area. Oz woke up and saw Donna curled into him, her legs tucked up on the padded bench seat where they had been all night. He looked around and saw Jim curled up on a bench across from them. *Maureen must still be with Terry.*

He stretched, trying not to disturb Donna, and slowly lowered her onto the seat as he got up to see if he could find out how Terry was doing. He walked over to the admittance window and asked the woman behind the glass. She informed Oz that they had moved him up to the ICU on the second floor. Oz thanked her and walked back over to Donna. He gently touched her shoulder to wake her.

"Ozzy? What time is it?" she asked, all groggy.

"It's 7:30," said Oz. "Terry's been moved up to the second floor to ICU."

"Okay," she said, yawning. "Let's go."

Oz walked over and woke Jim to let him know. Jim yawned and stretched, trying to unkink himself from sleeping on the bench.

"Can I get you guys a coffee?" asked Jim. "Because I sure need one.

"That would be great sir. Two regulars please," said Oz.

"You got it. Meet you up there," said Jim.

Oz and Donna followed the signs, directing them to the elevators and up to the second floor ICU Nurses Station, and spoke with one of the nurses there.

"Excuse me, Ma'am. Can you tell me which room Terry White is in?" asked Oz.

"He's in room 2645, just down there on the left," she said.

"Thank you, ma'am."

Oz and Donna walked down the hall, reading the placards outside each room until they found 2645, and they knocked on the partially closed door.

"Come in," said Maureen.

"Just us, Maureen," said Oz.

They walked into the room and saw Maureen sitting bedside, holding Terry's right hand. His left hand connected to an IV that fed him fluids, blood, and painkillers. The bandage on his face covering the cross-face wounds that were now stitched closed. A massive bandage on his chest peeked out from the top of the hospital gown that was draped over him. He was awake and had been talking with Maureen.

"Hey, Ter. How are you, man?" asked Oz.

"You got your wish, kid. Now you're the pretty one of the two of us," said Terry.

"Terry, really?" said Maureen. "You almost died, and you're making jokes," said Maureen.

"Sorry, Hun. I don't know how else to be," said Terry.

"I'm so glad you're alright, Ter," said Oz.

"You're not gonna kiss me, are you?" said Terry.

"Not until you buy me dinner first, dickhead!" said Oz.

Oz and Terry laughed while the ladies failed to see the humor in the situation. Terry coughed and clutched his chest as the stitches ached from the strain.

"Easy, Hun," said Maureen. "I don't know how the both of you can joke at a time like this."

"Sorry, Maureen," said Oz.

"How are you, Terry?" asked Donna.

"I'm alright, kid. Thanks for taking care of my Maureen," said Terry.

"Don't even mention it. Honestly, I was more than happy to be there for her," said Donna.

"Ain't she a doll?" said Maureen.

"Yeah, not bad for an out-of-towner," said Terry as he winked at Donna with his left eye, since a bandage did not cover it.

Jim knocked on the door before entering the room. He had a tray of coffees and a tea for Maureen.

"I'd have brought you a coffee, Ter, but I thought it might be hard to drink it through a straw," laughed Jim.

"Cawksuckah, I'll remember that," said Terry.

"Good to see this didn't break your spirit," said Jim, handing everyone their drinks.

"Maureen, Hun. Can you give us a minute? I gotta talk to Oz, and Jim about last night," asked Terry.

"Sure, Hun. I need to freshen up a bit anyway," said Maureen.

"I'll come with you, Maureen. I could do some freshening up as well," said Donna.

Maureen and Donna left the room, leaving the boys to have their chat. Terry tried to see the door to make sure that they had really left and were not within earshot.

"Are they gone?" asked Terry.

"Yeah, Ter," said Oz.

"Mind telling me why you were out and didn't call your partner for back-up?" asked Jim.

"I thought I was meeting an old CI of mine. Called me out of the blue, and said that he heard something about this ghoul that was killing people," said Terry. "I would have never thought it was a setup."

"So what happened?" asked Oz.

"I got the call and left to meet them at the Civil War Monument, which, I thought, was a little odd since we never meet on this side of the Charles. I guess I just wanna catch this cawksuckah so bad, that I was blinded," said Terry. "I showed up, and that is when the fucking thing jumped me. It hit me like a freight train. When I came to, I was hanging there, and the thing was carving up my chest. It could have easily killed me if it wanted to."

"Can you describe the thing?" asked Jim.

"Just like the homeless guys and Oz described. It was fucking huge, flaming eyes, dark hooded robe," said Terry. "Crazy fast and wicked strong."

"Do you remember if it said anything to you?" asked Oz.

"Not that I can remember, kid. I just remember the thing breathing on me, its breath was so hot. Like I was next to a bonfire," said Terry.

"I'll get him, Ter. You just get better," said Oz.

"Yeah, kid. Can't leave you unsupervised," laughed Terry.

"Just take your time, Ter," said Jim. "If you or Maureen need anything, don't hesitate at all. Alright?"

"Thanks, Jim. That means a lot," said Terry.

"Just get well, Ter. I'm gonna bounce. I'm all kinked from sleeping on that bench," said Jim.

Jim slapped Terry on the knee and Oz on the back before leaving the room. Terry and Oz heard him saying goodbye to Maureen and Donna on their way back to the room.

"There they are, two scarlet-haired angels!" said Terry.

"Your vision is fucked after all," said Maureen.

"Aww, come here Maureen, gimme a kiss," said Terry.

"Sounds like that morphine is kicking in again," said Maureen.

"Can we drop you at home, Maureen?" said Oz. "I think we should let Terry rest up."

"I'm gonna stay, Hun," said Maureen.

"Hun, go home, get some rest, take a shower, and come back later. I'm fine, the worst is over," said Terry.

"Are you sure, Hun?" asked Maureen.

"Absolutely. Go with Oz," said Terry.

"Okay, Hun. I love you! I'll be back shortly," said Maureen.

"Love you too, Hun!" said Terry. "Thanks, Oz."

"Don't mention it Ter," said Oz. "Rest up."

"Bye, Ter. Get well," said Donna, leaning in and giving him a peck on the cheek.

Maureen gave Terry a kiss. Her eyes welled up with tears, not wanting to leave him there alone. She would be back before too long. She walked out of the room with Donna, Oz followed close behind.

"Oz?" hollered Terry.

"Yeah, Ter?" said Oz.

"When you come back, make sure you bring me a Dunkees, you cawksuckah!" laughed Terry.

***

Oz pulled into the driveway at Maureen and Terry's house. He reached into the pocket of his jacket and handed Maureen her keys. He held her hand as she collected the keys from him.

"Maureen, if you need anything, please don't hesitate to call. Any hour, any day, okay? Please, whatever you need. I'm here for you," said Oz.

"Thank you, Oz! And thank you for finding him," said Maureen.

"Just like the Lieutenant said, we're family. I would do it a million times over, without hesitation, for both of you," said Oz.

"You got a keeper here, Donna," said Maureen.

"Don't I know it," said Donna, reaching forward and placing her hand on Maureen's shoulder. "And seriously, anything you need at all, just ask. We'll be right here."

"Thank you so much. Both of you. We're so blessed to have you," said Maureen.

Maureen opened the door and got out. Donna released the seat and climbed out from the back. She gave Maureen a hug before Maureen walked to the stairs and up to the door. She unlocked it and went inside. Donna sat down in the passenger seat and closed the door.

"Never a dull date with you, Ozzy," she said.

"I'm so sorry, Hun," said Oz.

"Don't be silly. You saved Terry's life!" she said. "How can I ever be upset over that?"

"I know," said Oz. "But I'm still sorry. It always seems like there is something to interrupt us." Oz backed out of the driveway and headed for his apartment.

"Ozzy, I prepared myself for this, the moment that I found out that you were a cop. If I wanted it easy, I'm sure that I could find it. But I want you, and all that comes with that," she said, grabbing his hand from where he had rested it on the shifter.

"How did I get so lucky?" asked Oz.

"Everything happens for a reason, Ozzy," she said. "And all of this… the stuff that is going on… all just testing our resolve."

"You're incredible, do you know that? Really, undeniably incredible," he said. "What shall we do with the rest of our Sunday?"

"I don't know about you, but I need a shower and a nap," she said.

"Yeah, I could do with both of those, it was a long night," said Oz. "Hungry?"

"A little," she said.

"Craving anything?" asked Oz.

"Besides you?" she giggled. "Honestly, babe, I'm good with some toast."

"Sounds good to me," said Oz.

Oz pulled into the garage and backed into his parking space. They got out of the car, and Oz grabbed the blood-soaked shirt from the trunk before they headed to the elevator. Oz put his arm around Donna as they exited the elevator headed for his apartment. She put her hand into his back pocket. When they walked into the apartment, they both let out a sigh, so glad to be back somewhere that they could just relax.

"Shower or toast first?" asked Oz.

"Let's eat because if we don't, we won't eat until we wake up later," she laughed.

"As you wish, my dear," said Oz. Oz opened the fridge and saw a couple of fresh tomatoes. "How about a toasted tomato sandwich?"

"A what?" asked Donna.

"You've never had a toasted tomato sandwich?" asked Oz, slightly shocked.

"Clearly, if I don't know what it is," she said.

"Well, my dear, you are in for a treat. In just a few short minutes, you will be in flavor heaven," laughed Oz.

Oz washed one of the tomatoes, and started slicing it into quarter-inch thick slices, and put the slices on two stacked pieces of paper towel, to absorb some juices so that the bread wouldn't go soggy. He dropped two slices of bread into the toaster. When they popped, he spread the butter on both pieces. "Mayo?" he asked?

"Sure, just a little," she said, watching him work.

Oz spread a little mayo on one slice of toast. He dropped two more slices in the toaster and layered slices of tomato on the other slice of toast. He ground a little salt and pepper over top of the tomatoes, took the slice of toast with the mayo on it, and put it on the tomatoes. Finally, he plated the sandwich, and sliced it in half diagonally, before setting it down in front of Donna, who was seated at the breakfast bar.

"Voilà!" said Oz. "Bon appétit!"

"Thank you," she said, giggling.

"Drink?" asked Oz.

"Water?" she said.

Oz grabbed two bottles of water from the fridge and placed them on the breakfast bar. One in front of Donna, and the other where he was going to sit. Oz finished making himself a sandwich, plated it, and sat beside her at the breakfast bar.

"Well, what do you think?" asked Oz.

"Surprisingly, very delicious!" she said.

"I told you they were tasty," he said. "My mom used to make these for us growing up."

"Aww, really?" she said. "Are your parents still in Michigan?"

"Yeah, with my sister, her husband, and my two nephews," he said. "What about your family?

"Mom and Dad are still back in Ohio. I was an only child," she said.

"Were they sad when you moved out here?" asked Oz.

"God yes! You would have thought, by how they reacted, that they were never going to see me again, that I was moving to the other side of the world," she said.

"Well, you are their only baby. It makes sense," he said.

"Were your parents upset when you moved to Boston?" she asked.

"Mom was. Though I think she was more upset when I wanted to become a cop," he said. "She's a worrier."

"That was the perfect breakfast, officer," she said, laughing.

"Are you making fun of me?" he asked.

"No, really! It was yummy and so hit the spot," she said. She leaned over and gave him a kiss. "Now, Mr. Officer, I'm going to hop in the shower quickly."

"Enjoy, babe. I'll see you after," he said.

Donna went off to the bedroom to grab a couple of things before heading into the bathroom. Oz collected their plates, washed and dried them, along with the knives that he used to make the sandwiches. He tidied the kitchen and headed into the bedroom. He pulled a fresh pair of boxer briefs from the drawer and set them on the dresser.

Donna came out of the bathroom, towel wrapped around her, as she came into the bedroom. Oz couldn't help but stare at her. He pulled off his shirt and tossed it in the hamper.

"I'm gonna throw a quick load in the washer. Can I put anything in for you?" he asked, undoing his jeans.

"No, thanks. I'll throw a load in after work tomorrow," she said.

"Where did the weekend go?" he said.

"I know," she said.

"Are you staying over tonight?" he asked.

"As much as I would love to, I probably should go back to my place. Be fresh for work tomorrow," she said.

"Alright," he said.

He walked over and gave her a kiss as he took the hamper out to the stacked washer and dryer in the hall closet. He put a load of laundry in, came back into the bedroom and grabbed his underwear from the dresser, and headed into the bathroom.

The shower felt so good. Exactly what he needed. He could feel all the stiffness from sleeping on the bench in the waiting room melt away. He scrubbed away any of the blood that had dried on him. *Why did this thing go after Terry? Is this what it meant by me suffering? It was going to go after those that I care about? This has now become personal between us because I disrupted it?*

Oz got out of the shower, dried off, and walked back into the bedroom. Donna was in bed, under the covers. Oz lifted the covers and crawled in behind her, spooning against her. He slid his left arm under the pillow that supported her head, and his right arm over her, grasping her hand and pulling it to her chest. He kissed her on the neck. She moaned and wiggled her backside into him.

"I'm worried about you being alone tonight," he said.

"What do you mean?" she asked.

"I think that I should spend the night at your place, make sure that you are safe," he said.

"Ozzy, don't be silly. I'll be fine," she said.

"Are you really that ashamed of your place that you don't want me there?" he said.

"Not at all, babe. I always want to be with you, but honestly, I think that you are just scared because of what happened to Terry," she said.

"Is there anything wrong with being cautious?" he said.

"There is being cautious, and there is being overprotective," she said.

"Okay, Hun," he said. "Maybe you're right."

"Now, just hold me, and let's get some rest," she said.

Oz squeezed her tight and kissed her again on her neck. They drifted off to sleep, snuggled into each other.

***

Oz woke to the sound of the washer chiming its tune. Donna was still fast asleep. He slid out of bed, and quickly transferred the laundry from the washer to the dryer, and started it. He threw the last load of clothes into the washer and slid back into bed behind Donna.

Laid there next to her, his eyes closed. He couldn't shake this feeling that he had about her safety. This feeling was stronger than the feeling that he had the day of the attack at the Hatch Shell. *But why didn't I have the same feeling when Terry was attacked? He's like an older brother to me, my best friend.*

Oz had finally drifted off to sleep when the dryer chimed. He slid out of bed again and folded the clothes from the dryer and put them away. The washer chimed when he hung up the last shirt. He threw the remaining clothes into the dryer and went back to bed.

Did I get the feeling before Terry was attacked? Did I ignore it, or was I too preoccupied to notice? Could I have stopped this from happening? How do I even stop this thing if I do catch it? I know that the bullets hurt it, but not enough. Not even enough to slow it down. Do I need a bigger gun? Different bullets? Shockingly, he was able to fall back asleep cuddled up to Donna.

He woke again, this time to Donna caressing his face. He blinked his eyes, focusing them on her, and he smiled at her. The day's light seeped through the closed blinds, glowing behind her.

"What time is it?" he said.

"Does it matter?" she said.

"As long as it's not time for you to go, then no," he said.

"Did you manage to get some sleep?" she asked.

"Yeah. How about you?" he replied.

"Mmm, I slept great!" she said.

"Feeling recharged?" he asked.

"Absolutely. Must have been the toasted tomato sandwich," she laughed.

"You know you'll be begging for another one of my sandwiches very soon," laughed Oz.

"Begging, huh?" she said.

Oz pulled her against him and kissed her. She draped her leg over him as he grabbed a handful of cheek before he maneuvered so that he was on top of her. She moaned with his display of power, and ran her nails down his back.

25

Donna packed her things into her bag to take home, while Oz pulled the clothes out of the dryer, folded and put them away. He walked up behind her and draped himself over her, embracing her from behind.

"I don't want you to go," said Oz.

"Aww, Ozzy! I don't want to go, but I need to," she said.

"I know," he said. "I've really loved having you here so much this week."

"It's been amazing!" she said.

Donna zipped up her bag, and they walked out of the bedroom, down the hall to the entranceway. Oz carried her bag and set it down by the door. She put on her shoes and Oz helped her into her little denim jacket. He picked up her bag, and they walked down to her car that had been parked in one of the visitor's spots for days.

The sun had just withdrawn from view on the horizon. The sky clinging to what little light remained. The darkening hues of red and purple transformed into the night sky. Oz put her bag in the trunk of her car. She kissed him before opening the driver's door and getting in.

He leaned in and kissed her one last time before closing her door and sending her on her way.

Oz couldn't shake the sickly feeling in the pit of his stomach that this might be the last time that he saw her alive. The feeling was getting worse with every passing second. He walked back up to his apartment, grabbed his phone from the countertop, and sent Maureen a message, checking in on her and Terry. She replied a couple of minutes later, with a message that said she was fine and with Terry, who was in and out from the medication, but his spirits were well.

Maureen will probably stay with Terry until they kick her out, and even then, knowing her, she will kick up a fuss and stay just a while longer. I really just can't shake this feeling that something terrible is going to happen tonight.

Oz went to the bedroom and opened the safe in his closet. He pulled out his pistol, removed the clip, checked to make sure that he had a full 9 rounds in the magazine, and slid it back in. He checked the chamber, then slid the pistol back into the holster on the left side of his shoulder rig. He pulled the two reserve magazines from the right side of the shoulder, checked to make sure they were both fully stocked as well, before holstering them again.

Oz laid the stocked rig on the bed, returned to the closet, opened a footlocker that was stored on the floor. Inside was his Point Blank Executive Body Armor. A sleek black vest designed to be concealable and maneuverable.

Oz pulled the vest over top of his shirt, grabbed his shoulder rig from the bed, and put it on. He grabbed a beaded steel chain from the wooden tray that sat on his dresser for his badge. Returning to the kitchen, he clipped his badge onto the chain and put it on over his head, hanging the badge right in the center of his chest. He removed his police windbreaker from the closet near the entrance and put it on. With his keys in hand, he exited the apartment and headed down to his car.

"*Agony awaits you, Ozwald!*" the voice said.

Oz crooked his neck, making it crack as he tried to ignore the voice, and got in his car. He pulled out of the garage and headed for Donna's apartment. "*You will know true suffering and pain!*" said the voice. "*I can not be stopped!*"

The voice seemed to talk more the closer he got to Donna's place. "*Your partner got a taste! That was just the beginning!*"

Oz parked his car on the street, out in front of Donna's apartment. He looked around, trying to see anything odd. He knew that Donna's place was at the rear of the building, on the top floor of the two-story building.

Oz exited his car and closed the door gently. The night air was very still, and all was quiet. Oz made his way quietly to the building and around the back. He could see that the lights in Donna's place were on, but couldn't see any movement of shadows projecting against the window coverings. He pulled his cell phone from his back pocket and messaged Donna.

'*I miss you already,*' he wrote.

The sickly feeling in his stomach exacerbated waiting for the reply. *Come on, babe… answer!* Oz crept down to the parking lot at the back of the building, hopping over a wrought-iron fence and down a concrete embankment to get a better view of the windows of her apartment.

Oz looked around, trying again to see movement, unsuccessfully. He checked his phone. There was still no response. *Why the fuck is it so quiet?* Suddenly, a breeze kicked up, and he was hit with a putrid, musty odor. Oz crouched by a nearby car.

The smell increased and made his eyes water. He knew whatever it was; he was downwind of it. He was reminded of hunting deer with his father back in Michigan. His father constantly checked the direction of the wind, being sure to stay downwind of the buck they were tracking.

The breeze seemed to travel with this pungent odor, as if the source of the smell was also the source of the breeze, like an evolutionary advantage, allowing the predator to stay downwind of its prey. If this was the case, this gave him a tremendous advantage. He reached into his jacket, pulled his pistol from the holster. With his barrel pointed at the ground, Oz stayed crouched and moved along the side of the vehicle to see if he could get a better look at where the smell was coming from.

He peeked up across the hood of the car, across the parking lot, and he could see the large shadowy figure making its way towards the building. *If that thing is out here, then at least I know that Donna is just busy.* He glanced up at her balcony, and to his disappointment, he saw that the sliding door was cracked open a few inches. *What the fuck is she thinking?*

Oz clicked off the safety, getting ready to strike. Like a mongoose stalking a snake, he was going to have to keep the element of surprise, as this thing was dangerously fast and strong. He crept closer to the figure. As he did, it seemed to get smaller. Oz got within twenty feet of it when he watched it change its form. *What the fuck! Did I really just see that?* Instead of the 10-foot tall hooded figure he was following across the parking lot, he was now twenty feet from an average height male in a black hoodie and jeans, with a menacing look, but definitely human. Oz reached into his pocket, unlocked his phone, looking for a reply, with no luck. He opened another app and tapped the screen before pressing the power button and returning the phone to his pocket.

The man approached the illuminated walkway from the light above the rear entrance to the building. He approached the door and pulled on the handle. The door opened as if it were not locked or latched. Oz popped from cover as the man pulled the door open.

"Freeze!" said Oz. "Don't move!"

The man turned around.

"Don't do it, Price! I'm warning you!" said Oz.

"Nathaniel Price is no more, Ozwald!" said the man. The voice was dark, evil, and threatening.

Looking the man in the eyes, Oz saw this. This was just a vessel in front of him. The eyes were glowing orange, as if the sockets were filled with flames. He approached Oz.

"If you aren't Nathaniel anymore, then who are you?" asked Oz.

"I am Azazel," he said.

"Azazel, huh? And what makes you so special?"

"How dare you! You're just a weak mortal! I am one of the seven princes of Hell!" said Azazel.

"You just look like a human to me," Oz said sarcastically.

"You mock me? Have you not seen enough of what I am capable of?" said Azazel?

"I've seen your work, torturing and killing all of those innocent people. But if you're so powerful, why are you always hiding in the shadows?" asked Oz.

"Innocent? None of you are innocent?" said Azazel.

"None of them seemed evil or bad to me, or their friends and families," said Oz.

"And I thought your partner was the tougher of the two of you. How quickly I learned the opposite when I carved him up, and he cried for his mother," said Azazel, taking a step toward Oz.

"I said don't move!" demanded Oz.

"Or what, Officer Friendly? You'll shoot me again?" said Azazel.

"It stopped you before," said Oz.

"Did it? Then why am I here now? You can never stop me," said Azazel.

"We'll see, asshole! I'm gonna send you back to whatever Hell you came from," said Oz.

"This would be an impressive feat for someone as spiritually void as you are," Said Azazel.

"Spiritual or not, just give me a reason to fill out the paperwork for pulling the trigger," said Oz.

"I am going to enjoy killing you slowly," said Azazel, taking another step towards Oz. "After I use your little woman to bring forth my beloved."

Bang!

Oz fired a single round into Azazel's left shoulder. He let out a blood-curdling screech as the bullet seared and forced its way into the flesh. He stepped back, grimaced, and stared at Oz. Lights in the apartments turned on after the sound of the shot.

"Silly mortal, you will suffer for that!" said Azazel. He stood up and stepped to Oz again.

Bang!

Oz fired another round, this one hitting him square in the right knee. The .40 caliber round exploded the joint on impact from this range. Azazel screeched again and dropped, clutching at his knee.

"Sure seems like this hurts?" said Oz.

"Oz? Is that you? What is going on?" Donna yelled from her balcony.

"Back inside, Hun! Close and lock the doors!" he yelled up to her, not moving his eyes from the downed Azazel.

"Hey, what's going on out there?" yelled a tenant from the neighboring balcony.

"Sir, I'm Detective Shields, Boston PD. For your safety, please go back inside," said Oz.

"What's happening?" she said again.

"Just do it! Please!" he pleaded.

The tone of his voice was serious and stern. Donna and the neighboring tenant receded back into their apartments and closed the door.

"Such an obedient woman! She will make the perfect vessel for my goddess!" said Azazel, trying to get to his feet.

"Shut up! Stay the fuck down!" said Oz.

"Together we will open the gates of Hell, and bring forth the end of your world," said Azazel.

Bang!

Oz fired a third bullet into the left knee. Azazel dropped, as if he was about to pray to a higher power. Oz approached cautiously. Azazel screeched in pain again.

Onlookers watched from behind curtains inside their apartments.

"Could being in this weak human body have its downside?" said Oz.

Azazel screamed in frustration and anger, trying to stand. Pools of black blood oozed from the wounds. Sirens could be heard approaching. Someone from the building must have called 9-1-1 when he fired the first shot.

"Oh good! Here comes the cavalry. Maybe I'll just put you down now, and save us all the trouble," said Oz.

"You'll never kill me! I'm immortal!" said Azazel, snarling at Oz. "This body is just a doorway to your world. Strike me down, and I will be back."

"I may not be able to kill you, but I'll never stop trying," said Oz, lifting his pistol and pointing the barrel between the eyes of the being in front of him.

Oz pulled the trigger. Azazel's head was forced back from the impact of the bullet. The bullet exited the skull, spraying the wall behind him with blood and matter. Oz fired 2 more rounds into the chest. The flaming eyes extinguished as the body crumpled lifelessly to the ground.

Oz holstered his pistol and pulled his cell phone from his pocket. He swiped it to unlock and stopped the recorder that he had running. Donna came rushing to the back door. She was wearing a short t-shirt and pajama pants, her hair pulled back in a ponytail. She pushed open the door and ran out to him.

"What is going on?" she asked.

"This is our killer," said Oz.

"I thought you said he was ten feet tall?" she said.

"I know, and moments before I shot him, he was," said Oz.

"Babe, you're talking crazy right now," she said.

"I'll explain later. Right now, I have to figure out how this was a justified shooting because he is unarmed," said Oz. "You should go back inside, Hun."

"No way, I'm not going anywhere," she said. "Your positive. This is the killer?"

"I have him confessing to cutting up Terry," he said, waving his phone.

"That won't be enough?" she asked.

"Not these days," he said.

The first cruiser rolled up on the scene. Lights flashing and illuminating the street. Oz turned to greet the incoming officer with his badge on display.

"Detective Shields, Homicide," he said.

"Detective! What happened here?" asked the officer.

"I spotted a murder suspect entering this building," said Oz.

"And how did he end up dead?" asked the officer.

"I shot him," said Oz.

"Obviously. Was he armed?" asked the officer.

"It doesn't appear so," said Oz.

"What were you doing here?" asked the officer.

"I had a hunch that something bad was going to happen here tonight," said Oz.

"I'm not gonna sugar coat it, Detective, this looks really bad," said the officer.

"I don't disagree," said Oz.

"You… uh… wanna call your lieutenant?" asked the Officer.

"Probably not a bad idea," said Oz.

"Look, Detective, I'll do what I can for you, but you gotta give me something here."

"I have a recording of him admitting to carving up a detective, who's laying in the hospital as we speak," said Oz.

"This fucker cut up a cop?" asked the officer.

"Not just a cop, but a good cop, and my partner," said Oz.

"I gotta call in, Detective, but while I do, I suggest you call Lieutenant," said the officer.

"Thanks, Officer," said Oz.

Oz dialed Jim from his recent calls. The phone rang twice before the Lieutenant picked up the call.

"Oz? What's going on?" asked Jim.

"Sir, I got the killer and the guy that cut up Terry," said Oz.

"Great work, kid!" said Jim.

"Could be better, sir," said Oz.

"Why?" Jim asked, the elation leaving his tone.

"I have an audio confession of him cutting Terry up, but he's unarmed sir… and… uh… I killed him," said Oz.

"Where are you right now?" asked Jim.

"Outside of Donna's building, Wait Street and Pequot Street," said Oz.

"Don't say a fucking word to anyone. I'm on my way," Jim said.

"Yes, sir," said Oz. Oz hung up the call as the officer returned.

"Did you get him?" asked the officer.

"Yeah, I did. He's on his way," said Oz. "What's your name?"

"Gibbs, Aiden Gibbs," said the officer.

"Gibbs, good to meet you. Listen, I can't ask you to stick your neck out for me, man," said Oz.

"Let me hear that recording, and you won't be." said Aiden.

Oz unlocked his phone and handed it to the officer. He took off his windbreaker and put it around Donna. The officer listened to the entire conversation and handed back the phone.

"So, your girlfriend called you because she heard some strange noises, so you came right over. You saw this guy heading into the building, you confronted him, and it sounds like he gave you a full confession, and threatened a peace officer. That's how this all sounds to me." said Aiden.

"Thanks, but that still doesn't get me out of shooting an unarmed suspect six times," said Oz.

"True. Let's just wait and see what your lieutenant has to say," said Aiden. "For now, I've called off all other units. The paramedics are still on their way."

Tenants began collecting inside the door to the building, all trying to get a glimpse at what had happened. Officer Gibbs headed over to them and attempt to get them all to return to their homes.

***

"Oz," said Jim as he exited his car.

"Yes, sir," said Oz.

Jim walked over to Oz, Donna, and Officer Gibbs, looked down at the body on the ground and assessed the situation.

"Six shots, kid?" said Jim.

"Wanted to make sure he was dead, sir," said Oz.

"Donna, Hun. How are you?" asked Jim.

"A little shaken. Apparently this thing was here for me," she said.

"What can you tell me, kid?" asked Jim.

"Well sir, just like the other night with the Hatch Shell, I had this feeling that I just couldn't shake, that Donna was in danger. And that after I interrupted this thing the other night, it told me it was going to make me sorry for that. He started with Terry, and was going to go after Donna next," said Oz.

"Alright, so a hunch has you here at the scene. Cops follow hunches all the time," said Jim. "Then what happened."

"I pulled up out front and messaged Donna. I waited for a reply, and when I didn't get one, I got out of the car and went around back to see if I could see her moving around her apartment," said Oz. "I couldn't see her shadow moving around, and there was still no reply from her. I smelled this musty odor, like the one that the vic from the Hatch Shell described to Terry and me. I crouched behind a vehicle, and that is what I saw: this massive figure walking towards the building. I snuck closer for a better look, and as I got closer, it was transforming back into… him. The blood found at the Hatch Shell scene from FSD is a perfect match for this man, Nathaniel Price. I unlocked my phone, started a voice recording, and then, well, once I had confirmation from him he was our killer, well… the rest is history."

"Let me hear that recording," said Jim.

Oz unlocked the phone and handed it to Jim. He listened to the recording twice before handing the phone back to Oz. Jim reached up and ran his fingers through his snow-white hair and scratched his head, thinking.

"This is gonna be a bit of a tough sell, kid. But I'll do all that I can for you. This is, after all, our killer. FSD will be able to confirm that for us," said Jim. "But since he was unarmed, you're probably gonna be off for two weeks, without pay."

"Honestly, sir, if that is the least that happens, I'm ok with it. I made sure that this guy isn't going to hurt anyone else."

"I may have to call in a few favors with BPSD, but I agree with you, kid. All of Boston will sleep better with this cawksuckah dead," said Jim.

"Trooper?" asked Jim.

"Gibbs, sir," said Aiden.

"What's your take on this?" asked Jim.

"My take sir?" asked Aiden.

"Yeah, how do you plan on reporting this?" asked Jim.

"Like I told the Detective, his girlfriend called him because she heard some strange noises, so he came right over. He saw this guy heading into the building, he confronted him and based on the recording that guy threatened a peace officer, and the Detective defended himself from a dangerous criminal," said Aiden.

"Good boy," said Jim. "I'll make sure that you're looked after."

"No need, sir. The Detective was just doing his job. And so am I," said Aiden.

Jim patted Officer Gibbs on the shoulder, then reached into his jacket and pulled out his cell phone. He made a call and walked away, just out of earshot of them. When he returned, he was smiling.

"I didn't expect to see you smiling, sir," said Oz.

"I just got off the phone with the Herald, gave them the scoop that ah mystery killer has been put down tonight by Detective Shields, thanks to his hard work and dedication," said Jim. "This will make BPSD less likely to dig into this. Either way though, tomorrow morning we will go to them, first thing. We won't wait for them to come to us."

"Yes, sir," said Oz.

"Great job, kid. No matter what, I'm proud of you!" said Jim. "Trooper Gibbs. I look forward to reading your report."

"Yes, sir," said Officer Gibbs.

The paramedics arrived on-scene and hopped out of the ambulance. Jim walked over to meet them. Since he was the highest-ranking officer on site, he was controlling the scene. Jim informed the paramedics that the suspect was deceased so that they could prepare for transporting a dead body. The paramedic in charge radioed back to dispatch to inform them that the patient is deceased and to notify the Medical Examiner.

"Why don't you go back upstairs, Hun," said Oz.

"I'm not leaving you," said Donna.

"You've got work in the morning. It doesn't sound like I'm going to be working a full day. So please, go get your rest. I'll be fine," said Oz.

"Ozzy…" said Donna.

Oz placed his hands on the side of her face, stared into her eyes so that she could see exactly what he was thinking and feeling when he spoke with her.

"Donna, please! Go get yourself ready for tomorrow, try to get some sleep. I'll speak with you tomorrow," said Oz.

He kissed her on the lips, then held her tight in his arms. She wrapped her arms around him and didn't let go.

"You sure that you are going to be fine?" asked Donna.

"Importantly, you're safe. I'll be fine," said Oz. "Now go, get a good sleep."

"Okay, Ozzy! Call me tomorrow?" said Donna.

"You know I will," said Oz.

He kissed her one more time before saying goodnight. Donna went back into the building and headed up to bed. Oz walked over to the Lieutenant, who was standing with Officer Gibbs.

"Oz. It's all good, kid. Why don't you go home, get some rest, and we'll go and see BPSD in the morning," said Jim.

"Are you sure, sir?" said Oz.

"Why? You wanna shoot more people tonight?" joked Jim. "Go, I've got this. Don't worry. You got our guy, that is the most important thing."

"Yes, sir," said Oz. "Sorry for the extra hassle."

"Would you go already? I'll take care of this, and see you first thing," said Jim.

"Yes, sir. Thank you. Goodnight," said Oz, as he started to walk towards his car.

"Oh, and Oz!" shouted Jim.

"Yes, sir?" replied Oz.

"Coffee, regular. Thanks!" said Jim.

"You got it, Lieutenant," said Oz.

Oz walked back to his car and got in. He sat there a moment in the driver's seat, staring out the windshield. *Went a little overboard tonight, Ozzy! Six fucking shots? Really? Didn't think it through, did you? A shot to the shoulder and head would have been plenty. Now, your dumb ass has to try to sell this to BPSD. Good luck with that.* Oz sighed, started the car, and headed for home.

26

Oz arrived at the station with two large regular coffees from Dunkin'. He walked upstairs to the detective pool, past his desk, and straight to the door of the Lieutenant's office. He knocked on the door. Jim looked up from his computer, removed his reading glasses, and smiled when he saw Oz at the door with his hands full of coffee.

"You're a good kid," said Jim.

"Regular, just like you asked for, sir," said Oz.

Oz entered the office and handed Jim the coffee before sitting in one of the chairs on the opposite side of the desk from him. He took a sip of his coffee and sat nervously, bouncing his right leg, waiting for what was to come.

"I called Maureen to see how Terry was doing. She said he's still heavily drugged, but she said if he may be able to come home by the end of the week," said Jim.

"That is great news!" said Oz. "I was going to go over and see him after work, or earlier, depending on what happens."

"Oz, it will be okay. Trust me," said Jim. "Let me make a call."

Jim picked up his phone and made a call. Oz couldn't hear who he was speaking with, but he figured it was someone with the Bureau of Professional Standards and Development. Oz could feel his stomach churning. He was a ball of nerves. He knew he killed the killer, but he wasn't sure how the BPSD was going to see it. Especially since the killer was unarmed. It didn't matter that he had a nearly full confession recorded. Jim hung up the phone and looked at Oz.

"Put on your dancing shoes, kid. It's showtime," said Jim.

Jim stood up, grabbed his suit jacket from the coat rack in the corner behind his desk, and put it on. He adjusted it before he buttoned it up. Oz stood up. His legs felt like rubber. Like they could give out at any moment. Jim grabbed his coffee off the desk and walked around to Oz. He put his hand on Oz's shoulder.

"C'mon, kid. Let's do this," said Jim.

Oz took a deep breath and followed Jim out of the office and down the hall to the elevator. They took the elevator to the top floor. Every time the elevator notified them they were on the next floor, Oz's stomach turned over. Jim could sense Oz's nerves and put his hand on Oz's shoulder.

"Take a breath, kid. Just go in there and answer their questions. Don't say anything more than that. They have my report, and Trooper Gibbs' report," said Jim.

"Yes, sir," said Oz.

The elevator doors opened and Jim guided Oz out and down the hall to the Bureau of Professional Standards and Development. The office was completely encased in partially frosted glass. The division's crest was etched into the glass double doors as you entered the department.

Jim opened the door, Oz entered the office, Jim followed him in, and they walked up to the reception desk. The receptionist behind the desk was a dark-haired woman in her 40s, her hair was pulled back into a tight bun, and she looked up from her desk and her glacier blue eyes and bright smile greeted the two men.

"Good morning, Gentlemen, how may I assist you?" she said.

"Lieutenant Roberts and Detective Shields, here to see Dan De Luca," said Jim.

"Sure, just a minute," she said.

She picked up the phone on her desk and dialed a four-digit extension. The phone rang twice before she began to speak. She informed Dan De Luca that Jim and Oz were there to see him. Hanging up the phone, she told Oz and Jim to take a seat on the chairs in the lobby, and he would be right with them. Oz and Jim grabbed a seat while they waited for Dan.

Dan De Luca was a lieutenant with the BPSD. He was 59 years old and had an immaculate record as an officer in Boston with over 30 years of service. He was 6' tall, and silver-haired, and fit. His suit was perfectly tailored to fit his physique. He came out to the reception area and greeted Oz and Jim.

"Gentlemen, thank you for coming," said Dan. "Please, right this way.

Jim and Oz stood up and followed Dan to a conference room behind the reception area. Dan opened the glass door to the conference room, holding it open for them. Jim and

Oz entered and took a seat at a large, dark-stained oak conference table in the middle of the room surrounded by eight desk chairs. Dan sat across from them at the table, where a file folder was placed. Dan opened the folder and pulled a pen out of his suit jacket.

"Detective Shields, thank you for volunteering to come in and see us this morning. This should go smoothly," said Dan, giving Oz a small smile.

"Absolutely, sir. I have nothing to hide," said Oz.

"Perfect. So let's get right into it then, shall we?" said Dan.

"It says here in the report that 'Nathaniel Price', the victim of last night's shooting, was the suspect for seven murders, assaults of…" said Dan, as he paused searching for the name in the file. "A 'Miss Shannon Russo' and 'Detective White'."

"I think it is more the attempted murder of Shannon Russo and Detective White, sir," said Oz.

"Right. And you have evidence that this is your suspect?" asked Dan.

"Yes sir. There was traceable blood evidence from Mr. Price at the scene of the crime with Shannon Russo, and I have a recorded confession from him on my phone from last night," said Oz.

"Did Nathaniel know he was being recorded?" asked Dan.

"No sir. Since I didn't have a body cam and the fact that I was alone, I thought it was best to record the events just in case something were to happen to me. It was not planned to get a confession from him. That occurred under his own free will," said Oz.

"There is a chance that this recording may be inadmissible," said Dan.

"Inadmissible? Are you fucking kidding me?" erupted Jim. "This cawksuckah killed innocent people, and harmed a cop. My Detective, there is no way that this recording is not gonna be the nail in the coffin for this sick son of a bitch."

"Please, Jim. Let me just do my job. If you keep erupting like this, I will have to ask you to leave," said Dan.

"Sorry, Dan! I'm good," said Jim.

"May I hear the recording, Detective Shields?" asked Dan.

Oz pulled out his phone and played the recording, laying his phone down on the table. Dan listened intently as the events unfolded on the recording and made notes while it played out. The recording ended, and Dan sat back in his chair and held his pen to his lip, in thought about how he would proceed.

"Well?" said Jim.

"I'm not going to say that we can't accept this recording as evidence. I can't ignore the confessions on it. But…" said Dan. "In the recording, he claims to be a prince of hell. This could be seen as evidence of insanity."

"Crazy people have killed before, this isn't new," said Jim. "Is anyone mounting a defense for this killing?"

"No. There was no next of kin to notify. But it will only take a bleeding heart attorney to get wind of this, and they might," said Dan.

"So let's squash this," said Jim.

"Detective Shields, why did you fire so many rounds?" asked Dan.

"Well sir, the first round was planned in a non-lethal location, to halt his movement towards me, knowing how dangerous this man was. The next two shots were targeted to keep him alive, but to ensure that he would stop progressing toward me. Seeing that this was only making him more enraged, I put him down," said Oz.

"So you felt threatened?" asked Dan.

"Yes, sir. My partner was armed, and you saw what this man was able to do to him," said Oz. "I did what I felt I needed to do, sir, to make sure that this dangerous person could not cause further harm. It's there on the recording, I provided clear direction to halt."

"You did. I will agree," said Dan. "I'd like to bring FSD in on this if I can. Do you mind? I will call them right here from the conference phone?"

"Not at all, sir. Please go right ahead. I have nothing to hide," said Oz.

Dan called down to FSD. The phone rang three times before Jared answered the call.

"FSD, this is Jared," he said.

"Jared, this is Lieutenant De Luca with BPSD. Do you have some time to answer a couple of questions?" asked Dan.

"Absolutely, sir," said Jared.

"The victim of last night's officer-involved shooting. Do we have a confirmed ID?" asked Dan.

"Yes sir, the victim was identified by the ME as Nathaniel Price," said Jared.

"And I have been informed that Nathaniel Price's DNA was found to be a match for some evidence collected at one of the crime scenes. The attack on Shannon Russo at the Hatch Shell?" asked Dan.

"Yes sir, that is correct," said Jared.

"Anything notable with this victim that we should be made aware of?" asked Dan.

"Funny that you ask, sir. As hard as it may be to believe, the ME has informed us this morning that the victim had been dead for at least 10 days," said Jared.

"But he was shot last night?" said Dan.

"That is correct, sir," said Jared.

"How is this possible?" asked Dan.

"Well, sir, I don't have an answer for that. What I can say is that the samples that we collected from the Hatch Shell were depleted of oxygen, and had the consistency of blood found in a corpse. I couldn't exactly explain it to Detective Shields at the time either, but it was noted in the case file," said Jared.

"Thank you, Jared. I appreciate you taking the time to speak with me," said Dan.

"No problem, sir," said Jared.

Dan hung up the phone, sat back in his chair again, pressed his pen to his lips, tapped it while he was deep in thought. Oz and Jim just sat there in silence. Dan closed the file folder, clicked his pen, and put it back in his jacket.

"Detective Shields, I can find no reason to proceed with this investigation any further. If anyone would like to charge you with the desecration of a corpse, then this investigation may be re-opened. Other than that, can you send me that recording?" said Dan.

"Sure, I'll send it right over. So, that is, it?" said Oz. "I'm free to resume normal duties?" asked Oz.

"That will be up to your lieutenant, but as far as I am concerned, this investigation is closed," said Dan.

"Thank you, Lieutenant," said Oz.

Oz and Jim stood up and shook Dan's hand. They walked out of the conference room, headed back towards the elevator. Jim pressed the button, calling for the elevator.

"I told you there was nothing to worry about, kid," said Jim.

"Only because you can't kill a dead guy, sir. Otherwise, I was screwed," said Oz.

"Same shit," said Jim.

"How many cases can we close on this?" asked Jim as they stepped into the elevator.

"All six. Just the one vic at the baseball diamond that we don't know the identity of, but it wouldn't be the first case closed to a John Doe," said Oz.

"Great! Why don't you close as many as you can and then take the rest of the day off? Go see Ter, and check on Maureen," said Jim.

"Are you sure?" asked Oz.

"Yeah. I don't want him getting used to life without you. You two are a good duo," said Jim.

"Thanks, Lieutenant," said Oz.

The elevator doors slid open now that they were back on the second floor. Jim walked out of the elevator first and Oz right behind him as they headed back into the detective's pool.

"I've known Terry many years, and I think that you're the first partner that he has had in a long time, that he didn't ask me to transfer after two days. That's saying something," said Jim. "Glad things went our way this morning."

Jim patted Oz on the back and went into his Office. Oz went to his desk and sat down. He pulled his phone from his pocket and messaged Donna, letting her know how things went this morning, and that he hoped that she was having a good day.

Oz turned on his computer and logged in. One by one he went through the case files, entering the identity of the perpetrator into the reports and closing them. Oz's desk phone rang. The call display showed an outside number assigned to the Office of the Medical Examiner.

"Detective Shields, homicide," he said, answering the call.

"Oz, it's Brad. Can you talk?" asked Brad.

"Yeah, what's up?" asked Oz.

"So I was doing the exam on the body that they brought us last night…" said Brad.

"Yeah, if this is about all the bullet holes, I apologize," said Oz.

"No, if only that was my problem," said Brad.

"What's up?" asked Oz.

"Well, I've found some really strange things," said Brad.

"Stranger than the fact that he was dead 10 days before I shot him?" asked Oz.

"Well, yeah. Weirder than that is that there are some interesting marks all over his body… like stretch marks," said Brad. "How soon can you get down here?"

"I was just closing case files. I can be there in like ten minutes," said Oz.

"Great, I'll let the receptionist know that I'm expecting you," said Brad.

***

Oz entered the reception area of the Office of the Medical Examiner and proceeded to the front desk. He presented his badge to the receptionist.

"He's expecting you, Detective. I'll buzz you in through those doors there," she said.

"Thank you," said Oz.

He walked through the doors to the right of reception, headed to Brad's office, and knocked on the door. Brad looked up from his computer, pushed his glasses up his nose.

"Oz, thanks for coming down here so quickly," said Brad as he got up from behind his desk.

"It sounded like this was important," said Oz.

"Y... Y... Yes, very. Come, come with me," said Brad.

Oz followed Brad down the hall to one of the exam rooms. In the middle of the room, under a white sheet, was the body of Nathaniel Price. Brad grabbed a pair of blue nitrile gloves, put them on, and walked over to the body, and pulled back the sheet, exposing the upper half.

"What did you need to show me, Brad?" asked Oz.

"These..." said Brad. "See these marks here and here?"

He pointed out elongated marks on the body.

"Stretch marks?" asked Oz.

"When was the last time you saw stretch marks on a skinny guy?" asked Brad.

"What are they then?" asked Oz.

"That's just it. They appear to be stretch marks, but the length of them is extreme. Almost as if he doubled in size or something," said Brad.

"This is going to sound crazy, but I was twenty feet from him when he transformed from this massive ten-foot monster down to… well, this," said Oz.

"Are you messing with me?" asked Brad.

"If only. I feel even crazier saying it out loud," said Oz.

"Not any crazier than I sounded, telling everyone that this guy was dead at least ten days before you shot him," said Brad.

"Yeah, how is that possible? I spoke with this guy before I shot him," said Oz. "I recorded the whole thing."

"You did?" said Brad. "Can I hear it?"

"Sure, I don't see why not," said Oz.

Oz pulled his phone from his jacket pocket and played the recording for Brad. He listened to the recording like a kid listening to a radio program in the '40s. His attention was fully captured by the back-and-forth exchange between Oz and the dead man.

"That's unbelievable!" said Brad. "This man was possessed?"

"That's what he was claiming," said Oz.

"You said that you saw him morph?" asked Brad.

"Yeah! He shrunk as he approached the light from the building," said Oz.

"This was the second time that you saw him?" asked Brad.

"Yeah, the first time I saw him was days before at the Hatch Shell, where I shot it three times in the chest," said Oz.

"That would explain the nine bullets that I removed from the body," said Brad.

"So I hurt it before?" said Oz.

"I don't know about that," said Brad. "I recovered three bullets from the chest, but there were no signs of entry wounds."

"How is that possible?" asked Oz.

"I'm spitballing here, but when you first shot him, was he human or monster?" asked Brad.

"He was huge, I interrupted it," said Oz.

"Maybe that has something to do with it. When it was morphed into the creature, it was invulnerable, and when it was in its human form it was vulnerable," said Brad.

"So, by shooting it in its human form, it was like killing the host?" asked Oz.

"In a sense, yes. As much as the host body was already dead, or mostly dead, this demon needed the body," said Brad. "In the recording, he called it a doorway to our world."

"That's interesting," said Oz.

"And maybe, this is why the killings seemed to evolve. As it passed more into our world, it transformed this body, until it could remain in our world fully," said Brad.

"With each murder, it grew stronger and changed more. That this body really was just a vessel to our world?" said Oz.

"Certainly seems that way, and you just managed to kill it when it was most vulnerable," said Brad.

"Huh, that's interesting," said Oz. "Did you find anything else during your examination?"

"To go along with the elongated marks on the flesh, the bones were also strange, the marrow was depleted, so they were hollow, but they were also rubbery. That's a bad term. There was evidence of osteomalacia, which is a softening of the bones because of calcium and vitamin D deficiencies. This may have aided with the rapid growth of the being," said Brad.

"So bizarre," said Oz.

"You can say that again," said Brad. "So what is going to happen to you? I heard he was unarmed when you shot him."

"Well, thankfully you can't kill a dead man, so I'm off the hook, so to speak. Unless someone wants to come after me for desecration of a corpse," said Oz.

"That is a relief," said Brad. "If this is, in fact, our killer, then I, personally, don't care how he was stopped, it's just more important that he has been stopped."

"Yeah. I have to agree with you there," said Oz.

"How is your partner?" asked Brad.

"Recovering. They think he may get released from the hospital by the end of the week," said Oz. "I'm heading over to see him after I leave here."

"That's good news. Give him my best. I'll let you know if anything else comes up," said Brad.

"Will do, Brad. Thanks again for your help," said Oz.

"Anytime, Oz. Thanks for coming down here and helping me fill in some gaps," said Brad.

"No worries," said Oz.

Oz shook Brad's hand and left the exam room and headed down the hall to the double doors. When he got outside to his car, he pulled out his phone from his pocket and called Maureen.

"Oz? Is everything okay?" she said, answering the call.

"I should be asking you that," said Oz.

"We're fine, Hun," said Maureen.

"I'm on my way to come and see Terry. Can I bring you anything?" asked Oz.

"No, thanks, Hun. I'm fine," she said.

"Tell that cawksuckah, he better not show up without my Dunkees!" said Terry in the background.

"Tell Terry that the nurses have informed me it is not a good idea for him to have that right now," said Oz, laughing.

"God, as if he isn't in enough pain," she said. "I'll see you soon, Hun."

"Alright, Maureen, see you shortly," said Oz, hanging up the phone.

***

Oz walked into the room with a large coffee in hand, set it down on the small over-bed rolling table in front of Terry. He turned to Maureen, who was sitting bedside, and gave her a hug and a kiss on the cheek.

"You're a lifesaver, kid," said Terry. "Maureen told me you caught the cawksuckah?"

"Shot him dead, outside of Donna's apartment," said Oz.

"Atta boy!" said Terry. "So, did BPSD take your badge away?"

"Nope, apparently there is nothing they can do if I kill a dead guy," said Oz.

"What?" said Terry, puzzled.

"The ME said that the man that I shot, died ten days earlier," said Oz.

"You're fucking with me?" said Terry.

"How is possible?" asked Maureen.

"I wish I knew?" said Oz. "If you think that is crazy, I spoke with the dead guy before I shot him," said Oz.

"Who gives a shit, he's dead, and now we can move on," said Terry.

"Speaking of other shit, how are you feeling, old man?" joked Oz.

"Much better now that I've got a Dunkees in my hand," joked Terry. "Can't wait to get outta here."

"How's life on the morphine?" asked Oz.

"I'd suck a cock for a good shit right about now. I'm so fucking backed up," joked Terry. "I'll be glad to get off it."

"Jim said that you may be able to come home by Friday?" said Oz.

"I'm hoping for sooner than that," said Terry.

"How are you holding up, Maureen?" asked Oz.

"I'm alright, Hun. It's hard not having Ter at home," she said.

"Can I do anything for you? Get you anything?" asked Oz.

"So sweet, Oz! But I'm good, Hun. Thank you," she said.

"Anything you need, Maureen. Please don't hesitate. I mean it!" said Oz.

Maureen reached over, grabbed, and squeezed Oz's hand. Oz looked at her and gave a warm and comforting smile.

"What are you doing with the rest of your day, kid," asked Terry.

"Go home and take it easy. Nothing else really to do," said Oz.

"Where's your girl?" asked Terry.

"Working," laughed Oz.

"What does she do?" asked Maureen.

"She's the Administrative Assistant for the DA," said Oz.

"A working girl, huh?" said Terry.

"Yeah, today is her first full day of work. All this went down outside her apartment last night as she was getting ready for today," said Oz. "She's going to be exhausted today."

"Why was the killer outside her place?" asked Terry.

"Same reason he targeted you," said Oz.

"What do you mean?" asked Terry.

"I interrupted him at the Hatch. I pissed him off. I also shot him, and hurt him," said Oz. "This was him getting back at me. Attacking you, going after Donna. Trying to make me suffer, by attacking those I care about."

"This didn't happen to me because of anything that you did, kid," said Terry.

"That's sweet of you to say, Terry, but this is because of me. I'm so sorry. Both of you. I'm so sorry," said Oz. "I should have been there to stop this. I should have been there to keep this from happening."

"Oz! I'm alive because of you! You have nothing to be sorry for. You hear me?" said Terry. "Nothing. I made the call to go alone. I could have called you to join me. I didn't.

I was a dummy and went in alone. And you saved me from that mistake. I owe you my life."

"You don't owe me anything, Ter," said Oz. "You're my partner, I'd live and die a million times for you, man."

"I know you would, kid. That's why you're a great cop and an even better partner," said Terry.

"I'd hug you if you weren't so jacked up right now," said Oz.

"The coffee is good enough, kid," said Terry.

"Do either of you need anything?" asked Oz.

"Nah, kid. We're good," said Terry. "Are you leaving already?"

"Yeah, I'll leave you lovebirds alone. You don't need me being a third wheel here," said Oz. "I've already said it, but I mean it, if you need anything at all, just let me know."

"Thanks, Oz!" said Terry.

"I love you both, take care of yourselves, okay?" said Oz.

"You too, kid," said Terry. "Have a good night, say hi to Donna for us."

"For sure, will do. Take care, guys," said Oz.

He leaned down, hugged Maureen, and kissed her on the cheek. She squeezed him long and hard, so grateful for what he had done for them. Oz stood up, grabbed and squeezed Terry's hand, and giving him a smile before he left.

27

Ring... Ring... Ring...

"Hey, Hun! How'd it go today?" asked Oz.

"Hey, Ozzy! It was busy, but more importantly, how did you get on?" said Donna.

"You can't get into trouble for killing a dead guy, so I'm good," said Oz.

"What? That doesn't make any sense?" He wasn't dead," said Donna.

"Apparently he was dead before I shot him," said Oz. "Are you home?"

"Just got in the door," she said.

"Any plans for dinner?" asked Oz.

"Hadn't even given it a single thought. I'm kinda wiped," she said.

"How about I grab us a pizza and bring it over?" he asked.

"Ozzy, you're a doll, but you really don't have to do that," she said.

"I just want to be with you," said Oz. "You're already tired, and just got home, so it doesn't make any sense for you to come here. What do you say?"

"I can't say no to seeing you," said Donna.

"So, what would you like on your pizza?" said Oz.

"Meat, lots of meat," said Donna.

"You really are like no woman I've ever met," said Oz. "See you in about thirty minutes?"

"If you're late, do I get it for free?" joked Donna.

"If I'm late, take the whole thing and tell me to leave," said Oz.

"Guess you better not be late then," laughed Donna. "I'm gonna hop in the shower. See you soon!"

They hung up the phone. Oz called the little pizza shop down the street from his place and ordered a large meat lover's pizza. It was a delicious, thick, but light crust pizza, doused in the most savory tomato sauce covered with a healthy layer of mozzarella cheese, pepperoni, bacon, sausage slices, and meatballs.

Oz grabbed his wallet and keys off the breakfast bar and left the apartment. He walked a short distance down the street to the pizza place. The owner of the pizza parlor was at the cash register, his white apron stained with tomato sauce. His name was Giuseppe Romano, but everyone in the neighborhood called him "Little Joe". Little Joe was anything but little. He was about 325 lbs, and 5'8" tall. He was bald and had a thick bushy gray mustache and the ends were twisted and curled up with mustache wax. He smiled at Oz when he saw him walk in the door.

"Detective, how are you?" said Little Joe, in a thick Italian accent. "I've not seen you around for some time now!"

"Joe, I'm good, how are you?" said Oz. "How's Maria?"

"Ahh, she's a pain in my ass as always," said Little Joe.

"I heard that," said Maria from the back kitchen area.

"Evening, Maria," shouted Oz.

Maria came out of the back with Oz's pizza fresh from the oven, sliced, and boxed up, and set it on the counter. Maria came around the counter, pulled Oz down, hugged him, gave him a kiss on the cheek, and then pinched his cheek between her fingers.

She was Little Joe's wife and an absolute sweetheart. She was 5'2" heavy set, and bandy-legged, and waddled when she walked, troubled by arthritis in her knees. Her dyed black hair always curled and kept under her hairnet. She and Little Joe had been married for 52 years. They picked on each other a lot, but anyone who knew them knew they would be lost without each other.

"How's my boy, Ozzy?" said Maria. "I saw you on the TV the other week, you looked so handsome."

"I'm good, Maria. How are you?" said Oz.

"Well, you haven't been called to take me away for killing that lump of shit, so I'm good," said Maria. "Who's the pizza for, Ozzy, it's not your usual."

"It's for me and my new girlfriend," said Oz.

"Aww, you found a nice Italian girl?" asked Maria.

"Maria, why are you busting his balls? Ozzy, forget about her," said Little Joe.

"No, Maria. She's not Italian, but she's a sweet girl, you'd love her," said Oz.

"Well, you bring her by sometime, okay?" said Maria. "I'll make sure she's a good girl for you."

"You bet, Maria. I will," said Oz. "What's the damage, Joe?"

"For you, it's $22," said Little Joe.

"Here's thirty. Make sure that you be nice to my Maria, eh," said Oz.

"You hear that Joe, you be nice to me!" said Maria.

"Yeah, yeah, yeah," said Little Joe.

"You guys are the best. Love you both. See you soon," said Oz.

"You too, Ozzy, take care of yourself," said Little Joe.

Oz grabbed the pizza from the counter, leaned down, kissed Maria on the cheek, waved goodbye to Joe, and left. He walked back to his building and through the garage to his car. Oz placed the pizza on the passenger seat and pulled out of the garage, headed for Donna's place.

***

Oz parked his car in the parking lot at the rear of the building in one of the spots marked 'Visitor' in yellow paint on the pavement. He grabbed the pizza and walked to the rear entrance, and pulled the handle, the door, still not latched or locked. Oz shook his head and went inside, and took the stairs to the second floor.

Knock… Knock… Knock…

"Who is it?" said Donna.

"It's not Domino's," said Oz.

Donna opened the door and greeted Oz with a big, bright smile before giving him a kiss and taking the pizza from his hands. Her hair was still damp from the shower, and she wore a long baby blue t-shirt. He followed her into the apartment.

Donna's place was a very open floor plan. The kitchen was off to the right of the entrance, and the living room just to the left. There was a short hall with a single bedroom and bathroom off it, and at the very end of the hall behind a bi-fold door was the washer and dryer.

"This smells amazing!" said Donna.

"This lovely Italian couple owns this great place just down the street from my place," said Oz.

"Go there often?" she asked, opening the lid of the pizza box.

"Not as much anymore, but I've been going there since I moved here, they've become like family," said Oz.

"Aww," said Donna. "Water?"

"Please," said Oz. "In the fridge, here?"

"It's not in the closet," joked Donna.

Donna dished out two slices of the hearty pizza onto a plate for Oz, and a single slice for herself. She carried the plates over to the dining table she had set for them. Oz grabbed two bottles of water from the fridge and brought them over to the table before sitting down.

"This is so good,' said Donna, after taking a bite of the pizza.

"I told you, Maria and Little Joe know what they are doing," said Oz.

"What's on this?" asked Donna, taking another bite.

"Pepperoni, sausage, meatballs, and bacon," said Oz.

"Oh my God, it's so good," said Donna.

"Maria makes the meatballs herself and I think they even make and age their own pepperoni," said Oz.

"It really is, oh my God! And her sauce is so good too," said Donna, with a mouth full of pizza.

"So work was busy?" asked Oz.

"Yeah," said Donna. "I hit the ground running today. Prepared lists of potential witnesses for a couple of upcoming cases, typed up a couple of subpoenas, filed some reports. It was a busy one."

"But good?" said Oz.

"So good," said Donna. "The way that you and the Lieutenant were talking last night, I thought for sure that you were going to get into trouble."

"So did I," said Oz. "We went to see the Internal Affairs guy this morning, and it went way better than I could have imagined. The ME's report came back saying that the guy I shot was already dead ten days ago. The IA guy didn't know what to do after that. There is nothing in the rule book for killing an unarmed dead guy."

"That is so crazy!" said Donna.

"Yeah, so not what we were expecting at all," said Oz.

"What did you do the rest of the day?" asked Donna.

"Closed case files, and I stopped by the hospital to see Terry and Maureen," said Oz.

"How's he doing?" asked Donna.

"Better. He can't wait to get out of there. He was more like his old self today," said Oz.

"And how about Maureen?" asked Donna.

"She's so strong. I reminded her of our offer, but she just kept saying that all she needed was for Terry to come home."

"How long before they let him go home?" asked Donna.

"This week, if he keeps progressing the way that he is, he could be home before Friday," said Oz.

"Wow, that's amazing," said Donna.

"Terry is one tough son of a bitch, for sure," said Oz. "Can I get you another slice?"

"I shouldn't, but it's so good," said Donna. "Okay, just one."

Oz smiled, grabbed their plates, took them to the kitchen, and put another slice on each of their plates. He walked back over to the table. Placing Donna's plate in front of her, he leaned down and kissed her.

"Mm, I missed you last night," said Donna.

"It was a long, lonely night without you. I'm so glad that I didn't let you talk me out of coming over," said Oz.

"Me too. This pizza is incredible!" joked Donna.

"You're trouble," said Oz. "I may have to teach you a lesson for being so cheeky."

"Oh, yeah?" said Donna. "Whatcha gonna do, officer? Handcuff me to the bed?"

"That would be a start," said Oz.

Donna gave Oz a playful smile and winked at him. They finished their slices of pizza, and Oz cleared the plates away. Washed them, dried them, and put them away.

"Ugh, I'm so full," said Donna.

"That's the point of eating," said Oz.

"Funny, smart guy. Come, join me on the couch!" said Donna.

Oz folded the dish towel and hung it back on the handle of the oven door before joining Donna on the couch. He sat beside her, and she snuggled into his chest. He wrapped his arms around her and embraced her, inhaled her deep into his chest.

"This is where I'm happiest," said Oz.

"Mm, me too, Ozzy," said Donna. "I really could have used you beside me last night."

"Why didn't you say so? You know that I would have stayed," said Oz.

"I didn't want to seem needy or like some scared little girl," said Donna.

"After what happened, you wouldn't have seemed like either of those. I'm an idiot, I'm sorry. I should have thought about how you were feeling, but I was too wrapped up in my own mess," said Oz.

"Don't be. It was a pretty crazy night," said Donna. "Is work going to be quieter now?"

"It should be. Boston doesn't usually have many murders," said Oz.

"I picked a good city to come to then," said Donna.

"You definitely did. I know I'm glad you picked it," said Oz.

"Are you staying here tonight?" asked Donna.

"I didn't have a plan one way or the other, I was just winging it. I just knew that I wanted to see you today," said Oz. "Do you want me to stay?"

"I'd feel so much better if you spent the night," said Donna.

"Then I'm spending the night," said Oz. "Do you have PJ's I can borrow?"

"As much as I would love to see you try to fit into some of them, I don't think that you'll need any," said Donna.

Oz laughed and gave Donna a poke in her ribs and made her twitch. She playfully hit him, and he poked her again. She straddled him and kissed him. He kissed her back; the passion soared between them. He stood up, and she wrapped her legs around him, and he carried her down the hall to the bedroom.

28

Oz awoke just before the sun rose. Donna laid there asleep, while Oz eased out of bed, trying not to disturb her. He grabbed his clothes from the floor and dressed. He gently kissed Donna's forehead and left the apartment.

Back at his apartment, he took a shower and changed before heading to the office.

Oz walked into the detective's pool, poured himself a coffee. *Ahh, that is a perfect cup!* Oz sat down at his desk and pulled out his cell phone and messaged Donna.

'Good morning, babe! I didn't want to disturb you this morning when I left. Have a great day. Thanks for another amazing evening. Hopefully, you aren't sick of me and would like to get together again tonight!'

Oz logged into his computer, continued to sip away on his coffee, while he opened up his Outlook. There were confirmation emails for the closure of the case files from the day before. So far, things seemed like they were going to be very quiet as he finished his coffee.

Vrrrt... Vrrrt... Vrrrt...

Oz pulled his phone from his pocket to see a message from Donna.

'Hey, Hun! Just got to the office. I slept great thanks to you. I missed not waking up to you! Talk to you later, have a great day xx!'

Oz smiled and put his phone back in his pocket. He pulled his notepad out of his desk drawer and tore off the pages that contained his notes. He dropped the pages in an empty file folder and wrote the case numbers and the killer's name on the lines for the file name tab. He slid the folder into one of the empty hanging folders and closed the drawer.

The morning seemed to fly by, which was so unusual for a Tuesday, and given what little work there was to do now that the killer had been stopped. Days like these were boring, but there was a comfort in knowing that no one in the city of Boston was being killed.

"Shields!" shouted Jim from his office.

Oz got up and walked over to Jim's office, and popped his head inside.

"Yes, sir?" said Oz.

"Oz, I need you to go to the packies on Parker Street," said Jim.

"Packies, sir?" asked Oz.

"Right, I forgot. You're not from here. The market and liquor store," said Jim.

"Gotcha," said Oz. "What do we know?"

"Double homicide during an attempted robbery," said Jim.

"You got it, Lieutenant. I'm on my way," said oz.

Oz left the office, grabbed the keys to DET 35, and headed out to the parking lot. He unlocked the car on the way and got in the car. He pulled out of the spot and headed for Parker Street. *I should have just brought my car. This is so close to home, but there is a bit too much day left.*

Oz pulled into the parking lot off Gurney Street. He parked the car next to a BPD cruiser, exited the vehicle, and headed to the store entrance on the Northside of the building. Inside the liquor store were two officers. One was speaking with an eyewitness at the back of the store by the coolers, and the other officer was by the door.

"Officer," said Oz, displaying his badge.

"Detective," said the officer at the door.

"What do we know?" asked Oz.

"Owner is behind the counter and this guy here was the robber. The owner took three shots to the chest, and the perp here took a shotgun blast square in the chest!" said the Officer. "My partner's just getting a statement from the witness now."

"Did anyone check the security footage?" asked Oz.

"No, sir, not yet. We just secured the scene," said the officer.

"Thanks, great work," said Oz.

Oz walked over to the officer with the witness. The witness was a male, around 35, with dark brown skin and a short black afro. He was 6'3" tall, and he wore a tattered navy-blue Patriots hoodie, a pair of dirty blue jeans, and an old pair of three-stripe Adidas shoes.

"Good afternoon, sir! I'm Detective Shields. How are you doing?" asked Oz.

"I just saw two muthafuckas kill each other. How the fuck do you think I'm doing?" said the man.

"That's understandable, sir. If you don't mind, I just need to ask you what happened? Are you alright to do that?" asked Oz.

"Yeah, I ain't no pussy," he said.

"Great! Can I get your name?" asked Oz.

"Quashawn Allen," he said.

"Quashawn, what did you see here today?" asked Oz.

"I was over here right, grabbing some Henny you know. Then this muthafucka comes in yelling "open the register, gimme the money" right?" said Quashawn. "The owner was all like, "fuck you! I ain't giving you shit!" So, the dude was like, "Give me the money, or I'll shoot you and take it." The owner told him to go fuck his-self, and he pulled out his shotgun and they both started firing."

"Did the robber not see you in the store?" asked Oz.

"Hell no! I skooched down here outta site," said Quashawn.

"So he didn't see you at all?' asked Oz.

"Nah, man! He came in and went straight for the cash," said Quashawn. "Pretty amateur if you ask me."

"Was there anyone else in the store?" asked Oz.

"Nah, it's usually pretty quiet here, that's why I come here," said Quashawn.

"Thank you, Mr. Allen," said Oz. "I appreciate your help."

"No prob!" said Quashawn.

Oz walked into the back of the store and headed towards the office. Inside the small office on a wire shelf were a couple of monitors on top of some digital recording equipment, next to an old metal desk with a wood top. The desk was littered with papers and a couple of old Dunkin' cups with a mouthful or two of coffee left in them.

Oz watched the monitor as he rewound the recording. Pressing play, the events unfold just as Quashawn had described. It was hard to see from the video who shot first because the flash from the guns messed with the cameras. What could be seen was both men dropping dead from the shots that were fired.

Oz returned to the front of the store where the officers were. The crime scene photographer was there with them, snapping pictures. Oz pulled a pair of blue nitrile gloves from his coat pocket, kneeled beside the body of the robber, and searched for ID. Oz pulled a wallet from the back pocket of the baggy jeans that the perp was wearing. He slid the driver's license from one of the card slots in the brown leather bifold wallet.

The name on the driver's license was Rafael Morales. Date of birth, August 1st, 1991. Lived around the way on Annunciation Road in the apartments there. Oz slid the license back into the wallet, and the wallet back into the pocket of the jeans of the perp. He pulled his notepad and pen from his jacket pocket and recorded the ID of the robber and the name of the witness.

"Do you guys know the name of the owner there?" asked Oz.

"Diego Benitez," said one of the officers.

"That was quick," said Oz.

"I've been patrolling this area for a few years. Been in here quite a few times," said the officer.

"What can you tell me about the owner?" asked Oz as he stood back up.

"He was a really nice guy, but he was getting sick and tired of guys like this coming in here and robbing him. His insurance was going through the roof because of it," said the officer.

"How often was he getting held up?" asked Oz.

"It was happening more and more. I would say an average of a couple of times a month. It was getting so bad that we had to up our patrols here," said the officer.

"When did he get the shotgun?" asked Oz.

"That was really recent. The baseball bat wasn't deterring anyone anymore," said the officer. "A real shame. Like I said, Diego was a great guy."

"Do you by chance know his next of kin?" asked Oz.

"His wife, yeah. I know her," said the officer.

"Would you mind breaking the news to her? It may be best coming from a familiar face," said Oz.

"Yeah, I can take care of that," said the officer.

"Thanks. I'm going to head to the perp's apartment and see if there is a next of kin to notify," said Oz. "You gents have this scene locked down, so I'm going to get out of the way."

"Sure thing, Detective," said the officer.

Oz left the store, got in the car, and radioed back to dispatch to update on the call before heading to the apartment of the robber. Oz informed dispatch that was his next stop, and that he would call for assistance if required.

***

Oz pulled up to the address on the driver's license of Rafael Morales. He approached the door to the building and found there at the entrance was a list of the tenants and their apartments. On the list, he found the name of R. Morales, located in apartment 1D. Oz pulled open the door and entered the building and walked down the hall to the door marked '1D' and knocked.

"Yes? Who is it?" said the voice of a Latin female inside the apartment.

"Ma'am, this is Detective Shields, BPD. Is this the home of Rafael Morales?" asked Oz.

"Yes!" said the woman.

The chain was being slid from the door and the deadbolt unlocked before the door swung open just enough for the woman to see Oz standing on the other side, presenting his badge. She opened the door fully.

The woman was 5'3" tall, jet black hair pulled back into a ponytail, olive skin, with a beautiful complexion. She wore a tight tracksuit with a crop top, so her navel piercing was on display. She wore large hoop earrings to complete the stereotypical attire.

"Afternoon, ma'am. Are you the wife of Rafael?" asked Oz.

"Yes, what about him?" she asked.

"Ma'am, I regret to inform you that your husband was killed today while trying to rob a liquor store on Parker Road," said Oz.

"You're joking?" she said.

"No, ma'am. I'm not joking. The Medical Examiner's office will contact you to come and identify the body and make arrangements," said Oz.

The woman crumbled to the ground, muttering something in Spanish that Oz couldn't make out, as she began to sob. Oz put his hand on her shoulder and extended his condolences to her again.

He helped her to her feet and back into the apartment and onto the couch. He apologized again before letting himself out of the apartment, heading back to the station.

Back at his desk he opened a case file, and put in all the details, and closed the case all in one session, as he had enough evidence and detail to show that the incident involved a mutual killing.

Jim emerged from his office and saw Oz at his desk, working away on the computer, so he came over and sat across from him at Terry's desk.

"How was that one, kid?" asked Jim.

"Mutual kill," said Oz.

"Easiest to solve," said Jim.

"Yeah, that is for sure," said Oz.

"Your solved case numbers are gonna rock this month," said Jim. "We don't have an employee of the month, though. So, all you get is an 'atta boy'."

"Thanks, Jim," laughed Oz.

"Did you see Ter yesterday?" asked Jim.

"I did. He's doing good. He is dying to get out of the hospital and off the morphine," said Oz.

"Sounds like his old self," said Jim.

"Oh, he's definitely back to being Terry," said Oz. "If it's ok, I was going to take off and bring him a coffee?"

"Sure, kid. That's work-related," joked Jim. "Tell him that vacation is over, and he has to get his ass back to work."

"Thanks, Jim. I will," said Oz.

"Good job, kid!" said Jim.

Jim stood up and walked out of the detective pool. Oz packed up his desk, got up, and pushed in his chair. He dropped off the Impala keys with the motor pool and left work for the day.

***

"I'm not a delivery service, so don't get used to this!" said Oz, entering the hospital room with a coffee in hand for Terry.

"Just when I thought I had you trained," said Terry.

"Hi Maureen, how are you?" asked Oz as he leaned down to Maureen, seated bedside, and gave her a hug and a kiss on the cheek.

"I'm good, Oz. Thanks for cheering this grumpy asshole up," said Maureen.

"That bad, is it?" asked Oz.

"Hey, I'm still in the room!" said Terry.

"Yeah, we know," joked Oz.

"Fucking cawksuckah!" said Terry. "How was work, kid?"

"Quiet. I had a mutual kill today at a liquor store near my place," said Oz.

"I missed that?" said Terry. "Those are the easiest to solve."

"Don't listen to him, Oz. He's high as a kite," said Maureen.

"I'm not high!" said Terry.

"Uh-huh, of course, you're not, Hun!" said Maureen.

"Any good news, Maureen?" asked Oz.

"Well, if his levels are good tomorrow, then he can come home," said Maureen.

"That's amazing news!" said Oz. "How soon before he can come back to work?"

"Why? Do you miss me?" said Terry.

"Actually, the Lieutenant said vacation is over, and it's time to get your ass back to work," said Oz.

"Jim said that? Cawksuckah," said Terry.

"The Doctor said he can resume light duties as soon as he's released," said Maureen.

"Even better. Do you want me to come and pick you up in the morning until you are 100% again?" asked Oz.

"Oz, that would be so great of you!" said Maureen. "You don't mind?"

"Not at all, Maureen," said Oz.

"You're a doll!" said Maureen.

"That means you're picking up coffee on the way to get me," said Terry.

"Sure, Ter. No problem," said Oz.

"Ahh, you're a good kid!" said Terry.

"Will you shoot me a text if he gets cleared to go home tomorrow?" asked Oz.

"You bet, Hun.!" said Maureen. "Thanks again for everything, Oz!"

"Don't mention it, Maureen. It's my pleasure," said Oz.

"Not just the carpooling, Hun," said Maureen.

"I know, Maureen. I'd do it again in a heartbeat," said Oz. "You two have a good night, I love you both."

"You too, kid!" said Terry.

Maureen stood up and escorted Oz to the door of the hospital room. She grabbed his hand, and Oz turned around to face her.

"Oz, thank you so much for everything that you've done for us," said Maureen.

"No thanks needed, Maureen. He's my partner. My best friend. I love you guys, and I'd do anything for you, anytime, without hesitation," said Oz.

"You're an angel, Oz!" said Maureen.

She wrapped her arms around him and kissed him on the cheek. She placed both of her hands on his face and stared straight into his eyes. Oz put his hands on her shoulder to reassure her. Her eyes were full of tears. Oz pulled Maureen in for another hug.

"Hey, shh. It's all good, Maureen. He's getting better and will be home before we know it," said Oz. "Come on now, dry those tears."

"I just don't know what we'd do without you, Hun," said Maureen.

"Exactly what you did before me. Be strong for each other," said Oz. "Text me tomorrow when you know more, okay? Go, be with Terry. Chin up. I'll see you both tomorrow."

"Okay. Thank you again, Oz!" said Maureen.

Oz smiled at her, and Maureen wiped her tears with the palm of her hands, sniffled, and said goodbye to Oz. Oz squeezed Maureen's hand one more time and then headed down the hall, leaving the hospital. Maureen walked back over and sat with Terry.

"You alright, Hun?" asked Terry.

"I'm just so glad that you're alright, babe. I can't wait to have you home," said Maureen.

"I love you, Hun!" said Terry.

"I love you too, Ter!" she replied.

29

Knock… Knock… Knock…

"Ozzy!" said Donna excitedly, as she opened the door of her apartment. "What are you doing here?"

"I just came from visiting Terry and Maureen. I saw your car in the parking lot on my way past, so I thought I'd surprise you," said Oz.

"I'm so surprised!" said Donna.

She wrapped her arms around his neck, pulled him down, and gave him a kiss. He kissed her back, putting his hands on her waist, slid them down to her ass, and lifted her up and into his arms.

"Come in, come in!" she said before kissing him again.

Oz carried Donna inside her apartment and kicked the door closed with his foot as he continued to kiss her. She tasted so sweet. Oz put her down, back on her feet, and kissed her once more.

"How'd it go today, babe?" asked Oz.

"It was great, and it just got a million times better," she said.

"Had dinner yet?" asked Oz.

"No, I was actually just gonna throw some of that delicious pizza in the oven. Can I tempt you with some?"

"Sounds as perfect as you," said Oz.

"Mm, you're the best!" said Donna.

Donna gave Oz another kiss before heading into the kitchen. She pulled the pizza box out of the fridge and turned on the oven. She pulled a cookie sheet from the warming drawer under the stove and put the last five slices on it. Donna closed the pizza box, and Oz reached for it.

"Is there a recycle bin?" asked Oz.

"In the garbage room down the hall," said Donna.

"Perfect, I'll be right back, don't lock me out," said Oz.

Oz grabbed the box from the counter, leaned down, and gave her a kiss. He opened the door to the apartment and walked down the hall to a door marked 'Garbage'. He opened the door and placed the pizza box in the large recycle bin in the room's corner. Oz turned and headed back to Donna's apartment.

"Ozwald!"

Oz stopped dead in his tracks. A chill ran up his spine. The fine hairs on the back of his neck stood at attention, like soldiers. He knew there was no point in looking around. This voice was in his head.

"I warned you! Now, I'm coming for you!"

Oz took a deep breath and walked the last few steps to Donna's apartment. He pushed the door open, entered the apartment, and closed and locked the door behind him. As he turned around, Donna was there, looking at him.

"Are you alright?" asked Donna. "You look like you just saw a ghost!"

"I'm fine," said Oz.

"You heard the voice again, didn't you?" asked Donna.

"Yeah, just in the hall there," said Oz.

"But you killed the guy? I saw it," said Donna.

"Yeah, well, apparently, I killed the host and not the demon," said Oz.

"Then how in the world do you kill a demon?" asked Donna.

"I don't have the slightest clue. But for this to end, I'm gonna have to find a way," said Oz.

"Who do you even talk to about something like that?" asked Donna.

"I don't know, a priest or something? Who would know about demons?" asked Oz.

"I grew up catholic, but I don't ever remember our priest talking about demons," said Donna.

"I didn't think it would be back so soon," said Oz.

"There isn't anything that you are gonna do about this tonight, so I say we eat our pizza, curl up on the couch and watch something on TV before bed," said Donna. "You're staying the night, aren't you?"

"I have no plan to go anywhere," said Oz. "Especially now."

"Good," said Donna.

Donna pulled the cookie sheet full of pizza out of the oven and dished it out. She brought the plates over to her little dining table. It was just as tasty as it was last night.

"So, how are Terry and Maureen?" asked Donna.

"Terry may get released tomorrow," said Oz.

"No way? That is incredible!" said Donna. "How long will he be off work?"

"They said that he can come back as soon as he is released from the hospital," said Oz

"Seriously? That is so soon?" said Donna.

"I thought so, too. I've offered to come and pick him up in the mornings so that he doesn't have to worry about driving," said Oz.

"I swear, if you were any better, you'd have wings and a halo," said Donna.

"He's my partner. How much of a horrible human being would I be if I didn't at least offer that?" said Oz.

"Well, I think it is super sweet," said Donna.

"Maureen is gonna message or call me tomorrow when they know for sure," said Oz.

"How did I get so lucky?" said Donna.

"Lucky? What are you talking about?" asked Oz.

"Yeah, what did I do to deserve someone so good as you?" said Donna.

"I'm not that good. I just shot an unarmed man," said Oz.

"Yeah, an unarmed possessed man, that was coming to kill me," said Donna.

"I'd kill a million unarmed men if they were coming to hurt you, or anyone else I love," said Oz.

"Ozzy? Did you just say that you love me?" asked Donna, a little in shock at the words that he just uttered.

"I mean, I guess… yeah, I did. I mean, I do," said Oz.

"Oh, Ozzy! I love you too!" said Donna.

Donna got out of her seat, walked over to Oz, and sat on his lap. She wrapped her arms around him and kissed him. Her eyes welled with tears of happiness. Oz embraced her, pulling her close to him. He could feel a sense of calm rush over him. His fear and uneasiness at hearing the voice again dissipated.

They cleaned up from dinner and sat together, cuddled up on the couch, and watched a movie on Netflix. Donna unbuttoned a few of the buttons on Oz's shirt and slid her hand inside, and gently scratched the muscles hidden underneath with her nails. Oz held her close and massaged her backside. When the movie ended, Donna turned off the TV and straddled Oz. They kissed and Oz stood, lifted her up, and carried her off to the bedroom.

**

Ring… Ring… Ring…

"Detective Shields, Homicide," said Oz, woken by the phone.

"Oz, it's Jim. A body was found at Fort Hill Tower in Highland Park," said Jim.

"Yes, sir. What time is it?" asked Oz.

"Time for you to get your ass outta bed, and go to the crime scene," said Jim.

"Yes, sir. Sorry, sir," said Oz.

"I'm fucking with you, kid. It's 1:30 in the morning," said Jim. "The body isn't going anywhere, so gather yourself and drive safe."

"Will do, sir. Thank you," said Oz, hanging up the phone.

Oz groaned and stretched before rubbing his eyes and sitting up on the edge of Donna's bed. He sat there hunched over, his elbows resting on his legs, as he took some deep cleansing breaths.

"Will you be coming back?" asked Donna.

"Probably not, Hun. I don't want to disturb you more than I already have," said Oz. "Get your rest. I'll just head to my place after."

"Okay, Ozzy. I love you. Please be safe," she said, getting up to her knees and embracing him from behind. "Will I see you after work tonight?"

"Only if you want to," said Oz.

"How about I make us a nice dinner tonight?" asked Donna.

"Your place or mine?" asked Oz.

"Why don't you come here? Bring an overnight bag," said Donna.

"You want me to stay over?" asked Oz.

"Don't be stupid," said Donna.

"Alright, Hun," said Oz.

"You're not allergic to anything, are you?" asked Donna.

"No, babe, not at all," said Oz.

"Okay, good," said Donna.

Donna kissed Oz on the neck and kept her arms wrapped around him as he tried to put his clothes on. Oz stood up, breaking her grasp on him as he pulled up his pants and did them up. He turned around, putting his shirt on, and stared at Donna, kneeling there in front of him. There in the moonlight, peeking in her window, she looked adorable as she looked up at him with her big beautiful eyes.

"I enjoy watching you get dressed, almost as much as I enjoy watching you get undressed," said Donna.

"I've said it before. You really don't make it easy to leave," said Oz.

Oz leaned down to kiss her goodbye. His fingers combed through her hair to the back of her head. They kissed again passionately before he stood upright again.

"Get some sleep, babe. You've got a busy day tomorrow. I'll message you to let you know I got home safely. I love you!" said Oz.

"Mm, I love you too, Ozzy!" she said before they kissed one last time. "Good luck, and be safe!"

"Always," said Oz. "Make sure you lock the door behind me! Goodnight, babe!"

Oz walked out of the bedroom and out of the apartment. He heard the lock click when he was a couple of steps away from her door. There was a sigh of relief, hearing the door lock. He left the building, got in the car, and headed South to Highland Park.

***

There were three police cruisers on-scene, one on Fort Avenue, and the other two on Fort Avenue Terrace, close to where Oz pulled up. Officers on-scene were securing the area so that no one could enter Highland Park. Oz exited his car and approached one of the officers at the south entrance to the park.

"Officer, Detective Shields, Homicide. What can you tell me?" asked Oz, presenting his badge to the officer.

"Pretty messed up, Detective!" said the Officer.

"Where am I going?" asked Oz.

"Head to the Northside of the tower, can't miss it," said the officer.

"Thanks," said Oz.

Oz walked up the path and cut across the dew-covered grass to the Northside of the Fort Hill Tower. There, against the side, he saw the body hunched, sitting against the North wall of the tower. He approached the tower and saw a large amount of blood smeared on the white stone wall. Oz pulled out his flashlight from the inside pocket of his sport coat and turned it on. He was ill-prepared for what he saw.

Written in blood above the body was his name. Blood trickled down the wall from the lowest points of each letter of his name to the slouched body below. Oz examined the body as closely as he could without touching it. The head was torn from the body and may have been used as the paintbrush to write his name. He looked around the body for the head, but could not see it anywhere.

Oz crouched close to the body. *Looks like we have a Caucasian male, placed against the tower wall here after he was killed. The body is intact except for the head. There is a blood spot above the body right where the head would have been. A perfect circular impression, as if the head was slammed into the wall.* Oz put the end of the flashlight in his mouth and pulled out his notepad and pen and recorded what he saw.

"Detective," said a voice approaching from behind him.

Oz turned to see the officer that he had first spoken with approaching him. He was accompanying the crime scene photographer.

"Right on time! I need to check the body for an ID," said Oz.

"Sure thing! Just gimme a couple," said the photographer.

The photographer snapped several shots from various angles. The flash highlighted the horrific scene every time it flashed. Oz looked around the scene as the flashes illuminated it. Just like all the scenes, there was very little surrounding the body.

"Oz," shouted another voice from the darkness.

Oz turned to see who it was. He could see a figure approaching from the south. As the shadowy figure approached, Oz could begin to see who it was.

"Hey, Jared. You guys are early tonight," said Oz.

"Maybe you're just slower without your partner?" said Jared.

"Don't see how that would be possible," joked Oz.

"How's he doing, anyway?" asked Jared.

"He's doing well, could be back to work tomorrow," said Oz

"Really? That's a relief," said Oz.

"Yeah. Big time," said Oz.

"What do we have here tonight?" asked Jared.

"Caucasian male, decapitated, and a personal message to me," said Oz.

"What?" said Jared.

"Yeah, come and see for yourself," said Oz.

They walked back to the north side of the tower. The photographer gave Oz a thumbs up, letting him know he was all done and that Oz could resume his investigation.

"Jesus Christ!" said Jared.

"Yup," said Oz.

"Who did you piss off?" asked Jared.

"You wouldn't believe me if I told you, man," said Oz.

"Try me," said Jared.

"Remember the dead guy that I killed?" asked Oz.

"Yeah, kinda hard to forget," said Jared. "What about him?"

"He was possessed by a demon," said Oz.

"Get the fuck out of here! Really?" said Jared.

"As crazy as it sounds, man, I have it all recorded. It actually happened," said Oz.

"I guess that is one explanation of why you shot a dead man," said Jared. "So do you think this is the demon telling you he is back?"

"Highly possible. I don't have the most common name to be writing on monuments in blood," said Oz.

"You can say that again," said Jared.

"Mind if I look for an ID?" asked Oz.

"Go right ahead. But you could leave that to us, and you can head home if you are done here?" said Jared.

"I could, but I have to know who died so that I could have my name so nicely written," said Oz.

"Have at it then, boss," said Jared.

Oz walked back over to the body and knelt down beside it. He began fishing through the pockets of the dead man. In the back pocket of the jeans on the right side, Oz found a wallet. He turned on his flashlight and searched through the wallet. In one of the card slots, he found a driver's license. He pulled it out and examined it for the name. Ezra James Miller, born October 8th, 1989. Oz put the driver's license back in the wallet and put the wallet back in the pocket. He stood back up and walked back over to Jared.

He put his flashlight back in his pocket and pulled out his notepad and pen and recorded the name and date of birth of the victim, beside the notes that he had taken down of the scene.

"Well, at least there was an ID," said Oz.

"Good! I've seen far too many John or Jane Doe's lately," said Jared.

"Let me know if you guys find anything, though if this is our guy again, I'm thinking that it is going to be pretty clean," said Oz.

"You got it, Oz," said Jared. "Get out of here and get some rest."

"Thanks, Jared. Don't drive yourselves crazy looking for things that aren't there."

"Thanks, Oz," said Jared.

Jared finished suiting up as the rest of his crew showed up at the scene and set up the lights and the generator. Oz saluted Jared and walked back towards his car, unlocking it as he got close. He got in the car and rubbed his tired eyes before starting the car and headed home.

30

Oz grabbed his duffle bag that he had packed with a change of clothes and toiletries to bring with him to Donna's place after work and left the apartment. He tossed the duffle bag into the trunk of the Mustang, hopped into the driver's seat, and headed to work.

The sun was shining between the buildings on the drive to the station. The sky was a brilliant orange hue, littered with small clouds. It was cool, only 53 °F. A layer of dew covered the parked cars on the streets, and grassy patches of people's lawns and parks.

Oz parked his car and went into the station. When he arrived in the detective pool, he made himself a cup of coffee and walked over to his desk, and sat down. He sipped on his coffee as he opened and worked his report for last night's victim, referring occasionally to the notes that he jotted down on his notepad while at the scene.

Ring... Ring... Ring...

Oz pulled his cell phone from his pocket and saw that it was Maureen calling him. Oz swiped the screen to answer the call.

"Hey Maureen, is everything okay?" asked Oz.

"Hey, Oz! Everything is great! Terry and I are leaving the hospital now, and heading home," said Maureen.

"That is great! Do you need anything today?" asked Oz.

"I don't think so, Hun. But you are more than welcome to come by the house later if you like," said Maureen.

"Sounds like a plan, Maureen. I'll let you know when I'm coming, and you can let me know if you need anything," said Oz.

"Thanks, Oz. Talk to you soon," said Maureen.

Oz made sure that the call had been ended before tucking the phone back into his pocket. He got up from his desk and approached Jim's office. Approaching the office, he heard Jim on the phone with someone. Oz waited outside the office door until Jim had finished the call.

"Sir, do you have a second?" asked Oz.

"Always, what's up, kid?" asked Jim.

"Sir, I just got off the phone with Maureen. Terry has been released from the hospital," said Oz.

"That's great news, kid! So, when's he coming back to work?" asked Jim.

"Tomorrow, sir. I'm going to pick him up in the morning," said Oz.

"Partner and driver. Terry is a lucky guy!" joked Jim.

"Yeah, guess so," said Oz. "I'm going to head over to Terry's place after work tonight."

"Mind if I join you?" asked Jim.

"Not at all, sir. You want to ride with me?" asked Oz.

"Nah, I'll take my car, but thanks," said Jim. "Let's leave here about 3:30. That way we won't interrupt their supper."

"Sounds like a plan, sir," said Oz. "I have to go chase down the next of kin for last night's victim. I'll catch up with you later."

"Great work, kid!" said Jim.

Oz went back to his desk and opened the NCIC database and typed in Ezra James Miller and his date of birth. The search populated one result in the Boston area. Oz clicked open the link, and the screen displayed the picture that he saw last night on the victim's driver's license. Oz read the file. There was no next of kin listed and his parents were deceased. The victim was also an only child, according to the file. Doesn't look like there will be anyone to notify for this poor guy.

Ring... Ring... Ring...

Oz looked at the display on the phone on his desk and saw that the call was from the Office of the Medical Examiner. Oz grabbed the receiver and answered the call.

"Detective Shields, Homicide," said Oz.

"Oz, It's Brad," he said.

"Hey, Brad! What's going on?" asked Oz.

"I was doing a lot of thinking and research after our last conversation..." said Brad. "And I'm glad that I did."

"Yeah?" asked Oz.

"I did a deep dive after hearing that recording that you played for me," said Brad. "Azazel is a prince of Hell according to several publications that I read, and from some Satanic radicals that I called."

"You called Satanists?" asked Oz.

"Yeah, don't worry. I blocked my number and only gave them your name," said Brad, laughing awkwardly. "I'm kidding, I used a fake name."

"You had me going for a second there," said Oz.

"Yeah, sorry. Anyway, I did more digging on demons and went down a rabbit hole there. There is a way to send them back, not permanently, but for a long time. The Kurds figured this out centuries ago," said Brad.

"Kurds?" asked Oz.

"Yeah, Kurds are an Iranian ethnic group, that were mostly Muslim, but many converted to Catholicism over time. There are stories of Roman Catholic Priests in Turkey that forged these Kurdish daggers that they used against demons to kill them in their physical form and send them back to Hell."

"You're losing me," said Oz.

"Sorry, I am looking for a Kurdish Priest to see if we can get our hands on one of these daggers so that we can finally end this," said Brad

"We?" said Oz.

"Well, you, and me as kinda your sidekick," said Brad.

"You're a huge help, Brad," said Oz.

"I'll let you know as soon as I track down the dagger," said Brad.

"Great! Thanks, Brad," said Oz.

Oz hung up the phone and opened Google on his computer. He typed in 'Kurdish Dagger' into the search bar. The search result populated and there were images of all types of daggers, and many links to tales and folklore, but the results were mostly Islamic related. He added 'demon' to the search bar and hit enter. This populated a few more results this time, and some reference Catholicism.

There was one particular link that spoke of a blade forged from bone with writing carved into the blade. The blade was curved and extremely sharp; the hilt was leather-wrapped with the butt exposed, displaying a polished distal epiphysis. *This thing looks deadly. How would I get close enough to use it? Especially if this thing is as strong as it is. There is no way that I could overpower it. I sure hope that Brad can figure something out soon. We need to stop this thing before it kills too many more and becomes far too powerful.*

Oz logged off his computer, got up from his desk, took his coffee cup over to the kitchenette, and put it in the dishwasher. He adjusted his sport coat and walked out of the office. He wandered out to the parking lot and started walking back towards home. His mind raced, thinking about all that Brad had told him, and what he had read about the Kurdish Dagger online. Before he knew it, he was standing in front of the pizza parlor just up the street from his apartment. He opened the door, and a bell chimed overhead as he entered.

"Hold your horses, I'll be right there," shouted Little Joe.

He waddled out from the kitchen, arthritis in his knees almost crippling him today, as he winced with every step.

"Ozzy my boy! Come va?"

"What's good today, Joe?" asked Oz.

"Oh, you're in for a treat today, my boy! How would you like a fresh chicken parmigiana sandwich, on a nice a fresh homemade Italian bun, a little sautéed onions, and some greens peppers, mama's sauce, and fresh Parmesan cheese, huh?" said Little Joe.

"How could I possibly turn that down? You make it sound so good," said Oz.

"That's my boy! We'll make it good for you, huh," said Little Joe. "Maria, chicken parmigiana sandwich for our boy Ozzy, huh!"

"Coming right up," shouted Maria from the kitchen.

"You wanna drink with that?" asked Joe.

"Sure, how about a bottle of Orangina, please," said Oz.

"That's $6, Ozzy!" said Joe.

Oz handed Joe a ten-dollar bill and gave him a wave to keep the change. He always did that for Joe and Maria. Oz always felt like they could work a lot less if they just charged a little more for everything. But that wasn't their way. It seemed as though they really loved doing this, and it was never about getting rich, it was all about making the most delicious food. And as far as Oz was concerned, they had that part of the business nailed.

Maria emerged from the kitchen with the sandwich wrapped in foil paper and a handful of napkins. Little Joe grabbed the bottle of Orangina from the fridge and put it on the counter. Maria put the sandwich on the counter next to the bottle and walked around to greet Oz. Like always, she pulled him down to her and gave him a big kiss on the cheek, followed by her pinching the same cheek.

"Twice in one week. Is it my birthday?" said Maria.

"If it is, and I forgot, I'm in big trouble," said Oz.

"Such a good boy," said Maria, pinching his cheek again.

"You two take care, alright? I'll come by for a coffee and a chat soon, okay?" said Oz.

"Sure thing, my boy. We'll be here. Godere!" said Joe.

Oz grabbed his sandwich and drink from the counter and headed back to the station. He unwrapped the sandwich partially and ate it as he walked back. *My God, this is delicious! How do they make everything taste so incredible?* The sandwich exploded with flavor. The chicken was so juicy. The combination of sauce, onions, and peppers were incredible. The fresh, crusty Italian bun, still warm and perfect for what was layered between the top and bottom after being sliced in half. He devoured the sandwich. It never stood a chance.

Oz tossed the wrapper in one of the bus stop trash bins on his walk back to the office. He gently shook and opened the bottle of Orangina, taking a sip. It was so cold from the fridge and was just the perfect mix of tart and sweet. He didn't drink sodas or soft drinks often, but now and then he would enjoy an Orangina from Joe and Maria's place, and it always satisfied him, like some magical elixir.

Back at the office, he sat at his desk and saw that his desk phone flashed, letting him know that there was a voicemail for him. He picked up the receiver and pressed the button to access the voicemail. He listened to the automated voice that prompted him to enter his passcode, which he did, and the message began to play.

"Oz, it's Brad. Uh… Brad Walker. I need to talk with you as soon as you get this. I found some information that is very useful. It involves a small road trip. Well, maybe not so much of a road trip, but there is someone that we need to talk

to. Anyway, give me a call back at the office, when you can. Thanks!"

Oz deleted the message and hung up the phone by pressing his left index finger on the hook switch. He dialed the number for the Office of the Medical Examiner and asked to speak with Brad when the receptionist answered.

"Oz! Did you get my message?" said Brad, answering the call.

"Yeah, what's going on?" said Oz.

"I spoke with a priest at a Roman Catholic Church that is willing to speak with us in person. And he has a Kurdish Dagger," said Brad.

"You're joking?" said Oz. "That was quick!"

"Well, I didn't think this was something that we could sit on," said Brad.

"So, where and when?" asked Oz.

"As soon as you're available," said Brad.

"I can go now if you can?" said Oz.

"Really? Okay, then. I need you to meet me at the Basilica of Our Lady of Perpetual Help. Do you know where that is?" asked Brad.

"It is basically next door to my apartment," said Oz.

"Perfect. I'll meet you there in ten minutes," said Brad.

"See you there," said Oz.

Oz hung up the phone, walked over to Jim's office, and knocked on the door frame. Jim looked up and took off his reading glasses, placing them on the file that he was reading.

"What's up, kid?" said Jim.

"Sir, I got a lead to follow up on, so do you mind if I take off and check it out, and I'll just head to Terry's from there?" asked Oz.

"You're a grown boy, you don't need my permission," said Jim. "I'm not watching your hours."

"Just a courtesy, sir. So, you're all good?" said Oz.

"Go on, get outta here. I'll see you at Ter's," said Jim.

"Thanks, sir," said Oz, turning to walk away.

"Oh, Oz?" shouted Jim.

"Yeah, sir?" said Oz.

"Grab a napkin and wipe the lunch from your face before you go see anyone else," said Jim.

"Shit! Thanks," said Oz.

"Next time bring me back one of those," said Jim, laughing.

"You got it, sir!" said Oz.

Oz stopped by the washroom, wet a paper towel, and wiped his face clean. He felt a little embarrassed that he didn't even think to check his face when he got back to the office. He laughed at himself as he wiped the orange sauce stains from around his mouth, looking like a kid who just finished a big spaghetti dinner. Oz tossed the paper towel in the trash, left the washroom, and headed out of the station to his car.

***

Oz backed his car into his spot in the parking garage of his building. He figured that if he was this close to home, he may as well park there, and then he can grab a few things before heading to Terry's.

Oz walked up the street and crossed over to the other side where the Church was. The Basilica of Our Lady of Perpetual Help was a masterpiece of stone architecture. It seemed to tower over the street and neighborhood with its tall twin bell towers. The stonework was two tones of gray, elegantly decorated, and accentuated with arched carvings and stained-glass windows. There were three pairs of brown double doors under three archways, letting parishioners into the church.

Brad was standing on the stairs by the middle set of brown double doors. He waved at Oz when he saw him walk up. Oz climbed the stairs to Brad and shook his hand.

"Thanks for coming," said Brad.

"No worries! So, who are we here to see?" said Oz.

"Father Emre Denkel, a Turkish priest," said Brad.

"What does he know already?" asked Oz.

"Just what little I told him, about a possible demonic possession that was responsible for several deaths," said Brad.

"Sounds good. I'll follow your lead on this one," said Oz.

Brad pulled on the handle of one of the double doors, opening it. Oz followed Brad into the church. The inside of the church seemed larger than the outside. It was like entering some holy dimension. Inside was brightly illuminated from the sun shining through all the stained-glass windows. Oz followed Brad down the main aisle, approaching the altar.

"How may I help you, gentlemen?" asked the priest in a thick eastern European accent, almost appearing from nowhere.

"Sir, my name is Brad Walker. I am looking for Father Emre Denkel," said Brad.

"You have found him," he said.

Father Emre Denkel wasn't a very tall man, to begin with, but his 5'6" height seemed even shorter because he was hunched over permanently. He was 71 years old, his hair balding on top and the sides were short and white. His thick long white beard hung down about 6" from his chin, bordered on either side from the bright red stole, with embroidered gold crosses and gold fringe at the ends, that draped around his neck. His surplice was white with black embroidered patterns on the ends of the sleeves and at the waist. The surplice hung large and loose over the solid black cassock that draped to the floor.

"This is Detective Oz Shields, from the Boston PD. I spoke with you earlier and said that we would be coming by to speak with you," said Brad.

"I remember. Please, this way. We can speak in my chambers," said Father Denkel.

Oz and Brad followed Father Denkel down a corridor to a large, heavy wooden door. The hinges groaned from the weight of the door as Father Denkel opened it. He held out his hand, offering Oz and Brad a seat in the two wooden and upholstered seats in front of his bureau. He shuffled his way around the desk to his desk chair and sat down.

"How may I help you, gentlemen?" asked Father Denkel.

"Father, thank you for seeing us on such short notice. Detective Shields shot a man who was possessed by a demon the other night, and we believe this demon has taken possession of a new host and is killing more people. We were hoping that you may be able to help us stop him," said Brad.

"A demon? This is something that I have experience in," said Father Denkel.

"You do? That is great!" said Brad.

"Father, may I play a recording for you?" asked Oz. "I think this will help you more than us talking about my experience."

"Sure, sure," said Father Denkel.

Oz pulled out his cellphone and played the recording for Father Denkel. As the voice on the recording spoke, Father Denkel leaned closer and closer to the phone, listening intently. His eyes widened, and his complexion drained of all color when the name "Azazel" was said. He sat back in his chair as the recording ended.

"This is not just some demon. This is a Prince of Hell!" said Father Denkel.

"So this dagger that you have, Father, will this kill him?" asked Brad.

"I'm afraid not, my son. This is no ordinary demon, no routine possession," said Father Denkel.

"Can he be defeated?" asked Oz.

"He can, but it's not easy," said Father Denkel. "To defeat a Prince of Hell, we will need the help of an angel."

"An angel?" said Oz.

"The last time a Prince of Hell was defeated, was thanks to an archangel," said Father Denkel.

"And how exactly do we get an archangel's help?" asked Oz.

"This is very risky. This would involve an angelic possession," said Father Denkel.

"Angelic possession?" asked Brad.

"Yes, we would hold a ceremony where we would pray to God, for an archangel to come and help us fight Azazel. If God is willing, they will come down from Heaven and possess our warrior, and then he will be strong enough to fight Azazel," said Father Denkel.

"Okay," said Oz. "How soon can we do this ceremony?"

"Our best chance of success is to attempt this on Saturday night," said Father Denkel. "But this is not something to take lightly, it is very risky."

"It's a risk that needs to be taken to stop this guy," said Oz.

"I don't think you understand," said Father Denkel.

"I understand perfectly, Father. I have to stop this demon before he kills too many more people. He is already too dangerous," said Oz.

"Okay, okay! You're the boss! Be here Saturday night at eight o'clock," said Father Denkel.

"Thank you, Father," said Oz.

"Yes, thank you, Father," said Brad

Oz and Brad stood up, shook hands with Father Denkel, and left the office. They walked through the church and exited through the doors in which they had entered the church. They did not speak a word to each other until they were outside on the steps of the church.

"You aren't even the slightest bit curious of the risks?" asked Brad.

"It can't be any greater than the risk of having this asshole continue to murder innocent people," said Oz. "And have his plan come to fruition."

"But what if…" said Brad.

"Brad, there is no risk too great!" said Oz, interrupting him.

"Okay, Oz. I was just asking," said Brad, now staring sheepishly at the ground.

"I'm sorry, man," said Oz, putting his hand on Brad's shoulder. "I just need this to be over with before too many good people get hurt or killed. Know what I mean?"

"Yeah. I get it," said Brad.

"And Brad?" said Oz.

"Yeah?" said Brad.

"Thank you. I would not have figured out any of this without your help. You're the best sidekick anyone could ask for. Forget Watson, man," said Oz.

"Thanks, Oz!" said Brad. "That means a lot."

"Don't even mention it, man. I really appreciate everything," said Oz.

"So I'll meet you here Saturday night?" said Brad.

"You don't have to do that, man," said Oz.

"I'm not bailing on you now, Oz. I'm with you the whole way," said Brad. "Besides, it's not like I'm doing anything else."

"Alright. I'll see you on Saturday. Again, I appreciate everything," said Oz.

Oz shook Brad's hand and slapped him on the shoulder before crossing the street and walking to his building. *I should message Donna and let her know that is where I will be coming from and to see what time she will be expecting me.*

31

Oz pulled up to Terry's house and parked behind his Malibu in the driveway. He got out and walked up the stairs to the front door, and rang the doorbell. The door opened, and Maureen greeted him, with a big smile on her face.

"Oz," she said, giving him a big hug. "Come in, come in."

"How's it going, Maureen?" said Oz. "Jim said he would be coming by."

"Where's my Dunkees?" shouted Terry.

"Oh, it's at the store until tomorrow morning when I come and get your ass," said Oz.

Terry laughed as Oz entered the living room. Terry stood up from the chair he was seated in and shook Oz's hand, pulling him in for a hug.

"How are you, kid?" asked Terry?

"Good. Heading over to Donna's for dinner tonight," said Oz.

"How's she doing, Hun?" asked Maureen, taking a seat on the arm of the chair where Terry was sitting.

"She's great! Loves her new job. She's been asking about you both," said Oz.

"She's a real sweetheart, Oz. Hang on to that one," said Maureen.

"I plan to," said Oz. "How about you, Ter? How are you feeling? Happy to be home?"

"Not too bad, kid," said Terry. "Some cuts are still pretty fucking sore, but I'll be glad to get back to work."

"Do you need extra time to put make-up on in the morning, or should I be good to be here for 8?" asked Oz.

"Cawksuckah!" said Terry, laughing. "Just be here with a fresh Dunkees in hand, and I'll be ready!"

"I swear you guys are awful to each other," said Maureen.

"Nah, this is just playing," said Terry.

Ding dong... Ding dong.

Maureen got up and went to answer the door. Terry leaned toward Oz to say something so that Maureen wouldn't hear him.

"I saw in the paper that our guy is back?" asked Terry.

"Looks that way, Ter. But I have a lead on how to stop him for good this time," said Oz.

"Tell me all about it in the car in the morning," said Terry.

Oz gave Terry a nod. Maureen opened the door. Jim was standing there, happy as always to see Maureen. He leaned in and kissed her on the cheek as they greeted each other.

"Alright Mo, where are you hiding Frankenstein?" shouted Jim from the door.

Maureen hit Jim playfully as he entered the house. Jim just smiled and squeezed her bicep gently, and gave her a playful wink.

"Jim, thanks for coming by. Oz wasn't abusing me enough," said Terry.

"I thought you couldn't get any uglier, but here you are," said Jim.

"Do you believe this fucking guy? Went from Lieutenant to comedian overnight," said Terry.

Jim gave Terry a hug before taking a seat next to Oz on the couch.

"All good, kid?" asked Jim.

"Yes, sir," said Oz.

"You ready to get your ass back to work tomorrow?" asked Jim.

"I was thinking, why don't I just start back on Monday, you know?" said Terry.

"Sure. Why not just take off the rest of the month while you're at it?" said Jim.

"That would be great, Jim. Thanks! Maureen and I could do a second honeymoon," said Terry.

"Should I put in the paperwork for your retirement too, while I'm at it?" said Jim.

"Your too kind," said Terry.

Oz and Maureen were laughing while Jim and Terry went back and forth at each other, getting more sarcastic with every response. They were like watching Jack Lemmon and Walter Matthau go back and forth at each other in the movie Grumpy Old Men.

"Oz, maybe it's best if you leave Frankenstein in the car when you talk to people," said Jim.

"Always great to have you come by, Lieutenant," said Terry, jokingly hinting that Jim should leave.

"Aww. He's so sensitive," said Jim. "Kidding aside, how are you feeling?"

"I was telling Oz, not too bad, some cuts are sore, but for the most part, I'm back to 100%," said Terry.

"Good to hear. I still can't believe how quickly you recovered," said Jim.

"Do you boys want to stay for supper?" asked Maureen.

"Thank you, Maureen, but I'm having dinner at Donna's tonight," said Oz.

"Aw, lovely. Enjoy yourself. Jim, how about you?" said Maureen.

"I don't want to impose," said Jim.

"Don't be silly!" said Maureen. "You're always welcome here, you know that."

"How can I say 'no' to that?" said Jim. "Thank you, Mo!"

Maureen got up and went into the kitchen to start making dinner, leaving the boys to talk shop. Terry adjusted himself in the chair, getting more comfortable.

"That was quite the scene last night," said Oz. "Want me to come and get you tonight if he strikes again?"

"Fuck that! I'll start back tomorrow after a good night's sleep in my own bed," said Terry.

"Sounds good, Ter," said Oz.

"You think he'll strike again tonight, kid?" asked Jim.

"It fits the MO," said Oz.

"Can you handle it solo again, or do you want me to join you?" asked Jim.

"I'm good, Jim. Just stay home after the call," said Oz.

"Okay, kid. Don't hesitate to call if you need me," said Jim.

"I will, sir," said Oz. "Ter, you alright?"

"Yeah, kid," said Terry.

"Alright then, I'm gonna split. I'll be here for eight tomorrow, with coffee," said Oz.

"You're alright, kid, I'll see you in the morning," said Terry.

"See you, Lieutenant, enjoy yourself tonight," said Oz

"Have a good night, kid!" said Jim.

Oz got up from the couch, patted Jim on the back, and Terry on the shoulder on his way to the kitchen to say goodbye to Maureen. He walked into the kitchen. Maureen was at the sink washing potatoes getting ready to peel them. Oz put his hand on the small of her back and kissed her on the cheek.

"Take care, Maureen. Call if you guys need anything. Otherwise, I'll be by in the morning to get Grumpy."

"Give Donna my love, have a great time tonight!" said Maureen.

"Do you want anything from Dunkin' in the morning, since I'm bringing it for the old man, anyway?" asked Oz.

"No, thanks, Hun. I'm good," said Maureen.

"Okay then, I'll see you in the morning. Have a great night!" said Oz.

Oz kissed her again on the cheek and left the kitchen. He waved one last time at Jim and Terry before opening the door and leaving the house.

***

Knock… Knock… Knock…

The door swung open and Donna leaped into Oz's arms, kissed him, and wrapped her arms and legs around him. Oz carried her into her apartment, kicking the door closed behind them. He dropped his duffle bag on the floor just inside the door.

"Mm, hard to say what smells better, you or your cooking?" said Oz.

"As long as you are prepared to devour both, who cares?" said Donna, kissing him again.

"How was today?" asked Oz, setting Donna back down on her feet.

"Great! It flew by," said Donna. "Oh shit, dinner!"

Donna ran into the kitchen and turned off the burner on the stove, and moved the pot to one of the burners. She stirred one of the other pots with a wooden spoon that she had resting on a small red spoon rest.

"So, what are we having, babe?" asked Oz. "Can I help at all?"

"Nope, I've got this. You just sit there and look pretty," said Donna.

Donna grabbed one of the plates that she had on the counter. She dished out some white rice and then topped the rice with the Pork Chili Verde that was stewing in the larger pot. She set the plate on the counter, opened the oven door, and pulled out and folded two flour tortillas that were in the oven getting warmed. She repeated these steps for the second plate, turned off all the burners and the oven, and carried the plates over to the table that was already set for them.

They sat at the table across from each other and clinked their glasses of Riesling that she had selected for them. Donna smiled at Oz as he took a sip from his glass. Oz smelled the dinner in front of him. The aroma and presentation were spectacular. Tender chunks of pork, slices of carrots, jalapeños, smothered in green enchilada sauce seasoned to perfection. Oz loaded his fork with some pork, rice, and carrots, blew on it, and put it in his mouth.

"Babe, you've outdone yourself again," said Oz.

"Glad you like it. I wasn't sure how it was gonna turn out. I've never made this before, but I found the recipe while I was on lunch, and thought it sounded good," said Donna.

"You are an incredible cook," said Oz. "This is so good!"

"It's definitely a recipe I'll save, that's for sure!" said Donna. "How are Terry and Maureen?"

"They're good. Terry was taking jabs, as usual. The Lieutenant came by and was going to stay for dinner," said Oz.

"Aww, nice. Is he still going to work tomorrow?" asked Donna.

"Yeah, picking him up tomorrow at 8," said Oz.

"Looking forward to having him back?" asked Donna.

"I am. I won't tell him that, but it will be nice to have him back," said Oz. "I'm stuffed! This was wonderful. Let me clean up."

"Don't be silly," said Donna.

"I insist, babe. You made this incredible meal. The least I can do is clean up the mess," said Oz.

Oz cleared the table, much to the protest of Donna. He poured her a fresh glass of Riesling and took her over to the couch. He walked back to the kitchen and Donna guided him to the containers for the leftovers to go in. Oz filled the containers and began washing the dishes. They chatted randomly about things while Oz did the dishes. When he finished, he joined her on the couch and snuggled up with her.

"Wanna watch a movie? Go for a walk?" asked Oz.

"Mmm. Both sound great, but I have a better idea," said Donna.

"Oh? You do, do you?" said Oz.

Vrrrt… Vrrrt… Vrrrt…

"Shit! Really?" said Donna.

Oz pulled his phone from his pocket and swiped it to unlock it and answer the call.

"Detective Shields, Homicide," said Oz. "Yes sir, the Esplanade Outdoor Gym… Yes, sir, North of Fenway on the Charles… No, sir… I'm good to go alone… Thank you, sir. I'll see you in the morning… Yeah, take care!"

"Gotta go?" asked Donna.

"Unfortunately," said Oz.

"Are you coming back?" asked Donna.

"It's 8:45 now. If I'm done there by 10, is that gonna be too late for you?" asked Oz.

"Hell no! I'd rather have you here than not," said Donna.

"Okay. I'll message you when I'm done to see if you're still up. I'll just leave my bag here if that is okay?"

"Leave anything you like here, Tiger," said Donna. With her arms around his neck, pulled him in for another kiss. "Be safe, Ozzy. I love you!"

"I love you too!" said Oz.

***

Oz parked his car on Back Street near the Silber Way Overpass. He took the overpass over Storrow Drive to access the bike path that would take him right to the Esplanade Outdoor Gym. An officer greeted at the scene Oz.

The officer was a young black man, about 24 years old, standing about 6'3" tall. His name was Devon Butler. Devon was in great shape, very broad-shouldered, a towering figure. Not many would get the best of him in a one-on-one situation. His voice was very deep, almost like a soft growl.

"Butler, how are you doing?" said Oz, approaching the scene.

"Detective, I could have gone the rest of my shift without seeing this shit, but other than that, I'm alright. Just you tonight?" said Devon.

"Yeah, Terry isn't back until tomorrow," said Oz.

"Heard he got messed up pretty bad. How's he doing?" asked Devon.

"Other than uglier, he's still the same," said Oz.

"Shit! That's cold!" laughed Devon.

"What do we have here tonight, man?" asked Oz.

"A fucking mess!" said Devon. "Follow me."

"Any sign of FSD or the crime scene photographer yet?" asked Oz.

"Nah. Not yet," said Devon.

"Who else is here tonight?" asked Oz.

"I don't think anyone that you know," said Devon.

They walked up to the outdoor gym, and Oz could begin to see what happened. It looked like the body had been dragged from one end of the helix-shaped gym to the other, leaving a trail of blood behind. As Oz and Devon approached the body, the scene worsened.

"I think someone is trying to send you a message, bro," said Devon.

"You think?" said Oz.

Oz crouched near the naked torso that remained. The arms, legs, and head had all been torn from the body. 'Ozwald' was carved into the flesh on the back of the torso from the left kidney area diagonally to the right shoulder.

"Any sign of the limbs or head?" asked Oz

"Nah, man," said Devon. "I did a quick search of the area after I arrived."

"Who called it in?" asked Oz.

"The other officer. Bike cop patrolling the paths here," said Devon.

"Did they see anyone else around? Anyone suspicious?" asked Oz.

"Nope. He said it was the quietest night that he has ever had. Like he was the only one out here all night. It gave him the creeps," said Devon. "Weird right?"

"Dude, if you had seen the shit I have over the last two weeks, you wouldn't say that," said Oz.

"So, why is your name carved into the back of this person?" asked Devon.

"I don't have a great explanation for you, but the killer doesn't like me and is sending me a message with each kill," said Oz.

"You're joking?" said Devon.

"Nope. Last night's victim had his head caved in, and they wrote my name in his blood above him on the Fort Hill Tower," said Oz.

"Shit! That's fucked up, man," said Devon.

"I just hope to track this asshole down, before he kills too many more," said Oz.

"Good luck with that, because he left nothing here to trace back to him," said Devon.

"Yeah, FSD isn't a fan of this guy, either. Makes their life hell," said Oz, standing up and heading back over to where Devon was standing. "Speaking of which, where are they?"

"You don't have to stay if you got somewhere else to be. I got this," said Devon.

"What's your guess? Male or Female?" asked Oz.

"Did you cheat on your Detective's exams?" joked Devon. "You know many guys who get a butterfly tramp stamp, Detective?"

"I thought you had one?" joked Oz.

"Nice try," laughed Devon. "I think it's worse, that you were right down there at the body, and you missed it. Maybe you should get your eyes checked."

"Haha, alright man. You got me. I fucking missed it, alright," said Oz.

"Just when I was starting to think you were getting to be a good detective, too," joked Devon.

"Alright, smart guy," said Oz.

"My silence will cost you a beer," said Devon.

"You got it, man," said Oz.

"You alright, Oz?" asked Devon. "You don't seem yourself?"

"Just distracted, man. I'm alright, though," said Oz.

"Go on, get out of here. I got this. I'll send you my report," said Devon.

"You sure?" asked Oz.

"Yeah, man. Go on. Tell Terry I said hey," said Devon.

"Will do, brother. Thanks," said Oz.

"No worries," said Devon.

Devon grabbed Oz's right hand in a hand hug, and pulled him in for a hug, patting him on the back with his left hand. This seemed to relieve Oz of some of the stress he was feeling.

Oz left the scene and messaged Donna on his way back to the car. She responded almost immediately. Oz couldn't wait to get back to her.

32

Oz pulled up in front of Terry's place just before eight o'clock. The front door of Terry's house opened and Terry stepped out, with Maureen right behind him. Terry turned to kiss Maureen goodbye before heading down the steps to get into Oz's car. Maureen waved to Oz from the doorway.

Terry gingerly walked down the steps, as he was still quite sore. He eased his way into the Mustang and put on his seatbelt. He eyed the two coffees in the cup holders.

"Morning, kid! Which one is mine?" asked Terry.

"That one there," said Oz, pointing to the cup furthest from the shifter.

"Thanks, kid! So, how was your night?" asked Terry.

"Lieutenant called just before 9, and had me go to the outdoor gym on the Charles, North of Fenway," said Oz.

"How bad was it?" asked Terry.

"Just a torso of a woman left behind with my name carved into the flesh. No arms, legs, or head. Blood from one end of the gym to the other," said Oz.

"This is one sick fuck!" said Terry.

"You can say that again," said Oz. "Butler was there last night. He said to say 'hi'."

"How's Butler?" asked Terry

"He's good. Said he could have gone all shift without seeing that last night," said Oz.

"He'll end up in Narcotics for sure," joked Terry.

"How was dinner with Jim?" asked Oz.

"Pretty good. Had some laughs. He left about 7:30 or so," said Terry.

Terry and Oz pulled into the station, and Oz parked the car, and they headed into the office. As they walked into the detective pool, applause and cheers greeted them. There was a banner that said 'Welcome Back Terry!' Terry hated this kind of thing. Jim knew it, which is precisely why he did it. Terry just said 'thanks' and walked to his desk. Sitting there on his desk was a Frankenstein mask.

"Fucking comedians!" said Terry.

"Aww, c'mon Ter, you know we're just messing with you," said Jim. "Good to have you back!"

Terry said nothing, just gave everyone a half-smile. He sat down at his desk and drank his coffee. The rest of the detectives knew that the moment was over and went back to their desks and their business. Oz sat down, turned on his computer, and opened a case file for the victim of last night's murder.

"You really know how to kill a party, Ter," said Oz.

"Jim knows I hate that shit!" said Terry.

"Yeah, but you could at least fake it," said Oz.

"What? Like you being a detective?" said Terry.

"Don't be a dick," said Oz.

"What are we doing today?" asked Terry, changing the subject.

"Nothing on the agenda so far. First, vic had no next of kin, and there wasn't much left of last night's victim to identify. So just like last time, we are sitting in the middle of the lake with no paddles," said Oz.

"Why did I come back?" asked Terry.

"You don't wanna hang out with me?" said Oz.

"Not here, kid," said Terry. "Anywhere but the office."

"C'mon, let's get out of here then," said Oz.

"Where are we going?" asked Terry?

"Breakfast," said Oz.

"For real?" said Terry.

"Absolutely, come on," said Oz.

Terry and Oz got up from their desks and headed out to his car. They got in and Oz drove them to a small diner not too far from the station that Oz knew about.

***

Returning to the office, Oz noticed that there was a message on his desk phone. Oz picked up the receiver and connected it to the digital mailbox. It was a message from Brad Walker about the victim from last night. Brad asked for Oz to call him when he got a chance. He sat down and dialed the ME's office, and asked for Brad.

"Brad Walker," said Brad.

"Hey, Brad, it's Oz," said Oz.

"Hey, Oz. How's it going?" said Brad.

"Good, I'm just returning your call," said Oz.

"Right, right, so, the two most recent victims, there has been no trace of the barbiturate," said Brad.

"So, these victims felt everything until the time of death?" asked Oz.

"The last victim, for sure. I believe that the carving of your name into the young woman's back was done before she was killed," said Brad.

"You're sure about that?" asked Oz.

"Positive. And the sick bastard cut her deep too," said Brad.

"What about the limbs? What can you tell me about how they were removed?" asked Oz.

"They were ripped off. Not cut. Literally pulled off. The flesh was tattered," said Brad. "Viciously removed."

"Posthumously?" asked Oz.

"I'm afraid not. Again I can't say in which order they were removed, but the head was definitely last," said Brad.

"Fuck!" said Oz.

"Yeah, it seems like this time around he is intent on making each victim suffer more and more. Probably because you made him start over," said Brad.

"All the more reason to stop him this time for good," said Oz.

"For sure," said Brad. "Are you worried at all?"

"Why worry about something that I can't control?" said Oz.

"I guess, but it's not even me, and I'm shitting myself," said Brad.

"Don't worry, man, it will all work out," said Oz. "Anything else that we need to know about our victims?"

"No, that is all for now. If anything else comes up, I'll let you know," said Brad.

"Thanks, Brad," said Oz.

"No problem, Oz," said Brad.

Oz hung up the phone and pulled out his notebook. He jotted down some notes on the victims. Terry looked up from his computer, tossing a scotch mint in his mouth from his desk drawer.

"What's up, kid?" asked Terry.

"That was Brad, the ME. He said that the barbiturate substance hasn't been found on any of the victims so far and that all the trauma that has been inflicted on them was done before he killed them. He is making these people suffer more this time around," said Oz.

"That ain't good," said Terry.

"No, that's why this time I have to stop him for good," said Oz.

"You got any idea how to do that?" asked Terry.

"You won't believe me," said Oz.

"Oz, I'm so far from not believing you after what happened. Try me," said Terry.

"I've spoken with a Kurdish priest, and on Saturday we are going to attempt an angelic possession," said Oz.

"A what?" said Terry.

"We are going to attempt to have an angel possess me so that I can fight and kill this thing," said Oz.

"You're kidding me, right?" said Terry. "Kid, what if something goes wrong?" said Terry.

"Terry, we gotta stop this thing! How bad will it get if we don't?" said Oz.

"I know what you're saying, kid, but at what cost?" asked Terry.

"I'm not willing to find out the cost if we don't do something," said Oz.

"You're nuts! Do you know that?" said Terry.

***

The rest of the day was pretty quiet. It was probably for the best, since it was Terry's first day back. It was good for him to ease back into things. They didn't say much to each other for the rest of the day. Terry spent the day reading the news and sports articles on his computer, while Oz tried to look into angelic possession, though every search came up with references to demonic possession. Apparently, angelic possession was far rarer.

The ride back to Terry's place was quiet until Terry finally couldn't hold it in anymore. He turned off Oz's radio and started to speak to him like a father.

"Tell me more about this possession thing?" said Terry.

"Brad and I went to see this priest, and he said that there is an ancient ceremony that he will perform, requesting that God let an archangel come down and help us," said Oz.

"Did this priest tell you anything else?" asked Terry.

"He mentioned a couple of times that it is risky," said Oz.

"Risky, how?" asked Terry.

"I didn't ask. I just said, let's do it," said Oz.

"Are you fucking retarded?" said Terry. "Kid, what if you get killed?"

"Terry, I faced this thing before, and it didn't kill me. If I have an angel on my side, it can only be better, right?" said Oz.

"Let's say this works, and you kill this demon. How do you stop the angelic possession?" asked Terry.

"I never asked," said Oz.

"For fuck's sake, kid," said Terry. "Tomorrow we are going to see this priest, and I'm gonna ask the questions that you didn't."

"Ter, seriously man, it's not a big deal," said Oz.

"Oz, you wanna hear how 'not a big deal' it is? When we get to my place, come in and tell Maureen what you wanna do," said Terry. "Better yet, call Donna right now and tell her."

"No, thanks," said Oz.

"You're fucking right, 'no, thanks'. You know she'll lose her shit on you. I assume that Donna doesn't know either?" said Terry.

"No, I didn't tell her," said Oz.

"Of course you didn't. Because she'd lose her shit on you, too!" said Terry.

"I just don't want her to worry any more than she already does," said Oz.

"And how do you think she's gonna feel if something like this happens to you?" said Terry, pointing at his face.

"Ter, I know you're right, but this thing has to be stopped," said Oz.

"Then let's find another way. We'll talk to the priest and see if there is another way," said Terry.

"Alright, Ter," said Oz.

Oz pulled up in front of the house and put the car in park. He felt somewhat deflated from the strong arguments that Terry had made, not just out of genuine concern for his well-being, but also for being so logical and rational about it all.

"Have a good night, kid," said Terry. "Think about what I said."

"You too, Ter," said Oz. "Do you need a hand getting inside?"

"Nah, I'm good," said Terry, exiting the vehicle.

33

Oz got out of the shower and dried himself off. He wrapped the towel around his waist and went to his bedroom, picked up his cell phone from the top of the dresser. There was a message from Donna, checking on him. He replied.

'Hey, Hun! Everything is good. Just out of the shower.'

'Am I gonna see you tonight?'

'For sure! I just had to come home first. Any idea what you wanna do tonight?'

'How bout you grab us something from that Italian place, and I'll come to you tonight?'

'You sure? I don't mind coming to your place.'

'Absolutely. I'm just gonna get myself ready, and I'll see you shortly.'

'Ok Hun. I love you!'

'I love you xo!'

Oz got dressed and left the apartment, walking just up the street to the pizzeria. He walked inside and, like always, there was Little Joe, behind the counter.

"Maria, come! Our boy Ozzy is back," shouted Little Joe.

"Don't lie to me, Joe," shouted Maria from the kitchen.

"He's not lying," shouted Oz.

"Oh! My boy, what brings you in tonight?" asked Maria, coming from the kitchen out to the front of the restaurant and greeting Oz in her usual manner.

"Well, my lady is coming over for dinner tonight, and she asked me to get something from here for us to enjoy. Any suggestions?" asked Oz.

"Is she fussy?" asked Maria.

"No, not at all," said Oz.

"How about I make you a special spicy sausage penne arrabbiata, huh?" asked Maria.

"Where's that on the menu?" asked Oz.

"Silly boy, I make a lot of things that are not on the menu," said Maria.

"What's in it?" asked Oz.

"I love you like a son, but you're not getting my recipes," joked Maria.

"I don't know what I would do without you, Maria," said Oz.

"You'd be a lot skinnier, that's for sure!" said Little Joe.

Maria slapped Little Joe on the arm as she went back to the kitchen to prepare the dish. Little Joe just laughed, shaking his belly.

"What's the damage, Joe?" asked Oz.

"That will be $15, Ozzy," said Little Joe.

"C'mon, its gotta be more than that," said Oz.

"Nope, that's it," said Little Joe.

Oz gave him $20 and put his hand up, letting him know he didn't want the change. Oz hung out with Little Joe, chatting away, while the dinner rush began to hit. There was some young help for Maria in the kitchen, and of course, the delivery drivers coming and going.

Maria came out from the kitchen carrying a large covered aluminum pan, placing it on the counter. She walked around the counter, gave Oz a hug and kiss, and gave him a big smile.

"You and your lady friend enjoy, okay?" said Maria. "Always so good to see you, Ozzy!"

"Thanks, Maria, we will," said Oz. "Love you both! Be good!"

Oz grabbed the tray and left the shop and walked back to the apartment. As he got to the door, Donna pulled up to the curb and parked the car. Oz stood there and waited for her to join him so they could head upstairs together.

Donna greeted Oz with a kiss, then smelled the tray that Oz was holding. The smile that was already on her face from seeing Oz grew bigger and brighter. They took the elevator up and entered Oz's apartment.

Oz pulled a couple of bowls down from the counter and Donna grabbed cutlery from the utensil drawer and some paper towels to fold into napkins. Oz dished up the pasta into the bowls and took them over to the table. He grabbed the Parmesan cheese shaker from the fridge and the red pepper flakes from his spice cupboard. Donna pulled out a bottle of red wine from her overnight bag.

"Is that all you have in there?" asked Oz.

"Let's just say, that bottle is bigger than anything that I brought to sleep in," said Donna.

"Let's dig in," said Oz.

Donna poured the wine into the glasses that she brought over to the table. They dug into the hearty pasta dish that Maria had made for them.

"Oh, my God! This is incredible! What is it called?" asked Donna.

"Maria called it Penne Arrabbiata," said Oz.

"I'm definitely gonna order this again!" she said.

"It's not on the menu, so, good luck!" laughed Oz.

"It's not on the menu? How did you get it?" asked Donna.

"I went in and told them you were coming over, and I needed something nice for dinner. Maria was the one who said that we would like this," said Oz.

"She really does like you!" said Donna.

"Loves me like a son," laughed Oz.

"I'll say. Not many people get this kind of special treatment from a restaurant," said Donna.

"What can I say, people like me," said Oz.

"How was Terry today?" asked Donna.

"He was pretty grumpy when we got to work. The boys surprised him with a 'Welcome Back' celebration," said Oz.

"Why did that make him grumpy?" asked Donna.

"He hates stuff like that. Especially when it is for him," said Oz.

"He seems like such a different person at work," said Donna.

"He's a lot harder at work than he is outside," said Oz.

"Was it a good day, though?" asked Donna as she finished her dinner.

"Yeah. Terry got a little upset with me at the end of the day," said Oz.

"Why?" asked Donna.

"I have something to tell you, and I don't want you to get upset with me too," said Oz.

"Ozzy, what is it? Why would I get upset with you?" asked Donna.

"The demon has returned, and is growing stronger and more violent every day," said Oz.

"Right, you heard it the other day," said Donna.

"Yeah. Well, the ME and I have been looking into how to stop him for good, and we think that we have found a way, but it is risky," said Oz.

"How risky?" asked Donna.

"I never asked," said Oz.

"Never asked who?" asked Donna. "Can you stop holding back and just tell me what is going on?"

"Okay, okay," said Oz, taking a deep cleansing breath. "We read about a Kurdish dagger that has the power to kill demons, so we went to speak with this priest who supposedly had one."

"That's great, so the risk is that you need to be close enough to use the dagger?" asked Donna.

"No. I played the recording for the priest so that he could hear exactly what we are dealing with, and he said that the dagger will not work on a Prince of Hell," said Oz.

"So what will?" asked Donna.

"He said that we need to perform a ceremony requesting that an archangel come down and help us," said Oz.

"I'm still not seeing the risky part, Hun," said Donna.

"The priest said that in order for the archangel to come, there needs to be an angelic possession," said Oz.

"So, this angel needs to possess a body?" asked Donna.

"Yeah, and I may have volunteered for this," said Oz.

"What? Why would you do this?" asked Donna.

"I can't just keep killing the host. We need to send this demon back to Hell for good," said Oz.

"But why you?" asked Donna.

"I just feel like this is something that I have to do," said Oz. "That it's something that only I can do."

"Babe, I don't want you to do this," said Donna.

"This is why Terry yelled at me too," said Oz.

"And you are still going to do this?" asked Donna.

"Terry and I are going to see the priest again tomorrow. He has a lot more questions he wants to ask before he even considers this as an option," said Oz.

"At least someone has some sense," said Donna.

"Babe, please don't be upset," said Oz.

"How can I not be? I love you! Your job is dangerous enough as is. That risk I can accept, but this… this is beyond. This is you volunteering to put yourself in danger without any consideration for those who care about you," said Donna.

Oz just lowered his head in defeat. This is the very reaction that Terry said he would get. Donna got up and walked around the table to Oz and sat on his lap, wrapping her arms around his shoulders. She put her forehead to his and closed her eyes.

"I love you, Oz! You are the greatest man I have ever known. Please don't do anything that would take you away from me," she said.

A single tear rolled down Donna's cheek. Oz wrapped his arms around her and embraced her. His heart was aching with the thought that he was making her upset.

"I love you too, Donna," said Oz. "I'm sorry. I wasn't thinking."

Donna squeezed him tighter. She sniffled and buried her head in his shoulder. Oz ran his fingers through her hair, trying to calm her.

Donna sat up and wiped her tears and looked into Oz's eyes. She could see the guilt he was feeling and gave him a reassuring smile. She got up from his lap, went to clear the bowls, and Oz grabbed her hand.

"Go and sit, babe. I have this," said Oz. "Can I pour you some more wine?"

"Please," she said, sniffling.

Donna went and sat on the couch, and Oz brought her another glass of wine. He turned to go and clear the table and Donna grabbed a hold of his hand. He squeezed her hand and lifted it up to kiss it.

Oz cleared the table and washed the dishes before joining her on the couch. Oz sat on the couch and Donna laid her head on his lap. He caressed her cheek and pet her head. She rolled onto her back to look up at him.

"I'm sorry," she said.

"Sorry for what? You did nothing wrong. I'm the idiot," he said.

"You're not an idiot, babe. It's the hero in you. The savior. You will do whatever it takes to protect. I understand that, as much as I don't like it," she said.

Donna sat up and straddled Oz. She kissed him long and deep. Her hands laid on either side of his face. Oz embraced her, wrapping his arms around her.

***

Vrrrt… Vrrrt… Vrrrt…

"Detective Shields, Homici…" said Oz.
"I know who the fuck I'm calling!" said Terry.
"Ter? What time is it?" asked Oz.
"After midnight. Put your boots on, we've got another one," said Terry.
"Right. I'll come by and get you shortly," said Oz. "Where are we going?"
"My side of the Charles. Flagstaff Park," said Terry.
"Alright, I'll be there in fifteen," said Oz.
"Sounds good, kid," said Terry. "Oh, hey?"
"Yeah?" said Oz.
"Bring coffee!" said Terry.
"Sure thing, boss," laughed Oz.

Oz hung up the phone and cuddled up to Donna from behind. He kissed her on the neck and squeezed her tightly. Donna moaned and wiggled into him.

"Gotta go, babe. I'll be back shortly. Stay right here, just like this. I love you!" said Oz.

"I love you!" moaned Donna.

Oz gave her one last kiss before getting out of bed and getting dressed. Oz grabbed his keys and his police windbreaker and left the apartment. He hopped in his car and headed out to get Terry, stopping at Dunkin on the way.

Oz pulled up in front of Terry's house, and Terry came out. He was watching from the front window for Oz to pull up. Terry came down the stairs and to the passenger side of the car, getting in and sitting down. Terry grabbed his coffee from the cup holder, popped the top before taking a sip. It began to rain.

"That's a good coffee!" said Terry. "How was your night going?"

"I told Donna what was going on," said Oz.

"Yeah? Did she lose her shit on you?" asked Terry.

"In so few words, yeah. She was pretty upset," said Oz.

"No fucking shit, genius!" said Terry. "I'm not an expert on women, but I know what'll piss them off."

"You were right, man. Need me to say any more than that?" said Oz.

"So, you're not gonna go through with it now, right?" said Terry.

"I didn't say that. We should still go see the priest tomorrow though," said Oz.

They pulled up to the Harvard Bus Tunnel (more like a laneway) and parked near the two squad cars blocking the entrance. They got out of the car and headed toward the scene, showed their badges to the officer standing near the squad cars, who waved them through.

Halfway down the lane was the FSD Truck. Jared and the crew were out and suiting up. Jared gave Terry and Oz a wave, and they headed over to him.

"Welcome back, Terry! How are you?" asked Jared.

"Not bad, kid. Thanks!" said Terry.

"Know what we are looking at here tonight?" asked Oz.

"I know what you aren't looking at if you aren't twenty feet tall," said Jared.

"What?" asked Terry.

"Head to the monument and you'll see," said Jared. "We'll be over there shortly."

"Sounds good," said Oz.

They turned and walked towards the monument. The rain was light. As they approached the monument, they could see something near the top. Oz pulled his flashlight from his pocket and shined it up the pole. Atop the monument was a golden-colored eagle with its wings spread, looking like it was ready to take flight. The wings were pierced through the upper torso of the body that was suspended there.

At first, Oz thought the body was just stripped and covered in blood, but as they got closer, he realized that like the priest, it had been skinned. Worse than that, it had been skinned and the muscles on the arms and legs butterflied open, exposing the bones.

"How good are your eyes, kid?" asked Terry.

"Pretty good, but I can't exactly say what I'm seeing," said Oz.

"Give it a go," said Terry.

"I'd say we have another male, just based on the size of the victim. The skin has been removed, and the muscles on the arms and legs opened up," said Oz.

"How the fuck did this thing get the body up there?" asked Terry.

"No clue, but it did. We gotta stop this thing, Ter. It's clearly more powerful this time around," said Oz.

Suddenly, from above, there was a ghastly cry. The body twitched, and the legs kicked. It let out another scream in pain before the scream trailed off and the body fell limp.

"Jesus! He's still alive!" said Oz. "Jared!"

Jared poked his head out from behind the truck to see Oz waving him over, and yelling for him again. Jared came running over, the Tyvek suit ballooning open as he ran.

"What's up?" said Jared.

"The victim may still be alive, but won't be for long," said Oz.

"You're shitting me!" said Jared. "Sharon, radio dispatch, we need an ambulance now!"

"What?" yelled Sharon.

"Ambulance! Now!" yelled Jared.

Sharon darted to the driver's door of the truck, flinging it open, and got on the radio. They could hear her yelling on the radio, stressing the urgency of the situation.

The faint sound of sirens could be heard, getting louder with every passing second. Within just a few minutes, they saw the two cruisers part, letting a firetruck and an ambulance through. Sharon hopped in the FSD truck and moved it ahead, making room for the firetruck and ambulance.

The ladder on the firetruck began extending towards the victim on the monument. Two firefighters walked the ladder as it extended. Not wasting a single second, the trailing firefighter carried a backboard. The ladder extended to within inches of the monument beneath the victim. The first firefighter arrived at the victim, reaching up and C-collar on the victim, before attempting to move him.

The second firefighter arrived and laid out the backboard on the rails of the ladder. As the first firefighter lifted the victim from the wings of the eagle and rotated to lay the nearly lifeless body on the backboard. The two firefighters positioned the victim on the board and strapped them down before descending the ladder.

When they reached the fire truck, they passed the backboard down to the rest of the truck crew, waiting to transfer the victim to the gurney. The paramedics went to work the second the victim hit the gurney. Oz and Terry rushed over to the ambulance just as the paramedics lifted the gurney into the back.

"Is he alive?" asked Oz.

"Barley, the pulse is very weak," said the paramedic, closing the rear doors.

The other paramedic hopped into the front seat and the ambulance sped off, headed for the Cambridge Health Alliance Hospital, lights flashing and siren blaring.

"If that guy is still alive, I'm sure that he doesn't wanna be anymore," said Terry.

"Ter, that's awful!" said Oz.

"Kid, think about it! No skin, all hacked up… would you wanna live?" said Terry.

"I get what you're saying, but still," said Oz.

"Kid, I wasn't half that bad, and until you showed up, I was ready to go," said Terry. "I'll bet that poor son of a bitch has no fight left, no desire to stay alive. And no one would blame him."

"Yeah, you're probably right," said Oz. "I'll be right back."

"Where are you going?" asked Terry.

"I'm going to go speak with one of the officers. I want to find out who called this in, who found him," said Oz.

"Alright, I'm coming," said Terry.

They walked back to the two officers who were blocking the entrance to the laneway. Oz was kinda kicking himself that he didn't ask on their way by, but maybe they weren't meant to.

"Officer," shouted Oz.

"Yeah, Detective?" one of the officers replied.

"Who called this in?" asked Oz.

"I did," said the officer. "I was driving down Peabody, and I just happened to glance at the monument there. Didn't know what it was until I shined the spotlight on it. When I saw it was a person, I called it in right away."

"Did you see anything else?" asked Oz.

"Not that I can recall. The park was empty, and there was no traffic. Not unusual for this time of night here," said the officer.

"Thanks," said Oz.

"C'mon, kid, let's call it a night," said Terry. "We can find out in the morning if this is a homicide or not."

"Alright, Ter."

They walked over and got into the Mustang. Oz headed off towards Terry's place. Terry winced and shifted in his seat.

"You alright, Ter?" asked Oz.

"Yeah, just time to take some Tylenol and go to bed," said Terry.

"We're almost home, man. You gonna be alright for 8 tomorrow?" asked Oz.

"Yeah, kid. I'll be good," said Terry.

"Ok, I'll bring the coffee," said Oz.

"Damn right you will," joked Terry.

Oz pulled up to the front of Terry's place and parked the car beside the curb. Maureen left on the porch light and an upstairs light for Terry.

"Thanks, kid. Get home safe, and get a good night's sleep," said Terry.

"Thanks, Ter. You too," said Oz.

"I am home, dummy," joked Terry.

"Get the fuck out of my car, old man. I'll see you in the morning," said Oz, laughing.

Terry laughed and slapped Oz on the front of his right shoulder before getting out of the car. Terry slowly climbed the stairs to the front door. Oz waited by the curb until he saw Terry was inside. Terry gave Oz a wave, closed the door, and turned off the porch light.

34

Oz woke to the sound of his alarm. He rolled over and shit it off, stretched and groaned, before rolling back over to spoon and hug Donna. Donna moaned as he kissed her neck.

"Good morning, gorgeous!" he whispered into her ear.

"Mm, good morning, Detective," she replied.

"I'm gonna go and take a quick shower. Are you getting ready here or at your place?' asked Oz.

"No, I'm gonna finish getting ready at my place," she replied.

"Want me to pack you some pasta from last night for lunch?" asked Oz.

"Mm, that sounds lovely," said Donna.

"You got it, babe," said Oz.

Oz got out of bed and went to the bathroom to get ready for work. Donna fell back to sleep and awoke twenty minutes later to Oz getting dressed. He smiled at her when she rolled over and looked at him.

"Morning, Sunshine!" said Oz.

"Mm, morning!" said Donna. "My turn to get ready?"

"Totally up to you, babe. I don't care if you want to stay right there all day," said Oz.

"I wish," said Donna.

"I'm gonna go and pack your lunch," said Oz.

Oz leaned down and gave Donna a kiss and left the room for the kitchen. Oz pulled down a mid-sized plastic container from one of the cupboards and dished some pasta from last night into it. He snapped on the lid and set it on the breakfast bar.

Donna came out of the washroom with her overnight bag in hand and came into the kitchen where Oz was. She gave him a kiss and wrapped her arms around him. Oz wrapped his arms around her.

"Let's go out for dinner tonight," said Oz.

"Where do you want to go?" asked Donna.

"Depends. What do you think you feel like?" asked Oz.

"It will be hard to top last night's dinner," said Donna.

"Seafood?" asked Oz.

"I'm intrigued," said Donna.

"How about just a nice restaurant down on the harbor?" said Oz.

"You're on, Mr. Shields!" said Donna.

"I'll call today and get us a table for 7 or 7:30?" said Oz.

"Sounds good," said Donna.

They grabbed their things and left the apartment. Oz walked Donna to her car, kissing her goodbye before watching her drive off. Oz went back into the building, entered the garage from the stairwell, and got into his car.

***

Oz pulled up in front of Terry's house. Terry opened the front door, turned, and kissed Maureen goodbye before gingerly heading down the stairs. Maureen waved to Oz, and Oz waved back. Terry opened the passenger door and got in, groaning as he sat down.

"Morning, Ter! You alright?" asked Oz.

"Yeah, kid. Just a little tired and sore, but this magic elixir will fix me right up!" said Terry. "How are you?"

"I'm good. Finally, Friday," said Oz.

Ring… Ring… Ring…

"Detective Shields, Homicide," said Oz, answering the call through the Bluetooth in the car as he began driving away from Terry's house.

"Shields, it's Lieutenant Roberts," said Jim. "Have you picked up Terry yet?"

"I'm here, Jim," said Terry.

"Damn, I'm good," joked Jim.

"What's up, Lieutenant?" said Oz.

"Last night's victim was alive until arriving at the hospital, where he succumbed to his injuries. So, it's back in your house," said Jim.

"No offense, but thank God he didn't live," said Terry.

"I agree with you there. I hear it was pretty bad," said Jim.

"Yeah, sir, it was," said Oz.

"Stop by the ME's office before you come in. I'll see you when you get into the office," said Jim.

"Yes, sir," said Oz, hanging up the call.

"Starting my Friday with Doctor Dickhead, perfect," said Terry.

"He's not that bad, man," said Oz.

"So says you," said Terry.

"Just shut up and enjoy your coffee, old man," said Oz.

"Don't mind if I do," said Terry.

Oz pulled up in front of the ME's office and parked the car. Terry let out a sigh, dreading the thought of going inside. Oz looked at Terry, smiled, and patted him on the leg.

"C'mon, buddy. Let's go! Behave and I'll buy you a refill on the way to the office," said Oz.

"Fine," said Terry in a child-like protest.

They got out of the car and walked into the reception area of the ME's office. The receptionist looked up from what she was doing to greet them. She recognized them straight away and called Brad to let him know they had arrived. Seconds later, the double doors off to the right of the reception desk opened, and Brad appeared in the doorway.

"This way, gents," said Brad.

Oz and Terry followed Brad down the hall to one of the exam rooms, where the body was sitting on an exam table covered. Brad grabbed a file folder from a stainless-steel table just inside the door of the room.

"Cause of death was similar to the priest who was crucified, traumatic cardiac arrest, and hypovolemia, but far more blood loss this time, because of the deep cuts through the muscle tissue," said Brad.

"Did you find anything unusual?" asked Oz.

"Not any more unusual than the way that this poor guy was murdered," said Brad.

"Any luck with identification?" asked Oz.

"Unfortunately, no. DNA is not a match to anything in the database," said Brad.

"Any trace of the saliva or the barbiturate?" asked Oz.

"No, none. So, again, this victim felt everything, right to the end," said Brad.

"Sick fucker," said Terry.

"He definitely seems more sadistic this time around," said Brad.

"Are the cuts the same as before?" asked Oz.

"Definitely! Just as sharp and with the same precision," said Brad. "No hesitation cuts, which shows just how intentional all of these cuts are."

"Thanks, Brad," said Oz.

"Sure, no problem. Any idea where he is gonna strike next," asked Brad.

"No. Nothing yet," said Oz.

"Well, good luck! This sick fuck needs to be stopped," said Brad, trying to pander to Terry.

"You got that right," said Terry.

"We'll leave you to it, Brad. Thanks again!" said Oz.

"No problem," said Brad.

Oz and Terry shook hands with Brad and left the room. Neither said a word as they walked down the hall towards the double doors to the reception area. Oz opened the door for Terry as they entered the reception area and waved goodbye to the receptionist on their way out of the building.

***

Jim came out of his office and walked over to Oz and Terry sitting at their desks. He pulled out the chair at the desk beside Terry and sat down.

"How'd it go at the ME's office?" asked Jim.

"It's definitely our killer," said Terry.

"Any idea how to catch him?" asked Jim.

"We're just getting ready to go and see someone, and see if we can get some information about how to stop him," said Oz.

"Keep me posted," said Jim.

"You got it, Jim," said Terry.

Jim got up and walked over to the kitchenette.

"Want to go and see that priest and get a bite to eat for lunch?" asked Oz.

"I like the way you think," said Terry.

"I just know how you think," said Oz.

"I thought it was either that, or you could hear my belly yelling," joked Terry.

They got up and walked down to the motor pool, where Oz grabbed the keys for their usual Impala. Oz drove them to the Basilica of Our Lady of Perpetual Help, where he parked in the parking lot on the Southside of the building. They entered the church and headed down the main aisle towards the altar. As they approached, Father Denkel came down from the altar to greet them.

"Welcome, gentlemen. How can I help you?" asked Father Denkel.

"Father, I'm Detective Shields. I was here the other day with Mr. Walker," said Oz.

"Right, right," said Father Denkel, recognizing Oz.

"Father, this is my partner, Detective White," said Oz, introducing Terry.

"Com, come. Let's go to my chambers," said Father Denkel.

Oz and Terry followed Father Denkel down the hall to his chambers. He opened the heavy wooden door, and they followed him inside. Father Denkel walked around the desk and sat in his chair, and Oz and Terry sat down in the chairs opposite of him.

"Now, what can I do for you?" asked Father Denkel.

"Father, my partner was telling me about some plan to attempt an angelic possession?" asked Terry.

"Yes. That is what we spoke about," said Father Denkel.

"How dangerous is this?" asked Terry.

"This can be very risky," said Father Denkel.

"How risky?" asked Terry.

"Well, typically the risk is their life, as we are summoning a mighty entity, to battle another powerful entity," said Father Denkel.

"Kid, are you sure that you wanna risk your life for this?" asked Terry.

"Terry, we risk our lives every day just being cops. I think this is something that we have to do," said Oz.

"Your partner is very special. He has a guardian's spirit, a protector's mentality, and a warrior's spirit. He will always choose to preserve the lives of others over his," said Father Denkel.

"How successful is this type of thing?" asked Terry, ignoring what the Father said about Oz.

"Well, it depends on how powerful the entity has become. But unlike the demon, an angel does not need to build his strength in the possession. They come ready for battle," said Father Denkel. "Benefits of doing the Lord's work, perhaps."

"None of this is making me feel any better," said Terry.

"How bad will it get if we don't try this?" asked Oz.

"If the demon gets powerful enough, and finds a sacrifice for his bride, this could bring the apocalypse," said Father Denkel.

"You're joking?" said Terry.

"I'm not. It is the duty of a prince of hell to bring the end of days," said Father Denkel. "Opening the door for the other princes and the Devil, himself."

"This is so crazy!" said Terry.

"Azazel is the demon associated with the sin of Wrath. He is ruthless and will stop at nothing," said Father Denkel.

"Is there another way beyond possession to stop him?" asked Oz.

"Not that I know of," said Father Denkel. "Princes of Hell are not normal demons. They are stronger, more powerful. It's not just a possession."

"No silver bullets or something? Bullets soaked in holy water?" asked Terry.

"Weapons of man will only work on the host, not the demon," said Father Denkel.

Terry sighed and hung his head. With every question that he asked, his ability to stop this from happening slipped away, no matter how much he tried to think of another way.

"Thank you, Father. We appreciate you taking the time to see us," said Oz.

"No worries," said Father Denkel.

35

Oz and Terry returned to the office after grabbing lunch. Terry was quiet from the moment that they left the church. Oz didn't want to bother him. It was best to just let Terry think. Oz hated the silence between him and his partner today. He couldn't let this continue. If they weren't going to talk about the situation at the church, then Oz was going to find something else to break the silence.

"Ter, do you know a nice place to go for dinner?" asked Oz.

"Are you asking me out on a date?" said Terry. "You could do better than that."

"Funny guy! I want to take Donna somewhere for dinner tonight," said Oz.

"Have you been to 75 on Liberty Wharf?" asked Terry.

"No. Is it good?" asked Oz.

"Fucking delicious, kid. Nice, relaxed atmosphere, no need to really dress up fancy," said Terry. "Maureen, and I have been there a few times for our anniversary."

"Really? I think that is the nicest that I have ever heard you talk about any place," said Oz.

"You make me sound like a monster. I like things," said Terry. "You should call and make a reservation for tonight if you plan on going there tonight. Gets busy there, especially on a Friday night."

Oz googled 75 on Liberty Wharf and found the number. He picked up the desk phone and dialed the number. The phone rang three times.

"I'm going to kill you, Ozwald," said the voice.

"Pardon me?" said Oz, surprised by what he heard.

"75 on Liberty Wharf, how may I help you," said the voice of a young woman on the other side of the call.

"Yes, sorry. I would like a reservation for 4 people please," said Oz.

Terry looked up from his computer screen at Oz and mouthed the words 'four' to him with a questioning look. Oz covered the receiver.

"Call Maureen and tell her you two are my guests for dinner tonight," said Oz.

"What time would you be looking for, sir?" said the young woman.

"I was thinking around 7:00?" asked Oz.

"Just a moment… yes, sir, I can fit your party in for 7 tonight. Is it a special occasion?" she asked.

"Just dinner with friends," said Oz.

"Wonderful, sir. Can I get your name for the reservation?" she asked.

"Yes, Shields. S-H-I-E-L-D-S," said Oz.

"Thank you, Mr. Shields. We will see you and your party at 7 tonight," she said.

"Thank you so much. Bye," said Oz.

"All together, how perfect. You can watch them die," said the voice.

Oz hung up the phone. His expression was blank and his complexion, paling. Terry saw this and noted how his expression didn't match the conversation that he just heard.

"You okay, kid?" asked Terry.

"Huh?" said Oz.

"You okay?" asked Terry again. "Something wrong?"

"Uh, no. No, nothing's wrong. We're all good for 7 tonight," said Oz, recovering.

"You don't have to take us out for supper, kid," said Terry. "Plus, I'm liable to put people off their suppers."

"Stop, you're healing better well. I know I don't have to, but I want to take you guys out. So are you going to call Maureen or not?" said Oz.

"Okay, okay, I'll call her," said Terry.

"Shall I pick you guys up tonight?" asked Oz.

"Nah, Maureen can drive us," said Terry.

"You sure?" asked Oz.

"Yeah. Better than us all cramming into the Mustang," said Terry.

"We can all fit in the Mustang, fine," said Oz.

"Nah, it's all good, kid," said Terry.

"Alright, Ter. If you say so," said Oz.

"I'll call Maureen now and let her know," said Terry.

Terry grabbed his cell phone from his pocket and called Maureen to tell her they were joining Oz and Donna for dinner tonight. Oz pulled out his cell and messaged Donna, letting her know he booked them a table for 7. He didn't tell her about Terry and Maureen before joining them. He wanted that to be a surprise.

***

Oz gathered his things from the breakfast bar before leaving the apartment to pick up Donna from her place. He entered the stairwell and headed down the stairs to the door, accessing the garage. He unlocked the Mustang as he walked towards it.

"You will suffer!" said the voice.

Oz ignored it as he got into his car. It would be easier to ensure everyone's safety, since they were all going to be together. He started the car, and drove out of his parking spot, and left the garage. He pulled up to Donna's apartment and called her from the car.

"Hey, babe! Are you all set?" asked Oz.

"Hey! Yeah, I'll be right down," said Donna.

They hung up the phone, and a couple of minutes later Donna appeared. She looked beautiful, as always, wearing a flowery patterned spring dress. Her hair, down and slightly curled, bounced as she skipped into Oz's arms. She kissed him as he wrapped his arms around her and lifted her up. He set her back down on her feet and opened the passenger side door for her to get in. Donna elegantly got into the car, and Oz closed the door once she was inside and settled. He jogged around to the driver's side and got in.

"The first week under your belt, how was it?" he asked, pulling away from the curb.

"It was good. Fairly busy. Prepped a bunch of things for the weekend. But I'm glad the week is done. Which sounds horrible because I did have such a great first week," said Donna. "How'd you get on today?"

"Pretty quiet. Not much going on. No identity for last night's victim," said Oz.

"I think that would be worse than knowing the ID. At least if you have a name, as horrible as letting their loved ones know what happened, they at least know. Instead, you have people out there still worrying, you know?" said Donna.

"Yeah, that is true. Knowing would be better than not, for sure," said Oz.

"How's Terry doing?" asked Donna.

"He's good. He's been pretty quiet, but otherwise, he is the same old Terry," said Oz.

"That's good, I guess," said Donna. "Shit! I forgot my bag back at the apartment."

"That's alright. We'll grab it after dinner. There's no rush. We have all weekend together," said Oz.

"I know, but it's just a pain," said Donna.

"Maybe I'll make it worth your while," said Oz.

"Oh? Go on Detective, I'm listening," said Donna.

"Maybe I'll just make love to you when we get your bag after dinner, and then again when we get to my place," said Oz.

"And what's in it for me?" joked Donna.

"Funny girl," said Oz, laughing.

Donna leaned over and kissed Oz on the cheek, then grabbed his hand from the shifter and wove her fingers in between his.

Oz pulled into the parking lot on the south side of the Boston Fish Pier and parked the car in a spot as close to the restaurant as he could find. He hopped out of the car while Donna checked her lipstick in the vanity mirror on the passenger sunshade. He opened her door for her and helped her out of the car. They held hands as they walked into the restaurant.

"Welcome to 75 on Liberty Wharf," said the hostess.

"Reservation for Shields," said Oz.

"Ah yes, right this way, sir. Your party has also just arrived," said the hostess, escorting them to the table.

"Our party?" asked Donna quietly.

They approached the table, and Donna saw Maureen and Terry sitting there. Maureen saw the couple coming and stood up to greet them. Seeing Maureen stand, Terry slowly got up. The couples hugged and greeted each other before taking their seats.

"Oh my God! What a surprise, seeing you both here," said Donna.

"Oz didn't tell you we were coming?" asked Maureen.

"No!" said Donna.

"Oz, you shit. Why wouldn't you tell her?" asked Maureen.

"I thought it would be a nice surprise," said Oz. "Have you guys been here long?"

"Nah, just arrived. Haven't even ordered drinks yet," said Terry.

Within minutes, a tall, handsome young man showed up at the table. He was 6'2, with thick dark hair that was combed back. He had a friendly and warm smile.

"Good evening, folks. My name is Joey, and I'll be your server this evening. Can I get everyone started with a drink?" he asked.

"I'd love a glass of Red and White Sangria," said Maureen.

"I'll have a glass of Cab, please," said Donna.

"I'll have a lager," said Terry.

"And for you, sir?" asked Joey.

"I'll have a scotch neat," said Oz.

"Excellent. I'll be right back with your drinks, giving you a few more moments with the menu."

The talk at the table died down while they examined the menus, deciding on what to have for dinner. Terry was the first to put his menu down, almost as if he knew what he wanted before even getting there. Joey returned to the table with the tray of drinks, placing them down in front of everyone. He grabbed the pitcher of ice water from the tray and poured each of them a glass. Joey handed off the tray and the pitcher to a passing waiter and turned to take their orders.

"Has everyone decided?" he asked and received a unanimous 'yes' from the group. "Excellent, let's start with the ladies then."

"May I have the Beer Battered Fish and Chips?" said Maureen.

"Would you like a wedge of lemon for that?" asked Joey.

"Sure," said Maureen.

"Great! For you, ma'am?" he asked.

"I'll have the Pasta Primavera, please," said Donna.

"You'll love it," said Joey. "For you, sir?"

"Nantucket Seafood Stew," said Terry.

"Nice. And for you, sir?" asked Joey.

"I'll have the Liberty Fish Tacos, please," said Oz

"Excellent, sir," said Joey. "I'll get the kitchen started on this, and I'll be back to check on you."

Joey left the table, headed to the server station to input the order before disappearing into the kitchen. The couples sat at the table enjoying their drinks, sharing general conversation. It was good to see Terry and Maureen smiling after what they had just been through, especially Terry. His wounds were still tender but were healing well.

Joey returned to the table with a large tray and a scissor stand dangling from the ditch of his elbow. In an almost magician-like motion, he opened and set the scissor stand beside the table and rested the large tray on the stand. He placed the meals in front of them, picked up the stand and the tray and presented a Parmesan grater, and asked Donna if she would like some fresh Parmesan. She told him she did, and he cranked the handle of the grater and sprinkled her pasta with Parmesan cheese until she raised her hand for him to stop.

"Can I get anyone anything else?" asked Joey.

"I'll have another lager," said Terry.

"I'm fine, thanks," said Maureen.

"I'll have another glass of wine, please," said Donna.

"Atta girl," said Terry, smiling.

"I'll just take some more water," said Oz, handing his empty scotch glass to Joey.

"Excellent!" said Joey. "I'll be right back."

Joey left, and they all started to eat their meals. Everything was lovely. Oz could see why it was the first place that Terry recommended. Joey returned promptly to the table with the drinks. He cleared the empty glasses and refilled the water glasses. When he asked if everything were to their satisfaction, he looked around the table and received his response via smiling faces, all nodding with mouths full of food.

I swear they are trained to see when your mouth is full of food to ask that, thought Oz. Between bites, the couples carried out the typical small talk, sharing stories, and having laughs. This was definitely the setting that he had hoped that Donna would have met Terry and Maureen, rather than how she did. At this moment, no one was thinking about what had just happened a week ago, which was precisely what they all needed.

After dinner when Joey had cleared the plates, and brought cups of coffee for the couples that they requested instead of dessert. They sipped the coffees and continued the banter. Oz handed Joey his credit card to pay for dinner. There was some debate over this, but eventually Terry conceded. Terry insisted they should at least split it, but Oz would have none of it. They were his guests tonight.

When they finished, they all got up and walked out to the parking lot together. They hugged and said goodbye to each other. Terry and Maureen walked to their car. Donna put her arm around Oz.

"That was such a nice night," said Donna.

"It was, wasn't it?" said Oz.

"Was this your idea?" asked Donna.

"Everything but the restaurant, that was Terry's," said Oz. "He told me that this place was good so when I called to make the reservation, I made it for the four of us, surprising him, and insisted that he and Maureen were joining us."

Oz opened the door for Donna and helped her down and into the car. He walked around and got in the car. He backed out of the parking spot and headed for Donna's place to get her things.

***

Ring… Ring… Ring…

"Shields, Homicide," said Oz.
"Oz, it's Jim," said Lieutenant Roberts.
"Yes, sir. What's going on?" asked Oz.
"Meet me down on the Longfellow Bridge," said Jim.
"What's going on, sir?" asked Oz.
"It's Terry and Maureen," said Jim.
"Sir, all due respect, just tell me," said Oz.
"It's not good. Just get here ASAP," said Jim, hanging up the call.
"What's wrong?" asked Donna.
"Something about Terry and Maureen. I gotta go," said Oz.
"I'm coming with you," said Donna.
Oz was too frazzled to argue. They got ready and left the apartment as quickly as they could. Oz sped to the bridge. Arriving on the scene, all access to the bridge was closed. Officers had barricades up, blocking all lanes. Oz drove up to the barricade and presented the badge. The officer moved the barricade and let Oz through. Suddenly, Jim was standing in front of the car with his hand up, getting Oz to stop. He hopped out of the car. Donna got out of the passenger side.

"Sir, where is he?" asked Oz.
"Oz, calm down! It's not gonna help anything," said Jim.
"Where are they, Jim?" asked Oz.

"They're trapped in the car," said Jim.

Oz pushed Jim aside and ran towards the car. Maureen's Mini was on the roof. The car had rolled several times before, sliding and halting, wheels up. There was debris all over the road. Firefighters worked to stabilize the vehicle. Oz could feel tears welling up in his eyes with every step closer to the car. Donna came up behind Oz with Jim.

"What the fuck happened, Jim?" asked Oz. "We were just with them."

"From what I've been told, a tire blew, and Maureen lost control. The car rolled, hit the guardrail, and kept rolling," said Jim.

"Fuck!" said Oz. "I knew that I should have driven them home."

"None of this is your fault, kid," said Jim.

The firefighters worked away on the car, trying to cut Terry and Maureen from the wreckage. Medics were there, ready with backboards and gurneys. Oz could do nothing but watch through the flashing lights of all the emergency vehicles. Donna wrapped her arm around his waist. He put his arm around her.

"They are going to be okay," said Donna, trying to be reassuring.

Maureen was the first to emerge from the wreckage. They carefully placed her on a backboard. She had a C-Collar around her neck to stabilize. They strapped her to the board and lifted her onto the gurney. The medics immediately wheeled her into the Ambulance and left the scene. Terry was still trapped in the car. The passenger side of the vehicle took a hard hit against the guardrail. There was barely enough room for one person to work on the passenger side, the way that it had stopped resting against the guardrail.

Struggling to free Terry from the passenger side, the firefighters decided to try to pull him out of the driver's side of the vehicle. Oz, Donna, and Jim stood huddled together, nervously watching the firefighters work. They cut away the entire driver's side of the car, frantically working to get Terry free.

"Oz, I'm gonna head to the head to the hospital, and be there for Maureen. I assume you're not gonna leave until Terry is on his way to the hospital," said Jim.

"I'm not leaving, no!" said Oz.

"Can I catch a ride with you?" asked Donna. "I want to be there for her."

"Sure thing. That's sweet of you," said Jim.

"Good idea, Hun. I'll be there shortly," said Oz.

Donna kissed Oz on the cheek before walking to the car with Jim and leaving the scene for the hospital. One of the firefighters ripped the driver's seat from the car and tossed it aside. Finally, Terry emerged from the car. Three firefighters carefully slid him from the car and onto a backboard. They strapped him down and quickly lifted him onto the gurney. The medics rushed him into the ambulance and took off for the hospital.

"Oz, you want an escort to the hospital?" said Devon.

"Devon? What are you doing here?" asked Oz.

"What do you think, Detective? Dispatch called me to the scene," said Devon.

"Can you let me know what you guys find? What happened here tonight?" asked Oz.

"You know I will, brother," said Devon. "I'm serious about the escort, though. I can make it happen."

"Thanks, man, but I'm good. I'm just going to tail the ambulance," said Oz.

"Alright, bro. Get going. I'll call you," said Devon.

Oz got in the car and sped away from the scene, catching up to the ambulance. He followed it all the way to Massachusetts General. He quickly parked in the garage and ran across the street into the emergency room.

36

Oz paced around the Emergency Room waiting area. Donna sat next to Jim, his arm around her shoulders, comforting her like a father would comfort his daughter. *This doesn't make any sense. How could this happen?*

Vrrrt... Vrrrt... Vrrrt...

"Shields, Homicide," said Oz, answering his phone.
"Oz, it's Devon. Any word yet?" asked Devon.
"Nothing yet, man," said Oz.
"I found something here at the scene that doesn't fit," said Devon.
"What's that?" asked Oz.
"Well, initially we thought a tire blew out and Maureen lost control. But this doesn't look like a tire blew, man," said Devon.
"What?" said Oz.
"Oz, it looks like one of the tires was slashed," said Devon.
"Slashed?" said Oz.

"Yeah. The driver's front tire is sliced open," said Devon.

"You're sure about that?" asked Oz.

"100%, man. There is an 8" slice in the sidewall. Whatever did this was sharp as hell, too," said Devon.

"Thanks, man. Let me know if you find anything else. No word on either of them from the doctors yet," said Oz.

"Thanks, Oz. We're all praying for them here," said Devon.

Oz hung up the phone and put it back in his pocket. He reached up and ran his fingers through his hair as he walked back to Donna and Jim.

"Who was that?" asked Jim.

"It was Butler. He said that one of the tires was slashed," said Oz.

"Slashed?" said Jim.

"Yeah, he said there is an eight inch slash in one," said Oz.

"How?" said Jim.

"He didn't say. He just said that whatever did was sharp as hell," said Oz.

"Lieutenant Roberts?" said a nurse, coming into the waiting area.

"I'm Lieutenant Roberts," said Jim, standing and walking over to her.

"Lieutenant, Mr. and Mrs. White have come out of surgery, but they are not out of the woods just yet. They both suffered serious trauma from the accident. For now, we have done all that we can for them," said the nurse.

"Can we see them?" asked Jim.

"I can allow one of you to come back, but only for a few minutes. They need to rest," said the nurse.

"Oz, you go. I'll stay here with Donna," said Jim.

"Are you sure?" said Oz.

"Go. Be with your partner," said Jim.

"Thank you, sir," said Oz. "I'll be right back, Hun. I love you."

"I love you too," said Donna.

Oz followed the nurse into the Emergency Room. The nurse slid open a sliding glass door, giving Oz access to the room where Terry laid in a bed. Oz walked to Terry's bedside. Terry laid there connected to IVs and a Holter monitor. His neck was still supported in a neck brace. The Holter monitor beeped steadily in the background.

"Terry, if you can hear me. Hang in there, man," said Oz.

"Oz?" Terry said, faintly.

"Yeah, Ter. I'm here," said Oz.

"It was him," said Terry.

"Who?" said Oz.

"The fucking demon," said Terry. "Hit our car on our way home."

"Save your strength, man," said Oz.

"M... M... Mo..." started Terry.

"She's here, Ter. She is out of surgery. You both just need to rest," said Oz. "I'm going to get this fucker."

Oz grabbed Terry's hand and gave it a squeeze. Terry faded off to sleep from the morphine. Oz turned and exited the room, closing the sliding glass door behind him. He walked to the Nurses' station and asked where Maureen was. The nurse there pointed to a room two doors down from Terry's. Oz slid open the door and entered. Maureen lay there in a similar state to Terry, except Maureen was hooked up to a ventilator.

The scene was heartbreaking. Oz began to tear up, seeing Maureen laying there. A machine breathing for her. Just moments earlier, they were at dinner, sharing stories and laughing. Now they were clinging to life. *If you can hear me, you cocksucker. I'm coming for you.* Oz wiped his eyes and left Maureen's room, closing the door behind him. He returned to the Nurse's Station.

"Excuse me," said Oz.

"Yes, sir?" said one of the nurses.

"Can I leave you my card? If there are any changes in Terry and Maureen White's condition, can you please call me?" said Oz.

"Sure, Detective," said the Nurse.

"Thank you!" said Oz.

Oz walked out to the waiting room. Donna and Jim stood up when they saw him return. Donna could see that he had been crying. His eyes were a dead giveaway.

"Terry tried to speak with me but was very weak. Maureen," said Oz, choking back emotion. "Is on a ventilator."

"What did Terry say?" asked Jim.

"He said that they were attacked on their way home," said Oz.

"Attacked in a moving car?" said Jim.

"This thing we are hunting, it has no limits. It gets stronger every day. Stronger with every kill," said Oz.

"Are you sure it wasn't the drugs talking?" asked Jim.

"I'm positive, sir," said Oz. "This thing already tried to kill him once before, it was trying to finish the job."

"Fuck!" said Jim. "We gotta stop this thing, kid."

"I will, sir," said Oz.

"Go on, get outta here. I'm gonna stay awhile longer," said Jim.

"You sure, sir?" said Oz.

"Yeah," said Jim.

"Alright, please call if anything changes," said Oz

"Will do, kid," said Jim. "And Oz?

"Yes, sir?" said Oz.

"Whatever you need to get this son of a bitch, you have it," said Jim.

Oz shook hands with Jim, with Jim pulling him into an embrace. Donna hugged Jim and kissed him on the cheek before she and Oz left the waiting area, headed for the car parked in the garage. They held hands as they walked to the car, but didn't say a word.

***

Oz backed the car into the parking spot in the garage and parked the car. He and Donna exited the vehicle, and Oz grabbed her overnight bag from the trunk of the car. They were thoroughly exhausted, taking the elevator up to Oz's apartment. Oz opened the door to the apartment, and Donna entered first.

"Are you alright, Hun?" asked Donna.

"I should have insisted more on driving them tonight," said Oz.

"Ozzy, you can't beat yourself up over this," said Donna.

"But maybe I could have prevented this from happening. Maybe they wouldn't be laying in the hospital right now, clinging to life," said Oz.

"And maybe we'd all be dead or right there with them," said Donna. "You're still here to keep fighting, and that is what you are going to do. Don't be stuck on what happened, focus on what you are going to do."

"It was so heartbreaking to see them like that tonight. Especially Maureen hooked up to that machine breathing for her. She never did anything to anyone," said Oz.

"I know, babe. I know," said Donna.

Donna grabbed Oz and pulled him into her, hugging him. His head on her shoulder, he began to cry. Donna caressed the back of his head, trying to console him. Oz wrapped his arms around her and choked back the tears, forcing himself to be stronger, to not let this break him. Oz broke the embrace, wiped his eyes, and picked up the overnight bag, and walked it back into the bedroom, putting the bag on the bed.

"I need a drink. How about you?" asked Oz.

"Sure, is there still some wine?" asked Donna.

"I'm pretty sure that there is," said Oz.

Oz pulled down a wine glass and a small drinking glass from the cupboard. He grabbed the wine for her and poured her a glass and handed it to her. Then he pulled out a bottle of Glenlivet single malt from the cupboard by his knee, pouring himself a glass.

"To the health and recovery of Terry and Maureen!" said Oz, holding his glass out to toast Donna.

"To our friends," said Donna.

They clinked glasses, and Donna took a sip. Oz downed the glass of scotch and poured himself another. Donna put her hand on his arm.

"This won't make everything better, babe," said Donna.

"I know," said Oz.

He downed the second glass of scotch and then rinsed it out and washed it in the sink. Donna finished her glass of wine, and Oz washed it and dried it as well. Donna walked up to Oz and put her hands on his face, looked into his eyes with a soothing gaze, and kissed him. Then she grabbed his hand and walked him back to the bedroom.

37

Oz woke to the sun peeking through the blinds in his bedroom. Donna was still in deep sleep beside him. Oz eased out of bed. So he didn't disturb her, and got dressed in jeans and a t-shirt. He walked out to the kitchen and opened the fridge to see what was in there that he could make for breakfast. There wasn't much beyond half a dozen eggs.

He grabbed his keys from the breakfast bar and slipped on a pair of running shoes, and left the apartment. He walked to the Stop & Shop up the street and grabbed a few things to make breakfast for Donna and him.

Oz returned to the apartment and silently entered, snuck down the hall, and peaked in the bedroom to see Donna still there sleeping. He returned to the kitchen and began preparing breakfast. He chopped up some ham, red and green peppers, tomatoes, green onions, and spinach, placing each one in a small bowl to easily dispense. Finally, he cracked and whisked several eggs in a bowl while he preheated a frying pan. Donna emerged from the bedroom, rubbing her eyes.

"Good morning, Sunshine!" said Oz. "Can I make you an omelet?"

"Mmm, sounds spectacular! Is there coffee?" asked Donna.

"There can be, very quickly," said Oz. "What do you want in your omelet?"

"I'll have everything," said Donna, looking at all the bowls on the counter.

"Cheese?" asked Oz.

"Oh, hell yes," said Donna.

Oz dropped a pod in the coffee machine and brewed Donna a cup of coffee. He began making the omelet. He placed the plate in front of Donna, with a napkin, silverware for her, and her coffee.

"You're an angel," said Donna.

"Hardly," said Oz.

Oz made his omelet and coffee and joined her at the breakfast bar when it was all finished. He dashed a bit of hot sauce over his omelet and cut the first bit.

"This is pretty good, Ozzy!" said Donna.

"Glad you like it. I grabbed everything but the eggs fresh this morning," said Oz.

"Aww, you really do love me!" said Donna.

"You doubted it?" asked Oz.

"Never!" said Donna.

"I was thinking about going to the hospital after we get ready," said Oz. "Do you want to come?"

"Does it make me a horrible person if I say 'no'?" said Donna.

"No, not at all. I feel like I owe it to them to go," said Oz.

"Are you sure?" asked Donna.

"Absolutely, babe. What are you going to do?" asked Oz.

"Matt texted this morning. He needs some things done at the office, so I'm going to go into work for a bit," said Donna.

"How long are you going to be there?" asked Oz.

"Not sure. Why?" asked Donna.

"Just curious. I have to go to church at 8 tonight," said Oz.

"Church? You're still going through with that?" said Donna.

"After what happened last night, I have to, babe. This thing has to be stopped," said Oz.

"What about us?" asked Donna.

"I can only promise you I will do everything in my power to return safely to you. The same promise that I make every day I go to work," said Oz.

Donna fell silent. Her eyes welled with tears. Oz could see that she was upset. He went to her and wrapped his arms around her. He kissed her on her forehead.

"This thing is going after those I love. I'm not going to take the chance that you are next," said Oz.

"I don't want to lose you either," said Donna.

"Then only good thoughts today," said Oz.

Donna cried as Oz continued to hold her. She squeezed him in her arms and didn't let go. He ran his fingers through her hair, kissed the top of her head.

"I love you, Donna," he said.

"I love you too, Ozzy," replied Donna.

***

Oz walked to the main reception desk at Massachusetts General Hospital, presented his badge, and asked the receptionist for the location of Maureen and Terry. He assumed that by now they would have been moved from the ER to intensive care. The receptionist there informed Oz that they had been moved to the 3rd floor of the Blake Medical Intensive Care Unit. Oz walked down the halls, following the blue lines to the D elevators and taking them to the 3rd floor. Oz exited the elevator and headed to the nurse's station, asking for the rooms for Terry and Maureen. The nurse informed him they were in a shared room down the hall.

Oz walked down the hall to the room with the placard outside the door marked 'Room 308'. He slowly entered the room and saw Maureen first, still hooked up to the ventilator and the Holter monitor. Beside her in another bed laid Terry. He, too, was now on a ventilator. Overnight, his condition had deteriorated, and they had to hook him up to the respirator. The attack and the accident had taken their toll on his body.

Oz sat in the chair in the room's corner, watching their chests move up and down as the machines breathed for them. He sat there angry and sorrowful at the state of his friends… his family. *I'm so sorry. I should have prevented this from happening. I should have insisted on driving you guys. I knew this sick fuck was going to come after you again. He isn't going to get away with this! I promise! I am going to make him pay dearly for this. You didn't deserve this.*

Oz welled up with tears as his mind raced. For the first time in his life, he felt himself praying. Pleading with God to save his friends. He would do anything to have them alive and well again.

Vrrrt… Vrrrt… Vrrrt…

"Shields, Homicide," said Oz, trying to sound like he wasn't on the verge of crying.
"Oz, it's Brad. Is this a bad time?" said Brad.
"Not really the best time, but what is up?" said Oz.
"Sorry, I'll make this quick. Are you still going to the church tonight?" asked Brad.
"Yeah, why?" asked Oz.
"I just wanted to make sure. So, I'll meet you there just before 8?" said Brad.
"Yeah. Sounds good," said Oz.
"Okay, great. See you later," said Brad.
"Later," said Oz, hanging up the call.
Oz sat with Terry and Maureen for a while longer. He sent Jim a text message letting him know that Maureen's condition was unchanged and that Terry's condition had deteriorated and that he is now on a ventilator. Jim responded, thanking Oz for the update, and stated that he would be by the hospital later to see them.

38

Oz walked up to the stairs of the Basilica of Our Lady of Perpetual Help. Brad was waiting for Oz by the doors. Oz was surprisingly calm as he approached the church. He had no idea what he was in for, but at this point, retribution was his greatest motivator. Oz pulled out his phone and messaged Donna.

'Hey babe, I am just about to head into the church. I hope to see you after if you are feeling up to it. I love you!'

He hoped to get a response from her before heading inside, but it didn't come. He walked up the stairs and waved at Brad. Brad waved back.

"Hey, Oz," said Brad

"Hey, Brad. How are you?" said Oz.

"Nervous. How are you?" asked Brad.

"I have no clue what I've got myself into, but if this is what it takes to end this, then let's do it," said Oz.

Oz and Brad entered the church. As they walked down the main aisle, they saw Father Denkel up on the altar doing something that they couldn't make out until they got closer. When the two men reached the steps to the altar, Father Denkel heard them and turned around to greet them.

"Ah, gentlemen, welcome! I'm nearly ready for you," said Father Denkel.

Oz and Brad watched Father Denkel draw a circle using salt, with symbols drawn with precision just outside. He then divided the circle into four quadrants and wrote a single strange symbol in each quadrant. He placed a candle at the edge of each quadrant and lit the wicks. Finally, Father Denkel placed a bowl containing leaves, herbs, and petals, and a silver trinket near the circular sigil, and lit the bowl contents afire.

"What are those symbols?" asked Oz.

"They are Enochian symbols, my son," said Father Denkel. "The ones here, here, here, and here and Enochian letters," he said, pointing at the symbols inside the quadrants.

"So what do we do?" asked Oz.

"I will have you stand in the circle and wait. I will say the incantation, and if God accepts, we should have an angel to help," said Father Denkel.

Oz took a deep breath and entered the circle, being sure to not disturb the salt. He stood precisely where Father Denkel instructed him to, and closed his eyes. Father Denkel began chanting. The words that he spoke were like nothing that Oz or Brad had ever heard before. Father Denkel was reciting an Enochian incantation. The candle flames flickered. Brad stood to the side and stared in amazement.

Father Denkel finished the incantation and waited. Oz dropped to one knee and hunched down, his fist stabilizing him on the ground. His breathing was slower than normal. Father Denkel approached Oz cautiously.

"Are you alright, my son?" asked Father Denkel.

"Ol zir kures," said Oz, in a much deeper and resonant tone than normal.

"Who am I speaking with?" asked Father Denkel.

"Ol zir Michael, noco c Ascha," said Oz

"Thank you for answering our call to service. Can I speak with Oz now?" asked Father Denkel. "Are you alright, my son?"

"Father?" said Oz. "I feel so strange."

"Can you stand?" asked Father Denkel.

"I… I… I think so," said Oz.

Oz stood up and looked at Father Denkel. His already piercing blue eyes now seemed to have an electric glow to them, almost like they were neon lights. Oz tilted his head to the left, cracking his neck, then to the right, doing the same.

"Dude, your eyes…" said Brad, shocked.

"What?" asked Oz.

"They're glowing," said Brad.

"Oz, you are now with the Archangel Michael. He can talk with you in your thoughts," said Father Denkel. "Try it."

"Michael?" thought Oz.

"Why have you summoned me, child of Adam?" asked Michael. The voice was powerful and robust, deep yet soothing.

"We are being tormented by a demon named Azazel. He is torturing and killing people, and is now targeting those I love since I killed his previous host," said Oz.

"Azazel!" said Michael. *"We have battled before. It has been thousands of years since then. I'm surprised that we were unaware of his return."*

"How do we stop him?" asked Oz.

"Ask the priest if he has a cold iron sword in this house of God," said Michael.

"Why iron?" asked Oz.

"Cold iron is the only substance on your earth that can harm powerful, malevolent supernatural creatures," said Michael.

"Father? Do you have a cold iron sword?" repeated Oz.

"I do. In my chambers," said Father Denkel.

"Perfect! We must have this," said Michael.

"Come, come. Let's go get it," said Father Denkel.

Oz and Brad followed Father Denkel back to his chambers. Father Denkel opened the heavy wooden door and they entered. On the wall behind the door, crossed in an X behind a large metal shield, were two longswords. The blades were grooved down the center and highly polished to a mirror shine. The guards were thick brushed iron that flared out at the ends. They had brown leather-wrapped grips with brushed iron pommels with polished red stones encased within.

"Grab one of the longswords," said Michael.

"They look heavy!" said Oz.

"They should be if they are what the priest claims them to be," said Michael.

"Can I take one down?" asked Oz.

"Sure, sure. Be careful, they are very heavy," said Father Denkel.

Oz wrapped his right hand around the leather grip of one of the swords. He lifted it from its hooks and raised the blade, wielding the longsword as if it were light as a feather.

"Whoa!" said Brad. "You ever held a sword before?"

"Nope," said Oz. "This isn't me doing this."

"This is so crazy, man!" said Brad, almost excited.

"You're telling me," said Oz.

"Does anything else feel strange?" asked Brad.

"Not really. I feel like me, but I have this voice in my head and abilities like this, that I never had before," said Oz.

"So how do we find this demon?" asked Brad.

"No cl…" started Oz.

"Express our gratitude to the priest for the sword," said Michael.

"Father, if you don't mind, I need to take this sword," said Oz.

"Of course! Good luck, my son. May God bless your quest," said Father Denkel.

"Thank you!" said Oz.

Brad and Oz left the Father's chambers, walking back through the church. All that he witnessed stunned Brad. He felt as though he had been watching a movie unfold right before his eyes. Oz stopped halfway down the aisle.

"Ozwald! You will suffer!" said Azazel.

"What's wrong, Oz?" asked Brad.

"I just heard the voice," said Oz.

"The angel?" asked Brad.

"No, the demon," said Oz.

Vrrrt… Vrrrt… Vrrrt…

Oz pulled his phone from his pocket, and there was a text from Donna. Oz opened the messages app and there was a blurred image. He tapped on the picture to download it. The picture loaded and went full screen on his phone. Donna was bound and gagged. She bound hands over her head, hanging from a meat hook above her head. Tears ran down her face, making her make-up run.

The phone vibrated in his hand as a second message came through. He closed the picture and went back to the conversation. The message that came through read: *'you have thirty minutes to find her before I start the sacrifice to bring my beloved'*.

"Mother Fucker!" said Oz, slamming his fist on a nearby mailbox, crumpling it like a pop can being crushed, with his angelically enhanced strength.

"Whoa! What's going on?" asked Brad.

"The son of a bitch has my girlfriend!" said Oz.

"Where?" asked Brad.

"That's what I have to figure out," said Oz.

"Any clues?" asked Brad.

"Just this picture," said Oz, showing Brad the picture.

Brad looked at the picture, zooming in and messing with the brightness on Oz's phone, attempting to reveal something in the background that would give him a clue. Brad then taped on the picture and the menu to save it to Oz's phone. He exited the messages app and went into the picture gallery. Taping on the photo again, he accessed the photo properties. Under location, there were only coordinates given.

"I have coordinates from the picture properties," said Brad.

"Seriously? How did you know how to do that?" asked Oz.

"I'm a nerd. Before you say that I'm not, I'm totally alright with it," said Brad.

"What are the coordinates? Where are we going?" asked Oz.

"It says 42.336586, -71.077406. Let me just copy those, and paste them into the map... Boom!" said Brad. "Washington Street and Massachusetts Ave."

***

The mustang roared up and parked in front of a boarded-up five-story building on Washington Street. Brad looked at the building as Oz opened the driver's side door and got out of the car. Realizing that Oz exited the Mustang, he opened the passenger's side door and got out. Oz opened the trunk and pulled out the longsword.

"It's all boarded up. How are we going to get in?" asked Brad.

"We aren't. I am," said Oz. "It's best that you stay out here, Brad. I don't need anyone else getting hurt."

"But you can't go in there alone," said Brad.

"I'm not alone," said Oz.

Oz walked up to the main door that was raised three steps from the sidewalk and kicked in the plywood covering the doorway. The plywood exploded into splinters as the door behind it flew open.

"Azazel!" shouted Michael, taking control of Oz.

Michael's voice echoed through the empty halls of the building. The darkness suffocated the interior of the building. This would have been a problem for Oz, but with Michael, he could see everything. The darkness disappeared, as though he were looking around with night vision. The smell of mold and mildew filled the air.

The building hadn't been occupied in over thirty years, and throughout this time there had been several fires damaging the upper floors. Oz slowly made his way up to the second floor, looking in room after room as he made his way down the halls. The sword was in the air, ready to be swung. Oz turned the corner, heading down a hallway towards the stairwell.

"Michael, the last time that I confronted him, there was a distinct smell that got stronger and stronger the closer that I got. This building is so damaged from fire and water that there is no way that we can smell him this time," said Oz.

"Leave this to me," said Michael.

Oz made his way up to the third floor and started walking down the hall. The smell of mold was stronger on this floor. The water damage could be seen in the walls. Wallpaper that remained untouched from the fires curled off the walls.

Wham! Oz slammed through the wall opposite of a doorway he was passing. Dust whirled around the room above him. The dust intruded his eyes, causing them to sting and water. He looked up to see a dark figure coming through the hole in the wall. The figure was huge and cloaked. As the dust settled, he could see the figure more clearly.

Two massive horns protruded from just above the temples, curling upward. The flesh from the host was torn where the horns had ripped through the flesh. It had small spikes along the cheekbones and chin. He was easily ten feet tall and extremely muscular. More spikes pierced the flesh along the collarbones.

His fiery eyes locked on Oz as he skulked towards him. Oz somersaulted backward, getting to his feet. No longer in control, he grabbed the blade of the longsword with his left hand and ran his hand up the blade. The blade ignited behind his hand as it ran up the blade. The flame that engulfed the blade glowed blue. Now wielding a flaming longsword, he waved at Azazel to come and get him.

"That's a neat trick. Too bad it won't help you," said Azazel.

Azazel swatted at Oz, slashing him across the face. The claws were so sharp that Oz didn't notice that he was cut until he felt warm blood trickling down his face. Then before he could react he was pinned against the ceiling, as he was hoisted effortlessly then dropped, slamming onto the floor. The air rushed from his body, from the impact.

Oz winced in pain. He could feel that Azazel was toying with him. He was so powerful and fearless. *Michael, when are you going to take over? Is there going to be anything left of me before you do?*

Azazel grabbed the back of Oz's shirt and tossed him through a wall in the room where he ended up in a moldy bathtub. The faucet almost pierced through his back when he impacted it. It shattered two ribs with the impact. Oz was still struggling to catch his breath. Dust swirled around the room, getting in his eyes again, blurring his vision.

Any fucking time, Michael! Thought Oz. *Where's the sword?* Oz pulled out his pistol and pointed it at the doorway to the bathroom. He eased out of the bathtub, winced in pain as he tried to find a comfortable posture.

He crept to the door, and quickly pointed his gun into the room as he looked for the demon. The room was empty. The sword lay on the floor where he was first slammed to the ground, still aflame. The blue flame illuminated the room.

Oz scanned the room. His gun was still drawn. The demon was gone, toying with him again. Oz holstered his pistol and picked up the longsword. Now, using the ignited blade to light his way, he made his way down the hall, looking in all the open doors, trying not to get caught off guard again. He made his way to the fourth floor and continued his search. In the distance, he thought he could hear Donna whimpering.

There was a flash of light, and Azazel appeared in front of him. Oz got into a guard stance, readying for an attack. Azazel slowly walked toward him. Stared at him with his flaming eyes.

"I'm going to enjoy killing you slowly, Oswald," said Azazel.

"I stopped before, and I'll do it again," said Oz.

Oz tossed the sword at Azazel and drew his gun. Azazel dodged the flaming sword. It clanged as it crashed to the ground behind him. Oz drew his pistol and fired two quick shots while Azazel was distracted by dodging the flaming sword. The bullets hit Azazel in the chest and left arm. The demon shrieked in pain as the bullets seared into his flesh.

"They may not kill you, but they sure do hurt," said Oz.

Azazel growled and marched toward Oz. He dragged his claws along the walls as he approached. The dust filled the hall behind him. Oz fired three more shots to the dust-filled hall. Azazel shrieked again at the searing pain, but kept coming.

Dust stung his eyes again and blurred his vision. He tried to blink the dust from his eyes as he staggered back. Unable to see, Azazel pounced, striking Oz in the sternum. The impact robbed his lung of their contents and caused Oz to drop his gun. Oz dropped to a knee, gasped for air. Azazel laughed, his menacing laugh echoed through the hall. The demon struck again with a hammer fist to Oz's back, dropping him to the floor. Dust plumed from under him. Azazel picked Oz up and threw him like a rag doll through a nearby wall into another room.

Oz choked and coughed, still scrambling to catch his breath. He looked up to see Azazel climbing through the hole. His cloven hoof clacked as it hit the bare floor. Pieces of the wall fell as he passed through the opening. Oz pushed himself up and made a sprint toward the demon, spearing him back through the wall, and the hallway, and through the other wall.

Oz rolled off the demon and rose to his feet. Azazel groaned, sprung to his feet, and howled. He lunged and swiped at Oz. Suddenly, no longer in control, he dropped to a knee, ducking the swipe from Azazel. Oz punched into the right thigh of the great beast with crunching force and speed. Oz followed that strike with a lightning-quick left to the rib cage.

Azazel staggered and fell through the wall into the hall. Oz climbed through the hole and was met by an overwhelming hook from Azazel. Oz, stunned by the strike, fell to the ground, staggered to get to his feet. Azazel swiped across Oz's back, opening four parallel gashes. Oz cried out from the searing pain. Azazel kicked Oz down the hall.

Seeing the glow in the hall, Oz somersaulted to the flaming sword, picked it up, and spun to face Azazel coming down the hall toward him. Oz crouched in a guard position with the sword before lunging toward him. Azazel reached for Oz, and in a defensive swing, cut off the demon's right hand just above the wrist. The demon cried out a deafening howl.

Oz lunged toward the staggering demon, swung the sword at Azazel's right leg, severing the leg off at the knee, as Oz slid past him. Azazel fell to the ground, crashing down on the newly created stump, then into a heap on the floor.

Oz spun around and prepared to strike again with the flaming sword. Azazel cried out for him to halt, as he tried to get to one knee. Without mercy, Oz, controlled by Michael, swung the longsword diagonally, cutting through Azazel's left arm just above the elbow and into the side of the beast. Azazel cried out.

"Enough!" said Azazel. "I yield!"

"Did you show mercy to any of your victims, when they begged?" said Michael, drawing the blade from the side of the demon.

"No more!" said Azazel.

Oz slashed down with the sword, cutting off the horn on the left side of Azazel's head. Sparks flew as the fiery blade sliced through the horn. The horn fell to the ground at the foot of the demon. The blade swung back around and stopped, just cutting the flesh on the neck of the demon.

"Stop!" cried out Azazel. "Exercise me! Banish me back to Hell! Don't kill me!"

"The Prince of Wrath, begging for mercy. How fitting?" said Michael. "This is the end of the line for you, Azazel. God will always prevail! Good will always triumph over evil!"

"Please! I beg of you!" said Azazel.

Oz drew back. The longsword crossed over and came down diagonally. Azazel raised his right arm as his only defense as the fiery blade sliced through the arm and then the neck of Azazel. There was a gurgle as the head slid from the neck and dropped to the floor. Oz stood up and stepped back. The body collapsed to the floor and began to smoke before igniting and burning.

"Donna!" yelled out Oz.

Oz began checking every room, looking for Donna. He kicked open a door near the end of the hall, where Azazel appeared after the flash of light. There in the candle-lit room hung Donna. Oz dropped the sword and rushed into the room. He grabbed her and lifted her from the hook. He laid her on the floor and checked her for signs of life. Checking for a pulse on her neck, he could feel a faint pulse.

"Donna, stay with me! Come on, babe, stay with me," said Oz, welling up with tears.

He stroked her face and gently shook her. He looked down at her body and found slashes in her side. Oz scooped her up so that the wounds were against his body so that he could keep pressure on them as he carried her out of the room and downstairs.

Brad saw Oz emerge from the building carrying Donna and dragging the longsword. Brad grabbed the sword from Oz and opened the passenger door of the Mustang. Oz set Donna down on the passenger seat of the car and belted her in. Oz grabbed the sword from Brad and ran his hand down the blade, extinguishing the flame before tossing it into the trunk. Brad climbed into the car's back seat and Oz got into the driver's seat and sped off to the hospital. Brad held pressure on Donna's side as Oz held her hand, begging her to stay with them.

39

Oz rushed into the emergency room carrying Donna. The triage nurse came rushing out with a gurney, and Oz laid Donna on it. Two more nurses came rushing to the gurney to assess Donna's condition as they rushed her into the back. Oz followed them through the doors.

"What is her name?" asked one of the nurses.

"Donna. Donna Richardson," said Oz.

"Donna, Hunny? Stay with us!" said the nurse, rushing Donna into one of the Major Trauma rooms.

Oz was stopped at the door as the doctor closed the door, heading in to take charge of the situation. Oz helplessly watched through the window as they worked to resuscitate her. One of the nurses cut open her shirt, and another nurse brought over the crash cart. They attached the stick-on electrodes to Donna's skin, attaching cables to the electrodes.

The doctor called for Donna to be shocked by the defibrillator. A nurse grabbed the paddles and prepped for the first shock. She placed the paddles on Donna's torso and triggered the first shock. Donna's body contorted with the delivery of the shock. Oz's heart ached to watch her go through this. Her pulse was still weak, so they shocked her again. A tear rolled down Oz's cheek.

The monitor beeped in rhythm as Donna was now registering a stable pulse. Frantically, the doctor and nurses went to work. One nurse drew the curtain on the window, blocking Oz from seeing what was going on. Oz left the emergency room and headed down the hall to the chapel. He walked to the altar and knelt down to pray.

"Michael, I've never done this before. I'm going to need your guidance on this," said Oz.

"Speak from the heart, and the Father will hear you," said Michael.

God, I come to you seeking your mercy and help. I know that I have already asked so much in asking for you to give us your bravest soldier, but I need help that only you can give. Please see it in your heart to save my loved ones. Donna, Terry, and Maureen are innocent victims in these senseless acts committed against them. I would gladly give whatever is needed for them to be saved.

There was silence as Oz sat there, thinking of his friends in the empty chapel. Tears ran down his face.

"The Father has heard your prayer," said Michael.

"How do you know?" asked Oz.

"He speaks with me," said Michael.

"Why can't I hear him then if you are in me?" asked Oz.

"The true voice of the Father would kill a mortal. He speaks through messengers. Even his son, never heard his voice until he joined him in paradise," said Michael.

"What did he say?" asked Oz.

"He said if your friends are strong enough, they will pull through. Now is not their time," said Michael.

"So, there is nothing that even he can do?" asked Oz.

"The Father does not choose who or when. He only chooses how they will be welcomed into the kingdom of Heaven. Death chooses who and when," said Michael.

"Do I need to bargain with the Reaper, then?" asked Oz.

"Death makes no deals," said Michael.

"How do you get back to Heaven?" asked Oz.

"My host must pass on," said Michael.

"Well, isn't this just fucking great!" said Oz.

Oz stood up, brushed off his knees, and left the chapel, returning to the emergency room. The curtain was still drawn in the room where Donna was being worked on. When a nurse exited the room, Oz stopped her and asked her for an update. The nurse just told him he would have to be patient, as she ran off to get units of blood for Donna.

Oz paced outside the room, cycling through emotions, desperate for her to be okay. Desperate for Terry and Maureen, just a few floors up, to be okay. To be breathing on their own again. What he wouldn't give to feel Donna's sweet kiss, or hear Maureen's laugh, or get teased by Terry one last time.

The emergency room doors burst open as paramedics wheeled in a gurney with a man police had shot that in the stomach. An officer was close behind the medics as nurses rushed to act. The man screamed in pain and kicked violently as the nurses tried to restrain him. The officer moved in to help restrain the man so one of the nurses could sedate him. This only made the man thrash more.

"Get your fucking hand off me, pig!" shouted the man. "Get your muthafuckin' hands off me! I'll fucking kill you!"

Three nurses and the officer struggled to keep the man on the gurney. He got one of his arms freed and punched one of the nurses in the face. He flailed his free arm wildly, occasionally hitting those trying to restrain him. He grabbed hold of the officer's pistol from the holster and fired it point-blank into the officer's chest. The officer dropped to the ground. The nurses let go of the man and stepped back with their hands in the air. Oz drew his pistol from his holster and pointed it at the man, who now had a nurse hostage. He held her in front of him, his arm around her neck, and the gun at her temple.

"Drop the fucking gun, asshole! Let her go!" shouted Oz.

"You drop your gun, pig! You don't know me!" shouted the man.

"You're right, I don't. And you don't know me. You don't know the fucking day I'm having. So go ahead, give me a fucking reason. Give me a fucking reason to take you out, right now!" said Oz.

"Your ass is fucking crazy!" said the man. "I'll shoot everyone in this muthafucka! I don't give a fuck!"

"Just you try it, asshole!" said Oz.

Blam!

The man fired. The bullet tore through Oz's neck. He dropped to the ground, blood pouring from the wound. Two armed security guards burst through the double doors of the emergency room, opening fire on the man.

He never saw them. All shots hit him square in the back. Fortunately, the nurse was unharmed. After the third shot, his hold on her broke. The gun fell to the ground and the man along with it. Screams filled the ER.

Nurses rushed to the fallen officer and to Oz. Doctors came out from rooms to assist. The two security guards checked on the man, clearing the pistol from his reach. He lay there, dead. All life disappeared from him in an instant.

Oz choked as blood filled his airway. It spurted from his mouth as he exhaled, trying to get a breath. There was so much blood. The nurse applied pressure to the wound, but this only routed the blood to his airway. He grew weaker with every passing second. Then everything went black.

40

Oz opened his eyes, and the light was so bright that he could barely focus. He looked around to see that he was in the hospital, but had no way of knowing how long he was out. A nurse came into the room to check the IVs that he was connected to and noticed that he was awake.

"You're awake!" she said, surprised.

"Do…" Oz tried to speak, but nothing came out.

"Shh!" said the nurse. "I'll be right back with the Doctor."

The nurse left the room. Oz laid his head back on the pillow and looked at the ceiling. All he wanted to know was where Donna was, or if she was okay. How were Terry and Maureen doing?

"*Michael? Are you there?*" asked Oz.

There was no response. *Where is he? Did I die? How long have I been here?* Thought Oz. None of this helped to ease his frustration. The nurse returned to the room with an older, silver-haired gentleman in a white lab coat. Obviously, this was the doctor.

"Mr. Shields, welcome back. I'm Doctor Jones. Please no jokes. I've heard them all before," said the doctor, trying to break the mood. "How are you feeling? You went through quite a bit of hell. Do you have any pain or tenderness?"

Oz tried to speak, but again nothing but a raspy noise came out. Oz pointed to his neck where the bullet had ripped through, and winced at his face, to indicate to the doctor that he was experiencing discomfort in his neck.

"Well, I hope you weren't much of a talker before," joked Doctor Jones. "I'll get you some meds to relieve the discomfort. I just want to do a check while you are alert to make sure that there is no other damage that we weren't able to see while you were unconscious."

Oz made hand gestures to show that he wanted a notepad and a pen. The nurse left the room to go and get a bag of painkillers to add to the IV, and the pen and paper. The doctor began his examination. He pulled the covers off Oz's feet. He took out his pen and lightly dragged it on the underside of his foot. Oz pulled his foot away because it tickled.

"That's a good sign. No spinal or nerve damage," said Doctor Jones.

The nurse returned with the notepad, the pen, and the painkillers. She gave Oz the pen and paper while she connected and hung the bag of painkillers. Oz wrote on the notepad 'Where is Donna Richardson?' and presented it to the doctor.

"Donna Richardson?" asked Doctor Jones.

Frustrated, he wrote, 'What happened to me?'

"You were shot in the neck in the ER," said Doctor Jones. "You lost a lot of blood and were dead for around 6 minutes. You got very lucky. Any longer, there could have serious complications had we been able to bring you back any later than that."

'How long have I been out?' Oz wrote.

"You have been in a coma for nearly 2 weeks at this point," said Doctor Jones. "While you were out, we could stitch and remove the stitches on the lacerations to your face and back, as well as the bullet wound in your neck."

'Are the Whites still in the ICU? Terry and Maureen?' wrote Oz.

"Yes!" said Doctor Jones.

"Are they okay?" asked Oz.

"They are. They are looking at being discharged either today or tomorrow," said the doctor.

Oz sighed in relief. A single tear ran down his cheek. He sniffled and wrote, 'What happened to the woman in the ER? I was shot just outside where she was being treated.'

"Is that Donna?" asked Doctor Jones.

Oz nodded and pointed at the question again.

"Redhead?" asked the nurse.

Oz nodded.

"She has been by every day to see you. Usually in the evening, and doesn't leave until visitor hours are over each night," said the nurse.

Oz looked up at the ceiling and cried. He was so relieved that she was ok.

"Do you have any questions about yourself?" asked Doctor Jones.

Oz made a gesture about his voice.

"We will have to examine that and run some tests, but I am optimistic that you will be able to speak again. For now, just get some rest, and I will check in again on you later," said Doctor Jones.

The nurse took the notepad and pen from Oz and set them on the table beside the bed before she and the doctor left the room. Oz laid there, tears rolling down his cheeks. The drugs began to take effect, and he felt his eyelids getting very heavy. Unable to stay awake any longer, he passed out.

***

Oz was woken by the sensation of his hand being squeezed. He opened his eyes and turned his head to see Donna sitting bedside. She was looking down and sobbing.

"Hey!" wheezed out Oz.

Donna's head snapped up, and her tear-filled eyes connected with his. She smiled and wiped away the tears. He squeezed her hand, and she squeezed back.

"I thought you would never come back to me!" said Donna.

"I…" wheezed Oz.

"Shh. Don't talk!" she said. "Just hold me!"

Donna crawled into the bed with Oz and snuggled up to him. He wrapped his arms around her and kissed her on the head. She hugged him tight across his body. The nurse came into the room.

"You're awake?" she said. "Feeling alright?"

Oz nodded. Donna moved to get off the bed, and the nurse raised her hand, as if to say that it wasn't necessary.

The nurse came around to the side of the bed where the IV pole was located and checked the bags.

"Mind if I check your bandage?" she asked.

Oz strained to expose his neck where the bandage was giving access to the nurse. The nurse peeled back the bandage to check the wound. She pulled out some alcohol cleaning wipes from the nearby nurse's cart. She cleaned the area around the wound. The stitches had recently been removed, but the wound was still tender.

"Looks great! Healing nicely. I'll just change the bandage and get out of your way," said the nurse.

The nurse changed the bandage and left the room. Donna reached up and traced the tape on the bandage as she looked up into his eyes.

"I'm so glad you are alright!" said Donna.

"You," wheezed Oz.

"I'm here because of you. I hope my scars won't gross you out," said Donna.

"I… love… you!" wheezed Oz.

"I have an idea!" said Donna.

Donna got up from the bed and left the room. She returned a minute later with a wheelchair. She helped Oz out of bed and into the chair.

"Where?" wheezed Oz.

"We're going to go and see some friends," said Donna.

She wheeled Oz, IV pole in his hand, out of the room and down the hall to the room where Terry and Maureen were. She knocked on the door before wheeling Oz in. Terry and Maureen's eyes lit up, seeing Oz and Donna enter the room.

"Kid? How are you doing?" said Terry.

Oz responded, giving a thumbs up.

"Great! You're finally a silent partner," joked Terry.

"Terry, that's terrible!" said Maureen.

"What? I haven't busted his balls in weeks. Can't have him getting soft," said Terry.

"Home?" asked Oz.

"We are finally getting outta here tomorrow," said Maureen. "It'll be so good to be home and in our own bed."

"When are they gonna let you out, kid?" asked Terry.

"They haven't said yet," said Donna. "But, now that he is up and about, I can't imagine it being any more than a couple of days," said Donna.

"Good to hear, kid," said Terry. "How are you doing?"

"Good. There will be some scarring, but I'm alive thanks to Ozzy!" said Donna.

"Scars are nothing. Look at me, I am covered in them now, but Maureen still finds me pretty!" said Terry.

"Hun, you were never pretty!" said Maureen.

"You're feisty!" said Terry. "I love you!"

"I love you too!" said Maureen.

"Hey kid, I say we take another week off and go see us a couple of Sox games," said Terry.

"Desk," wheezed Oz.

"You're right, kid. The Lieutenant is gonna have us on light duty, which means he's gonna pay us to go to games," said Terry.

Made in United States
North Haven, CT
04 December 2021